Winter at Death's Hotel

ALSO BY KENNETH CAMERON
FROM CLIPPER LARGE PRINT

The Bohemian Girl
The Frightened Man
The Second Woman

Wint

Falkirk
**Community
Trust**

W F HOWES LTD

This large print edition published in 2012 by
W F Howes Ltd
Unit 4, Rearsby Business Park, Gaddesby Lane,
Rearsby, Leicester LE7 4YH

1 3 5 7 9 10 8 6 4 2

First published in the United Kingdom in 2011
by Orion Books

A CIP catalogue record for this book is available
from the British Library

ISBN 978 1 40749 350 3

Typeset by Palimpsest Book Production Limited,
Falkirk, Stirlingshire
Printed and bound in Great Britain
by MPG Books Ltd, Bodmin, Cornwall

CHAPTER 1

New York City, January 1896

The New Britannic was one of New York's smaller and finer hotels – the city's finest, in fact, it would have insisted, although people who judged by flash and size would have said otherwise. The very best service and tone, the hotel management asserted – service and tone and taste. *Good* taste, of course, the best taste, matched by hotels like the Criterion in London, as the service and tone were perhaps matched by Brown's.

Most certainly, if you were English and of a certain sort, you stayed at the New Britannic when you were in New York. Of a *certain* sort: not new money, not great peerages, not political power; rather, achievement and reserve and even fame – but of course, no notoriety.

The bronze front doors opened into a paneled space with narrow beams overhead, pillars that rose at intervals of fifteen feet to Egyptian capitals in dark oak. Bronze chandeliers reached down, all electric; real imitation Aubusson stretched away to the mahogany Reception. Around the periphery, straight chairs, heavily carved, not very sittable; towards the centre, leather chairs meant to look and be more comfortable; an occasional dark table, a lamp – again electric, of course. Sitting in a leather chair towards the periphery but facing the doors was a man in a dark suit and dark necktie and a very high collar, his face square, a little heavy, displeased; on his upper lip a moustache and a faint sneer of scepticism.

The group coming through the doors was small, only three people but with a lot of luggage, so that it took two 'boys' to carry it. The man was noticeable, the two women not: he was tall, heavy, self-confident, dressed in London tailoring and London shoes and a London hat, with a London overcoat, a sprinkle of snow on the shoulders. He strode past the dark man in the leather chair – never noticed him, in fact – and went straight to Reception and said in an oddly high-pitched but loud voice, 'I am Arthur Conan Doyle.'

'Of course, sir!' The eminence at Reception, still young but very grand, sounded both impressed and regal.

'Cook's have reserved a suite of rooms.'

'*Yes*, sir.' Said as if some question had been raised about what Cook's had done. He moved a register a fraction of an inch forward, followed it with an inkwell and a pen. 'If you would just sign, Mr Conan Doyle . . .'

'*Doyle*. "Conan" is not the patronymic.'

'Ah. Mr *Doyle*.'

Doyle wore pince-nez, which he touched with a finger as he bent over the register as if he feared losing them. Pen in hand, he read up a column of the names of those who had registered before him. His lips moved, slightly shaking the walrus moustache on the upper one. He occasionally made a joke, in fact, about his looking like a walrus because of his girth and that moustache, although inwardly he cringed at the idea that anybody would make the comparison but he.

'Our other guests at the moment,' the young man said, 'include Sir Henry Irving. Sir Henry is doing a season at the Lyceum Theatre. And two of the principals of his company are with us, as well. *And* Mr William Cody!'

Doyle looked up at him. 'I *know* Irving.' Indeed, he had written a play for him before he had become *Sir* Henry. 'I *don't* know a Cody.'

'Of the Wild West. They're completing an engagement at Madison Square Garden.' He waved a hand, pointing vaguely at Madison Square Garden a block away.

Doyle sniffed. 'You seem to have a superabundance of show people.'

'Oh – oh, and we have General Sammartino of Argentina. And Mr Cyrus Bickle of American Steel. And Miss Marie Corelli, the English novelist!'

A somewhat dour stare suggested that Doyle didn't think of Marie Corelli as a novelist. Or perhaps not as English. He said, 'I was assured

3

by Cook's that this would be a quiet, entirely respectable hotel suitable to British sensibilities.'

'We pride ourselves at the New Britannic on our Britishness, Mr Doyle. We go out of our way to come up to British standards. And as for quiet, this is the quietest hotel in New York. It was *built* to be quiet.' He pushed a pamphlet across the desk: *How the City's Quietest Hotel Was Constructed along the Most Modern Lines.*

Doyle sniffed again. 'We shall be here only a few days, anyway. I am embarking on a lecture tour of the United States.' He signed the register – 'Mr and Mrs Arthur Conan Doyle and maid.' He hid pretty well his profound annoyance that he couldn't add 'and valet,' as his man had got sick on the crossing and had been held for quarantine at Immigration. It left Arthur Conan Doyle – *the* Arthur Conan Doyle, author of the stunning novels and short stories about Sherlock Holmes, *the* Sherlock Holmes – about to begin an exhausting tour with no support except a wife and a lady's maid. Not that his wife wasn't a great help, a huge help, of course. Nobody knew his shirts as she did.

The personage behind the desk nodded to a uniformed inferior, handed over a key, and murmured something about a hydraulic elevator, then smiled and said, 'Lift.'

Doyle looked at the woman, looked at the lift, sighed and said, 'Come along, Louisa.'

★ ★ ★

4

If asked, she'd have said she adored her husband, and she'd have added 'of course.' That expression often invites an implied 'but,' but she'd never have intended such a thing. She *did* adore him. She was aware of what she called his whims and his eccentricities, but he was a man and so entitled to them; besides, he was a suddenly and phenomenally successful author, also her first and only lover and the father of her two children. When he said, 'Come along, Louisa,' she came along. Her eyes, however, did not stop flicking about the hotel lobby as if she were memorizing it. Those eyes were small, blue, shielded by spectacles; the rest of her was slightly plump, a bit settled about the hips and bosom – no doubt about her having had children. Her clothes were expensive and correct and no more than two or three years behind the fashion, as they needed to be to be thought really *proper*. And Arthur didn't like what he called 'faddish' clothing, by which he meant noticeable, and which she called 'cheap.'

Still, those blue eyes searched the big space as avidly as the eyes of a woman studying a roomful of other women's clothes. She had taken in the man in the dark suit at once, decided he was a hotel detective (she knew that Americans had such things), decided that that was slightly thrilling, filed it away. Now, as she turned to follow her husband, her eyes went to the bronze doors, through which were coming a pretty young woman with wonderful copper-coloured hair and a good-looking young

5

man. The woman looked nervous, the man pleased and as sleek as a wet seal. Louisa Doyle saw him trade a look with the hotel detective; something passed between them; the couple came on. (*How interesting*, she thought, *he's fixed it with the detective and they're having an illicit liaison!*) The woman was chattering – nerves, Mrs Doyle thought; she's never done this before – her voice gratingly American, quite astonishing, really. How they got those nasal sounds, she couldn't imagine. She must try it when she was alone. And what had happened to the letter G in their participles and gerunds? Thrown overboard to lighten ship so that they could talk as fast as they did?

The copper-haired woman's eyes touched Louisa's, started away but came back, and the two women looked at each other, and suddenly the young woman smiled as if she and Louisa were sharing a wonderful secret. As if they were sisters. The woman looked momentarily radiant, happy (*in love*, Louisa thought, *oh, my dear*), and then she swept past, still chattering in a whisper to the handsome man.

Louisa Doyle smiled her small, tentative smile. It all pleased her very much. New York had already rewarded her with a small thrill and something to write home about. How nice.

'Come along, Ethel,' she said to her maid.

The rooms were precisely what she'd hoped for, more for Arthur's sake than her own; he was particular to a fault ('too fussy to live,' her mother had said). Both rooms had windows looking down on Twenty-third Street; the sitting room had a small fireplace, the bedroom a bed large enough for anything they might get up to. Arthur could be surprisingly athletic for so large a man; of course, he still played football occasionally. And cricket. Cook's had suggested that the new American fashion was two matching beds, but she had refused, blushing, using the Italian term *lette matrimoniale* to buffer her embarrassment as she insisted on one bed for the two of them.

A woman friend in their young married days had told her quite a daring joke about marriage and what Arthur called S-E-X: If a newly married couple for their first year put a bean into a jar for every time they made love, and if at the beginning of the second year they took a bean *out* of the jar each time they made love for all the rest of their married life, they'd never empty the jar. That had sounded cynical and depressing to Louisa and still did: she believed that she and Arthur were still, after years, putting beans *into* the jar.

Perfect the rooms were, then, with a perfect bed, and she wished they might stay there longer than a few days before the railways would whisk them off to exciting places named Erie and Buffalo and Milwaukee. But Arthur's career came first.

'I hope *you* have a nice room, Ethel?'

'Oh, very nice, ma'am.' Ethel was unfastening the hooks and eyes at the back of Louisa's bodice.

7

'In the back and upstairs, but quite nice.' The boned bodice was grey velvet with a high collar and grey piping, dull silver beads next to the piping – all quite tasteful, and in fact one of her favourites.

'You must be tired, Ethel. Heaven knows I am. All that hurly-burly of the dock! And no man to help you oversee the luggage.'

'Mr Doyle helped, ma'am.'

'Well, of course, but . . .' She meant no manservant to help; Arthur was, after all, the man in charge, the *general*, as it were, of the campaign that had had to fight its way from the dock to this very pleasant hotel. 'I do hope that Masters will be released from quarantine quite soon.'

'Yes, ma'am.'

'The bustle, please, Ethel.'

The dress had a separate bustle, very dark red wool, almost a brown, the actual bustle *quite* small but with folds of the wool falling to the floor. When it was off, Louisa reached into the opening in the skirt, just where her right buttock began, and undid the ties there, first reaching into the pocket that hung below the opening and taking out her notebook, her pencil, and her beaded change purse. 'I'm always forgetting these things.'

'Yes, ma'am.'

Ethel gathered up the skirt as Louisa stepped out of it, leaving her in her grey silk petticoat and corset, also silk, boned, decorated around the top and over the breasts with ecru lace. 'Undo me,

8

please, Ethel.' Ethel was folding the skirt; she laid it on the bed, then undid the corset.

Louisa sighed with pleasure as it came off. 'Don't you *despise* corsets, Ethel? I simply loathe them. It must be lovely to live in the South Seas where they wear practically nothing at all.'

'Oh, madame.' Said rather perfunctorily.

'Oh!' Louisa stretched. She untied the side fastening of the petticoat and let it fall, leaving her, rather daringly, in form-fitting combinations. She wanted to say, *It's a good thing Arthur can't see me now*, by which she meant it was a too-bad thing, as Arthur would have been excited and they'd have made love. Arthur, however, was out walking, 'getting the lay of the land,' as he put it. At any rate, she couldn't say such a thing to her maid, so she said, 'Who helps you with your fastenings and corset and all, Ethel?' She meant, corsets were the devil to get in and out of, so did the maids help each other?

'I do myself, ma'am.'

Louisa saw her in a mirror. Ethel was blushing. She supposed it was the idea of having help in undressing, perhaps the idea of a man's helping. Ethel was plain, in fact quite homely – 'homely as a mud fence,' Louisa had heard a man say of a woman once, though she'd never seen a fence made of mud. And at forty, surely Ethel was far past any dreams of men. Surely. Not that Louisa was any raving beauty herself – not enough chin, rather too little nose, too – but she had never thought of herself as *plain*.

'I can fend for myself now, Ethel. You go and have a nap.'

'You should have a nap, ma'am; remember you've been ill.'

Louisa was supposed to have had tuberculosis, but she didn't acknowledge it and didn't accept the diagnosis and hated the idea. She'd had a stay in Switzerland because Arthur had insisted. She thought it was all nonsense. 'I'm quite fit now, Ethel.'

'I'll just hang these things up, then, ma'am.' One of the steamer trunks was open and sitting on its end; a cave full of clothes was visible. As Ethel hung her dress in it, Louisa moved about the handsome room in her combinations. She tried the bed, found it gratifyingly firm but bouncy; she stood by a window and looked down on the tops of carriages and people's hats. New York City! She had been told that New York was terrifically energetic and quick, full of people perpetually on the run. London seemed to her about as much city as the world could want or need. Could New York be bigger? Quicker, noisier, grittier? London had had its underground for decades; what did New York have? Something called 'the El,' trains that ran along next to people's windows, which she would hate, she knew. The idea of people looking in her windows, looking into her *life*, appalled her.

'I'm going then, madame.'

'Thank you, Ethel.'

She moved about the room again. She touched

things, smiled at nothing, realized that she was excited – *New York! A hotel detective! An illicit liaison!* She came to the full-length mirror and studied herself. Without her glasses, she looked, she thought, rather pretty – but then without her glasses, she couldn't see very well, so perhaps it was only her poor vision. Her figure had come back after the babies, although she'd been secretly pleased (and scolded herself for vanity) that her breasts had kept their size. So had Arthur been, she thought. Of course, there was the problem of her hips . . .

She began to unbutton the front of the combinations. She slipped a lacy strap from her left shoulder; her breast appeared, happily plump, rose-brown at the nipple. She exposed the other breast. Yes. She undid more buttons, pulled the garment over her hips. There. There was the soft hair, paler brown, she thought, than her head, so intricately coiled. Her own smell rose to her, clear through the scent of patchouli. She slid the combinations down, pulled one side over her left heel, then the other over the right.

And, naked except for her stockings, wondered if anyone could see her.

She threw her left arm across her breasts and cupped her right hand over her pubis. Crouched, she turned, as if she would surprise an intruder. (*And say what?* she asked herself.) There was nobody, of course. She looked at the windows, over which Ethel had pulled lace curtains. Could somebody see in? Some horrible creature several streets away with a telescope?

You fool. She had had these fantasies when she was thirteen. They hardly suited her at twenty-eight. Aloud, she said, 'Remember – you're a representative of Britain!' That was what Arthur had said to her as they had come down the gangway from the ship. Arthur could be rather stuffy sometimes, was the truth of it, although she'd never say so to anyone else. She said, 'Remember you're British!' and laughed and took her hands away and walked with deliberate slowness to the steamer trunk and selected a flannel Jaeger dressing gown and put it on with the same slow grace. Then she looked around the room and even waved (at nothing), as if to show that she had risen above the moment.

When Arthur came in, she was lying in bed, the robe exchanged for a sensible nightgown because of course she couldn't go to bed naked. ('What would people say?' her mother would have shrieked.) Arthur's cheeks were red, his pince-nez fogged, but he was grinning. 'New York is a hurly-burly!' he shouted. 'Are you asleep?'

She was laughing. 'How could I be?'

'I walked to Broadway. I walked *up* Broadway. I walked over to Fifth Avenue and I walked *down* to Washington Square! It is all quite magnificent in a somewhat *active* way. I've never thought of this before. London is magnificent for its static things – buildings and statues and places where great things happened: the Monument! Westminster! New York is magnificent for what *is* happening – the people, the traffic, an electrical feeling. Perhaps it's money being made. Are you tired?'

'Why would I be tired?'

'Remember that you've been unwell, Touie. You mustn't over-excite yourself. And it's been an exhausting day. Getting us and our goods and chattels off the ship and into a hackney carriage; getting here – all that. You must be tired.'

'You're having an idea, Arthur.'

'Oh, well – I only thought – it's an hour until we have to dress for dinner – perhaps a bit of a lie-down . . .'

'Well – lie down.'

That went well, and they both dozed a bit, and then she lay on his chest and told him how silly she'd been in fearing she'd been watched.

'Nonsense, little one.' He stroked her hair. 'Do you know that the walls of this hotel are two feet thick? And do you know why? It's what makes the hotel so quiet: They put up two brick walls separated by twenty inches of air and then filled that space with volcanic stone! Yes, hundreds of tons of porous, and therefore quite light, stone between the rooms! I read the pamphlet the little man at Reception gave me – wretchedly written thing – and it's quite remarkable, quite remarkable. Nothing like it in London. It's very . . . mmm . . . *New York*.'

'It is quiet, isn't it?'

'So nobody could possibly have seen you. What you were feeling were my spirit emanations.'

'You mean *you* were watching me.'

'From a distance, and only in spirit, my dear.'

'And then you came in, in the flesh.' She snuggled against him. 'How nice.'

At seven, they dressed for a very early dinner (really more a workingman's tea, she thought) with Henry Irving, who'd left a card and an invitation to join him, but who had to be at the theatre at what she thought of as the dinner hour. Louisa and Arthur managed, in a practiced but never-mentioned ballet, to avoid dressing in front of each other. Louisa needed the help of Ethel, anyway, and it would hardly have been proper for Arthur to be there when Ethel was and Louisa was less than fully dressed. Arthur, therefore, dressed first while she stayed in the bed. He smoked a cigarette, put on trousers and shirt and announced that he was now decent by walking around to her side of the bed as he talked.

'Perhaps I should take up smoking,' she said.

'Ladies don't smoke.'

'You make it look so nice.'

'Only fast women smoke.' He was trying to tie a white butterfly in his cravat. 'Drat! Why did Masters have to make himself sick!'

'I don't think he made himself. I think he caught something.'

'Because he's undersized and pale as a ghost and unhealthy – typical London lower class. I should never have taken him on.'

She smiled. 'What you need, Arthur, is some sinister Indian. A dacoit or a dervish – something from one of your stories.'

'Damn my stories. Drat! I can't get this tie right!'

She got into her robe in the shelter of the bedcovers and went to him. He had lit a new cigarette, had it jutting from his mouth as he raised his chin for her to tie the bow. She took the cigarette from his mouth, puffed, and put it back. He cried, 'Louisa!'

'Hush or I can't tie your tie.'

'You must never do that again. Promise me.'

He was using his serious voice, when he sounded like her father. She finished the tie and said, 'I promise,' but ended the promise with a silent *never to take a cigarette from your mouth again.*

'I shall be in the sitting room. Shall I ring for Ethel?'

She began going through her dresses. She had put only three evening dresses in this trunk. All were conservative, matronly, 'nice,' the sort of thing that the retiring wife of an eminent man should wear. She had picked out the bronze with the gunmetal stripes and the *pavé* over the breasts when Ethel came in. She had been out for a walk. It had been quite exciting! Louisa was left unsure why it was that Ethel could go for a walk alone but she couldn't. The difference was some nuance of

15

propriety, she knew that, but she supposed the real difference was Arthur.

A little after eleven that night, Police Commissioner Theodore Roosevelt was walking – it might more accurately have been said *marching* – up Sixth Avenue. He had been a commissioner for more than a year, the entire time devoted to what in military terms was called a 'forward strategy.' In police terms, this meant reorganization, the ripping out of dead wood, and the tearing up by the roots of corruption and graft from what had been (and, he feared, still was, thanks to his three fellow commissioners and a wickedly immoral Democratic Party) the most corrupt police force in the country. Soon, he promised himself, he would go on to better things, leaving, he hoped a legacy – or at least the reputation of a legacy.

Part of his project of reform was this nightly walk, every night a different part of the city, to check on the beat policemen: Were they on their beats? Were they on time? Were they sober? Terrible Teddy might appear anywhere, any time from nine to midnight, and now and then at three in the morning. He had found sleeping cops, drunken cops, cops sitting over fires in trash cans getting warm, cops getting their ashes hauled by prostitutes, cops doing everything that cops shouldn't. The broken careers of cops littered the paths of Teddy's walks; the ghosts of fired cops haunted them as the fallen haunt a battlefield.

Roosevelt in fact thought in military terms – thought, too, that he'd make a damned good general, if only he could find a war. And of course he'd *be* a general, not a private or a sergeant or even a captain: his career, having started at least halfway up the ladder because he was a child of privilege, was of course headed for the top. And he *had* to reach the summit of whatever mountain he chose to climb; it was no good enjoying the view from even a few feet down. He had to *achieve* – but he also had to be seen to achieve. At that moment, he was thinking that his next step should be to run for governor of New York State. And to be elected, of course. He'd already run for mayor of New York City but lost – finished a humiliating third, in fact – and he'd been appointed to the Civil Service Commission and to this job as a commissioner of police, but what could a man do as one of several members of a commission? Where was the glory in it? Where was the fame?

He swung his arms, as if to a military band, marched towards Twenty-second Street as if on parade. If eleven o'clock at night was at least theoretically a dangerous time to be out, let the crooks and bad men beware: Terrible Teddy was armed with both a police whistle and a revolver. He secretly hoped some fool of a criminal (criminals were stupid, he insisted) would try something. Action – he was a man of action!

He was aware of a horse-drawn wagon heading downtown. Somebody sat on the box. The rig-out didn't look criminal and so didn't interest him, and he barely looked at it before returning to thoughts of himself as governor; what he saw from the corner of an eye registered only as *Sheeny with a wagon*. Of no interest to a commissioner of police.

He walked on, glanced at his watch, thought that the beat policeman was thirty seconds late. Another deadhead! Another time-server, another—

A large bulk in heavy blue wool rounded the next corner, his truncheon spinning on its strap as if he were giving a display of fancy stick-work. He would be Irish. They were all Irish; that was part of the trouble: they stuck together; they owed more to their common Irishness than they did to law and order; they were the creatures of Irish politicians, who got them their jobs and paid for their funerals, and they were the pawns of the Sons of Erin and the Hibernian League and Tammany Hall. The only thing that could have been worse, to Roosevelt, was if they had been Italian. A few Italians had been let into the force, doubtless bringing the Black Hand and other criminal societies with them, because it was well known that all Italians were criminals. Trying to turn them into policemen was like making a bed for the fox in the henhouse and expecting it to lay eggs.

'Sure, and it's Mr Roosevelt hisself!' The Irish accent was probably laid on thick for his benefit; the beat cops knew it annoyed him. The man seemed so jovial that Roosevelt wondered if he had been warned. Or was drunk.

'You're a minute late, officer.'

'Aw, I was having a bit of a waterworks in an alley, your Eminence. Hard to concentrate on the police work if your bladder's screaming for a drizzle.'

'Report.' Roosevelt moved himself close enough to sniff the man's breath.

'Ah, very much a great deal of the usual tonight, Commissioner. Staying alert, being vigilant, preventing crime.' The man seemed to blow his breath out with greater force to make sure Roosevelt got its pungent cabbage-with-onions scent.

'That's what the handbook says you *ought* to be doing. When I say "Report," I don't want my own words recited back to me, man. I mean, tell me what's happening!'

'Oh, sure it's very quiet. Cold, not many of the bad boys and girls on the streets. And this is a decent neighbourhood, gentlefolk all, most of them tucked up in their beds by now. I been checking the locks on the businesses with rigour; all well and good there. Cautioned one young swell was three sheets to the wind and headed for a rap on the head by some lushworker and his pockets emptied if he didn't go home, so I put him in a hack and sent him on his way.'

'You'd better have found him a night in jail.'

'Indeed, indeed, but that'd of meant me walking him to the station and leaving the streets without

19

police protection, so I used me better judgment and let him go. And isn't it that we're supposed to be preventing crime more than punishing it? Oh, and I met you, Mr Roosevelt, which is a high point of the evening and will go in my report for sure.'

Roosevelt grunted in disgust. 'Well, you'll simply waste more time, standing here jawing at me. Good night to you.'

'Indeed, indeed, and to yous, your Honour.'

The fat cop went off whistling and spinning his stick. Roosevelt, deflated by the triviality of the encounter – not quite what Prince Hal found when he made the round of the campfires before Agincourt – turned right and walked back to Fifth Avenue and right again and so headed home.

The wagon that the Commissioner had hardly noticed made its plodding way down Sixth Avenue, its driver seeming to nod over the reins. At Fourteenth Street, it picked an erratic route by side streets down to that over-romanticized area called Greenwich Village, now a louche resort of the down-and-out, the Bohemian, and a good many of the Italians who were part of the latest tidal wave to break over New York. Respectable brownstone houses clustered near the bottom of Fifth Avenue and Washington Square (although the original families had already moved farther north), but south and east there was squalor. It was a village in name only, bleeding into the

Bowery to the south and the new tenement area that bulged into the East River in that direction. It had been a village when Washington was president; now, the city had engulfed it, eaten it, digested it, excreted it as a slum.

The wagon made its slow way down Bleecker Street, then east until it was in the Bowery itself – the Bouwerie, as it had once been when the Dutch were there, now a bower no longer. Paved, built on, decayed, fallen from whatever grace neighbourhoods achieve, it was at night the home of the preyed-on and the predator – rats and feral cats; men who staggered when they tried to walk and slept where they lay when they fell, and men who turned out the pockets of the fallen and would steal even their shoes while they slept. By day, it had its pool halls and its dime museums, its Yiddish theatres and its saloons and its scams and its whores, as well as its businesses and its churches, its almost new buildings with their cast-iron fronts and their hydraulic elevators, its mission for the destitute and its police stations, whose gas lamps burned in the dark like the last hope of any honest citizen mad enough to wander there.

The old man on the wagon seemed not of the place, neither predator nor prey. The horse clopped on; the old man's head stayed down. When, however, he reached a short alley that offered its dark opening like a narrow mouth to Elizabeth Street, he glanced aside down the alley but did not stop. At the next corner, however, he turned right again, then left to go south on Mott Street until he passed a beat policeman going slowly north. The old man glanced aside with only his eyes. The policeman opened his dark lantern and shone it on the wagon.

'*Shalom*, Mr Policeman.'

'And the same to you. You're in a rum neighbourhood, Ikey; they'll kill you for the rags in the wagon, much less the horse.'

'I am careful. Thank you.'

They turned away from each other. The policeman dropped the flap of his lantern. The wagon went on but turned left at the corner, then moved faster as the old man flicked the reins on the horse's back. The horse did nothing so noticeable as trot, but the wagon was moving now a good deal faster than the policeman on his parallel track. It went back up Elizabeth Street, slowed opposite the mouth of the same alley, and made a half-circle in the street so as to stop with the wagon blocking the alley.

The old man got down. He almost ran into the alley; muffled sounds came out – nothing more, perhaps, than a rat, the scrape of a trash can. Then the old man hurried back, and, with surprising agility, lifted a bundle of rags from the wagon bed and half-staggered with it back into the alley.

Now the sounds were furtive, unclear – the trash can again, the old man's wheeze, a grunt as if at some effort. Then a silence. Something soft falling. A couple of thuds.

The old man came out, wiping his forehead on his sleeve. He carried some of the rags, threw them into the wagon, and lifted out a burlap bag that looked wet in the dim light of a distant lamp. A strong stench of manure was carried on the breeze that blew dirt and a days-old newspaper along the pavement. The sack went with him into the alley; no sound, then a soft fall of something, a rustle, silence, then footsteps as the old man came out, threw the now empty sack into the wagon and climbed up behind the horse and touched it into motion. Forty-five seconds later, the street was empty.

Not, however, for long. Four minutes later, the beat policeman rounded the corner a street north of the alley and began his slow progress south. The dark lantern threw its soft beam into doorways; the policeman's hand tried every door. On he came, not pausing at the crossing of Grand Street because there was no traffic now, and then hardly pausing for two bodies crowded into the angle of an ancient brick house, now empty, and its broken front steps. The policeman flashed his light on them, assured himself that they were alive, moved on and crossed Hester Street.

Three buildings lay between him and the alley. He tried each door – one, long ago a merchant's home, now a warehouse; one new, with a neoclassical front, a jobber's in hardware goods; the third a near-ruin with a closed saloon on the first floor.

He came to the alley. He opened his dark lantern

and held it up to throw the light down its length. He was already poised to move on, ready to see nothing but a rat or two and perhaps a cat. But he paused.

He took a step back up the street to get a better angle. He moved closer to the building, almost leaning on it. He held the light out ahead of himself to try to get the beam closer to what he thought he had seen.

It hadn't changed: it still looked like a bare leg, not down on the pavement but up in the air.

Fear of the new commissioner drove him into the alley. In the old days, he'd have left it for the next man and for the light of morning, but now it would be hell to pay and no pension if he passed up something like a man naked and dying of cold. He had a pal who'd passed up a drunk who'd fallen off Gansevoort pier and drowned; that had been the end of his pal's police career.

Gripping his truncheon and the lantern – he carried a pistol, thanks to Know-It-All Roosevelt, but the nightstick was the weapon he trusted – he moved into the alley, the dark lantern thrust out ahead like a talisman that would protect him from evil. As he got closer, he saw that he had been right about the human leg. There it was, sticking out.

He went closer. Not a man's leg, but a woman's. Sitting on a trash can as naked as—

'Oh, Mother of God!' He bent to vomit.

CHAPTER 2

Louisa Doyle woke before six. She didn't
know that it was before six; she knew only
that she felt wonderful, that she was happy
and safe and loved, and that she was in *New York* and
her husband was beside her in a marvelous bed.
She put a hand out to feel the mound of him
under the bedcovers; she moved a foot to feel his
hairy leg, like a guarantee, a surety of marriage.
Of protection.

She stretched. Daylight waited behind the closed
drapes; streaks of it bled around the edges and
told her at least that it was day. She heard sounds
from the street, too, the rumble of iron wheels and
the clop of hooves. It was all very well to say that the
hotel was quiet, but, even with double glazing on
the windows (a particular point made of it in the
brochure), New York was too energetic and too
loud to be kept out completely.

She slipped out of bed. She was wearing a rather
too demure floor-length nightgown, ten inches of
frothy lace at the bottom and the cuffs of the
sleeves, a gift from Arthur's mother. She laughed
to herself, then at herself: Arthur's mother thought

that, even married, she should be fully covered at all times; she, who had been naked in bed with her athletic husband (they had made love again after the early supper: after all, it had been too early to go to sleep), but had got up in the night only to put on the nightgown. As he, she supposed, had got up to put on a nightshirt.

What funny things we are.

She peeked out between the curtains. An apparently grey day, although she couldn't see the sky because of the buildings across the street. Directly below, somebody was sweeping the pavement. A man in a bowler hat was pushing a barrow that was covered with a tarpaulin. A hackney carriage was already waiting on the hotel side of the street; as she watched, another pulled up behind it. Across the street and towards Fifth Avenue, a man in a duster and a black soft hat was opening the front door of a shop.

Life. Life was beginning. Had she ever felt like this in London?

Something pinged and hissed in the room. *Central heating.* Another of the New Britannic's boasts. There was a smell of warm metal. The hotel itself was coming to life.

She made a very quick *toilette*, promised herself to do better later, and, uncorseted, got herself into a favourite, very simple dress – the faintest plaid over dove-grey wool, the sleeves full to the elbow, its own tiny pillow of a bustle nestled up high on her rump. Shoes to match – grey, at any rate,

26

leather – no hat needed, surely; it would be like going out into a house to step into the hotel corridor.

She planted a feather-light kiss on Arthur's cheek, willing him not to wake, not to spoil her little adventure. She wrote a few words on a sheet of hotel paper, 'Gone for a newspaper for you,' and propped it where he would see it on the bedside table.

There was a key somewhere; Arthur had been given it by the boy yesterday. How vexing not to have one's own key. Well, she would demand one at Reception. Ask for one, anyway.

When she opened the door, she almost fell over a newspaper that had been dropped there. A glance told her that there was a newspaper in front of every door. The *New York Times*. Headlines about something American, in fact something New Yorkish; she'd look at that later. Staid columns of print. It seemed a let-down after the pleasure of seeing the city wake. She tossed it into an armchair and went out.

The corridor was carpeted, and so her feet went silently along. Did she dare to take the lift herself? She couldn't make it work, she was sure; but there must be a boy on duty. It made sense that there would be a boy on duty all night.

She rang.

After some seconds there was a sound overhead, as if something mechanical had been woken and didn't like it. Then there was a sound below, a clash of metal on metal. And then a kind of hum as the hydraulic (whatever that was; she must ask Arthur) began its work.

The doors flew open. A boy – a real boy this time, not an old man – grinned at her, said 'Down?' and then threw his weight into closing the doors again with the same clash.

'Rest'ernt ain't open yet, miss. Cuppa tea if yous ast fort at Reception.'

'Oh, tea would be very nice, thank you.'

'Juss ast fort.' He threw the gates open with a noise that he clearly enjoyed. 'Watcherstep!'

The lobby was empty except for two women, both apparently middle-aged, thick, one with a bucket and mop and one with a large can, into which she was emptying ashtrays. She had a rag tucked into the back of her apron; she whipped this out and wiped each ashtray clean. Neither woman looked at her.

Louisa felt pleased, as if she'd been allowed to look in on the hotel's secret life. She went to the Reception. There was nobody there, but there was a little metal bell, like a breast lying flat, and a sign, 'Please Ring for Service.' She touched it, got a silvery clang, waited. A man she hadn't seen before came out of some inner sanctum with a suggestion of pulling straight a tailcoat he'd just wriggled into. 'Madame?'

'Oh, I'm up terribly early, I'm afraid. I, uh, might it be possible to have a second key to my room? And a cup of tea at this hour?'

'Tea, of course, madame. What room?'

She didn't know what room. Arthur knew what room, but she didn't. She said, 'I'm afraid you'll have to look it up. Mrs Arthur Conan Doyle. I, uh, thought it would be nice if I could find a newspaper for my husband. To read, I mean. Oh, other than the *New York Times* which is a splendid newspaper, I know, but something – lighter?' Why was she babbling? She did this; she knew she did; flustered by a man younger than she with no power over her and no reason to care what she did or why. Almost angrily, she said, 'Where can I buy a newspaper?'

'News-stand right next to the hotel, madame – out the entrance and turn to the left.'

'Oh, thank you. Oh, I didn't bring a hat.' She said it to herself, but he heard it and immediately rang a different bell for a boy – like most of the 'boys' old enough to be her father – and said to him, 'Tell the kitchen tea for Mrs Arthur Conan Doyle, *now* – will that be tea here or in the room, Mrs, um, Conan Doyle? – here, then. Then come right back and hop it next door to get her a news-paper; she'll tell you which one.' He gave her a smile to tell her what a fine job he'd done of passing on her commands.

She had to wait only seconds while the boy trotted somewhere in back and shouted 'One tea now!' in a voice she could hear: the ground floor of the hotel was *not* to be congratulated for its quiet, then. And he was back, asking which paper.

'Oh, something, mmm, *masculine*. I should think something . . .' She was going to say 'literary,' but the boy said, 'Sporting, I'm on it,' and he was gone. Then he was back, she handed over a coin, and then she was seated in a leather armchair at one of the tables in the lobby holding a folded sheet of pink newsprint with POLICE GAZETTE across it in highly decorative, in fact vulgar, letters. Below that it said, EXTRA EDITION, the letters only slightly smaller, a jot more tasteful, and then in huge black type MURDERED AND DISFIGURED WOMAN'S CORPSE FOUND UNCLOTHED IN BOWERY ALLEY.

Tea, toast, something called gooseberry jelly, and milk and sugar were put down in front of her.

'Good heavens!'

'Ma'am?'

'Oh? Nothing. Oh, thank you.' A young woman was trying to spread a serviette over her lap.

'We got coffee, too. Just ast.'

'Yes, thank you, thank you so much.'

She turned the pink page. There was an engraving of a woman lying in what could have been taken for an alley – something cylindrical might have been meant as an ashcan – but the woman was fully clothed. There was also a smaller engraving of a decrepit building and another next to it with a large sign that said 'Bar,' under it the caption, 'A Scene in the Bowery.' The rest of the page was type:

'Worst Thing I ever Saw' Says Policeman
Veteran of Thirty Years

'She Shone in the Light of My Dark Lamp Like Marble'

One of the most hideous crimes in the history of that hideous place, the Bowery, literally came to light yesternight when a policeman's dark lantern picked out its disgusting lineaments from the gloom of an offalstrewn alley off Elizabeth Street. Making his rounds as was his wont, this grizzled veteran of three decades on the force, Patrolman James Malone, said to the *Gazette* of his awful discovery, 'It's the worst thing I've ever seen. I never knew that human hand could be so cruel. This is the work of a fiend.'

The unfortunate victim, undoubtedly a lady of the pavement who chose her Lothario neither wisely nor well, was mutilated in ways not fit to be described in print, nor will we stoop to give words to the disfigurement of a once-pretty visage. With flaming red hair and a statuesque physique, this broken blossom met her Destiny at the hands of a man – dare we say that word, *man*, for one so heartless? – whose savage use of the knife surpasses the worst excesses of such grisly legends as Geronimo and Bluebeard.

Readers of the *Gazette* will recall the murder a few years back of another fallen female, one who called herself 'Shakespeare' for her ability to quote at length from the Bard. We recall the ravaging of her body and cannot but wonder if a similar – nay, perhaps the same! – hand was busy here.

The Municipal Police are hard at work on the apprehension of the perpetrator of this atrocity before – it must be said – he might strike again. A member of the Murder Squad who must remain nameless told us that their eyes are turned towards the docks. 'This bears the marks of a foreign, probably an Oriental, mind. The knife may well have been one of those with a curved blade called the kris or the kukree.'

Officer Malone hinted that the victim was unclothed when found. More terribly, she seems to have been arranged deliberately in a place and posture that would emphasize the horror of her death. Although neither Officer Malone nor his superiors could speak to us in detail at the time of going to press, citing public safety and the strict moral code insisted on by Commissioner Theodore Roosevelt, we were able to infer from the small amount of blood noted by Officer Malone that the unknown woman was murdered elsewhere and brought to the place where she was found. The means of conveying her there is unknown, as of course is the identity of the person who did it.

We will say, after our long familiarity with the police and with crime, that neither the location nor the final position of the victim was accidental. This poor creature was not 'dumped' in the alley. What the policeman found when first he looked with his dark lantern was *deliberate*. It showed forethought and it showed a mad intelligence of the foulest kind.

What has been let loose among us?

On the facing page was a large photograph of a buxom young woman in what appeared to be a corset with a lot of frou-frou above the bosom – perhaps what was called a Merry Widow – and tights. And a large hat. Louisa was bewildered: was this the victim before the murder? No; a caption said, 'The Lovely Miss Adelaide Keecher, now Singing "When I Take You to My Heart" at Tony Pastor's Theatre on Fourteenth Street at Third Avenue. She's a peach!'

The only remaining page, the verso of the lovely Miss Keecher, was all advertisements – for pills of several sorts ('Men's Romantic Failure Cured!'), corsets (illustrated), pistols by mail, practical jokes (The Flatulence Pillow, The Drip Glass, The Rubber Snake), books on dreams, Masonic conspiracies, the Rosicrucians, Hindoo love secrets.

How extraordinary!

She looked again at the first page, then at each of the four; then she went back to the account of the murder and read it again. As perhaps was intended, she got more questions than answers from it: What sort of mutilation? What 'disfigurement'? What was that about 'posture' – was the dead woman standing up somehow? Why did the policeman say it was the worst thing he'd ever seen? He was a *policeman*; surely he saw ugly things often – wasn't that what the police were for, to serve as barriers between the ugliness of life and decent people?

She dawdled more than an hour away, thinking these thoughts, watching the first people drift into the lobby, then into the restaurant. She had all the time in the world, she thought. A great luxury.

She had some notion what the Bowery was. There was a song about it; she couldn't remember it, but she knew there was a song. And there was something in her guidebook, she thought, probably a mention in the section called 'Areas of New York City to be avoided.'

Murder was hardly surprising to her. She had followed the Ripper murders in London several years before; so had everybody, she supposed. And her husband, after all, had dealt at second hand with murder and all sorts of crimes; they were what had made Sherlock Holmes go. But this murder, she found, disturbed and fascinated her. Perhaps it was its happening on her first day in New York.

Or her first night, more precisely. It seemed foolish to be distressed by the murder of a prostitute (and of course she knew what prostitutes were; she hadn't been raised in a convent, after all). Nothing could be further apart than her night, in the arms of her husband in a luxurious hotel, and that of the woman who had been killed and mutilated (*how?*) and disfigured (*how?*)

She would ask Arthur.

She left a coin by her teacup and got up, turned and almost fell on her front as she tripped on a small wrinkle in the carpet. Well known in her family as clumsy, she blushed very red and looked around to find if she had been seen. The two charwomen had vanished. One of the 'boys' had been rushing towards her, now slowed as he saw she hadn't fallen. 'I'm quite all right!' she called, and turned her head and saw a man in a dark overcoat just coming through the bronze front doors. She realized it was the hotel detective. He smiled at her – he had seen her trip, the wretch, hardly a license for him to *smile*.

'You okay, Miz Doyle?' He had a hard voice and a manner she didn't like. Maybe it was the 'okay,' a word neither she nor anybody she knew would use.

'I'm perfectly fine, thank you.'

'We don't want you suing the hotel.' He laughed. His *want you* had come out as *wonchew.* 'I'll tell Carver to see to that rug.' *Tuh see tuh dat rug.*

She didn't know who Carver was, didn't care. 'That's hardly necessary. It was my fault.'

Again, he laughed. 'Accidents in the hotel're never the guest's fault. Ask any shyster.'

He swung around behind Reception and disappeared. She realized she was holding the pink *Police Gazette* in her hand. Could he have read the name? It would hardly have mattered; he'd undoubtedly be the type who read such a rag and would recognize it by the colour of the paper.

And what was a shyster? Something Jewish, from the sound of it.

She folded the newspaper and held it against her dress as she crossed the lobby to the lift. She was very formal with the boy who drove the lift up to her floor.

Arthur was exercising with his chest expander. It had handles and springs and was supposed to give him the chest of a circus strongman, but so far she hadn't noticed any change; not that she cared, as she liked Arthur exactly as he was.

'*Where* have you been?' he said as he pulled the handles apart as far as his arms could open. He was wearing trousers and a shirt, but no collar, and his braces were hanging down from his waist. He let the springs pull his hands back almost together and he exhaled.

'I was in the lobby, having a cup of tea.' She made herself sound very bright and happy.

'Oh, Louisa . . .' He pulled his hands wide apart again, and the springs twanged across his chest. He brought his hands back together. '. . . is that wise?'

'It seemed perfectly respectable to me. They

36

offered me the tea; I didn't ask for it.' (That was not quite true; it was the elevator boy who had offered it, and she *had* asked. *Oh, well.*) 'And toasted bread. I was the only one there.'

He pulled his expander apart again, was standing with his head thrown back and his large but soft chest thrown out. 'I don't think . . .' The expander twanged as his hands almost hit each other in front of him. '. . . that we should risk doing the wrong thing until we know the local mores. "When in Rome . . ."'

'I've brought you a newspaper.'

He threw the expander in a tangle on the bed. 'Why is it pink?' He took the newspaper from her.

'I've no idea.' She kissed his cheek. 'I think it means to be rather daring.'

Arthur was frowning at the *Police Gazette* and trying to get his wind back. 'Where did you get such a thing?'

She knew that tone, so she lied. 'I found it in the lobby.'

He stared at the front page, opened it to the second, stared at page two, then started to stare at page three and quickly closed it. 'I'm shocked that they would allow such a thing in a hotel of this reputation. I shall have a word with Carver.' He balled the *Gazette* in both fists and rather ostentatiously pushed it into a wastebasket.

'Who is Carver?'

'The manager. His father built this place. It's all in the brochure.'

'Oh, please don't say anything to him, Arthur.'

'Why not?'

'Well – suppose it had been left by one of the boys. Or that house detective. We might get someone into trouble.'

'Serve them right.' He thrust his arms over his head and bent down to touch his toes, or almost so.

She sat on the bed and watched him. 'Arthur.'

'Yes, my dove?'

'What does it mean when they say a woman has been "mutilated?" I know what the word means, of course, but only in a general way. This sounds to me like some sort of secret code – the kind of thing men say to each other when they don't want the rest of us to understand.'

'Where did you hear such a thing?'

'In that perfectly inoffensive paper you threw away. There's been a murder.'

'So I saw! Louisa, I forbid you to read such trash!'

'It was the only thing *to* read.'

'We have a perfectly good newspaper in the sitting room! The *New York Times*, quite a good newspaper, I believe.'

'But I wasn't in the sitting room.'

He stopped trying to touch his toes. 'Louisa, you're being obdurate.'

'And you're making mountains out of molehills! All I asked was, what does "mutilated" mean!'

They looked at each other. Like any couple who mean to make it work, they feared each other's

38

anger, she his more than the other way around – until, that is, she got really angry. He looked into her eyes, she into his. He broke the contact. 'I suppose it means that some atrocity was committed on the victim's body. Such things can't be talked about in detail, dear.'

'Your Sherlock Holmes would talk about them.'

'Only with Watson, because he's a doctor, and a fictional invention shouldn't be taken as an example of how we're meant to behave. Please do let's drop the subject.'

He was standing now with his back to her, ready to start jumping up and down or something of the sort, but they could see each other's eyes in a mirror. She went to him and put her arms around him from behind. 'I miss the children,' she said.

He put his hands over hers on his satisfyingly large abdomen. 'So do I. But we're here, and we knew there'd be a separation, and we shall see them again in six weeks. Eh?'

'I know.' She kissed the back of his shirt. 'I shall leave you to your muscles.'

'Don't be ironical, Louisa.'

She repaired her costume – meaning mostly that she struggled into a corset without anybody's help, felt quite righteous for having done so – and selected a hat.

'I'm going to buy something for the babies.' She was almost out the door when she said it.

'Don't leave the hotel, Louisa! Louisa – I forbid—'

Louisa went downstairs again, really to see whether nice people were using the lobby, as Arthur feared they wouldn't, but they were. Still, because she had another reason for going downstairs, she ascended a wide marble staircase to what was called the 'mezzanine,' which seemed to be an extra floor that wasn't counted in the number of storeys. ('Mezzo' meant half, like the singer, she thought, so perhaps a mezzanine was half a storey.) The mezzanine had a number of things on it – the ballroom, some offices, an elaborate ladies' convenience with a separate room for dressing or simply resting – but what she particularly wanted to see was what was called The Arcade. It wasn't really an arcade, as for example the Burlington Arcade was, but it was like a little street of shops, quite tiny things, really, but with windows on the corridor as if it were a street. The shops were just opening. She bought a picture-book for the younger child, foolishly because she'd have another five weeks of America in which to buy gifts, and she bought two shirts for Arthur at a price she wouldn't dare tell him, but they would come out of her allowance, and anyway he'd be pleased because they were of excellent quality and came from something called Brooks Brothers, which sounded to her like Bond Street.

When she was done she went down to the lobby again and wandered among the tables and chairs, which were rather like the furniture in somebody's drawing room, if not in a style she'd care to have in a house, and she sat at an empty table and again ordered tea.

She was halfway through her first cup when a shrunken yet fat woman came hobbling towards her on two canes. The woman was old, her face doughy, her clothes expensive but far too young for her. Louisa thought, *Oh, don't come here*, but on the old woman came, even though half the tables were empty, until she was standing next to Louisa's chair, breathing like a blown horse.

'You're sitting at my table,' the old woman said. 'You're the wife of Arthur Conan Doyle.'

'Yes, I . . .' Louisa was flustered and embarrassed; she tried to get up, sending Arthur's shirts cascading to the floor, half angry because no one had told her it was the woman's table – whatever that meant.

'Don't get up, dear; I'll sit down. I hate to sit alone.' Her voice was very American, the consonants hard and the vowels nasal. The woman clattered her canes together in one hand and pulled a chair out. Louisa was already on her feet, so tried to help her. 'I can manage alone, thanks very much; it's easier if I do for myself, you see?' The woman fell backwards into a leather chair, her face red from the exertion, panting. She said, 'I'm Mrs Amos Simmons.'

Louisa murmured something apologetic, but it was ignored because a servant had put a dish of ice cream and a plate of biscuits in front of the old woman without, so far as Louisa could see, any order's having been placed. The old woman said, 'I live here.' She started spooning up vanilla ice cream. 'I've lived here since the New Britannic was built. In fact, I was here before it was finished. They were still painting the rooms on the second floor when I moved in. I was the first guest, and I've been here ever since. Mr Simmons and I lived in Syracuse for years and years, I'd hate to tell you how many. He was in salt, that's why Syracuse. Why don't you sit down?'

The business about salt meant nothing to Louisa.

'Then we went into chemicals. Still in Syracuse. We made a pile of money and then my husband died and I came back home. Sit down, dear!'

Louisa picked up the shirts. 'My husband will be wondering where I am. I didn't know that this is your table.'

'I've sat here every morning for ten years, so I've staked a claim, but I like company, if it's the right kind, if you know what I mean.' She grabbed Louisa's wrist with a surprisingly strong grip and pulled her down. 'Now *sit down* and tell me who you are.'

'Well, really . . .' Louisa wanted to be angry but found she was laughing. The old woman was like somebody out of Tocqueville or Vigne, whose books she'd read to prepare for America. She said, 'You know who I am.'

'I know who you're the wife of but I don't know *you*.' She was spooning ice cream into her tiny mouth all the time she talked. 'Have a chocolate cookie. But don't eat them all; they're my favourite.'

She swallowed. 'There's Sir Henry Irving, the actor. He always bows.' And indeed Irving, heading for the front door, was bowing, then giving a smile to Louisa, who waved. 'And there's that man who calls himself Buffalo Bill, which is about as asinine a name as I ever heard – like calling yourself Cow Willie. Oh! And *her*.'

Louisa turned her head to see.

'Don't look! Every day, she waves at me and I don't wave back and she goes right on! You see?'

Louisa saw an impressively buxom woman, corseted to within an inch of asphyxiation, who looked fairly harmless to her. Becoming aware that Louisa was looking at her, she cocked her head and smiled the sort of smile that shows interest but also restraint, and Louisa smiled back. 'Who is she?'

Mrs Simmons dropped her voice to a whisper. 'That's *Marie Corelli!*'

'Oh, my husband mentioned her. She's a novelist.'

'She's a Roman Catholic, is what she is, if you ask me!'

Louisa decided to be wicked. 'Have you read her books?'

'Certainly not! I don't read fiction, anyway, except for dear Mrs Humphrey Ward. Fiction is usually unpleasant. Life is unpleasant enough without reading about it. There's that nephew of mine. He thinks he's English.' To Louisa's surprise, she began to recite: 'Little Boy Blue, Come blow your horn, The cow's in the meadow, The sheep's in the corn.' She put the empty spoon in her mouth, licked, and then began to scrape the inside of the glass for anything she'd missed. 'Well, here you are, Alexander.'

'Indeed, Aunt.' A very handsome man removed his bowler and smiled at Louisa. He was wearing a very blue suit – hence the poetry, Louisa decided.

As soon as he had been pointed out, Louisa had looked at him and agreed about his seeming English – the clothes, maybe, and his thinness – but what really rang in her head was a word that hadn't been spoken – 'safe.' *Safe!* What did that mean? What was a *safe* man? Especially such a good-looking one?

'This is Mrs Arthur Conan Doyle, Alexander. Her husband writes. My nephew, Alexander Newcome. He was born here but he chooses to live in London, so he's got to be more English than the English.' She eyed him. 'That suit's too tight.'

He smiled and bowed. 'Mrs Doyle. I am honoured.'

'Alexander, I want you to take me to Macy's,' Mrs Simmons said while he was still talking. 'Mrs Doyle, I'll say goodbye for now. They'll put all this on my bill. No, I insist; I'm sure I have lots more money than the wife of an author.' She laughed again. 'Anyways, I ate all the ice cream. And the cookies.' She tried to struggle out of the chair and managed to do so only with the help of both Newcome and Louisa. Panting, she stood there and stared at the bronze doors. 'Alexander, ring upstairs for my maid and tell her to bring me the winter cloak with the fur hood. I'm sure it's as cold as your stepmother's breath out there.'

Newcome smiled at Louisa over his aunt's head, making her his fellow-conspirator in tolerating the old woman. Again, he bowed, said, 'Mrs Doyle, I hope we meet again,' and he went off. She tried to say, *But we're leaving tomorrow*, but the old woman was rattling on about the house detective, whom she seemed to dislike as much as Marie Corelli. Louisa excused herself and hurried towards the lift.

Arthur, a little to her disappointment, hadn't missed her; he was happily reading his lecture on the future of the English novel, with which he was going to entertain people all over America. He looked up when she came in, grunted, and went back to admiring his own work.

She didn't quite dare take the *Gazette* out of the wastebasket right then, but she did as soon as he'd gone off to visit his publishers. His American publishers, that is. He was published first in London, then in America. He'd never met the Americans and wanted to get on with them; as he'd reminded her before he went off, they were paying the expenses of his lecture tour. 'But not mine,' she'd said, and he'd delighted her by saying, 'Not yours, but those I gladly pay because I can't do it without you. If you weren't with me, Louisa, I'd . . . I don't know what I'd do.'

45

That had been very nice. It made up for his reprimand about the lobby and the *Gazette*, which of course she knew was trash and which of course she'd been ashamed to have the detective see her carrying, so of course Arthur had been right.

Still, she wanted to know more about that murder.

She and Ethel took all her clothes out of the trunks and shook them out and hung them up to get the wrinkles out, although the clothes would all have to go back the next day because they'd be leaving. She and Ethel gossiped; she told Ethel about the murder. Ethel seemed to be frightened and said she would never go out of the hotel's doors again until they were headed to the train. 'Better to be safe than sorry.'

Louisa didn't see what there was to be frightened of. Ethel was not, after all, a lady of the pavement, and Louisa thought uncharitably (and, she admitted to herself, perhaps inaccurately) that murderous fiends surely preyed on better-looking women than Ethel.

Arthur had come back rather late from his luncheon with his publishers, and then he had rested (she had thought he was just a bit tipsy) and now he was working on his lecture. It appeared that the real purpose of the luncheon had been to tell him that although it was perfectly fine to talk about the future of the novel, what people really wanted to hear from him was what Sherlock

Holmes ate for breakfast, so he had to spice up his talk with some Holmesiana. This had caused Arthur to wake in a foul mood and with a headache, as he looked upon Sherlock Holmes and what he called 'detective stories' as an unfortunate means to the end of writing 'real' books, and, very much to that point, he had killed Holmes off and hoped to have nothing more to do with him.

Louisa got out on the pretext of taking Ethel with her to have a little walk. His last words were, 'No farther west than Broadway or east than Fifth Avenue! Mind, Louisa . . . !'

Now, without Ethel, she went out into the pale sunshine of Twenty-third Street, where the noise of the city was as abrupt and surprising as a blow. Hack drivers were shouting at each other; carriages were going by; horses' hooves and wheels hammered and ground the pavement; workmen with trash barrels on wheels were sweeping dung and trash and slamming it into their barrels; men and women were almost trotting along the pavements, their shoes clicking like watchmen's rattles.

She turned left, as much to go with the stream of the nearest walkers as because she had any destination that way. She had thought she might walk to Broadway (and beyond?) and have a peek at it: she was after all a married woman and so entitled to a little independence. Ethel had walked about; why couldn't she? She got, however, no farther than the news-stand at the corner of the hotel.

The afternoon newspapers were lying in piles in front of the stand, which was only a small wooden structure with a front that opened outward to make two wings that were festooned with magazines. Inside, a wizened man was watching as people threw down coins and snatched up newspapers. He grabbed the coins and dumped them into a shallow canvas apron. If he had to make change, a hand dove into one of the apron's pockets and distributed pennies as if he were planting seeds.

Louisa found that she was hoping to see another 'extra' of the *Police Gazette*, but she didn't see its pink newsprint anywhere. She had a bad feeling that in fact she would have to ask for it, and the wizened man would produce it from somewhere under the stand's narrow counter. Is that what the boy had done that morning? *Gimme a* Gazette, *will ya, Jimmy?* With a wink? How sordid. And yet, how thrilling.

She tried to stand in the middle of the pavement to look at the various newspapers, but she immediately became an obstacle to the city's foot traffic. She moved closer and got in the way of the newspaper buyers. She tried to stand at one end of the piles of newspapers, and the wizened man looked at her between wary glances at the coins the customers were tossing down – a sidelong look at her, a glance at the newspapers; a look at her, a look towards the piles. After some seconds, he said, 'Djou want somet'ing er dontcha?'

'I was . . . looking for a newspaper.'

'Jeez Cripes, whyntcha try a news-stand?' He was interrupted by somebody who was making off with a newspaper of great value: 'Hey, dat dere's fi' cents not t'ree. Hey, you—!'

The man had got only a step away. He looked a perfectly respectable businessman to Louisa, but the news-stand operator talked to him as if he were a criminal. 'Djou want me to call a cop? You t'ink ya can steal da bread off my plate? Dat's two more cents, Alfonse, or it's da Tombs fer yous!'

'I'm sorry!'

'Hey, sorry don't bring my two cents back! Fork it over!'

'I thought it was a three-cent paper!' Both men were shouting now.

'Where ya from, Cleveland? Go on!'

Two more pennies were thrown down on the counter; the wizened man shouted another insult; but Louisa missed all this. She had just seen a newspaper lifted from a pile, already falling half open in a practiced hand that was swinging it up to read as he walked. She saw 'murder' and 'horrible' and a sketch of a woman's face. Was it the same crime? Would it tell her exactly what had happened to this woman? (And did she want to know *exactly*?)

'I'd like this one, please.'

'So take it. Gimme t'ree cents – dey're da little ones, not like da big pennies you got back home, right, Limey? Am I right?' He laughed, showing

49

desperate teeth. She opened the paper and tried to read and he shouted, 'Get outa the way, lady – where djou t'ink you are, Bucking-ham Castle?'

Blushing, she moved quickly towards the shelter of the hotel, feeling embarrassed and bruised. How Arthur would have scolded the man if he'd been there! But better he wasn't, better by far; bad enough that she'd gone out into the street alone, and then to be scolded in public! And yet there was something about it . . . like seeing the hotel detective . . . something – *vibrant*.

She slowed as she approached the hotel's awning. She held the newspaper so she could read. There were the sketch and the article. 'Woman's Mutilated Corpse Found.'

Her attention was caught by the sketch. Her first thought was that there was no disfigurement; the *Police Gazette* must have had that wrong. Her second was that the conventionally pretty face looked familiar. But from where? Then she thought it was from a hundred similar newspaper sketches 'by our artist,' the face in fact the fashionable face of the moment, almost an abstraction of the idea of prettiness.

She was walking slowly. She stubbed her toe on the low stone step of the hotel, caught herself, thought as usual how clumsy she was, turned into the doors that were opened in front of her by a doorman, and passed into the lobby with a copy of the *New York Express* held up in front of her as if she were trying to hide.

'In the darkest hours of the morning, a grisly discovery was made by . . .' Well yes, she already knew that. And she knew Officer Malone and his years on the force. 'Unspeakable outrages were wrought on the body of this poor creature . . .' That was more like it, but as she read on she saw that there was no more detail than there had been in the *Gazette*'s extra. 'Lady of the evening as she may have been, the unidentified victim . . .' That was no help.

She turned to page five and read on, but the story seemed to be structured on some principle of diminishing returns: the farther she got into it, the less there was. The beginning was sensation; the end was gas: 'The Metropolitan Police are working on the matter and hope to make an arrest soon.'

She sat in one of the lobby's leather chairs and went back to the beginning of the article and read more slowly. Malone, shock, mangled (that was new), unidentified – aha! 'Our reporter and our sketch artist penetrated to the bowels of the City Mortuary to actually see the body. (See sketch.) What they returned with is a once-beautiful face, rendered horrible by maniacal violence, but reconstructed by the specialists of the city morgue and our artist for the express purpose of aiding the authorities, in hopes that someone in the great public will recognize her. Our reporter adds that she was of middle stature and had luxuriant hair the colour of a new-minted penny. Neither he nor our artist was able to see more than . . .'

New-minted penny. That meant copper. Copper-coloured hair, not 'flaming red,' therefore . . .

It was as if it had fallen on her from the ceiling. She remembered where she had seen the face.

It was the woman she had seen in the hotel when they had arrived. A woman who had been with a good-looking young man. A woman there for a tryst, the hotel detective bought off. The woman's radiant smile. *A lady of the night? A fallen flower?* No, she didn't believe that, wouldn't believe that. And even if she was . . . ?

Good God! She, Louisa Doyle, was the member of the great public who could identify the murder victim!

She was upstairs as fast she could push herself into a lift and cause the boy to make the thing go. She burst into their sitting room and shouted, 'Arthur! Arthur!'

He was in a corner, working by the light from a window. His forehead was on his left hand; he barely moved when he said, 'Not now, Louisa.'

'Arthur! I know who the murdered woman was!'

'Louisa, please! Tell me over dinner. Can't you see I'm working?'

'But, Arthur – *please*. This is so important . . .'

'And what I'm doing is not, I suppose.' He threw his papers to the floor. 'All right! Now that you've successfully interrupted me, *what is it?*'

'Oh – oh, I needn't discuss it just now – I'm so sorry, my love—'

'Louisa, tell me.'

'No, you're quite right; I was thoughtless.'

'You will drive me mad!' He showed her by pulling at his somewhat sparse hair. 'Are you my wife or are you not?'

'Of course I'm your wife, Arthur.'

'Then I order you to tell me whatever nonsense you have to say about a murder! So that I can go back to work!'

She considered being angry, perhaps weeping. She was hurt, no doubt of that; on the other hand, he was the man and he *had* been working. She settled for a somewhat girlish chagrin and utter simplicity. 'I found a picture of the murder victim in a newspaper. The murder in the Bowery that I told you about. I *recognize* her. I saw her in the hotel lobby yesterday.'

At least he didn't ask her where she'd got the newspaper; she'd have had to lie again. Instead, he asked for details of the murder, which he'd quite forgotten; he asked to see the newspaper sketch; he asked her to explain why she remembered the woman. Then he tore the newspaper sketch to bits and told her that she was being utterly silly and he never wanted to hear about the matter again.

'I have a duty to report it.'

'Duty to whom? To report what? I forbid you to do such a thing.' His voice fell back to the level of a patient father's explaining life to a child. 'What you think you know about the woman is pure surmise. And what in the world do you know about trysts and assignations? You know nothing about why she was in the hotel; you know nothing about the man. In fact, your "recognizing" her is pure female romancing and wouldn't stand up in a court of law for ten seconds. Louisa, what can you be thinking of? I think you are exhausted and have overexcited yourself. Remember that you have been ill! Low fever can lead women to hysterical invention – you have woven an entire tapestry of cobwebs, my dove!' He took her hands and sat them both down. 'My dearest wife, think how it would look if you went to the police with this tale. What would a sharp detective make of a perhaps non-existent encounter in a hotel lobby, and a newspaper hack's sketch that could be any of a hundred thousand women in New York? My love, think!'

'You always say that police detectives are the stupidest men in the world.'

'Don't throw my words back at me, Louisa! It's not becoming to you. I ask you to *think*. Think of what it means if Mrs Arthur Conan Doyle tells the police she has a clue in a murder case. Do you know what the newspapers would call you? "Mrs Sherlock Holmes." That's what they'd call you. "Mrs Sherlock Holmes Finds Novel Clue." Do you see? My dove?'

She drew her hands away. 'You think I'm imagining things.'

'No, dove, no – you're too bright and too much my shining star for such a thing! I mean you don't have *facts*.'

And of course, he was right. She didn't have any real facts, if by 'facts' one meant something like the date of Magna Carta. 'Of course you're right, Arthur. Please forgive me for interrupting you.'

He kissed her. 'You should always be able to interrupt me. I was rude and churlish to you. Forgive me?'

They kissed. He went back to work. She went into the bedroom.

But, dammit, that woman was the one I saw in the hotel lobby! I know what I saw!

A closed carriage assigned to Commissioner Roosevelt pulled up at a side entrance of the City Mortuary. Roosevelt was out the door before its wheels stopped grinding against the kerb. He bustled across the pavement and yanked open the door as if he expected to make an arrest on the other side. 'Well?' he bellowed.

'All clear.'

'You're Cleary, are you?'

'Yes, sir, Lieutenant Cleary. Murder Squad.' Cleary was a tall, sad-eyed man with black hair that stood up like a hog's bristles. He was in fact the commander of the Murder Squad, and if he was offended because Roosevelt didn't remember having met him twice before, he didn't show it.

Roosevelt dropped his voice. 'Harding's in my carriage. Everybody's out of the way?'

'All o' them. The body's been pulled out.'

'I want you to go ahead of us and make *absolutely* sure nobody will see him. Harding's an eminent man.'

Cleary went off into the building, and Roosevelt did an aboutface and marched back to his carriage and opened its door. Seconds later, a man stepped down, but he kept his shoulders hunched and his hat slightly raised and tipped so that it masked his face. The two men raced across the pavement, Roosevelt even faster than the other so that he could open the mortuary door.

They went through, then moved along a tiled corridor whose overhead electric bulbs seemed less to drive the dark away than to dilute it into some kind of grey-green soup. Both encountered, but neither acknowledged, a smell that was the odour of death: chemicals, rot. Roosevelt led the way towards Cleary, who waited at the far end; when they got close, Cleary vanished to their right. They followed; there was Cleary, holding a door; again he vanished; they hurried to the door, found a stairwell, Cleary at the bottom.

In the cellar, Cleary pointed at a chipped metal door.

The two men went through. On the other side was an enormous room with an arched ceiling. Seemingly far away, like something on a stage whose perspective has been manipulated, a table was covered with a white cloth whose undulations suggested a mountain range shaped like a female body.

Roosevelt led. Behind him, the other, no longer trying to hide his face, had straightened and revealed himself as a man of sixty or so with a deeply lined face and not much hair. Roosevelt reached the table. He grabbed a corner of the white cloth and, as if brutality were required, twitched it off so that a woman was revealed from her copper-coloured hair down to the tops of her breasts.

The other man looked and then bit his lip and nodded.

Roosevelt left him alone with the body and went back up the huge room and into the corridor, where he found Cleary. He said, 'This is never to come out. Can you handle it?'

'There has to be an investigation.'

'We'll leave it that an unidentified woman of the streets was murdered. It will be an unsolved case.'

Cleary was not stupid. He was not foolish, either. 'Are you ordering me to end the investigation, Mr Roosevelt?'

'I'm ordering you to keep the identity of the woman and of her husband out of the public record. Can you do that?'

The two men looked into each other's eyes for several seconds. Cleary said, 'I guess I can. I just hope you appreciate what I'm doing here, sir.'

Roosevelt stared at him some more. 'Mr Harding will be grateful for your help.'

Cleary gave the faintest of smiles. 'That's all any man could ask, isn't it?'

The departure from the hotel next morning was nerve-racking and mostly unpleasant, everything ready to go wrong, Arthur in the deep gloom he always fell into when he had to get somewhere on time. Worse, he grumbled that it was Sunday and they hadn't time to go to church. Louisa pointed out that they often didn't go to church at home. He said she was being 'light.'

Ethel had been put in charge of the luggage and had commandeered two boys; they had immediately mixed everything up, grabbing the smallest things first and marching off with them, although the smallest (and most female) things were the very ones that Ethel and Louisa had meant to carry themselves so they wouldn't get left behind.

'Where's my satchel with my manuscripts?' Arthur demanded halfway through the hurly-burly that was moving them out of the suite and down to the lobby.

'Oh, I'm sure the boys have taken it already, dear.'

'I didn't see it go! If I arrive in Buffalo without that satchel, I'll be finished! Cooked! Plucked and boiled!'

Louisa ran into the bedroom and corraled Ethel. Ethel swore that the satchel had already been taken. 'They grab the easy things first, the wretches! They hope I'll take the heavy ones myself.'

'It's quite all right, Ethel; don't let them upset you.'

'One of them called me "honey".'

'Well, that's probably a compliment, isn't it?'

She ran back to Arthur to tell him that the satchel was safe, but he was already fulminating about something else. 'The tickets! What in hell has happened to the tickets! They're not in that satchel, I hope. Dear God, if they're in that satchel and it goes into the baggage car – no, not in the baggage car, I want the satchel with me!'

He was carrying his overcoat on his arm; she lifted it and felt in the inside pocket. 'There are the tickets, dear. Right where you put them.'

'Well, thank God for small favours.' He kissed her. 'You are a *large* favour. I shouldn't get so exercised, should I.'

'Well, you don't want to risk apoplexy. Why don't we go downstairs? Ethel will take care of everything.'

'You *trust* Ethel?'

'Entirely.'

'If I had that damned valet, we wouldn't be having all this trouble!'

She led him towards the lift. It was her view that they weren't having any trouble. On the other hand, to be fair, he was a public man with obligations for every minute of the next month, so he had every right to be nervous. She looked at her watch, a little thing pinned above her left breast. They had two whole hours before the train left.

Arthur recoiled from the lift and trotted back towards the suite. 'I'd best tell Ethel to hurry.'

Downstairs, a number of parties were leaving, perhaps taking the same train, she thought. That would be an odd and fantastic thing, if they kept meeting the same people all across America.

But how exciting it was going to be, even without anything fantastic! Cleveland, Ohio, sounded as romantic to her as Timbuktoo. What places she was about to see – and what remarkable people she would meet!

'Leaving already, Mrs Doyle? It seems unkind, that we should meet one day and part the next.' It was Mrs Simmons's nephew, Mr Newcome. He looked extraordinarily slender and stylish and glossy, as if somebody had gone over him with a tool and burnished him.

'Perhaps we shall meet in London,' she said.

'Perhaps we shall.' It was idle chat, meaningless; they both knew it.

Arthur came up then and she introduced them, and Newcome murmured something about 'your wonderful books' (even though he didn't say which ones), but Arthur was distracted because he had to wait behind several other people at Reception. He said, 'Yes, yes,' a couple of times, and then excused himself and said rather loudly that he had to catch a train, and would anyone who was not on a schedule please stand aside?

Nobody stood aside.

'This is infamous!'

Newcome touched his arm and smiled. 'Allow me.' He went behind Reception and through a door, appeared seconds later to wave Arthur to him. Louisa was left standing alone. She looked about, saw Ethel with the luggage, waved. Over the shoulder of one of the men waiting near

60

Reception she saw part of a newspaper page, a small headline, 'Has Jack the Ripper Come to New York?' That would be more about that poor woman, she thought. Did she have time to run to the news-stand? No, Arthur would be furious. Perhaps there would be newspapers on the train. Not that she *deeply* cared, surely not; she was leaving it behind; perhaps she would never hear of it again . . .

Newcome came back and said, smiling down at Louisa, 'One gets special privileges, being the nephew of the oldest resident. I've put your husband with the awful Carver.'

'Who is that?'

'The manager – a bit slimy to the touch, but otherwise all right, I suppose. It may simply be professional surface – a glossy carapace, like a beetle.'

He seemed quite brittle today; she remembered her sense yesterday that Newcome was somehow 'safe.' Today, she didn't feel it, whatever she had meant by it. As if he knew what she was thinking, he said, 'My aunt thinks I'm not much better than Carver, I'm afraid. She thinks that London has made me "a poser," by which I suppose she means a *poseur*.'

'And are you?'

'Oh, isn't everyone?'

At that point, Arthur came out, smiling rather grandly. He shook Newcome's hand. 'You saved our lives. We'd have missed that train for certain if you hadn't done what you did. Capital!' He smiled at Louisa. 'Carver fixed everything in two shakes. Splendid man, splendid.' Suddenly, his face darkened. 'Where is Ethel?'

Louisa turned him towards the bronze doors. 'She's the woman with all the luggage piled around her.'

'Has she everything? Is my satchel there? Dammit, Louisa, if she's misplaced that—!'

He insisted on seeing the satchel and then on counting all the luggage. 'Fourteen, fifteen. Or did I count this one before? Damn! I shall have to start over!'

'You didn't count it before, and there are fifteen, and that's everything. Do calm yourself, Arthur.'

'Ha! Well – are we ready? Boy!'

The same two boys had been waiting at the outer limits of the luggage; now, each picked up a suitcase in each hand and started out. There was confusion about a carriage, then about the trunks – they'd have to come in a separate vehicle – but Ethel seemed already to have commandeered both, so off the boys went. Then came Ethel with the small bags (the lady's essentials); then the boys came back, and so a kind of revolving wheel of people and luggage went in and out until suddenly the carpet was bare.

'Louisa! Into the carriage – hurry. Louisa?'

She was looking back down the lobby. 'Oh, Arthur, I like this place! I shall miss it.'

'We're staying here on our way back; you'll see it again. Come – come!'

She waved at Newcome, who was still idling near Reception, and then she turned and took a step towards her husband, and then she felt a terrific pain in her right ankle as she sailed through the air, as completely free of the ground as an aerial balloon. She came crashing down on her hands and elbows and knees and eyeglasses, the breath and the consciousness knocked out of her. People screamed; men ran towards her. Somebody tried to pick her up, and some of her weight came on that same right ankle and it was her turn to scream, and she fell forward again.

'My ankle – I think I've broken my ankle!' She looked through tears of pain and saw Arthur standing by the bronze doors.

He said, 'Louisa, how *could* you! Now we shall be *late*!'

CHAPTER 3

The Murder Squad had a big room in police headquarters at 300 Mulberry Street that was no more squalid than the hallways of the average tenement. The room was forty feet on a side, matchboarded up to the height of a desk, then distempered in some colour long forgotten, now more or less that of cocoa powder. Along one wall had been set wooden chairs with pressed, imitation-leather seats; the wall behind them had a smear of darker colour from the heads that had rested against it. These were for witnesses and suspects. Overhead were giant fans and lights with green shades of the sort used on factory floors; the ceiling above them was filigreed with gas pipes that no longer carried gas, and the channels that carried electric wiring; and above those were sheets of pressed tin, cobwebbed and darkened by decades of tobacco smoke. In this room, murders that had proved too tough for the precincts or that involved more than one precinct were taken over and – in theory – solved.

The Squad had its own lockup just off the big room. Anybody who went in there was assumed to be a killer and would already have been 'downstairs,' meaning in the basement, where detectives 'softened them up,' usually with lead-filled rubber hose. As a result, the lockup smelled of urine and blood and worse. Even though the door to the two cells was kept closed, the smells came through to mingle with the smells of tobacco smoke, sweat, suits too long worn without cleaning, old dirt, floor wax, and aggression.

The reigning lieutenant had a separate office opposite a wall of windows that had remained unwashed and unopened for so long that nobody any longer tried to look out of them. They looked, anyway, at a brick wall a dozen feet away. The sky, two storeys above, was long forgotten.

Lieutenant Cleary, the Squad's commander, had called a meeting to give them his own version of what Roosevelt had told him at the mortuary, but first he was huddling in his office with a sergeant named Grady, who was, as other detectives put it, tight to Cleary's duff. Grady was in his forties. He looked tougher than a lot of his suspects, and he stank of cigars. He wore a wrinkled double-breasted suit in a fabric that seemed to be covered with fuzz; his high collar was tight enough to cause his neck to slop over it like a pie's crust. He had little eyes, often bloodshot, and an expression that made people of goodwill want to talk to somebody else. He was wearing a bowler hat, even though he was indoors.

Cleary kept his head low and almost whispered,

65

even though Grady was sitting just across his desk from him. 'Here's the situation. Roosevelt tells me yesterday to go to the City Mortuary and get everybody out of the way so somebody can view the murdered whore. "Somebody" turns out to be Roscoe G. Harding, who owns enough coal mines to keep the trains running for the next hunnerd years. *Rich.* The whore turns out to be his wife – he recognizes her from some goddam drawing in the papers.'

'What's Roosevelt in it for?'

'Harding's a big Republican moneybags. Roosevelt wants to be governor. Harding sees the picture in the paper, he telephones Roosevelt and says he thinks it's her and he wants it hushed up who she is.'

'Why? She's dead.'

Cleary sighed. 'Because she's his *wife*. He doesn't want people knowing his wife had her twot cut up by some crazy who takes her for a whore! Plus he's maybe sixty and she's young enough to be his kid and a *looker*, and he doesn't want people saying she was out looking for a little of the real meat because he hasn't got it! See?'

'Much ado about nothing, like they say.'

'It's all in his head, yeah, but the way it's gotta be is, nobody knows the whore's been identified, she isn't somebody's wife, she's gone off to Potter's Field and that's that! Enh? Get it? We gotta say the case is dead, nothing more to come. Get me?'

'Where's the whore at now?'

'Husband took her last night and is going to bury her someplace upstate.'

'Today?'

'Pretty quick, yeah, I think.'

Grady screwed his face around so it looked hesitant and deliberately stupid and said, 'Ya know, Jack, a case like this, the husband is the obvious suspect.'

'Jeez, don't even *think* it! He isn't! There is no suspect!'

Grady shrugged. 'Just thinking.'

'Don't think!' Cleary put his elbows on the desk and leaned forward. 'Now.'

'Yeah?'

'Harding's *rich*. I don't see it yet, but I will – some gelt for you and me. He *owes* me.'

'Just us two.'

Cleary nodded.

Grady said eagerly, 'We tell this Harding if he don't pony up we go public.'

Cleary sighed again. 'That's why I don't let you do the thinking. No!' He passed big fingers through his hair. 'I'll let you know when I work it out. Don't you do anything! It's gotta be done right.'

'What about Roosevelt?'

'Oh, fuck him. Let him go be governor; he'll be outa our hair. He owes me one now too for doing this, but it don't give me enough on him to squeeze, you know?' He stood. 'Come on, let's get this over with.'

He put Grady at the squad room door to keep

strangers out and the detectives in, and he walked the length of the room and got up on an old ammunition box that gave him even more height than Nature had. He looked around at them. 'Everybody here?' He wasn't really asking; he knew that everybody was there. Good Cripes, he knew all their faces. He knew all their clothes. He even knew them by their smell, for God's sake!

'All right. Now.' He looked around at them again. His look was menacing, and the menace was real. Every man there owed his job to him. Half the men there owed their extra income to him. He wasn't standing up there to be kind.

'Good. Now, you've heard of a case we got, a murdered whore that the papers are full of shit about. The "Bowery Butcher." I want you all to understand that there's interest in this case from upstairs – got it? That means *I don't want it all balled up*. Get me?

'What has happened, I can say flat out right now, this case is dead. The fucking precinct cops and their tecs put their big feet all over it, and you can forget so-called clues, and you can forget what they call your "investigative techniques."

'I took over the case late yesterday. I reviewed all the revelant notes and reports. I and Grady interviewed the one so-called witness, which is the cop that found the whore. There's nothing.

'Therefore, we're going to clean this case up and do the paperwork and pigeonhole it under "Unsolved." Are you all clear on that?' He looked

68

around again. Every sphincter in the room tightened.

'What I want to make sure is, nobody from this squad talks to the papers about it. You got that? Not one word. Not to your wife, either, not to your girl, not to your priest, not to *yourself*. You hear me? I hear that one of you's talked about this case, you'll be back in a uniform picking drunks out of the gutter. If you're *lucky*, that's what you'll be doing!'

Some of them glanced at each other; a few raised an eyebrow or gave the smallest smile that lips could manage. They all meant the same thing: *The fix is in, and we're not part of it.*

'Dunne!'

Cleary's voice was a harsh bark. Everybody knew that Cleary had no use for Harry Dunne, who was a detective-sergeant but who would never get any higher so long as Cleary was in charge. Dunne had the reputation of being a plodder: his nickname from the distant past was 'Never,' because he was so slow: Never Dunne. He was so careful that he never finished. And, to the other cops' disgust, he was honest. Dunne was in his forties, grey, hefty, offering a round face in which women found warmth and reliability but no excitement.

'Dunne, you're gonna take charge of closing this Bowery Butcher case. Take Cassidy to help out. Clear?' He looked around the room once more. More smiles and raised eyebrows: it was okay to show that they were amused by Cleary's dumping this crap case on Never Dunne, and it was okay to be relieved that they weren't involved. 'Okay, then, that's that. Dunne – my office. Cassidy – you too. Now.'

Cleary got down. Finn, the squad arse-kisser, whisked away the ammunition box. Men impatient to do their jobs left in a hurry; others, more in love with leisure, sat at desks and put their feet up and lit cigarettes.

In his office, Cleary sat but let Dunne and Cassidy stand in front of him while Grady, hands joined over his crotch, stood by the closed door as if he thought one of them was going to try to escape. Cassidy was a smaller, younger version of Dunne, only a plainclothes detective. He, too, to everybody's disgust, was honest.

Cleary said the same things he had said in the squad room. Then he added, frowning at Dunne, 'I don't want you getting ideas, get me? I'm giving this job to you because you're not pulling your weight here; you're not closing cases. This one is all closed but the paperwork. Your job is to close it and nothing else. I'm doing you a favour. Get me?'

'Who killed her?'

Cleary looked threatening. 'How the fuck would I know? It's unsolvable. Write it up that way and put it on the shelf.'

'So what am I supposed to do?'

'You're supposed to do nothing! You *don't* try to identify the victim, that's a dead duck; you *don't*

70

advertise for leads; you *don't* see what your snitches say. Just do the paperwork and close it out.'

'Close it out.'

'Now you're talking. Take Finn and the Wop.'

Dunne groaned. 'If there's nothing to be done—'

'Do like I tell you and shut up. Cassidy?'

'I get you, Lieutenant.'

Cleary pushed a brown accordion file across his desk. 'Then get outa here.'

Out in the squad room, Dunne walked a few steps – enough to get where Grady couldn't hear them through the door, because he'd be listening – and he said, 'It's fixed.'

'That's the message I get, yeah.'

Dunne and Cassidy shared the cynicism common to all cops, plus a little extra because of what they'd learned trying to stay honest. Dunne gave Cassidy a conspirator's smile. 'So what are we going to do?'

'Can't we get rid of the Wop?' The Wop was one of the few Italians in the force, a quiet young man named Forcella. Nobody wanted him around.

'Not if Cleary says we gotta take him.'

'He's a fucking Dago!'

'Not as bad as a rat-faced Mick like Finn.'

'Cleary puts his hand on a fly button, Finn puckers up. He'll carry everything we do to Cleary.'

'That's the idea. Well . . .' Dunne looked around the sordid room. 'We'll have a meeting every morning to feed Finn some eyewash he can peddle to Cleary. I'll find him something to do to keep him out of our hair – maybe send him down to the Tenth to copy all their paperwork. He'll take at least three days just to chew the rag with his pals down there. Then he'll take two hours for the free lunch at Shankey's, and he'll come back sozzled and take a nap. Hell, maybe we can make it last a week.' He grinned at Cassidy. 'You ever think police work was going to be important? Like . . . *important*?'

'Ha-ha.'

Dunne shook his head. 'Cleary's got some kind of boodle going, so we gotta find out what it is. If we don't, we're waxed. But if we do and he knows it, we're fucked.' He opened the accordion file. Inside were two pieces of paper, one a blank form, one a copy of the patrolman's statement. Dunne laughed. He tucked the file under an arm and headed for the door. 'I'm off to the crapper to have a think. Don't close any cases while I'm gone.'

'Arthur?'

She felt for his warm, comforting body with her left hand. The hand got caught in the counterpane; she whimpered. She thought she was back on the ship because she felt herself pitching slowly back and forth, but sometimes it was side to side and sometimes it was end to end, a motion that made her feel as if she would be sick.

'Mrs Doyle?'

She tried to open her eyes. They seemed to be

glued together. *Sleep*, she thought. That's what her mother had always called it, that stickiness that glued the eyelids together and that became granules along the eyelids when she woke – *You have sleep in your eyes.* She tried to move her hand to wipe her eyes but she couldn't, and then they seemed to open all on their own, and she was frightened by what she saw – nothing.

'Mrs Doyle? Are you awake?'

She was looking at a ceiling, of course, which was grey and dark because there was no light. No, there was light, dim light, only a kind of glow that became no more than a stain on the darkness. Leaning over her, one side made visible by the stain, was some sort of woman. Louisa tried to ask her who she was, but although her lips and her tongue moved, no sound came.

'You've had morphine, Mrs Doyle. You're in your own bed and you've sprained your ankle, but you're going to be fine. Mrs Doyle?'

In her own bed? Was she back in London? But she'd been in New York. On her way to a train. To go to Buffalo. *With Arthur!* Where was Arthur? She felt panic rise in her as if it were a fluid that spread from her heart, along her arteries until a great gout of it blocked her throat. She did manage to make a sound, nonetheless: 'Arthur!'

'Mr Doyle had to take a train, remember? He got on his train and you're back in your room. Mrs Doyle?'

If it was London, why did the woman have that

incredibly nasal accent? And it wasn't her own room; it wasn't at all. Her own room had a ceiling papered with flowers that she'd insisted upon, even though Arthur had been shocked by them and said that other people wouldn't understand, but she'd said that she wanted to wake to flowers, and what would other people be doing in their bedroom? She said, 'Flowers.'

'Yes, sweetie, lovely flowers from Mr Carver and Mr Irving and, oh, lots of people! Beautiful flowers everywhere.'

Louisa tried to move her head so that she could look around and see what flowers the woman was talking about. Or was the woman mad? Had she somehow got into a room with a madwoman? She thought through what she would say and enunciated carefully, 'Where am I?'

'In your *room*, honey. In the New Britannic Hotel.'

The hotel. But they'd left the hotel. Arthur had staged a little scene and then that pleasant man, what was his name, had got him in to see the manager, Carver – *oh, Carver had sent flowers, oh, that one, the slimy one* – and they'd put all the luggage into carriages, Arthur and Ethel, and— Then she remembered.

'I tripped. On the carpet.'

'Well, you sprained your ankle, honey. Mr Carver says it wasn't the carpet, but that don't matter, does it.'

'I fell.'

'Yes, and pretty bad, too, sweetie, although I wasn't there to see it. Right down on your poor face, I heard. Have you got pain, sweetie?'

Pain? Had she pain? She didn't think so. She wasn't sure that she had anything, not pain and not pleasure. She felt as if she had been wrapped in something quite neutral, cloud or soft batting that nonetheless didn't make her too warm, and the sense she usually had of her feet and her legs and her forehead had been drained away. Still, if she was back in the hotel – well, not back, because she'd never left the hotel; she remembered tripping now, a sense of terrible calamity happening, about to happen, and then nothing. She had hit the floor, presumably. Or perhaps Arthur had caught her?

'Arthur's on the train?'

'Yes, sweetie, I was told to tell you he'd made his train in plenty of time, and he knew you'd be worried. He's sent you two telegrams, which Doctor says you're not to try to read yet, but I can tell you they're both very loving and nice and he misses you. So you're not to worry.'

She wasn't worried, but she'd have been happier if he were here and were saying things like 'to hell with the damned train; you're my wife!' rather than sending telegrams. With that slightly depressing thought, she fell asleep again.

When she woke a second time, she knew where she was almost at once (the 'almost' was a fraction of a second of panic) – hotel, room, Arthur-on-train, fall – and she was aware that her ankle hurt like billy-o. She tried to move her leg, and the pain caused her to make a sound, not a ladylike scream at all but a kind of guttural *Aaaghh*.

'Oh, thank God, you're awake.'

'Ethel?'

'It's me, madame.' Ethel's bovine face loomed over her like a balloon that had floated in the window.

'I thought you were on the train.'

'Oh, no, madame! My place is with you. How are you?'

'I want to sit up.'

'Doctor said—'

'Sit me up! Aaagh! Like knives in my ankle. Is it broken?'

'Sprained, madame. Mr Doyle and the hotel doctor had quite a set-to about it. Mr Doyle – *Dr* Doyle he is, really, isn't he? as he reminded the hotel man – said it was only a sprain and you could recover on the train, and they'd only need a litter and two attendants to get you on and off the train, which could be done through a window, but the house doctor said it was broken and he was going to hospitalize you. And then Mr Carver called in a specialist and *he* said you'd only sprained your ankle and bed rest was called for, and Mr Carver said of course the hotel would provide the very best care without you having to move to a hospital or some such. By that time, Mr Doyle and I had divided up the luggage again, and I got

76

all his into one carriage and off he went to catch his train, and the boys and me brought everything back up here – one of them calling me honey again to my face, and didn't I give him what for! – and they brought you up on a freight lift, and here you are!'

Louisa was absorbing the fact that her husband had gone away before he had known how badly she was hurt. She said in a somewhat slurred voice, 'I suppose Mr Doyle wasn't really worried for me.'

'He was, madame, oh, he was! But you kept saying, "You must go, Arthur, you must," and telling him to go, and it was you ordered me to divide the luggage.'

'I did?' She thought how noble of her that must have been. 'I must have struck my head, for I don't remember.'

'Oh, you took a terrible crack on the noggin, madame! Head first it was, and you've rather a black eye, I'm afraid, although it don't show so much if you keep that side in the dark. And your glasses broke to smithereens.'

'A black eye?' She was horrified. It seemed . . . unseemly. Then it seemed rather thrilling. 'Get me a mirror. The hand mirror from my little case will do.'

'Oh, madame, I wouldn't if I was you.'

'Oh, havers, Ethel! Anyway, you're not me.' *Good heavens, where did 'havers' come from? That's one of my mother's words.* 'Fetch the mirror, do, please.'

Ethel's balloon floated away, then reappeared.

Hands tried to push her up in the bed; there was a lot of stacking and smacking of pillows. The mirror was put into her hand. 'Doctor said not to upset you.'

It wasn't simply a black eye. It was a swollen cheek, a cut eyebrow, and a large purple-blue bruise with rather disgusting yellow edges that went from her forehead down almost to her jawbone. Louisa stared at it. She moved the mirror so as to get different angles on it. 'Well,' she said, 'I've never looked like this before.'

'No, madame.' Ethel was almost whispering.

'I shan't be able to go out.'

'Well, madame, with the ankle . . .'

'You mean I can't go out anyway. Is that what's meant by compensation? Or is it fortunate coincidence? There's something called the fortunate fall, which is I suppose what it might be said I had, if getting the face and the ankle at the same time were what was wanted. I'm babbling, aren't I. It must be the morphine.' She tried to focus, to clear her fuddled brain, but couldn't. 'Some woman was in here who said I'd had morphine.'

'That was the nurse, madame. Mr Carver insisted on bringing her in.'

She handed the mirror back, then held on to it to have another look at herself. It made her smile, then grimace as she moved her ankle. 'Vanity,' she said aloud. She remembered admiring herself in the mirror the day before. Served her right, her mother would have said.

The room began to drift away. She managed to say, 'I'll need my other eyeglasses, Ethel.'

She lay back and sighed. *Oh, Arthur.* What had she done now? She had worried him; she had made him almost miss his train; she had probably ruined his preparations for his first lecture. *It's all my fault.* She said, 'What time is it?'

Ethel's voice came from a far place. 'It's only a little past eight in the morning, madame.'

'It was yesterday I fell, was it?' She had a hard time pronouncing 'yesterday,' and by the time she got to 'was it,' she was asleep again.

Then she woke and realized that Arthur's first lecture had already been given and he must be headed somewhere else – Cleveland, was it? No, something with an Indian name – and she slept and woke, fuddled again – something about the doctor – and slept, and the windows were dark and the lamps were on and the strange woman who called her sweetie was there, and so she slept.

Telegram to Mrs Arthur Conan Doyle, sent from the Union Depot, Buffalo, NY:

MY DARLING DEAREST WIFE STOP RACKED WITH GUILT FOR LEAVING YOU STOP FORGIVE MY CHURLISHNESS STOP MY SELFISHNESS UNFOR-GIVABLE STOP HOPE RECOVERING AND WILL JOIN ME SOONEST STOP LOVE LOVE LOVE ARTHUR

Telegram sent to Mrs Arthur Conan Doyle from the Iroquois Hotel, Buffalo, NY, same day:

MISSING YOU UNBEARABLY STOP AMERICAN TRAINS PECULIAR STOP NO COMPARTMENTS STOP LECTURE HERE DISASTER STOP NO INTEREST FUTURE OF NOVEL STOP THINKING RETURN ENGLAND SOONEST STOP LOVE YOU MISS YOU STOP HAVE INSUFFICIENT UNDERWEAR STOP LOVE ARTHUR

And Louisa woke. Morning again. Knowing where she was but feeling muddled.

'Ethel?'

'Yes, madame.'

'He gave me more morphine, didn't he.'

'Oh, yes, madame; you were groaning in pain.'

'Well, I don't appreciate having been rendered unconscious for almost – good heavens, how long is it, nearly two days now – however well intentioned the physician. I want to get up.'

'Oh, no, madame! Doctor strictly forbids it!'

'Ethel, I have a call of nature!'

Ethel produced a hideous enamel pan from under the bed. Louisa looked at it. She was expected to straddle it, as she had had to do yesterday, she remembered now. For not the first time, by far, she envied Arthur for his ability to project urine to a distance. She said, 'I suppose the doctor isn't a woman.' She slowly pulled back the bedclothes and tried to move her legs to the edge of the bed. 'Aaaarghhh!'

'Madame, madame—'

'Hush, Ethel! I'm not going to sit ever again on some cheap enamel object that looks as if it was made for scooping goldfish out of a pond! Give me your hand.' She gripped Ethel's hand so tightly that Ethel made a face. 'Now I'm going to hop to the WC. You're going to hold on to me so I don't fall and smash the other side of my face. Ready? Off we go . . .'

She had done a lot of hopping as a little girl, but she had not then been feeling the after-effect of morphine. It was as if she had a ten-pound weight tied to her good foot. Still, she managed to get to an armchair, on which she leaned until she'd recovered her balance and her breath, and then she hopped on and at last got to the lavatory door. 'I can make it from here alone. Don't leave.' She started to close the door, then looked out. 'I want to send a telegram, so get a form. And Mr Doyle's itinerary. And a boy to carry the telegram to wherever they send them from. Or perhaps the hotel has its own office. Find out.' She half-closed the door again, then opened it. 'And order me some breakfast. I'm ravenous. Tea, toast, a three-minute egg, some jam but not that horrible gooseberry stuff. And a cup of tea for you as well if you want some.'

Half an hour later, enthroned in a huge pile of pillows and dressed in a clean nightgown and an ecru satin bedjacket of which she was particularly fond (an almost military cut – rather a joke, even

81

to lace epaulettes), she was finishing her breakfast and studying her right ankle, which she had left poking out of the bedcovers. It was as black-and-blue as her face but far more swollen. 'Elephantiasis,' she said aloud. There was nobody to say it to: she had sent Ethel out for the newspapers – 'All of them!' – because she had remembered that poor woman who had been murdered. She sighed. 'You really are a clumsy juggins, Louisa.' She tried to move her foot a fraction of an inch side to side. 'Aaarghh!' She reread Arthur's two telegrams for the sixth or seventh time and thought how really sweet he was. What did he mean about the underwear, she wondered.

When Ethel came back with the newspapers, she said that the doctor and Mr Carver were coming up. Louisa swore – or as nearly swore as she dared in front of Ethel – and tried to object but failed. She decided that the best thing was to seem busy, even to *be* busy; she had Ethel bring the cards from the mostly hideous flowers she could now see all around the room, and a pencil and paper for making a list.

Some of the flowers seemed to be from people she knew in the hotel – Henry Irving; the remarkable Mrs Simmons; even her nephew, Mr Newcome; Carver – but others were from people she had never met: 'the wait staff and kitchen workers of the New Britannic,' somebody named Mrs Alonzo Gappert, several enthusiastic lovers of Sherlock Holmes (who, she suspected, really wanted an introduction to her husband). There was a small bouquet from Marie Corelli, the novelist, whom she remembered smiling at after Mrs Simmons had said something disparaging; she also remembered Arthur's giving some sort of look when the name was mentioned at Reception. Well, she had this to say for the woman: hers and Newcome's were the most tasteful flower arrangements of the lot. Both were fairly small, subtly coloured – far superior to the two dozen blood-red roses of Carver's or the three-foot-tall monstrosity of lilies and ferns from one of the Holmesians.

As she wrote her thank-you notes, she thought of poor Arthur, far away somewhere; of that dead woman, disfigured – is that what the word meant, that her face had been like Louisa's own, bruised and discoloured? – murdered, left in an alley; of her children, whom she missed and wanted with her: how lovely it would be to snuggle into the bed under the flowered ceiling, a child on either side of her, a pile of children's books, their warm, scented small bodies—

'Mr Carver and Dr Strauss, madame.'

Carver *was* obnoxious – Uriah Heep crossed with Mary Shelley's creature – as she saw the instant he oozed around her doorframe, as if he had no more skeleton than a leech. He said he'd come to make sure she was recovering, but what he really wanted was her signature on a 'little paper' that absolved the hotel of any fault for her fall. He had a fountain pen ready in his hand. She remembered a bit of her mother's advice: *Never sign anything if they bring their own pen.* It was much better than her mother's advice about sex had been.

'No, Mr Carver, I won't sign. I'm afraid I'm not compos because of the drugs *your* doctor has given me. How would that look if it ever came to law?'

He went away, to be replaced by the doctor, a large man with a beard, his suit mostly unpressed, a gold chain crossing his waistcoat as if anchoring one side to the other, a general look of failure, and a German accent. He told her his name was Strauss; he tried to give her more morphine, which she rejected; and he said he wanted her to be seen by somebody named Galt, who took care of 'old Mr Carver upstairs.' Galt was recommended as an expert on sprains – 'old people, they fall a lot' – and she said she'd see, although privately she thought that the doctor ought to be the expert on sprains, not somebody upstairs. What good was he?

'Not a new word in a one of them!' Louisa cried. She pushed the newspapers off her bed. She was testy because without morphine her ankle hurt, just as the doctor had said it would, and besides the pain itself she hated his being right about it. 'There wasn't a single new word about that woman in today's papers. Nothing new at all – not a syllable! That isn't right, Ethel. It isn't normal. The police are supposed to find clues, witnesses,

84

all of that! And the newspapers are supposed to report it. And it's as if nobody's doing anything!' She thought of the young woman in the lobby, that brilliant smile. 'It's as if she never existed! As if she'd been . . .' She searched for what she meant, couldn't quite yet face the word *erased*.

'She was a fallen woman, madame.'

'Was she? How do we know? Did the newspapers say how they knew? "A lady of the pavement." What an expression! Who writes these things? Who makes these judgments?' She pushed herself up again, groaned, and motioned for Ethel. 'I had a newspaper that had a sketch of that poor woman in it. I want a copy of that sketch.'

'Oh, dear me, madame.'

'I want . . . I want . . . I don't know what I want! Yes, I do – I want that woman not to have been murdered!' She stared into the distance. 'I want a telephone.'

'There are telephone boxes off the lobby, madame.'

'And I can't get down to the lobby! Oh, blast!' That was a curse word of Arthur's that he had told her would pass muster in good company. 'Drat!' So was that. 'Oh, dammit to hell!' That was not.

'Madame!'

'I want to know who wrote that article for that newspaper – it was the *Express*, I'm sure it was the *Express* – that had the sketch with it. *He* must have known something. As soon as I'm able, I shall use the telephone to talk to him.' She let herself fall back, then propped herself up again. 'Although he'll be perfectly awful. Some poorly shaven drunkard in a collarless shirt and a bowler hat, I daresay. Smoking a cigar. With his feet up on his desk and holes in the soles of his shoes. Smelling of onions. And it's men like this whom we allow to write things like "lady of the pavement." It's *men* who do that, Ethel, vulgarians like this cigar-smoking brute who wrote the piece in the *Express*. I *must* talk to him. Next time you go downstairs, Ethel, tell Reception that I *particularly* want a copy of two days ago's *New York Express*, and they're to send it up the instant they have it!'

She lay back and closed her eyes and waited for sleep to come, as it had come so easily throughout the day before. But morphine, which takes its name from the god of sleep, becomes a demon of wakefulness when it fades from the body: now, images chased each other like playful dogs across her brain: the lobby, that woman, the house detective, Arthur, 'mutilation,' the awful Carver; that poor woman . . .

Erased, she thought. *It isn't right. I shall have to—to—?* To what? Go to the police? What police? Did they have divisions here, as in London? Would she have to go to a division in the horrible Bowery because the murder had been discovered there?

And then a name popped into her head. A name that Arthur had mentioned: Theodore Roosevelt, whom Arthur had said something good about because he was cleansing the New York police of corruption. And he had written an admiring letter to Arthur about one of his non-Sherlock Holmes novels.

She would write to Theodore Roosevelt!

'Ethel!'

Ethel, who was sitting near by and was almost asleep, jumped up and gave a yelp.

'Ethel, pen and paper! At once! And I shall need a messenger!'

In his office at police headquarters an hour later, Terrible Teddy was striding up and down, smacking one fist into the palm of the other hand and dictating a memo titled 'To All Officers of the Rank of Lieutenant and Above.'

'—the tidal wave of corrupt behaviour that smashed upon the shores of this city years ago must be strangled at the very root!' He stopped, fist in palm. 'No, strike that last part; it's a mixed metaphor. Tidal wave – mm, ah – back to, where was I . . . ?'

'Tidal wave of corrupt behaviour that smashed upon the shores of this city years ago must be—'

'Right. Yes. Must be, must be – ready? – must be driven back by an effort – make that concerted effort – by all members of this department with every fibre of their beings! No, make that singular – being. Every fibre of their being. Therefore – new sentence, got that? – Therefore, I am directing that every officer of the rank of lieutenant and above

87

will make a full accounting each July first of all bank accounts, real estate, business holdings, mmm – let's see, where else do they put money . . . ?'

A mahogany door opened; a head appeared. 'Can you be interrupted?'

'What now!'

A young man pushed through into the room and held up a piece of paper. 'Interesting letter, sir!' He had an accent like Roosevelt's, rather British in its dropped Rs, rather New England in its precision and its flat vowels, recognizable as probably Harvard, as his clothes were recognizable as certainly bespoke.

Roosevelt looked at the stenographer, another young man, but one who had a New York accent and inferior clothes. Roosevelt said, 'Leave us, but stay handy.' *Handy* was a word he'd learned in the West. He thought it made him sound both manly and democratic.

When the stenographer was gone, Roosevelt said, 'Well?'

'Chief, you remember the woman whose body was found in the Bowery? She'd been—'

'Of course I remember; don't go into it!'

'Pree-cisely! Well, here's a note to you on the stationery of the New Britannic Hotel from a woman who says she saw the victim in the hotel *with a man* on the day before the body was found.'

'Another crank.'

The young man grinned. 'She's the wife of Arthur Conan Doyle.'

Roosevelt frowned, then took off his pince-nez and stared at the young man. 'The newspapers.'

'There's that potential, Chief, but she's appealing to you to "keep this poor woman from being erased." Her words.' He said, with the satisfaction only the young can know when they think they're scoring on their elders, 'Maybe she's a crank even though she's the wife of Sherlock Holmes.'

Roosevelt took the letter, replaced the pince-nez, and said as he was reading, 'I'm attending a dinner for Doyle when he gets back from some tour he's making. Why the devil isn't she with him? Women have become so unpredictable.'

'I could find out.'

'No! "No fuss" – those are the words to go by. I don't want any public fuss about poor Harding's wife. I promised him that . . .' Roosevelt shook his head, then shook the letter. 'This woman says she saw the victim with a "young man." I don't think a man of Harding's calibre need hear that sort of thing about his wife, and certainly not read it in the gutter press.' He handed the letter back. 'Turn it over to the Murder Squad and have them deal with it. Tell them only that none of this is to come out and the watchword is "No fuss." He thought of what he'd said. 'Watch*words*. Are.'

The young man saluted. 'Right, Chief.'

'And send back that stenographer.' He began to walk up and down, smacking a fist into a palm. Where was he when he had been stopped? Tidal wave – fibre – aha, listing assets . . .

CHAPTER 4

Telegram to Mrs Arthur Conan Doyle, New Brittanic Hotel, NY, from Iroquois Hotel, Buffalo, NY:

MY DARLING STOP CHANGING LECTURE ENTIRELY STOP PRIVATE LIFE OF SHERLOCK HOLMES INSTEAD STOP ERIE PENNSYLVANIA TOMORROW STOP FOOD WRETCHED SO FAR STOP THINKING OF YOU STOP ALL MY LOVE DEAR ONE STOP LEAVING FOR ERIE TEN MINUTES STOP YOUR ADORING HUSBAND

Telegram to Mr Arthur Conan Doyle, Cattaraugus Hotel, Erie, Pennsylvania:

DEAREST ARTHUR MISSING YOU EVERY MINUTE STOP OH THE FOOLS STOP FUTURE OF NOVEL WAS BRILLIANT STOP DO YOU HAVE ENOUGH SHIRTS STOP DITTO UNDERSHIRTS STOP YOUR LOVING WIFE

Telegram to Mrs Arthur Conan Doyle, New Britannic Hotel, NY, from Cattaraugus Hotel, Erie, Pennsylvania:

SWEET DOVEKINS STOP ARRIVED ERIE I HOUR
LATE STOP MUCH VEXATION AT HOTEL OVER
MISPLACED RESERVATION STOP LECTURED 50
OVERWEIGHT WOMEN STOP QUESTIONS RE
HOLMES' SHAVING SOAP, COLOUR OF TOWELS,
BEDLINEN STOP DITTO WATSON STOP AM GOING
MAD STOP WHEN WILL YOU JOIN ME I NEED YOU
STOP ARTHUR PS CLEVELAND TOMORROW 2
DAYS 3 WOMEN'S CLUBS STOP THIS IS HELL
STOP MISPLACED RUBBER OVERSHOES SOMEHOW
STOP SNOWING HERE STOP YOUR ARTHUR

'Mr Doyle is unhappy,' Louisa said, waking on
the third morning after her accident.

'I should think so, madame! Worried sick about
you and in a strange country – it's a wonder he
can go on.'

'Well, it's only been three days.'

'Will you get up today to go to the convenience,
madame?'

'Of course I will; I did yesterday, didn't I?'

'You spent a restless night, nurse said.'

'Oh, that nurse! Every time I did go to sleep,
she woke me to ask how I was feeling. And that
voice! I've been trying to make some of the
sounds she does – "*naow*" – no, that isn't quite
right; I can't get quite far enough up into my
nose. "*Naow, Miiiz Doy-uhl, haow arrrre we.*" No,
I can't do it. Perhaps Americans have different
nasal passages.'

91

'What she says, madame, is she can't understand a word you say.'

'I suppose that would make sense.' She leaned back, focused, said, '*Naow.* No, I can't get it right. Well, practice, practice.' She handed Ethel the telegrams and told her to put them somewhere. 'I shall write Mr Doyle several real letters and send them ahead so they'll be waiting for him. Telegrams are finally rather irritating. I keep reading STOP as an imperative that begins the next sentence, so that if he's written "Missing you," I read "Stop missing you." I'd think they could have found a way of sending the full stop instead of having to spell out "stop."' She put her hands on the mattress and swung her legs over the edge of the bed. 'I'm getting up.'

'Oh, wait – wait—'

'Nonsense! I feel a thousand times better today, Ethel! I feel *energized – because I did something!* And I have a task for you, Ethel. I want you to summon that house detective.'

'Oh, madame, is that wise?'

'I wrote to Commissioner Roosevelt, and I need to have all my thoughts and ideas marshaled for when he wants to talk to me about the matter. Anyway, I shall go mad if I don't do *something.* I can't just lie in bed! I feel like one of those whales that washed ashore on the Irish coast. Beached! Out of my element. How bored they must have been! When they weren't terrified, I mean. That hotel detective, you see, knows things. And *I* know something – that that woman was in his hotel, and he saw her, and so he knows who she is. And obviously he's done nothing about it, or it would be all over the newspapers! Therefore, I shall talk to him. Get him.'

'But – a detective, madame – I don't know what to say . . .'

'Say, "Mrs Doyle wishes to see Mr" – what's his name? Find it out – ask at Reception. Anyway, he'll be sitting in the lobby, looking masculine. Say to him – "Mrs Doyle wishes to see you at once on an important matter." You may say "Mrs Doyle demands" if you like. You could also say "requires." But not "needs," that sounds so sort of wilting. "Requires" may be a bit too royal. Well, you decide.'

'Now, madame?'

'After I have my breakfast.'

Ethel looked terrified. Louisa supposed she would have to give Ethel something special. A pay rise? No, she couldn't afford that, and thinking so brought up the problem of money. Now that she thought about it, she had only what she had had in her handbag when she had suffered the fall.

Lieutenant Cleary was sitting in his office. His door had a pane of glass in it so that he could look into the big room and see who wasn't pulling his weight, an expression he used a lot to cover the responsibilities of the Murder Squad, which included investigating murders, beating suspects senseless, and finding illicit sources of money.

Cleary was looking through his window, but he wasn't focusing. He saw a D named Francotte reading a dirty book he'd taken from a suspect, but he didn't react. His real concern lay on his desk.

He looked down at it. It was a piece of heavy notepaper, slightly off-white, deckle-edged. At the top, 'Mrs Arthur Conan Doyle' was embossed in letters that looked to Cleary like some of the adverts for girlie shows. There was also a smaller piece of paper clipped to it; on it, in a very neat hand, were the words 'TR says see to this at once. The watchword is No Fuss. Keep Roscoe Harding in the dark. Shut the woman up.'

Cleary lifted the paper and read what Mrs Arthur Conan Nose-poker had written. He made a face, then surged from his chair like a sea lion coming out of the water and pulled open his door.

'Grady!'

Without waiting to see whether he had been heard, he collapsed back into his chair. He had been heard, of course; the entire Murder Squad had fallen silent for a few seconds, then started up again: a few chuckles, several sarcasms aimed at Sergeant Grady, a few farts.

'Yeah?'

Cleary blew out his breath to show disgust. 'Harvard Harry brought this down.' He flicked the note across the desk with a finger.

Grady pulled a chair that matched those for suspects to the desk and sat without being asked. He read the note that was clipped to the embossed paper, then read the embossed paper itself. 'Jeez,' he said.

Cleary grunted. 'This case is supposed to be sewed up.'

'Tighter'n a virgin's twat! Finn says Dunne's doing the paperwork.'

'Well, whaddya think? This bitch thinks she saw Harding's wife at the New Britannic, for fuck's sake.'

'Aw, it's bullshit. Women.'

'TR's arse-kisser says the word is No Fuss.'

'I thought the word was Crime Prevention.'

'That was last week.'

'Fucking Teddy is gonna be the death of us, Jack.'

'Look, what I see here is some aggravation and a chance to make some spondoola, just the two of us, okay?'

'I don't see it. What, shake down this nit-brain woman?'

Cleary leaned in. He tipped his head a little on one side; his voice became soft, slightly impatient, condescending. 'The husband, Grady. The *hotel*. Do I make myself clear?'

'The note says leave the husband alone.'

'Fuck him. You go to Harding, *from me*, and you say we have a witness saw your wife in a hotel with a good-looking guy; what's it worth to you to keep it quiet? Get it?'

'Harding ain't an easy guy, Jack. Oh, yeah, boo-hoo, my wife is dead, all that, but this is the guy put down a miners' strike with fucking *Gatling* guns, Jack. He won't be easy.'

'Sure he will. You go to him at home; he's got a house in Murray Hill someplace. First, you remind him I was the one helped him at the mortuary, I'm the one – you can include yourself in this part – quashed the investigation, Then you say how sorry you are to intrude on his grief, all that bull, then you tell him about this bitch saw the wife, then you say Mr Roosevelt wants to keep this quiet but we're committed to the pursuit of criminals and so on. Harding's gonna climb all over you trying to keep it quiet. You think an old guy like him wants everybody to know his young wife was getting laid by some gigolo? Fuck, he'll take your dick out for you and offer to kiss it, he'll be so anxious to keep it quiet. Then you say, well, you gotta buy off the papers for so much, and there'll be overtime, and like that. Harding knows how things are done. He'll pay.'

'How much?'

'Get a thousand. He's got it, what the hell? Then the hotel. We'll go together, right to the manager. Tell him we have this witness, we want to give it to the newspapers so's other people will come forward. We're looking for the gigolo, right?'

'I get it – he don't want his fancy hotel in the papers.'

'Damn right. We'll try to get another thousand.'

'That's pretty good money.'

'Well, we don't take less than five hundred. This is just you and me – samee-samee split.' Cleary grinned. 'The word is No Fuss.'

'What about the bitch?'

'We'll do her together. Scare the shit out of her, tell her she's nuts, shut up or we'll arrest you for criminal libel.' He squinted his eyes. 'Who's the house john at the New Britannie?'

'Not one of ours; I don't know him.'

'Well, we'll square him after we do the manager. Lay twenty on him. Tell him he never seen anything and this Conan dame is loony.'

'She's a missus. Maybe the husband—'

'I'm terrified.' Cleary waved him away. 'Go deal with Harding. The word is Make Hay While the Sun Shines.'

Grady went to the door and stopped with his hand on the knob. 'You think fucking Roosevelt is ever gonna leave?'

Cleary looked grim. 'He can't last. He's costing everybody too much money.'

'Mr Manion, madame. The hotel detective.'

'What?' She had been asleep again. Now, she floundered up, calling for a hairbrush, the eau de cologne. She put a hand over her mouth to exhale and sniff her own breath. 'Am I decent?' She had hopped into the sitting room with Ethel's help to wait there for the hotel detective, and of course her body had chosen that moment to put itself to sleep.

'Everything is in order, madame.'

'All right – produce this Manion.'

The detective came in quickly, his head up, showing a lot more manly confidence than Carver had when he had tried to get her to sign whatever it had been. *He looks as if* he *owns the hotel*, Louisa thought. He wasn't wearing a bowler hat or smoking a cigar, as she had more or less expected. In fact, he was a good-looking man. She thought *dangerous*, and then wondered where that had come from.

'Mrs Doyle.' He looked around at the flowers people had sent her, then at her. 'That's some eight-ball.'

'I beg your pardon?'

'You need a sirloin on that eye. That's a beaut. Can I sit?' Not waiting for an answer, he fetched a chair.

She was nonplussed. She had expected him to be diffident, even fawning, as if he had already known that she knew about the woman in the lobby, but of course he couldn't. She was being foolish – was it the morphine, some sort of after-effect, what was called a hangover? 'I don't like your being so very familiar, Mr Manion.'

'Was I? Gee, I'm sorry. Trying to break the ice.'

'There is no ice to break.'

'So to speak. We talked in the lobby the other day, didn't we?'

It was as if *he* had summoned *her*. She was beginning to think that summoning Mr Manion was a mistake. 'That isn't why I want to talk to you, Mr Manion.' She was trying to be regal, in response, as she now saw, to a definite sexual pull from the man.

'Okay, shoot.'

'Mr Manion!'

'Figure of speech.'

'Your figures of speech may be thought colourful in some circles, but I do not appreciate them. I am a guest; you are the house detective!'

'Low life.' He grinned.

'Sir?'

'"Low life." Maybe it's American. What I guess you'd call working-class. Or worse. The house Hawkshaw.'

She felt as if she should take deep breaths. 'Mr Manion, I wish to speak to you about a young man and woman who were in the lobby of this hotel when my husband and I arrived.'

'Yeah?'

'A handsome young man and a very pretty young woman with quite lovely copper-coloured hair.'

'No kidding. She sounds like a peach. Wish I'd seen her.'

'Oh, you saw her, Mr Manion! You saw her very well, and you and her escort exchanged a *look*.'

'We did, eh? A look. Gee.'

'A significant look, Mr Manion. You were *colluding*.'

'In cahoots, you mean? No kidding.'

'You may make vulgar jokes all you want,

Mr Manion, but I *saw* you, and I know what I saw. I also recognized the young woman as the victim of a vicious and horrible murder that same night. Now: who was that young woman, and why haven't you gone to the police with what you know?'

Manion gave her a look that suggested he thought she'd broken more than her glasses when she fell, but before he had got the look on his face there had been a flash of something else – fear? astonishment? horror? 'I think you're putting the horse in the wrong stall.'

'No, I am absolutely right about this. I don't like putting this sort of thing into words, Mr Manion; it isn't quite nice; but as you seem to like to put things as bluntly as possible, I shall say that the young man and woman were using the hotel for illicit purposes, and *you* were letting them do it!'

'Oh, hey . . . !'

'For money, I suppose.'

'Now just a minute—'

'I suppose I could ask the desk clerk, whom you also gave one of your looks, as I clearly remember.'

'You got the wrong end of the stick.' He wasn't smiling any more, she was pleased to see; in fact, he looked rather angry. And dangerous. And – disturbing.

'No, I have the right end of the stick, and I have a good grip on it. I wonder if you haven't a little sideline here of letting certain men bring women of a certain sort. What do they pay you, five dollars or some such magnificent sum? Is that what integrity goes for in New York nowadays, Mr Manion?'

'I never sold my integrity in my life!' Then he grinned. 'I never had any to sell. Where I come from, they cut your integrity off at birth.'

'You deny allowing this couple into the hotel?'

''Course I do. Ask anybody who knows me.'

'Then you won't object if I go to Mr Carver and the police with what I saw.'

He was silent. He wasn't flustered, however; after that single flash of fear or panic, he had remained as solid as when he had come through the door. Nor was he threatening or blustering. He said, 'I don't think Carver would fire me over a look, Miz Doyle.'

'Do you not, indeed. Mr Carver is very worried for his hotel just now; he's terrified that I'm going to make a fuss over my fall. Do you think he'd like to see his hotel in the newspapers – "Hotel Detective Allowed Murdered Woman's Love Tryst"?' She thought that was rather good, and made up in an instant, too.

Manion put his hands on his knees as if he were about to get up and said, 'No offense, but you got nothing. A look? Go ahead – tell a cop you saw a look. Cops love a good laugh.' He stood. 'You got anything else for me?'

'I recognized that woman, Mr Manion! I want to know who she was!'

'Go look in the register. Not there? Didn't the guy give Reception the dame's name? Why would

101

he? You think he had his head screwed on wrong? Guys who bring dames to hotels probably don't even *know* their names! You think a hotel D's gonna jump up and say before she gets in the elevator, "Could I have your name for my dance card, please?"' He shook his head in disgust.

'You are quite offensive.'

'Oh, yeah? Try being told you're a crook sometime.'

'I saw you!' That had no effect at all. 'I *will* tell Mr Carver!'

'Do a lot of that as a kid, did you? What we call a tattle-tale? You're a sweetheart, you are.'

'How dare you!'

'"How dare you!" I been waiting all my life to hear somebody say that! I never heard it this side of a two-bit melodrama.' He threw a ten-cent piece on the sofa next to her. 'Worth the price of admission.'

'Get out! Get out, you vulgar lout!'

Manion laughed. 'You could have that maid of yours put me out.'

She threw the dime at him and missed by several feet. She thought he would laugh at her again and then saunter out, but to her surprise he sat again in the chair, his face closed. After some seconds, she said, 'Get out,' again.

Manion sighed. 'You could send for the hotel detective.' He didn't smile. He seemed to have to think about what to say. 'Whadda you mean, you recognized the woman you say I gave a look to the guy she was with?'

Louisa had folded her arms over her breasts and pulled her bare ankle under the skirts of her brocade robe, as if to hide as much of her flesh from him as she could. 'I recognized her.'

'How?'

'From a sketch in the newspaper.'

Manion frowned and picked at something on one leg of his trousers. 'I wouldn't go spreading that around unless I was real sure.'

'I'm sure.'

'From a newspaper sketch?' He sat there. He frowned some more at his trouser leg. He said, 'Yeah, I remember the woman. Okay? I won't say I was conniving in anything. But what I remember was you and your husband, and me thinking he wrote Sherlock Holmes and how funny that was, me being a detective. And I remember seeing you and thinking how . . . thinking you weren't my kind. Then, yeah, I remember the woman. And you think she was the one murdered in the Bowery?'

'I'm sure.'

He pursed his mouth as if to whistle and blew out air, but not so as to whistle. 'Not good.'

'Because you'll get caught?'

'Nah. Oh, it'd make me look bad, letting them get past me, but no. What it is, a murdered woman and a connection with the hotel, that *is* bad. For that, I could get the axe.'

'I don't care what you get, Mr Manion.'

'I see that.'

'I care about that poor woman. She was *happy*. And you and all the rest of them, you want to erase her!'

He stood. 'Maybe you oughta do the same. Get that ankle better, go join your husband, forget it.'

'I will not!'

'Best advice you'll get today.' He headed for the door. 'The cops have decided to bury the whole thing – I can tell by what isn't in the papers. You don't want to mess with the New York cops, Miz Doyle – you really don't.' And he was gone.

Louisa pushed herself against the sofa pillows. She wanted a swear word and didn't know one strong enough. She did find that she had forgotten about the pain in her ankle, however.

What had he meant by saying she wasn't his kind?

'There's a boy with a message asking if a Mr Galt can come up, madame.'

'Galt.' She was back in her bed, pondering Manion's visit. 'Galt? Oh, dear heaven, he's somebody that dreadful doctor's sent. *Another* man to visit me in bed. You'd think I was a courtesan at Versailles. Oh, let him come in – but stay in the room, Ethel.'

Five minutes later, Ethel said, 'Mr Galt, madame.'

She saw a decently tall, balding, fair man in the doorway. Silhouetted against the light from the sitting room, he looked round shouldered, a posture she disapproved of. Perhaps he was tired.

He said, in a surprisingly deep voice, 'I do apologize, Mrs Doyle. Dr Strauss sent me.' *Doctor* came out as 'doc-tuh' – was this the Southern accent?

'Yes, yes.'

'May I come in?'

'Yes, please.' Trying not to sound as irritated as she felt.

He came in three steps and looked at Ethel. He said, 'I'm sure Mrs Doyle prefers having you here.' *Havin' you heah.*

'Oh, well . . .' Ethel looked at Louisa.

Louisa said, 'Yes, I do.' She sounded impatient, she knew. What was Galt afraid of – that she was going to fling her arms around him if Ethel weren't there? More kindly, she wondered if he had had trouble before, perhaps a misunderstanding. Yes, now she thought about it, having Ethel there was a kind of insurance for both of them.

'You have a sprained ankle, I hear,' Galt said, coming closer. As if it were all part of the same speech, he said sidelong to Ethel, 'If you can put your hands on a measuring tape, I'd surely like one.' He was looking down at the ankle, which was sticking out of the bedcovers like something that didn't belong to her. It was now as much yellow-green as blue, still swollen. He said, 'That must hurt like all get-out.' His voice was pleasing to her, soft despite its deepness, the hard American sounds rounded by what she was now sure was a pleasant, not at all insistent Southern accent.

Galt had on a buff-coloured linen jacket like a

105

shop assistant's, and dark trousers and canvas shoes with rubber soles, the sort of things that men called 'brothel creepers.' She didn't know why; was one supposed to pussyfoot about in a brothel? He wore a stiff collar with rounded fronts and a dark necktie that certainly wasn't new. He was, she thought, somewhere about fifty, looking it not because of lines and grey but because of a look of wear, even of perpetual fatigue. 'I'd like for Miss . . . mmm, ah . . .'

'Grimstead,' Ethel said, blushing.

Galt smiled at her. 'Miss Grimstead. Yes, I'd like you to measure up Mrs Doyle, if that's all right.'

'Of course it's all right!'

There was some measuring of her ankle and her foot, but Ethel was the one who touched her, not Galt. Would she have minded if he had touched her? He had rather long, masculine fingers, big in the knuckles. She thought of Manion's rather square hands, his short but strong-looking fingers. Square thumbs. When had she noticed all that?

'I guess it isn't news to you that you've got some pretty good swelling there, Mrs Doyle. Also some pretty fine bruises. But the other foot is all right, is it? Because if the other foot's all right, then you got something to walk on. I'm a great believer in patients walking.'

'Now?'

He chuckled. 'Not right this very minute, no, ma'am; we'll make haste slowly, as the saying is. But I'll send some crutches up just in case you get the urge. You're what height, Mrs Doyle – about five foot four? And a half, yes, ma'am.' He smiled. 'A hotel keeps all sizes of crutches, just in case. You'd be surprised the things that happen in a hotel.'

She said, both because she was curious and because she wanted to be something other than the poor body in the bed, 'You're a nurse, are you, Mr Galt?'

'Not a nurse, ma'am, no, not as you'd say a *nurse*, unless you meant a Sairey Gamp kind of a one. I'm more what I'd call a caretaker for the elderly, though I do have a certificate of completion from the Sanders College of Chiropracty.' He smiled. 'By correspondence. But it fits me to take care of old Mr Carver.'

'And old Mr Carver is . . . young Mr Carver's – that is, the hotel manager's – father?'

'Yes, ma'am, his father.'

'And they live in the hotel?'

'Oh, no, ma'am; Mr Carver, the younger one, I mean, he lives out. With his wife and all.'

'So he's put his father in one of the rooms?'

'Oh, no, ma'am! Old Mr Carver and me have the penthouse.' He pointed upward. She remembered somebody else's doing the same thing; now she understood. 'Mr Carver had it put up there for himself.' Seeing that she still didn't understand, he said, 'Mr Carver *built* the hotel.'

This surprised her, she wasn't sure why. She said, 'I don't believe I've seen him – in the lobby or the restaurant, I mean.'

'Oh, no, ma'am. Old Mr Carver don't go out any more.' He was writing in his book; he said to Ethel, 'Could you find us some ice, do you think? You could ring for a boy and tell him to bring it.' Galt looked again at the side of Louisa's face. 'I think that some ice in a towel would bring that swelling down, Mrs Doyle, and maybe take some of the bruising off, too. I'm a great believer in ice. You'll hear people say to use hot towels, and they have their place, but in the early days, I like ice.' Ethel had left the room – there seemed to be no worry now about being alone with Louisa – and while Galt was waiting for the ice, he looked out a window.

'Your work must be very rewarding.' She was being polite.

He smiled again but stared the window. 'Old people are sometimes surprisingly strong. They can have forgotten their own children and not know where they are, forgotten even who *they* are, but they still can be a handful. I saw Colonel Beauregard throw a grown Negro man off the piazza once.' He turned to her. 'I was taking care of Colonel Beauregard. He'd been in the war, which is why he was called "colonel." It taught me to be careful, seeing him throw a grown coloured man like that.'

Still Ethel hadn't come back. 'Is old Mr Carver a handful?'

'He's all right. I shouldn't talk about him, should I. He's all right.'

'Does Dr Strauss tend to him?'

'Dr Strauss is his physician, yes.'

'I think that Dr Strauss relies too much on morphine.'

Galt seemed to withdraw from her, then to come back. 'Dr Strauss's wife died two years ago. Dr Strauss is *lonely*.'

'Oh – I didn't mean . . .' It wasn't a matter of what she had meant; it was what he had meant: that the doctor relied too much on morphine in his own case because he was lonely. Could that be what he meant? She blushed. He was looking away from her.

Ethel came back. Galt showed her how to make a sort of sling for Louisa's ankle out of a strip of torn cotton he produced from a pocket. The idea was that the sling would hold her injured foot off the floor and tie to something at her waist so as to relieve her of carrying the foot around if she used crutches. 'It isn't much of an invention as medical improvements go,' Galt said, 'but it seems to work. I'd suggest you choose a skirt that's not too heavy, too, because it'll catch on your heel and weigh the foot down even more.' He smiled at Louisa, her gaffe about the doctor apparently forgiven. Or forgotten. He explained how she was to use the crutch and how careful she would have to be on stairs, especially going down. 'Or down goes McGinty!' They all laughed.

The ice came, and he showed Ethel how to fold it into a towel (which she hardly needed to be shown, Louisa thought) and apply it to the side of Louisa's face; then the two of them filled another towel with ice, Louisa watching with one eye, and put it on the ankle. Ethel's colour was quite high.

'Too cold?' Galt said.

'It's very nice.'

'Cold does the job. Heat feels good, but cold's the ticket.' Galt looked around, found what he wanted in the bedside clock, said he had to go. 'Time to get old Mr Carver up from his morning nap.'

'Can't he get himself up?'

'Sometimes yes and sometimes no. He pretty well has to be carried about sometimes. Or pushed in his chair.' Galt hesitated, then gave her an apologetic smile. 'You don't want to get old if you can help it, ma'am.'

When he had gone, Ethel seemed fluttery. This was unusual, in fact unprecedented, but Louisa couldn't see how Galt could have had this effect on her and so let it go. Instead, she started to write a letter to Arthur – where would he get it? Somewhere days and days and miles and miles from now – but her mind sloped off to her letter to Commissioner Roosevelt and what effect it must be having. She had sent it by special messenger (her stock of ready money that much more depleted), so it must be there by now; had Roosevelt been spurred to action? Invigorated in his pursuit of the criminal element? On the track already of the killer?

She was writing on a lap desk provided by the management – she thought that Carver probably wanted her to have it in case she was ready to sign his paper. *Oh, Louisa, don't be cynical. Cynicism is so cheap.* She was sitting in an armchair by a window.

She was surprised at how commercial the street seemed to her now. It was jarring that this elegant hotel would be across from a men's haberdashery, a knick-knack shop, and a dealer in 'fur findings,' whatever they were. Directly opposite her at her own level were a furniture store of rather low quality and a large window on which the words CUSTOM GENTS DUDS were hideously prominent. Above these were other display windows with large signs that advertised jewelry and something called Fashion Frocks and fabrics by the bolt. How, she wondered, were New Yorkers to see the signs? Were they really expected to walk along with their heads back and a crick in their necks? The only pedestrians she could see seemed to have their eyes on their own shoes, moving far too fast and with far too much purpose to be bothered with things two and three storeys above them.

She tried to concentrate on her letter, but her thoughts wandered.

That poor woman.

Arthur will need warmer underwear when he gets to Minnesota, but that's still a week away.

What is Mr Roosevelt doing? Will he visit me personally to thank me?

111

'A Miss Corelli, madame.'

'Oh, dear.' Her first thought was to say she didn't want to see anyone. Her second was that she didn't know a Miss Corelli, corrected at once to memory of a woman – one of many – whom Mrs Simmons didn't like. Her third was to wonder why Arthur disapproved of her. But Arthur's disapproval suggested possibilities. 'Show her in, Ethel.'

She straightened herself, fluffed her hair, and hoped that Miss Corelli would be exotic and outrageously worldly.

'Ah, Mrs Doyle, you poor thing!'

Marie Corelli was fortyish, handsome, dominating, and about as exotic as the Houses of Parliament. She was, however, quite stylish.

'Miss Corelli, how nice of you to visit me. Thank you so much for your flowers.'

'Oh, flowers, they're easy, aren't they.' Miss Corelli sat down and looked at Louisa as if she were an article she was considering buying. She said, 'I feel as if we've known each other ever so long – I think perhaps we were friends in another life. Don't you believe that we've had other lives? I love your bedjacket.'

'My husband tells me you are a novelist, Miss Corelli.'

'Actually, I didn't set out to be an authoress; I set out to be a singer, which is why my name isn't the real one. If one is going to be a singer, one ought to be Italian. Do you mind if I smoke? So I took Corelli, after the composer, of course, and

112

Marie. And then when I was Marie Corelli and dyed my hair black, it turned out I hadn't the *push* to succeed with the materialistic demands of managers and that lot. So I took up writing. Just like your husband.' She had taken a cigarette from a shagreen case, which she now offered.

Louisa thought she was, if not exotic, at least odd, and she was going to say no to the cigarettes, but part of her rather liked Marie Corelli, so she said, 'Yes, please.'

'Lucky you, staying in bed,' the woman said. 'I just go and go and go. Yesterday I was in Boston. Tomorrow I go to Baltimore – three days. If it weren't for this hotel, I'd go back to Paris.' She exhaled, looked around the room, said, 'I was educated in Paris – a convent. I live there now. I think in French.'

'My husband's on a lecture tour, too.' *Convent* was tinkling in her brain; Mrs Simmons had said something about Catholicism. Heavens – a Papist! That was rather exotic in itself.

'Yes, well, mine isn't lectures and it isn't a tour, because I told them if I couldn't stay in one place, I wouldn't come, so I stay here and go out and come back, you see? *Bon*. Because of the hotel. This hotel keeps me sane. It has *emanations*.' She inhaled again on the cigarette. 'Are you *spirituelle*? I am a sensitive. I knew the instant I walked in the front door that there were many, many really old souls here. Did you know that the American Indians were the Lost Tribes of Israel? It's been

113

proven. In print. They landed here and I think they built a temple right on this spot to one of the deities they'd acquired in their travels, because they'd fallen away from Jehovah, just like the ones who worshipped the golden calf. Not that we should be concerned with a narrow-minded idea of the one God.' She exhaled smoke. 'I sense the name Azul here.' She took a book from a large handbag. 'I've brought you a copy of my *Romance of Two Worlds*, which will clarify for you my cosmology. As you will see, Azul is a figure of great importance.'

Louisa, familiar with authors and their affection for their own works, made appropriate sounds. She opened the book, looked into it, as she knew she should – words, a great many words.

Marie Corelli was marching on. 'And it isn't only the *sense* of Azul that holds me here. There are *sounds*, you know. The sounds are, of course, Azul's entourage. For those who have ears to hear, this place is full of a divine music.'

Trying to be polite, Louisa said, 'Is Azul a spirit?'

'Most people who use that word mean ghosts or some other such rubbish. The idea that the dead wish to hang about this dreary world and try to get into touch with living beings whom they didn't much care for when they were alive is nonsensical. No, Azul is more on the order of what is called an archangel. He is an emanation of the One, you understand.'

'With wings?'

114

'I depicted him with wings in my book, but I shan't really *know* until I have seen him and bathed in his effulgence. As I hope to do in this hotel. I feel him so strongly here!'

Louisa, a bit fuddled by the cigarette, said that it was nice that Miss Corelli liked the hotel, but what a shame she had to leave it every other day to give lectures, or whatever they were.

'One has to touch one's readers. One has often to explain one's philosophy. One has to listen to know what it is they want from one.'

'I think my husband believes that he should be the one to decide that.'

'That's the way men think, isn't it?'

'I supposed it's the way authors think.'

'Only authors who are men.' She stubbed her cigarette out in a little lidded box and closed it, as if she were saving her cigarette ashes. She stood. 'I have fatigued you, I fear. But, if you will permit, we shall meet again, yes?' She moved towards the door, her progress smooth and steady, as if she were on wheels. 'I shall bring you more of my books. *Wormwood* would show you how close I am able to come to realism without being guilty of either bad taste or sensationalism. Realism – and materialism – have doomed our civilization. *Au 'voir.*' And she was gone.

Spirits? Materialism? The Lost Tribes of Israel? Louisa wondered why she had associated Marie Corelli with the risqué – something Arthur had said? Arthur disliked what he called 'lady novelists' in general, those who wrote about what he called S-E-X most of all. He had said of one woman's work that he 'wouldn't have such a book in his house,' not knowing that Louisa had a copy in her sewing basket. Had Arthur actually read Marie Corelli? But if he had, he'd have known she wasn't risqué. He'd also have known that she was what Arthur called 'incorrect,' meaning that she didn't believe in the same sort of spiritualism that he did.

As a rule, Louisa was indifferent to other people's beliefs, except her husband's, of course. She had to concede, however, that Marie Corelli's spiritualism seemed rather impressive – archangels, effulgences, the One – whereas Arthur's seemed to her an eccentricity that she was to tolerate. And Miss Corelli had good taste in clothes and flowers. And seemed quite kind. Although disappointing because she didn't write about S-E-X.

Louisa was no stranger to S-E-X and had in fact had a precocious knowledge of it even as a child, some of it wrong, some confused, some incomprehensible until later, but by age ten she had known a lot. Her clergyman father had got a church on one of the islands off the west of Scotland; there, Louisa had met little girls who knew all about S-E-X and were eager to educate her. In the summer she had gone with her best friend, Tenny McLean, to the shielings, the remnant, then dying, of an old custom that had women forming their own summer communities where the grazing was good and where they built 'shielings,' temporary little houses. Here she learned about penises (*They look like sausage and they get big so they can stick them into you.* Shocked, Louisa had said, *Where?* Tenny had been contemptuous. *In your hole, ye daft sapskull!*) and kinds of copulation (*Duncan Moy's been took off to Oban by the polis for topping his ewes*) and other behaviours (*Mrs McCrae and Mrs Brown got caught playing with theirselves together in the shieling*).

She learned none of it from her parents: her mother was shy and usually speechless; her father was a distant monarch who showed in every syllable that he had married beneath himself and that his wife had produced children who were beneath him and that his parishioners were beneath him, too. When Louisa had applied what she had learned from Tenny to her mother and father, she had been dumbfounded.

However, all that knowledge had later proved useful.

Louisa wrote three long letters to her husband and put them into envelopes addressed to his hotels in Dayton, Ohio, and Detroit and Ann Arbor, Michigan. She found it tedious writing three letters, because the first letter seemed to exhaust everything she had to say. She had avoided saying anything about the murder; Arthur had not been very understanding about that. Perhaps when there was a happy outcome of her letter to

117

Mr Roosevelt, she would tell him. Well, of course she would. He would see that she had been right all along, that she could think for herself, and that even though she was in pain, she was living in the world.

'Madame?' Ethel was whispering from the bedroom door.

'Whatever is the matter, Ethel?'

'The police are here.' Ethel looked terrified. 'What shall I do?'

'The police?' Like all good people of her class, Louisa had been raised to fear – and of course respect – the police, while at the same time doing everything possible to avoid ever dealing with them. But she thought, *Police – Roosevelt – my letter*.

'*And* Mr Carver, madame. What shall I do?'

'Well, of course you will show them in, Ethel! I'll see them in the sitting room.' It was very quick work by the New York police, she thought, and showed how seriously she was being taken. Wouldn't Arthur be pleased!

She managed to get out of bed by herself, and she hopped to the clothes cupboard and took down one of the dressing gowns that Ethel had unpacked for her. It was, she thought, quite appropriate and decent, and of course the police would understand that under the circumstances of her injury and their commitment to solving the crime, they must over-look her appearing *en déshabillée*, as it were. The dressing gown was wool, a rather deep brown, quite nun-like in its cut, with flowing sleeves. Entirely appropriate for police work.

Her crutches had arrived, but she hadn't practiced with them. Better not to take the risk, she thought. Using one of them as a cane, she moved rather clumsily to the bedroom door and stood there looking at the three men who were already in the room, until a flustered Ethel got her wits about her and came to help.

'I'm so sorry, I'm rather slow,' Louisa said as she crossed to an armchair. 'I had rather a fall.' She sat, one hand on the now-vertical crutch. 'Do sit down, please.' She tried not to include Carver in the invitation, as she was still angry with him over the paper he'd wanted her to sign. Anyway, he was hovering near the door as if ready to bolt.

There were two of them. Neither sat. One was very large, as large as her husband. He had what must have started life as an almost handsome Irish face, now rather ruined by pockmarked skin. The other one was smaller, darker, glowering, and wore a remarkable suit. A smell of tobacco and old clothes reached her.

The big one looked at Ethel, then jerked a thumb towards the bedroom. Ethel, apparently frightened, looked at Louisa and, seeing her nod, fled.

'You're Mrs Arthur Conan Doyle?' the big one said.

'Yes, I am.' With a smile and a girlish shake of the head that was supposed to set her curls a-dancing. Or at least charm the socks off the visitors.

'Are you the author of a missive to Mr Theodore Roosevelt, the President of the Commissioners of the Metropolitan Police of the City of New York?'

'Yes.' She felt a stab of uncertainty. All she knew of the manners of policemen was what her husband had written about made-up London ones, who were even stupider than Watson but always polite to their betters. These two, it seemed to her, were not so polite as they should be. Nor so deferential – or was she simply misjudging American mores?

'Is this the letter?' He held up her note.

'Yes, of course. I recognize my notepaper.'

The two men exchanged a look as if their worst fears had been confirmed.

'So you made this allegation about seeing a murder victim in this hotel?'

'I reported what I believed I saw, yes.'

The shorter man said in a growling voice, 'Which may be libelous.'

'I hardly think so!'

The big one said, 'Reflecting on the integrity of this hotel.' In the background, Carver nodded and wrung his hands. She understood why he was there, at any rate.

Louisa said, 'I did nothing of the kind.' She tried to say that as politely as possible, although she was irritated.

'Commissioner Roosevelt was real unhappy to hear this kind of insinuation being talked around.'

Real unhappy? How in the world could he be? An important man could hardly be made unhappy by a *note*. She said, 'I should like to know your names, if you please.'

The big one looked at her. He had dead eyes when he wanted to, she saw. He was used to frightening people, and he enjoyed doing it. She said, 'Your *names*.'

'I'm Cleary, Lieutenant. He's Grady, Sergeant. Now about this here letter—'

'Don't you have badges or warrants or some sort of identification?'

Cleary's eyes narrowed. 'You trying to give us trouble?'

'I am trying to find out who you are.'

The small one – Grady; *Good heavens, both Irish* – said, 'What d'you think you'll know if you know?'

'I shall know what names to write to Commissioner Roosevelt if you continue to be as rude as you have been so far.'

Cleary deadened his eyes some more, but she sat up straighter and stared right back at him. Cleary broke first; his eyes shot away and he gave a great, false explosion of laughter. 'The little lady's scared of us, Grady! Well, well, my gosh, Mrs, um, Conan, let's see what we got . . .' He reached into a pocket and pulled out a gold badge, which he held up, then held out as he walked towards her, as if it were a crucifix and she an evil spirit.

Grady, without moving from where he was, flashed a badge and put it away as quickly. Louisa

121

thought that they'd probably done as much as she could expect, so she thanked them and said that she supposed they could proceed.

Cleary looked as if he wanted to say 'Where were we?' because he looked at Grady and rubbed a finger under his nose and glanced back at Carver before he said, 'Now about this here letter.'

'It's a note, really.'

'About these here allegations.'

Grady raised his shoulders and let them drop and shook his shoulders like a bird having a dust bath. 'You got a husband?' he said.

The question was so rude she was shocked. More loudly than she intended, she said, 'Of course I have a husband!' She looked at Carver for support, for confirmation, but he was nodding at everything the policemen said and frowning at her.

'Where's he at?'

She was going to tell them, and then she thought that she was being abused, and she said, 'What has that to do with my note to Commissioner Roosevelt?'

'We ask the questions!'

'Then ask them politely, if you please.'

Grady looked at her as if he had never heard of politely. He looked at Cleary. Cleary said, 'Your husband isn't here, that it?'

'He is away, yes.'

'Deceased?'

'That is not what "away" means.' She remembered his name. 'Officer *Cleary*.' She enunciated it to show she would remember it.

Grady thrust himself in again. He even pointed a finger. 'You're being uncooperative! And it's *Lieutenant* Cleary!'

'And you are being offensive. Do not point your finger at me!'

Cleary put a hand in front of Grady as if he were afraid the man might attack her. 'We understand if your husband's away, Mrs Conan. Ladies get ideas if their husbands aren't around. Know what I mean? They get lonely, they see things. They misinterpret. Know what I mean?'

'If I thought I knew what you meant, Officer Cleary, I would be insulted.' She wanted to stand, but she didn't think she could make it in a dignified way. She needed Ethel.

'What Commissioner Roosevelt wants us to say to you, Mrs Conan, is that we get reports from all over from ladies who think they see things, and it doesn't work for the police to go chasing around like chickens with their heads cut off to follow up hysterical inventions, you follow me?'

'Hysterical? You think what I saw was the product of *hysteria*?' Arthur, ever the physician, had explained to her that the word came from the Greek for womb: the Greeks had believed that the womb took over women's thinking from the brain. He had laughed when he had told her. She said it again – '*Hysteria?*' – picturing her womb moving somehow to her head. And then she added for good measure, 'Inventions?'

'Mrs Conan, where did this idea you saw the victim come from?'

'From my seeing her!' She saw, beyond Cleary, Carver shaking his head and frowning.

Grady crossed his arms and sneered. 'You knew her, did you?'

'I recognized her. Later.'

'Oh, *later.*' He looked at Cleary and they chuckled. 'Later – like after a little wine, maybe?'

'I recognized her from the sketch in a newspaper.'

'A sketch! That wasn't even a sketch of the victim! That was just a sketch they keep around to use!' He looked at Cleary. 'She recognizes her from a sketch in a rag!'

She *must* stand. Cleary would tower over her, anyway, but she wanted to be on her feet, if only to show them she *could* stand on her own two feet. Or one foot, in this case. 'Ethel!'

The bedroom door opened a crack. 'Ethel! Now!' To her credit, Ethel came straight to her, and if she eyed the two men, she didn't quail. 'Help me stand, Ethel.' What followed was neither elegant nor impressive, but it got her upright with her crutch under her right armpit. When Ethel started to withdraw, Louisa said, 'Stay.' She drew herself up. 'I think, gentlemen, that you have had sufficient fun at my expense. If you are done, the door is behind you.'

'We're the New York City police – we leave when we want to!' Cleary hooked his thumbs in the armholes of his vest. 'Now I'm telling you, lady, don't you peddle this story of yours around no more. You're just gonna make yourself look bad. And your husband, too!'

'It is not a story, and I don't intend to "peddle" it. To the contrary, I have shared it only with Commissioner Roosevelt, who should be ashamed of his office that it produced the likes of you two in response! I shall now write to him to thank him for sending two such examples of his police, who have given me such *good* advice. And so politely, too!'

'Just you leave the Commissioner out of it, now.'

'Not for a moment! I think he deserves to know how his officers behave. I say again, the door is behind you.' She looked at Grady, then at Carver. '*All* of you.'

Grady said, 'It won't look good in the papers if we say you're nuts.'

What had Arthur said? Something about 'Sherlock Holmes's wife'? Surely they wouldn't put it in the newspapers! But they were crude enough to say anything.

But now they were going. Ethel ran ahead of them to the door and showed the policemen out; Carver had already oozed across the door sill. When Ethel came back, she said, 'Oh, madame! They were so unkind to you!'

Louisa wasn't looking at her, but at the door. 'What does "nuts" mean?' Her hands, which she had been holding in fists, were shaking.

'I think, madame – "mental."'

She absorbed that, considered it, put it away.

They had frightened her. As if she were a child and they adults – like her father when she'd done something wrong, punishing her with his voice, his size, his presence. *She couldn't let them do that to her!* She put her head up, stood very straight despite her ankle, and said, 'I shall dine downstairs tonight, Ethel.'

'Your poor foot!'

'We mustn't give in to physical discomfort, Ethel. Come help me dress.' Then she remembered that even if she mastered the crutches, she would need help getting about. She said, 'And you, too, Ethel, of course. You will need a dress.'

'Oh, no, madame!'

Personal servants of people staying at the hotel had their own dining room, undoubtedly with somewhat inferior food, but of course they preferred it that way (or so everybody said), so it was natural that Ethel preferred to be with people of her own sort. Nonetheless, Louisa would need her. She said, 'We'll fit you into that old blue one of mine with the flounces. It will be lovely.'

It wasn't, but with a good deal of pinning and a letting down of the hem, it more or less fitted, although it took four rolled-up stockings to fill out the bodice. Ethel was unenthusiastic but obedient.

When they entered the dining room, there was a moment's silence and then applause. Men stood. A few ladies waved their serviettes. Embarrassed, pleased, Louisa thought how she would describe it to Arthur in her next letter. *But of course the*

126

applause was really for you, my darling. I was only the – what do they call it in the theatre? – the understudy. Had it been you yourself, how much greater the applause would have been!

If, of course, he had sprained his ankle.

She ate mostly in silence. Ethel was all but flattened by eating in the dining room. It was the sort of place, after all, where men wore tailcoats and white ties and ladies evening gowns, although there were a few of the new, shorter black coats on more daring men here and there. Ethel was not a practiced conversationalist at best; here, she was monosyllabic and looked around her after each word to see who might have heard. On the other hand, she had impeccable table manners and knew more about the finer points of table silver than Louisa did: she had, after all, been a serving maid for part of her life.

Towards the end of dinner, a tall man with a pointed beard and quite long, greying hair came to their table and bowed. His evening clothes were impeccable, but the first words out of his mouth told her who he was. 'Ma'am,' he said in a nasal American voice, 'I do salute you.'

'Colonel Cody, is it not?'

'Ma'am, it is, and I know that in your country to come to your table this way without an introduction is thought *oo-tray* and then some, but I wanted to tell you what a gallant little lady I think you are. Trying to get about on those toothpicks can't be easy.'

'Colonel Cody, your kindness is your introduction. I'm delighted to meet you. I remember when you first came to London some years ago.'

'Nine years ago, to be exact, ma'am, and many times since.' Cody took a calling card from a pocket and put it down next to her hand. 'If you and your friend would be good enough to present this card – when you're up and about, when you're up and about! – at the box-office window at Madison Square Garden, you may lay claim to the best seats in that house of entertainment to see my Wild West. Knowing you were in the audience, ma'am, would gladden my heart and lift my spirits.'

Louisa thanked him, glanced at Ethel and saw her blushing – the 'your friend,' probably – and lifted a hand to return his wave as he left the dining room. A little later, Sir Henry Irving stopped, chatted, and left two tickets to his play at the Lyceum. Louisa sat on, enjoying the feel of life in the busy room, the change from what had been, after all, a day both boring and painful. Ethel said once that maybe they should go up, but Louisa shook her head. She ordered coffee for them both after a perfectly splendid dessert that involved both ice cream and meringue. She considered liqueurs.

When she was at last readying herself to leave, Arthur Newcome appeared.

'It's a relief to see you up and about, Mrs Doyle. I feared you were seriously hurt.'

Louisa gestured at the crutches. 'Seriously enough, though not seriously at all, of course.'

'I hope that one afternoon soon you will be able to go out for a drive. I have the use of a friend's carriage.'

'How good of you, Mr Newcome.'

'I thought perhaps Central Park. The hotel could pack us a picnic.' He smiled at Ethel. 'And you'd of course be most welcome, too.'

'And necessary,' Louisa said. 'I can't move without Ethel.'

'*Any* time, Mrs Doyle, that you have need of a carriage, I am ready to take you – anywhere. Consider me your personal driver.'

They chatted about her ankle, about Arthur, about two new novels they had both read. He had only just come into the dining room and hadn't dined; she said she would release him and gathered her things. They all rose together; Ethel maneuvered her into the crutches as if they were a difficult costume, and Louisa launched herself forward. A path opened in front of her, smiling, well-dressed people on either side. It was all very flattering and very pleasant. Until she accidentally hit her ankle on a chair.

Back in her rooms, she said, 'We must buy you a proper dress, Ethel. I shall have to dine down there every evening until I'm quite well, I suppose.' As she said it, she wondered where she'd get the money for a dress for Ethel. Perhaps put it on the hotel bill, if she could find something on the mezzanine?

Ethel said, 'I'd rather you didn't buy me anything, madame, if I may put it that way. I think that if you'd buy me a length of silk for a sash, and a bit of lace for a collar and cuffs, I could do very well in my good black dress. If you wouldn't mind, I mean.'

Louisa didn't mind.

Arthur Newcome left the hotel after his dinner and walked west, then south, then west again. He wore his evening clothes under a black overcoat; he swung a walking-stick in his right hand. On his head was one of the new 'Homburg' hats, thought not quite correct by the old guard (he should have been wearing a silk topper, they'd have said) but adequate for what he meant to do and the neighbourhood in which he meant to do it, where a top hat would have attracted too much attention. If not thrown stones.

The stick hit the pavement each step with a light, metallic crack. The stick itself was ebony, the tip horn, but the grip was ivory tipped with a good-sized silver knob. Newcome had brought it from London and thought of it as his nightstick, a word that made him smile: it was what London policemen called the heavier truncheons they carried at night. He, too, was often out with his at night, and he carried it for the same purpose.

As he got farther west into streets that were less grand than the block off Fifth where the New Britannic stood, he put his left hand into the pocket of his overcoat and gripped a flick-knife that lay there. He had bought it in Italy; he supposed it was illegal here, didn't care. Its stiletto blade was as slender and bright and sharp as a filleting knife, in fact sharper – sharp enough to have shaved with, as he knew. He gripped the stick, swung it, pictured the defensive guards to which he could put it. The stick and the knife, his night-time companions.

In a street west of Tenth Avenue, he walked slowly, looking for the buildings' numbers. He had been there that afternoon and found the one he wanted; still, in the dark the buildings looked alike.

He stayed on the outside of the pavement. Where there was a cluster of men or boys, he went on without looking but raised the stick a little extra at each step. They let him go.

He found his building and went up the red-brown sandstone steps, let himself in and went up the stairs. He wanted the third floor, which would have been the second floor in London. The light was poor, only a gas lamp on the wall of each flight of stairs, another in the ceiling of each corridor that bored back into the house. Grit rasped under his feet. The light caught bits of paper kicked into corners of the stairs. He smelled recently cooked suppers, urine, dirt.

He knocked at a door. In his pocket, he gripped the knife and put his thumb on the silver button that would release the blade. As the door opened, he moved the stick across his body in a low version of the hanging guard.

'Yes?'

Light shone behind the woman. He could make out the silhouette of piled-up hair and light on bare shoulders. She smelled of makeup and eau de cologne.

'I was told to ask for Lady Jane.'

'Who told you?'

'A London friend. He said to use the name Aloysius.'

He could see the light change on her cheek as she smiled. 'Come in.'

She moved away into the light. If she had possibly more width of shoulder than most women, and if she was perhaps somewhat taller, Arthur Newcome either didn't notice or didn't care. He let go of the knife and used the now free hand to close the door behind himself.

CHAPTER 5

Louisa didn't, as it turned out, write to Roosevelt a second time. She had lain awake much of the night, partly because of her ankle and partly because of the two awful policemen. The truth was, she admitted to the darkness, they *had* frightened her. They had frightened her with their size and their rudeness, which seemed to say, *You're nobody; we don't care about your husband or your hoity-toity Limey manners; you're in our city and we're the* police. And they had frightened her with their threat – and yes, it had been a threat – to put her in the newspapers. That would be horrible for Arthur, even unbearable. Arthur was really a shy man who liked using his books as a kind of shrubbery, from whose protection he peeked at the world. She would do anything to keep him safe in that private place.

So if she didn't write again to Roosevelt (and what sort of man was he, anyway, to have foisted those two oafs on her?), what could she do? It had shaken her that the big one – Cleary – had said that the newspaper sketch was not of the murder victim. Could that be true? Were newspapers that cynical?

She remembered that the *Police Gazette* had featured a drawing of what was supposed to be the murder scene, but it hadn't had anything to do with the description of the actual scene, so that it must have been a picture they just had lying about. Would they have done the same thing for the woman's face? The face was so personal, so very much one's possession – would they have dared?

At three o'clock, that low hour of the night, she had admitted that of course they might have.

Now, in the flat greyness of the morning, she saw that she must find out how authentic the sketch of the woman's face had been. She was sitting up in bed, sipping tea and waiting for her breakfast to arrive. In the chinks of her tormented thoughts about the murder and the policemen, she was also thinking of Ethel and what Ethel did for her – dressing her, waiting on her, running out on errands for her, being terrified by policemen because of her. And Ethel dressed herself and hung up her own clothes and ran her own errands. As in fact Louisa had before she married.

'We're maun poor,' her mother had told her when she was a girl. Again and again, and then even more often after her father had died. 'You might as well get used to it, as it's our lot.'

But she never had. She loved not being poor. How did Ethel bear it?

She put the teacup in its saucer and put both on the bedside table. She sank lower in the bed, the comforter pulled up to her chin in both fists.

Outside, there was no sunlight, only a leaden sky above (she had looked) and a city like a black-and-white engraving below. There was snow on the pavements.

I should go to join Arthur.

'Ethel!'

'Yes, yes . . .' Ethel hurried in from the sitting room. 'The breakfast is on the way, madame; I ordered it when you said, but—'

'Hang the breakfast! Ethel, do I overwork you?'

'Oh, no ma—'

'Of course I do. All I can offer is more money, as I need you, especially with this ankle. Would another four shillings a week do it? Would it justify the extra work?' Ethel began to protest, blushing, confused, but Louisa was already thinking about something else. She said, 'I shall have to talk to that hotel detective again. I despise him, but he will know how the newspapers operate. And the police, as well!' She was thinking that the hotel detective was every bit as rude as the two policemen, but in a different way. Not so – aggressive. Not as if he had contempt for her. In fact, as if he were playing . . . She dismissed that idea and swung her legs out of the bed. 'Crutch, Ethel.'

'But your breakfast, madame . . .'

'I shall eat it in the sitting room. That way, you won't have to carry it so far. I'll *try*, Ethel, I'll *try* not to demand so much of you. And I will pay you more. Will that help?'

She was making her clumsy way to the bathroom.

'And I shall draw my own bath. I will!' She wished she could talk to Arthur about it. Arthur, of course, would scold her for raising Ethel's wages. Well, they had plenty of money. Or Arthur had plenty of money; she in fact had almost none. 'Ethel! Remind me to ask Mr Doyle for some money.'

She drew her own bath and lay in it, feeling virtuous. She would talk to the hotel detective, but no longer than was absolutely necessary, and then, if he hadn't been any help, she would find out whether that sketch had been authentic. But how? Well, somehow.

Her breakfast had arrived while she had bathed; now it was cold. She waved away Ethel's offer to carry it back, instead asked for a telegraph blank, and wrote, a piece of cold toast in her left hand, her mouth chewing, MY DEAREST HUSBAND STOP MONEY RUNNING LOWEST STOP PLEASE WIRE YOUR BANK NEW YORK DELIVER CASH HERE STOP HUNDRED POUNDS ADEQUATE FOR NOW STOP YOUR LOVING DOVE.

He would be most put out, she knew. Well, better that than that she and Ethel starve.

She wrote him a long letter, as well. Where would it catch up with him? Chicago? Somewhere called Cheboygan?

Of course, if she could get herself on a train she could meet Arthur somewhere . . .

She tried to move her ankle. She sighed. Not yet.

'Ethel, please take my telegram down to the Western Union office, and on the way stop at

136

the hotel detective's office and tell him that I wish to see him again.'

'Yes, madame.' Ethel hesitated, her hand in the air between them to take the wire form. 'It's Thursday, madame.'

'Is it?' She was offhand, then realized that Ethel meant something. 'Oh – your half-day.'

'Yes, madame. But I can stay if you need me, of course.'

'No, Ethel, of course not. I'd forgotten, is all. You deserve your half-day. Whatever will you do? It looks frightful outdoors.'

'I thought of doing the shops, madame. What they call the Ladies' Mile. That's Broadway. They have shops that are ever so big – they take up a whole and entire street, some of them.'

'But Ethel—' She started to say that Ethel hadn't any money.

Ethel, as if she knew exactly how Madame's mind worked, murmured, 'It's only looking.' She took the telegraph form. 'Shall I help you dress before I go downstairs?'

Louisa wanted to say that she could do for herself, but she pictured it, standing on one foot and fastening a corset, then a bodice in the back. 'I suppose you had better.'

She was ready for the newspapers to have nothing in them. Certainly, the front pages did not – nothing, at any rate, that she wanted to read. The murdered woman was gone and forgotten; the world had raced on – a blizzard in the Midwest (was that where

137

Arthur was?), political chicanery in Albany (the state capital), canals seen clearly on Mars through a new telescope. But nothing about the copper-haired woman. It wasn't right; it wasn't *just*.

Until she got to the *Express* and a story halfway down an inside page: she saw that again it was by A. M. Fitch, that unshaven, beery, vulgar lout she had conjured up a day or two ago. 'Where Are the Police in the Bowery Butcher Case?' It started well, challenging the police to produce results, but then it dribbled off into the same old stuff that Fitch had retailed earlier about the horrors of the crime, but in essence, that was that. The copper-haired woman was still erased.

She put the newspaper down. She thought about the visit of the two policemen. And Carver. What had Carver been doing there with the two policemen, anyway? What had he to do with Louisa's having written to Roosevelt? Nothing. Carver had probably come with Cleary and Grady to make sure that they protected the reputation of the hotel. But if that was so, then he *knew* – knew why they were there, knew that they were going to tell her that her story was nonsense. No, they had been more forceful than that – *he knew that they were going to shut her up!*

But how could he have known unless they had told him? And why would they have told him? Out of the goodness of their hearts? Because they were worried about the good name of the New Britannic? No – it was a conspiracy.

'Mr Manion, madame.'

'Oh? Oh, good, Ethel. You may take away the newspapers now. And perhaps Mr Manion would like coffee.'

Manion was wearing a different suit today but of the same doublebreasted cut. It looked like armour on him, as if made from something uncompromising and rigid. His face had the same look, too – closed, hard, wary. But handsome – no, not handsome: *dangerous*.

'Mr Manion, I won't get up. My ankle. Do sit, please. Coffee?'

He shook his head. 'Thanks.' He asked about the ankle, hardly listened to the answer. He said, 'I thought you were mad at me.'

She had to translate 'mad' to mean 'angry.' 'We got off on the wrong foot, yes.'

'Wrong foot?' He laughed, not pleasantly. 'That was as neat a piece of blackmail as I ever saw tried.'

'Mr Manion! I had hoped this would not be unpleasant.'

'Oh, really? What now?'

She was ready to get up, crutch and all, and tell him to leave. He was as boorish as Bleary and Leary or whatever their names had been. 'I thought you might be able to give me some information.'

'Without us fighting the Battle of Bull Run over it?'

'About the woman who was murdered.'

'Here we go again.'

'There was a sketch of her in the newspaper. How accurate do you think it would have been? I ask you in your professional capacity. And as a New Yorker, too.'

'What newspaper?'

'The *Express*.'

'Not the *Police Gazette*?' He laughed. She blushed. 'If it's the *Express*, it might have been okay. The artist there is kosher – the real article. Guy named McClurg. I've seen him in a couple of trials, you know, in court – he'd catch a likeness in about thirty seconds, as good as a photo.'

She had had to translate *kosher*; on first hearing it, she had thought he meant the artist was a Jew. However, what he seemed to mean was that the sketch would likely have been authentic.

'Are you aware that the police were here?'

He started to say something. She saw his wariness increase, as if he suspected her of something. Very slowly, drawing the word out, he murmured, 'Ye-e-e-s.'

'How did you know?'

'I saw them in the lobby, didn't I?'

'How did you know they were police?'

He laughed. 'Lady, I'd know a couple of bulls at a mile and a half.'

'Did you speak to them?'

Again, he hesitated. 'Let's say I didn't. So what?'

'What did they do? Did they go straight to the lift?'

He processed *lift* and said, 'They maybe stopped at the office.'

140

'To speak to Mr Carver?'

'I didn't ask.'

'Did you see them with Carver when they came up here?'

'I said I was in the lobby. But maybe I saw them go with him to the "lift."'

Allowing a little of her annoyance to show, she said, 'Your *maybes* are not helping me, Mr Manion!'

'Well, *maybe* that's why I use them. *Maybe* I don't want to help you.'

She looked at him, found he was already looking at her. She made herself hold the look, thought that she was showing her determination, her grit, her . . . But the trouble was that she was showing something else. She felt herself blush but still didn't look away. His face seemed to get more and more solemn but less and less closed, and then his lips allowed a small smile. She realized that he was looking at her as a woman, and she was looking at him as a man. Swallowing hard, she said, 'I had hoped you would want to help me.'

'You didn't give me much reason the last time.'

She looked at him again, met his eyes – grey, rather light; not so many eyes like that – and looked down at her hands and said, 'I'm sorry. But I thought . . . you had . . .'

'You thought I was a dishonest D who'd laid down for five bucks. Well, you were right. Like I said, it was harmless. You said the woman smiled at you. Yeah, she was smiling. She wanted to be

141

there, and the guy wanted to be there. What's so terrible about that?'

'So you did see her.'

'I told you that yesterday.'

'Did you see her leave the hotel, too?'

'No.'

'The man?'

'Yeah, he left while I was still on duty. He went out the front door like he owned the place.'

She was thinking about what it might mean if the woman hadn't left the hotel: *Then she could have been murdered here. No, that couldn't be . . .*

She said, '*Did* you talk to those two policemen who came to see me, Mr Manion?'

'What if I did?'

'What did they say?'

He hesitated. He rubbed his big hands together. 'They said I didn't see any woman that day with a guy in this hotel. She was never here. They said that Carver was sure I didn't see anything.'

She raised her head and looked at him again. 'Did they give you money?'

He returned the look. His voice was bitter. 'Twenty bucks. The tall one put it in my pocket.' He put a hand over his breast pocket as if he were putting it on his heart. 'Like I was some flunkey he was giving a tip.' He took his hand away. 'I guess they got it back from Carver.'

'How?'

He laughed at her. 'They went into the office and stayed about four minutes. They didn't go in there to tell him what a swell hotel he's got, did they? I expect they told him they were going to have to tell the newspapers that a witness had seen a murder victim in his lobby unless he came up with some of the old spondoolicks.' He rubbed a thumb and two fingers together. 'I expect Carver paid. Through the nose.'

'Are the police so corrupt as that?'

'The New York police would pull a drowning man out of the river so's they could take his wallet and then throw him back. That's all the police are about, is money. Money, money, money.'

She swallowed. 'Commissioner Roosevelt, too?'

'Terrible Teddy? Naw, Teddy's straight. He lives in a fool's paradise where he thinks he's cleaning up the corruption. He's a dreamer.'

'All the other police? Corrupt, I mean?'

'Root and branch.'

'So the policeman who found her body in the Bowery – he was corrupt? He lied in what he said?'

Manion shrugged. 'Where'd the money be in that?'

'But you said—'

'An old footy like the guy who found the body would take a buck from a chippy not to bust her, or he'd take a free meal at a beanery or a free oyster off a pushcart. There's cops in this city haven't paid for a meal in twenty years. But there's also things cops gotta do to keep their jobs, which isn't because somebody, somewhere, is a good cop, it's just because the system's gotta look like it works. So the cop that found the body wrote his report. That's what the beat cop *does*. Unless somebody paid him to do it wrong, he did it the best he knew. Now, it could be that in some far-fetched detective story the murderer paid him to lie, but even the dumbest Mick bull on the beat knows that he could do better by telling the truth, unless the money was so big he could share it with his sergeant and his lieutenant and keep everybody happy. But somebody give him a lot of cash to hush up the murder of a professional girl? Nah. Nah, the beat cop probably told the truth.'

'Then his report would have the things in it that the newspapers left out.'

'Like what?'

'What "mutilated" and "disfigured" meant.'

'Yeah, probably, but you don't want to know stuff like that.'

She caught his eyes again. They started to hold each other's glance, but she broke it and said, 'Would he still have his report?'

'No, that goes to his sergeant. But if he's the ignorant mackerel-snapper I think he is, he'll have written it out a couple of times before he got it in words he could spell and could hand in. He might still have those.'

'How much?' Manion looked wary again. She said, 'How much to buy his rough drafts from him?'

'What if he threw them out?'

'If he didn't? Ten dollars? Twenty? A hun—'

144

'For ten bucks, the average bull would sell you his badge. For twenty he'd throw in the wife and kids. A hundred would scare him to death.'

'I'm a stranger to New York, Mr Manion. You're not. I don't know the police. You do.' She let a smile touch just the corners of her mouth. 'How much would you take to buy that policeman's report for me?'

His nostrils flared. 'I wouldn't take a penny from you! What the hell do you think I am?'

'I thought you said—'

'I took that cop's two sawbucks because I didn't want trouble, but if you think he bought me, you're crazy! And you're not gonna buy me, either.'

'I'm confused.'

'I'll say!'

Irritated again, she said, 'I can hardly go to that policeman myself.'

'What difference does it make? What d'you care what happened to that woman?'

She hesitated. A picture leapt into her mind: two naked people on a bed – the joy of it, the pleasure. All she could say, however, was, 'She was happy.'

Manion started to say something, then got up and walked to a window. He took out a cigarette, lit it. He blew out smoke. 'You don't know it was the same woman.'

'*You* know.'

'I don't! That newspaper sketch could have been anybody.'

'You recognized her, or you wouldn't be here.'

He turned back towards her, then lowered his head and, with the same hand that held the cigarette, rubbed his forehead. 'I don't know what "disfigured" meant, but if she was all banged up, the sketch artist might have had to fake a lot. Or an editor could have pulled some old sketch from the morgue and printed it.' He drew in smoke and blew it out one side of his mouth. 'Tell you what. You get the artist to say that the sketch was a good likeness of the woman, then . . .' He shrugged.

'Then *what*, Mr Manion?'

'Then I suppose I'll help you get the cop's report. If it exists.'

'And then?'

'Then I hope you'll be satisfied.' He looked around for somewhere to put out his cigarette and, seeing nothing, supported himself with one hand on the back of a chair and put it out on the sole of his shoe. 'But I suppose you won't be.'

'Given your attitude, I am surprised you would help me under any circumstances.'

His face showed disgust, apparently with himself. He said, in a voice that was dredged from somewhere that he kept old and unused things, 'You might be surprised what I'd do.'

With Ethel gone for the afternoon, Louisa felt very daring as she maneuvered herself out through the hotel's great bronze doors. Still uncertain on her crutches, she lurched: lacking the strength of back and shoulder to do it gracefully, she had to gather herself for each controlled fall forward, then hunch down, shrink, and lunge up again as if coming up out of water. Yet she felt that she was setting off on a great adventure – her first real journey outside the hotel, and on crutches! Stepping across the threshold into cold outdoor air was like, she thought, what a prisoner must feel when released from prison. Reality!

She had thought she would take advantage of Newcome's offer to take her anywhere, any time, in his friend's carriage, but Mr Newcome was not to be found. Reception thought he was in his room, but he was not answering his door. Perhaps an indisposition. Or a late night.

Newcome, she decided, was one of those charming but insincere people who promise more than they ever mean to deliver.

The doorman wore some sort of bogus livery and a top hat, which he now tipped to her. She said, 'I want you to call me a horse-cab, and when it comes I want you to help me into it, and then I want you to tell the driver that he is to help me down when we get where I want to go.'

'Indeed, indeed.' He touched the brim of the top hat again, palmed the coin she gave him in a gloved hand (more cash gone), and charged into the teeming street as if he'd been fired from a siege gun. He blew a whistle, then waved a cab towards him with a gesture that looked as if he were batting a bird out of the air. Then he stood in the middle of the street and, hand raised, held up the instantly enraged traffic until the cab had ground its iron rims against the kerb. Other drivers and draymen and even some pedestrians hooted at him, but he was unmovable.

Louisa crutch-hobbled to the cab's narrow door. She lunged forward and got her left foot on the step, then felt herself boosted under the arms into the interior, where the doorman held her until she got her left foot on the floor and could pivot and fall backwards on the horsehair seat.

Breathless, she said, 'Thank you,' and dove into her reticule for another coin, but he waved it away and went to instruct the driver. He seemed to assume that the authority was all on his side, for he spoke very loudly and, to Louisa, very bossily, but the driver seemed to take it without complaint, for a moment later he bent down from his seat and said to her quite meekly, 'Where to, ma'am?'

She gave him the address of the *New York Express* and off they went, the hotel doorman now waving at the traffic – which he had stopped – to move faster. Flakes of snow were coming down; the day was dark; electric lights were on in the buildings, giving an impression of warmth, of life, close but unreachable.

It was a long trip, in fact several miles, most of the way down Manhattan. She hadn't looked at her guidebook's map, and she was shocked at what it would cost. When at last they arrived, the driver climbed down, opened the door, and stood there. Louisa looked at him. She realized that she had no more idea what to do than he did. She couldn't use the crutches inside the cab; she didn't think that she could stand on one foot at the cab's door and put the tips of the crutches on the kerb and so be able to let herself down, even with an assist from him.

Perhaps she could launch herself into the air and trust him to catch her? He was a fairly old man, and inside his ancient frock coat she suspected he was string-bean skinny; she'd probably flatten him, and there they'd both be, writhing on the pavement.

'I think,' she said, 'if you would take my crutches and put them down and then put your hand under my left arm, I should be able to descend.'

'Give 'er a try,' he said. 'But don't yous do nothing rash, please.'

It was all right until she was balancing on her left foot in the cab doorway, but she realized too late that she would have to hop down to the carriage step, which was a metal plate about as big as one of her hands. She was debating how catastrophic this could be when a male voice said, 'Allow me, ma'am,' and a tall man who seemed to be dressed for a costume party swept one arm behind her skirts and the other behind her shoulders and plucked her from the cab – Louisa said, 'Oh!' – and put her down as gently as if he were putting down an egg; then he waited until she had her weight on her left foot, waited to make sure the crutches were placed securely under her arms, and tipped his wide hat and disappeared.

'Wild West Show,' the driver said. 'Them fellas is all over town. *I* coulda done it m'self, if he'd waited.'

Louisa shook herself, pulled down part of her bodice that had got disarranged, and paid him off.

She was standing in front of a tall building with imitation Greek columns that went up and up, stopping at each storey for a different order of capital. On her level was a more or less Gothic doorway in grey stone, inside it double doors in somewhat grubby brass, only the parts immediately around the handles looking bright. There was no doorman, but a pretty regular stream of people were coming and going, mostly male – men in suits and bowlers, boys in cloth caps and some adult's cast-off overcoat or cut-down suit, an old man wearing a board fore and aft that advertised the very newspaper she meant to visit. Louisa tried to join the stream but was too slow; to her astonishment, one of the boys held a brass door for her. When she tried to tip him, he said, 'On the house, lady!' and trotted off into the building.

There was a lobby with a terrazzo floor and a lot of dark bronze on the walls – pillars, plaques, some sort of directory – and at the far end a stairway whose steepness made her gasp. She said to one of the men who was flying past, 'The *Express*?' and he never slowed but did turn his head and snapped, 'Editorial on seven, presses in the basement!'

She couldn't conceive why everybody was in a

tearing hurry, but they were, and she had to get out of the way or be run over. Huddling against a bronze pillar (vaguely Egyptian), she said to a boy, 'Is there an elevator?' She remembered not to say 'lift.' The boy, who was quite different from the first boy, said, 'Where yez from, Arkansas?' and hurried away.

Seeing that there was nothing for it but the stairs, she started hobbling towards the back of the building. The mob rushed past her, flung itself at the stairs, and went up mostly two stairs at a time, while another mob ran down the other way. It seemed to be like the streets outside, everything organized into one-way streams. She looked up the stairs as she got close; they were steep, their treads black, dirt and cigarette butts and paper ground into their corners. And she had to go to seven!

'Why don't you take the elevator, little lady?'

She turned her head to see who had spoken; somebody else jostled her from the other side. The same voice shouted, 'Watch what you're doing, there!' And he raised his voice another notch to bellow, 'Go easy, boy, there's a crippled woman here!' He was a very fat man in a very loud suit, but he looked to her like Galahad in a cheap engraving. She said, 'Oh, thank you!' as he piloted her to her left and into a side corridor she'd missed, and there was an elevator.

'Too slow for most of us,' he said. 'Have a good day.' And then *he* was gone.

It was her first experience of *real* Americans

– New Yorkers, anyway – in their native habitat, except for the news vendor next to the hotel. She concluded that they were generous, always in a hurry, vulgar, and somewhat improper in their easy dismissal of the proprieties. Yet how grateful she felt to some of them already!

The man had been right: nobody else was waiting for the lift. It was at that moment up above some-where. She could hear a noise like iron wheels grinding on cobblestones; the noise would start, go on, then stop, and there would be a clashing sound; then it would start again, stop, and the same sound. *Somebody* must use the elevator, obviously.

At last the brass doors parted. Behind them was a brass grating that made the clashing noise when the adolescent at the controls threw it to the side as if he meant to smash it, and the pivoted pieces, which formed diamonds the size of her notepaper, closed up as their sides folded together and became slender verticals.

'*Gongup!*'

Three large men got out talking and walked off, still talking. Louisa hobbled in.

'*Floor?*'

'Oh – ah – oh, I think seven. Is seven—?'

'*New York Express*, editorial, sports, news, and ads. Publishing offices're on eight. Wotcher want?'

'Seven.'

'You got it.'

He reached across her and grabbed the shiny

brass handle of the tarnished brass gates and pulled them across her and smashed the gate against the jamb. '*Gongup!*' He grasped a handle that stuck out from the wall, actually part of a kind of crank that was pivoted at the level of his knees. He threw the crank over and sat on a padded stool that rose like a mushroom on a brass column from the elevator floor. They started with a lurch; Louisa gulped and felt her stomach drop to the level of her thighs.

'*Three!*' He flung open the gate with its usual crash. 'Step back inna car, will yous, lady?' A man and a boy were waiting to enter. Louisa hadn't practiced going backwards and almost fell.

'*Gongup!*'

She lurched against the back wall and let her weight rest there until they reached seven and the car stopped, the gate crashed, and the boy shouted, 'Seven! You wanted seven, dintchoos, lady? Seven! You getting out or aintchoos?'

The man and boy parted without looking at her. She hobbled forward, head down so she wouldn't put a crutch in the gap between the elevator car and the seventh floor. Once she was on firm ground, she turned. The gate was already closing. She said, 'You needn't be rude, young man.'

'Yeah, yeah, yeah . . .' She heard this like a fading angelic voice as the doors closed and the car ascended.

She looked around. She was in a long corridor that must have run the width of the building;

others ran at right angles at its ends. Directly across the corridor from her was a grate like a theatre's ticket window, and a sign that said 'Inquiries and Deliveries.' She hoisted her weight on the crutches and made her slow way over. A very young man, hardly out of adolescence, was inside the window. He was reading something, turning brilliantined hair to her.

'Excuse me?'

He held up a finger without looking up.

'Excuse—'

He whirled away from her and scribbled something on a slip of paper, jammed it into a tube the size of a cucumber, and rammed the tube upward into a brass pipe that ran up the wall – one of seven that Louisa could see. There was a whir and a sucking sound, and the tube disappeared.

'Yes, lady?'

'I am looking for a Mr A. M. Fitch. He writes for the *New York Express.*'

'Newsroom.' He pointed with a pencil down the corridor. 'Third door onna left.' He didn't pause but looked away from her and said over her shoulder to somebody behind her, 'Yeah?'

An urchin was standing behind her. He was so small that he had to pull himself up to talk over the window's ledge. 'Gotta packet fer da compositor.'

The pencil pointed the other way. 'Second onna left.'

'Ya t'ink I doan know? Ya tink I was bawn

yestiday?' The urchin looked at Louisa. 'Some nerve.'

Louisa hobbled along the corridor, adding the young man and the urchin to her store of New Yorkers. *Very poor manners. But a kind of essential humour. Or resilience, at any rate.* She opened a door that said Newsroom and hobbled into chaos.

The room was enormous – at least the size of the New Britannic's lobby. A waist-high fence of once-varnished wood ran its length, dividing a narrow lane where Louisa stood from a vast area full of desks. Four pillars rose to the ceiling. Smoke hung in visible layers, swirled as men and boys moved among the desks. At the far end from her, three men sat on a kind of dais with a wall around it; people, most of them boys, were handing up sheets of paper. Intermittently, a bell rang, and a different boy would run to the far corner of the room. At the other end, five telephones hung on the wall; every one had a man slouched into it as if he had been hung up there, and every man was shouting.

The place stank. It stank of men. She knew the smell – tobacco, perspiration, their maleness (not unlike the after-sex smell), old clothes – and it reminded her of Arthur, from whom this smell was a pleasant emanation of the man himself, not a miasma as it was here.

She chewed her lip and looked around for someone to help her. If anybody thought it unusual to have a woman on crutches visit the place, he kept it to himself. Finally, she approached a wooden gate set into the long, battered fence.

'Excuse me?'

A man wearing a green eyeshade was leaning over something he was reading by the light of an electric lamp.

'Excuse me?'

He never moved. He had a pencil and he was making marks on the pages in front of him. Louisa knew what he was doing; Arthur did the same thing when a book was going to the press. But Arthur was at least polite if she interrupted him. Or more or less polite.

She sighed and moved along the fence and spoke to an older man who was sitting with his feet on his desk and a glass in his hand. He swiveled his eyes to look at her but didn't move his head. The strong odor of whiskey reached her as he swirled his glass. 'What's up?'

She thought he meant that she could interrupt him. Taking the folded newspaper article from her pocket, she said, 'I should like to see your sketch artist.'

'Wouldn't we all. I think if you look in the nearest dive, which is to say saloon, or, as they say on your native shores, "pub," you'll find him. Keep your eyes cast down, as he's likely to be on the floor.'

'His name is McClurg.'

'So it is. That won't keep him from being on the floor, though.'

156

She quailed at the idea of going into a saloon. Even with Ethel – even with *Arthur* – she wouldn't have dared go into a saloon. Her New York guidebook was very harsh about saloons. She smoothed the newspaper article with a gloved hand, supporting it with the other, and said, 'Would it be possible for me to see A. M. Fitch?'

'Would it be possible?' He held up his glass and spoke to it. 'Would it? It would. But I wouldn't advise it.'

His alcoholic calm, if that was what it was, irritated her. 'I should like to see A. M. Fitch!'

'Be it on your head.' He actually smiled. 'Little lady.' He stood, looked into a far corner of the room and bellowed in a voice that could have been heard on Staten Island, 'Hey, Fitch! You got a visitor!'

Louisa looked where he was shouting. It was like looking through the trees in a wood, trying to see something beyond them: between her and whatever was in the far corner were male bodies, standing, leaning, hurrying, chatting. A few of them looked up at the man's bellow; somebody laughed. Then two of them parted and she was able to see what she supposed was A. M. Fitch – a woman in leg o' mutton sleeves and a black straw hat the size and shape of a boater. Miss or Mrs Fitch (Louisa, shocked to find any woman there, supposed it had to be Mrs) craned her neck and saw Louisa, studied her, looked disgusted, and waved her in.

Louisa thanked the man with the glass and went to the gate, wrestled with a bolt on the inside and finally got it open and hobbled through. Nobody offered to help, but everybody watched. She had suddenly become the most interesting thing that had happened in the newsroom that day. As she lurched forward on the crutches, she was afraid that one of them would trip her, so strong was her sense of their dislike, yet their faces were merely interested, perhaps speculative. None of them moved. Blushing furiously, wondering how one was supposed to hold one's head up while moving on crutches for which one hadn't the strength, she moved through the desks, tacking around them like a clumsy ship, pulling up at last at the dock of Miss or Mrs Fitch's desk.

Close to, the newswoman looked to be a very young and freckled woman dressed in mannish clothes. The white leg o' mutton shirt-waist was cut mannishly; she wore a mannish necktie with it, and a man's paper cuff protectors next to her hands. Louisa supposed there was a skirt hidden under the desk, would have been horrified to find there were bloomers or even trousers. The woman had watched Louisa come towards her; now, she said in an apparently angry voice, 'What have you got for me?'

'I beg your pardon?'

'You got a story? A tip? What?'

'Might I sit down?'

'You might, if I had a chair. Anyway, you aren't staying, are you?'

'Why are you all so *rude*?' Her opinion of New Yorkers was changing.

'It comes with the territory, honey. Anyway, you're English and kind of hoity-toity, so I 'speck we'd seem rude no matter what. What's a woman like you doing here?'

Angry now, Louisa said, 'I *thought* I would be able to gather some information!'

'You kidding me? Sweetie, we're the ones who gather information. Sorry.'

'I might even have something to contribute to your story about the woman who was murdered in the Bowery, but I suppose that wouldn't interest you! Thank you so much for your time.'

Louisa put her right crutch behind her and prepared to turn around.

'Contribute what? D'you know something or you just shooting the squit? Hey, sweetheart, I'm talking to you!' The woman had come around her desk and caught Louisa by the arm; at least she'd revealed that she was wearing a dark skirt. She looked as if she were deciding whether to strike Louisa or shake her. 'Yes or no?'

'Do take your hands off me.'

'Oh, la-di-da!'

'You are being deliberately rude. No one could be so rude by mere chance!'

The woman put her face close to Louisa's. 'In-for-ma-tion – yes or no? You spikka da English? You *capisce* "information"?'

The woman frightened her; the audience of men

terrified her; but what had Arthur said? *Remember that we are emissaries of Britain.* She said very quietly, with not a tremor in her voice, 'Good day, *Mr* Fitch.'

Somebody laughed.

Fitch turned on him and said something about where he could put his laughter. She turned back to Louisa, folding her arms over the white shirt-waist. 'If you know something about the murder in the Bowery that's new and dazzling, tell me. That's my story! It's dead as a doornail right now, but if you got something good, I could goose it back into life. Look, lady – Miz . . . ?'

'Doyle. I am Mrs Arthur Conan Doyle.'

'Miz Doyle, everything's on deadline here; we're all in a rush. I know it doesn't look it; this bunch of vagrants are mostly asleep or telling dirty jokes or getting noodled, but that's because the early-aft edition's mostly in bed. Still and nevertheless, I can't stand jawing with you all day while you make up your mind whether you got something or not. Get me?'

Louisa looked at her with a blank face. 'I will tell you what I know if you will tell me what *you* know. And introduce me to your sketch artist. *Get me?*'

'But is it *good?*'

'I saw the murdered woman the day before the murder.'

'Where?'

Louisa smiled like the Sphinx, which she had seen on a trip with Arthur.

Fitch grabbed a chair from another desk, dragged it over and slammed it down close to her own, then signalled Louisa into it. She had placed it so that Louisa's back would be to the vast room; now, when she spoke, she whispered. 'These pissants would steal me blind if they got the chance, so keep your voice down, get me? They *hate* me. Because I'm a woman.' With Louisa seated, Fitch took her crutches and leaned them against a wall. 'You any relation to the writer Conan Doyle?'

'I am his wife.'

'That's a good angle. I can see it in a subhead. "Mrs Sherlock Holmes." Get it?'

'If there is a chance of any such thing, I shall tell you nothing.'

'"Nothing comes from nothing," sweetheart; it works both ways. But if you don't like it, I'll see they don't use it. Promise!' She smiled a smile that said that her promises weren't worth tuppence.

'Nor is my name or any hint of my identity to be used – no "wife of a famous author known for a certain English detective," or whatever circumlocution you would invent.'

'"Circumlocution"! We oughta put you on the copy desk. Okay, you're Mrs Anonymous. But it's a nice angle. Tell me.' But even as she said it, Fitch put up a hand and said over Louisa's shoulder, 'If your ears were any bigger, you'd fly, Musgrove! Beat it! Go on – can't you see I got a sob story here?' She shook her head, whispered to Louisa,

161

'This is no good.' She pushed herself halfway out of her chair and screamed 'COPY!'

She stayed in that position until a boy appeared, to whom she snarled, 'You took your time, you little varmint!' She grabbed a blank sheet of paper, folded it in half, and gave it to the boy, who was not unlike the urchin Louisa had seen downstairs, except that he had on a mangled necktie. Fitch handed him the folded paper and whispered to him, 'Go find McClurg. He'll be in the Aces and Eights. Tell him to meet me at Holtzer's in five minutes or he'll never get another loan from me as long as he lives.' She caught the boy's shirt. 'Now run with that paper like it's something I gave you to take upstairs pronto, and if McClurg isn't at Holtzer's in five minutes I'll take it outa *your* hide. Get me?'

The boy, unfazed, said, 'Yeah, yeah, yeah,' and ambled away.

Fitch sat down and sneered, '"Lo, how I fly."'

'Shakespeare!'

'Yeah, we have him over here, too.'

'There was another woman who was murdered whom they called—'

'Can it, sweetie; the walls have ears.' Fitch was on her feet again. She grabbed a cloth coat from a hook above her desk and an umbrella from its place in the corner and then helped Louisa to her feet. 'You new to the outriggers?'

'I've used them only last evening and today.'

'Well, do your best. We gotta haul ash here or

162

McClurg'll turn right around and go back to his saloon.'

'Where are we going?'

'Holtzer's.' She tried to hurry Louisa through the newsroom, but Louisa might as well have been told to swim. Again, everybody watched her. A few men made remarks to Fitch, most of them unintelligible to Louisa, although she did hear one of them call Fitch 'Lady Jam-rag.' Fitch seemed to understand them better, because she said to one, 'Try it, and I'll have your you-know-whats for oysters, Flynn,' and to another she said only, 'You'll never be that lucky, Jenks.' She didn't slow until she reached the elevator.

Louisa came puffing along behind her and was grateful that the elevator wasn't there – the crashing sounds were well below them – and she leaned against the wall. Immediately at her eye level, somebody had written in indelible pencil, *Fitch eats the hairy banana.*

She thought she knew what 'banana' meant but didn't understand the 'hairy' part, although she'd seen only the one and maybe other men had hair on theirs. 'Eats' was also somewhat murky; if it meant what she thought it did, eating was not what went on – no biting and chewing, she would have thought. She had never performed this act, which seemed to her particularly unappetizing, nor had Arthur ever asked her. Could she ask him about it? And about 'hairy banana'? Probably not.

The elevator doors opened and the gates crashed.

Two men stood at the back; both, to her surprise, removed their hats.

'*Goandown!*'

She was able to lean a shoulder against the wall of the car as they fell. She was already, she knew, worn out. She dreaded having to get herself a cab to go back to the hotel. Who would help her in? And out?

The two men insisted on waiting until Fitch and Louisa had left the car; then they came out and had to steer around Louisa and her crutches. Fitch said, 'It isn't far.'

'Must we walk?'

'Unless you can fly.' She held one of the heavy front doors until Louisa was on the pavement. Light snow was still coming down. Fitch said, 'You mentioned Shakespeare.' She pointed to her left. 'This way. Yeah, there was a murder on the Bowery six years ago, a whore who called herself Shakespeare, but it was too long ago. There's no connection.'

'She was mutilated. One of the newspapers said there was some talk of the Ripper's having come to New York.'

'Honey, they say that every time a woman cuts her finger with the bread knife. No, it's got nothing to do with our murder.'

Louisa registered the 'our' but said nothing. After another couple of slow steps, she said, 'Is it Mrs or Miss Fitch?'

'Call me Minnie. And it isn't "Mrs." Not that I

164

haven't had offers. And I like men, don't get me wrong – I'm not what those cretins in the newsroom call a "morphadite."'

'What is a morphadite?'

Fitch laughed. 'What you or I would call hermaphrodite, if we ever had a chance to use the word. A hermaphrodite – you know. Both sexes.'

'Oh – a gynander.'

'A *what?*' Fitch was walking almost backwards, looking into Louisa's face. 'Girls who like other girls, get me? You ever hear of a Boston marriage?'

'Like a Sapphist, you mean!'

'Saffist! Gee, I never heard that one. Is it dirty?'

'It's from the name of the Greek poetess.'

'You don't say! That's cute.' She had taken a notebook from some pocket in her skirt and was writing as she walked. 'S-A-F-F—'

'No, it's P-H.' She spelled Sappho.

'I'd think it'd be Sap-pho, but it's all Greek to me.' Fitch guffawed. 'Here we are.'

They had arrived in front of a narrow bakery. Fitch opened the door and showed Louisa into a long room with wooden counters on each side, glass fronted, with tray after tray of pastries and sweets and desserts, and behind them against the wall shelves full of many kinds of bread. Three tables were set in a row down the middle of the room.

Fitch pointed at a chair. 'Sit. My God, those things do get in the way, don't they.' She meant the crutches. She raised her voice at a woman behind one of the counters. 'Two coffees, Mamie. And some of those cookies with the powdered sugar.' She fell into a chair opposite Louisa. 'Okay, we can talk here. Shoot.'

'I haven't seen the sketch artist yet.'

'You're as tough a bird as I could find on the Bowery! Don't you trust me?'

Embarrassed, Louisa murmured, 'Well . . . No, actually.'

Fitch made a face and then reached across the table and lifted Louisa's veil. 'Hey, that's some mouse! Your husband do that?'

'My husband adores me, and I him! I suffered a fall at my hotel.'

'It would make a great little story – "Mrs Sherlock Holmes Married to Wife-Beater." I know, I know, I'm not supposed to mention you.'

'My husband is a *gentleman*, Miss Fitch.'

'Call me Minnie. I guess you'd be surprised how many gentlemen use their wives to tune up for a fight with Sullivan.' Her eyebrows went up as the shop door opened. 'Well, speaking of gentlemen – our sketch artist, and only a little the worse for wear. You're late.'

Louisa saw a quite dapper little man dressed in a dark lounge suit buttoned very tight, a bowler hat, and spats; she saw, too, that he was quite drunk. Yet he was one of those drunkards who remain upright and more or less coherent even though the drinking day had started at dawn. His eyes were bloodshot, his nose red, and his breath beery.

'I hurried every step of the way, Minnie, m'dear.'
True, he was puffing.

'This lady has a question for you, and get on with it so's I can do my business with her.'

Louisa tried to give him her best smile, but he was studying her face where her veil was still up. 'That's some eye,' he said. 'Your husband do that?' He pulled a chair around and more or less fell backwards into it, putting himself between Fitch and Louisa. 'My wife does that to me sometimes. Information?'

'I shall say once more, and once more only, my husband had nothing to do with my injuries, which were the result of an accident. I do not like rudeness, Mr McClurg!'

'She knows my name!' He had said that to Fitch, now turned bleary eyes back to Louisa. 'To put it in the plainest possible terms, Mrs – Mrs . . . ?'

'Doyle.'

'Irish gal, eh? Well, I've always been able to get along with the Irish. I say again, what's it worth to you?'

Louisa calculated how much was in her purse, how much pinned inside her corset, and how much more in her stocking case in the hotel. All of it together didn't add up to much. 'Two dollars,' she blurted out. A whole eight shillings! How carefully she'd have thought about spending eight shillings in London.

McClurg looked at Fitch and then at the table. 'That seems fair. Shoot.' He took a small pad from a pocket, then a pencil and a bit of red stick and a lump of something white and began to move the pencil over the pad.

'You drew a sketch of the woman whose body was found in the Bowery. I want to know if the sketch was accurate.'

The pencil stopped. 'Accurate? You accusing me of not being *accurate*?'

'I mean, Mr McClurg, if someone thought she recognized the dead woman from your sketch, would they be justified in saying it was she?'

''Course.' He finished whatever he was doing with the pencil and flipped the pad around for Louisa to see. Although he had been looking at her, it was a sketch of Minnie Fitch, and a very good one. McClurg laughed, showed the sketch to Fitch and turned to a new page.

Louisa said, 'Did you make the newspaper sketch from the corpse itself?'

''Course.'

'But it had been "disfigured."'

'Pretty bad, too.'

'In what way? How was she disfigured, Mr McClurg?'

He looked at Fitch. She said to Louisa, 'If he tells you, you may need the convenience in a hurry. Straight back through the door and turn left.'

Louisa said, 'Miss Fitch, I am a physician's wife.' That was sheer bravado; she hated seeing other people's blood. She looked at McClurg. 'Well?'

McClurg was drawing again but raised his

eyebrows. 'Well, her nose had been cut off. And both lips. And her eyes were gone.' He looked up, perhaps to see if she was going to be sick.

Louisa was afraid she was. She thought she might faint, as well: the idea of having her lips cut off – it was the lips that did it, the *lips* – was too much for her, and she made a great effort and cleared the threat of darkness from her eyes, then fought with her stomach. She breathed deeply. 'That poor woman,' she said in a strong voice.

'Hey, she's not so bad,' Minnie Fitch said to McClurg. For answer, he spun his sketchbook so Fitch could see it, then Louisa. It was a sketch of Louisa, bruises to the fore, done in pencil with touches of red and white. Louisa shuddered. He said, 'Just to show you I can be *accurate.*'

'But – if her nose and her l-lips were missing . . .'

'Sewed 'em back on in the morgue. They do a good job there, better than some taxidermists. There was swelling, and the stitches, but I know what to do.'

Louisa felt a little faint again. 'The eyes?'

'They didn't put those back. Stuffed the, you know, the cavities and sewed the lids shut in case some loved one wanted a peep at the peepers.' He was sketching again. 'I didn't show any of that stuff – the stitches, the swelling – I been at this thirty years, you think I don't know the tricks of the trade?'

McClurg spun the pad to her again. On the new page was the recognizable face of the murder

169

victim, but with the lines of sewing on the lips and nose. 'That's what I saw. But that doesn't go into the paper.'

Louisa looked at Fitch. 'And you didn't mention the disfigurement in your article.'

'I tried; I always try, but they always edit me. Can't put that stuff in a "family newspaper." I've actually been told that part of our job is "protecting the city's women." You like that? You feel protected? Myself, I think a little real horror might get us down the road to helping some of those girls.'

McClurg tore the three pages from his book and distributed them as if he were dealing cards, one to Fitch and two to Louisa. 'On the house,' he said.

Louisa produced a little purse. 'Of course, I shall pay you more, Mr McClurg.'

'Not for the sketches, you won't.' He put a hand over hers, looked into her eyes; beery breath flowed past her. 'For information, sure. For my art, no.' He took the two-dollar silver note she produced and smoothed it between his fingers. 'Man's best friend.' He stood. 'Back to the den of alcoholic iniquity. Nice to have met you, Miz Doyle.' He nodded at Fitch. 'Minnie.' He hiccuped. 'Editorial knows where to find me.'

They watched him leave. Minnie Fitch said, 'He's a nice fella. And a sad case. "His art."' She shook her head. 'Nobody's ever satisfied, are they.'

'I'm ready to tell you what I know.'

'At last, as they say in the mellers.'

170

Louisa told her about seeing the woman in the hotel, her letter to Roosevelt, then about the visit of the police. 'They tried to *bully* me.'

Fitch was excited. 'Because they were on the take and they thought you'd queer it! They *know something*! I wonder if Roosevelt knows. Jeez, could Roosevelt be on the take, too? That would be the greatest story of my life! Jehosephat, if I could nail that one down I could move to the *World*!'

'I hardly think Mr Roosevelt the type to be "on the take."'

'Honey, in this city, it's like leprosy – they come in pure and clean, and they get down in the dirt with the lepers, and in no time they've lost their noses and their ears and they've got their stumps held out for cash like all the rest. The biggest talkers are the biggest crooks. Oh, sweetheart, if I could nail Roosevelt!' She wiggled her eyebrows and rushed on. 'Cleary and Grady, huh? Cleary's a lieutenant, big, tried to scare you to death with a look? Yeah, Cleary of the Murder Squad. He must think he died and went to heaven, making money from your hotel on a dead whore. Murder Squad doesn't get so many chances to dip their hand in the till, y'know? It isn't like gambling or prostitution, where the protection money rolls in like the waves at Coney Island. The whorehouses over on Twenty-third pay by the month; it's like having a pension.'

'My hotel is on Twenty-third Street!'

'Yeah, but a couple of blocks away. You gotta go

west of Sixth Avenue to start seeing the whores.'
Fitch looked down into her cup of by then cold
coffee. 'This is great. You really handed me a story
on a plate.' She drank half the coffee in a gulp
and set the cup down hard. 'What am I supposed
to tell you in trade?'

'I think Mr McClurg told me. Although I'd like
to know the woman's name, I think. To . . . give
her reality.'

'You playing detective, Mrs Arthur Conan
Doyle?'

'Certainly not!'

Fitch put a coin on the table and started towards
the front, where the cashier sat behind a machine
on which she had been ringing up purchases with
a good deal of noise. Louisa tried to jump up to
say that she would pay, but her crutches had been
moved into an alcove by the door, and all she
could do was signal. By the time that that was
straightened out, the bill was paid, Fitch had
refused Louisa's money, and they were standing
on the pavement. The snow had ended.

'You gonna promise me you won't take this
anyplace else?' Fitch said.

'Why would I do that?'

'For money, most likely, but I guess you got a
lot of that.'

'Will you share what you find with me, Miss
Fitch?'

'Minnie.'

'Minnie, then.'

Fitch was leaning on her umbrella. She pushed out one side of her mouth and cocked an eyebrow. 'I'll share when I've written it into a story and it's gone to press. I can't do better than that. If I sit on anything, I'm gonna be doomed to spending the rest of my days in the newsroom of the lousiest paper in New York.' She grinned. 'Take pity on the working girl.'

Louisa thought that Fitch needed pity about as much as a steel dreadnought did, but she said, 'I think we should agree to share and share alike.'

'*If* I can scoop everybody else.' Fitch waved the umbrella towards the south and said that Louisa could get a cab 'down there' and now she had to hurry, because she had work to do. Louisa watched her go, feeling with an odd sadness that the story of the murdered woman was going with her – as if she had let go of the woman somehow, had given her up. It was a peculiar feeling, a sense of loss, a sudden loneliness. Was that what the murdered woman had meant to her – a kind of companionship? Or, even more crassly, merely something to think about, to entertain her?

Louisa felt abandoned. She was no longer the just-released prisoner; she was a tired woman with a hurt ankle who didn't know how to get home. She turned away, meaning to hobble to the kerb and hope to see a cab. She became aware of a rising cacophony to her left, a complex and hideous noise that was increasing as she crossed to the kerb. It rose and rose, threatening to deafen. She

173

wasn't mad; other people heard it, too; ahead of her in the street, the driver of a carriage looked behind him and whipped his horses up; two women who were crossing broke into awkward runs, their skirts lifted in their hands. A terrified dog put its tail between its legs and bolted.

The thing came near. It looked like a rather elegant carriage, with brass lamps and a leather top and shiny, spinning wheels – but no horses.

A motorcar.

She had heard of such things. Arthur had shown her a picture of one in, she thought, the *Graphic*. But here was one in horrible reality, shaking and coughing and rattling and growling as it pulled right in front of her and came to a stop. A tall man rose from the back and stepped down, removing his hat as he did so.

'Mrs Doyle, how brave of you to be out! May we offer you transportation back to the hotel? It would be terrible for you to have to find a cab.'

It was Sir Henry Irving.

Could she? What would Arthur say? What would *people* say?

Seconds later, she was spinning along Park Row at twelve miles an hour, frightened out of her wits. Forty-five minutes after that, she was back in her hotel room, trying to run to her bathroom to vomit because she couldn't stop thinking of a woman without lips or eyes.

When she had cleaned herself and brushed her teeth, she dug out the two drawings McClurg had given her – herself with her bruises, the dead woman with the stitches in her lips and nose – and put them in an envelope with a note that said, 'Are these accurate enough for you?' She wrote *Hotel Detective* on the outside and took it down to reception, despite an ankle that was now screaming for relief.

Detective-Sergeant Dunne had walked from police headquarters to the Tenth Precinct station, not because he liked walking – he hated it, in fact, as he hated all forms of exercise – but because it was only a few hundred feet away. It was one of the mysteries of city administration why the Tenth wasn't housed at 300 Mulberry instead of 205, but Dunne had learned long since not to look into that sort of thing. It usually had to do with money.

'Dunne, Murder Squad.' He flashed his card. 'I wanta see Jimmy Malone.'

'Down in the duty room.'

'Well, fetch him up, will you? And don't put it in the book; this is a social call.'

He looked at the notices on the board while he waited. They were the same notices he ignored every day at 300 Mulberry. He seemed amused by what he read.

'Sure, it's Never Dunne.'

'Hey, Jimmy; how's the lad?' They'd known each other when both were probationers in uniform. They'd taken different paths.

'Passable but getting older. Ye've come up in the world, Dunne.'

'Got a few minutes, Jimmy?'

'Wouldn't I have, and me on nights for the next week? Not going to fill me full of tales of the old days, are you?'

Dunne led him along Mulberry to a coffee stall, where they both got milky coffee in white china cups and leaned against the matchboarded side of the stall. Dunne said, 'It's the matter of the dead woman you found in the Bowery.'

'Worst thing I ever saw.'

'I'm sure it was, lad. Murder's given me the investigation to wind up.'

'They know who done it, then?'

'O' course not, Jimmy; you know better than that. What I meant to say was that we're putting it on the shelf until we get some new evidence. I'm just checking the loose ends and like that.'

'I tole everything I know to that lieutenant of yours.' Malone spat. 'He's a piece of work.'

'Now, now, Jimmy, we never speak ill of our betters. What I'm after, Jimmy, is just to ask you again if you saw anybody, anybody at all, around the place where you found the poor girl.'

'Poor girl, my arse, Dunne; she was a hoor.'

'You knew her, did you?'

''Course I didn't, man! Never set eyes on her. But you get to know the type in our work, eh?'

'Well, as she wasn't wearing any clothes, Jimmy, I wondered how you knew she was a working girl. Saw the wear on her back, did you?'

'Ah, ya scamp! It just figures, don't it?'

'Anyways, did you see anybody else, Jim?'

'Nary a human soul.'

'Not all night?'

'Aw, shit, Dunne, what are you saying? 'Course I saw some folk here and there, the usual layabouts and drifters and hoors, but that was earlier. By the time I found that Godawful mess, it was time for even the bad folk to be in their beds. The town was empty.'

'So, you saw nobody near by. Now let's see – you found the body in the alley off Elizabeth Street. You'd last passed there when?'

'Cripes, I don't keep all that in me book! But if it was the usual night, I come by there twenty minutes before, give or take.'

'Then you went . . . ?'

'Then I go on down Elizabeth and across Bayard to Mott, and so north for a few blocks, and then left on Broome, and so over that to Elizabeth and so start down Elizabeth again. That's my beat.'

'And you saw nobody in all that time.'

'Not a soul. It's God's loneliest job, y'know, walking the beat at three in the morning. Cripes, I was even glad to see some old Jew with a wagon.'

Dunne sighed. 'That was somebody, Jimmy.'

'What d'you mean by that?'

'You saw an old Jew with a wagon.'

'So I did; did I ever say I didn't?'

'You said you saw nobody.'

177

'Aw, so what? He says to me, "Hello, Mr Policeman,"
and I says hello and we went our separate ways.'

'And where was this?' Dunne got out a pocket
street directory that was a scant two by five inches
and unfolded the thin-paper map inside its cover.
He held it against the wall of the coffee stall. 'Now
just show me where you saw him, Jimmy.'

'Well – I ain't got me glasses with me; how did
I know we was going to do reading? – but find
me Elizabeth Street. Right, there it is and there's
Mott, and I guess I was coming north about here
and he was going south. What of it?'

Dunne looked at the map, then made a pencil
mark. 'He had a horse, did he?'

'What, you think he was pulling the wagon
hisself?'

'What did he look like?'

'I think he was sorta grey, maybe. You know, like
a horse.'

'The man, Jimmy – the old Jew. What'd he look
like?'

'Like a ragman.'

'Wearing a hat?'

'Aye, a hat, but don't ask me what kind.'

'Grey hair, was it?'

'More white. Hanging around his face, y'know.'

'Suit? Necktie? Shawl?'

Malone waved a hand. 'I hadn't bought a ticket
to study him with a glass, Dunne. He was an old
Jew in a wagon; let it go, will you?'

'How did you know he was a Jew?'

'Didn't he sound like one? He was a kike with a kike accent. Cripes, man!'

Dunne finished his coffee and slapped Malone on a shoulder. 'It's good to see you, Jimmy. Nice change from 300 Mulberry.' He put both cups on the counter of the stall. 'I'll walk you back to the station, shall I?'

'I wasn't no help, was I.'

'Evidence is like the Almighty, Jimmy – it moves in mysterious ways. I won't know if you were any help for weeks and weeks yet.'

But as they were walking along Mulberry, he was thinking that he'd give this to the Wop, who was proving a better cop than he'd expected. Forcella could go to the precincts that surrounded the Tenth and talk to the cops who'd been on the night beat and ask whether they'd seen an old man, maybe a Jew, with a wagon.

Because the wagon was the bit of light that showed through the trees. A wagon would explain how he'd moved the body.

New Brittanic Hotel, New York City
My Dearest Husband,
I have had the most exhilarating and terri-fying experience of my existence! If it can be said that terror is exhilarating, which I think it is or certainly was for me! I have travelled in a motor-car! I had just stepped out of the hotel when who should happen by in this remarkably noisy monstrosity but Sir Henry

179

Irving, out 'for a spin', as he put it, with his friend Mr Clapp the theatrical producer and the owner of the machine! The machine was made entirely by hand in Germany and cost a great deal of money! I was invited to join them which I did. Oh, forgive me darling Arthur if you disapprove, but it seemed to be quite decorous to be seen in the company of Sir Henry and his distinguished friend and in my condition of near-invalid, so anyone of any sense watching would know that a favour was being done me and nothing improper could be inferred! We went down Fifth Avenue to Washington Square, which is quite nice though I am told abandoned by the better sort of people, and then up again, seeing both the Brevoort House and the Fifth Avenue Hotel, and other sights I cannot remember but which I am sure were delightful. It was a glorious interlude in my rather dreary life without you, in which nothing happens and I am able only to sit and read and think. I yearn for the day (and the night, how naughty I am) when we can be together again.

Have you wired money for me to your banker? I have not heard from him. The hotel continues to allow me to live here without payment (as is of course only proper, as if we were to sue the sum would be enormous) and that is four dollars a day saved, but I have to pay for my meals and Ethel's (though it seems to me that they should in conscience pay for our food as well as our rooms, as we could hardly be expected to live here without eating, and our being here at all is of course their doing, as it was their carpet), but at any rate I have to pay and am running out of money. I assure you, dearest husband, that I am guilty of no extravagance, not being able to leave the hotel and so unable to 'do the shops' and commit those frivolities of which I know you disapprove, and our meals are of the simplest, as I insist to Ethel, chosen from the cheapest things on the menu, and if I were able to go out and find less expensive places to eat I would, but you know I cannot.

Louisa bit the end of the hotel pen. Was she being convincing enough? Pathetic enough? Not that she meant to be at all insincere, but sometimes Arthur was rather hard-headed when it came to money. She thought guiltily of the two dollars she had given to McClurg. Arthur would explode if he heard of it. She would have to make it up somehow – small sacrifices she could cite if he ever found out. Give up desserts? She would happily give up wine with dinner, but people didn't drink wine with dinner here; they drank ice water, and it was free. She was also spending more than thirty American cents a day on newspapers. Could she give those up? How would she ever know anything?

181

She thought again of the dead woman. She felt the same pang of loss, then the same nausea. Despite what she had learned from Fitch and McClurg, she was not satisfied: she had let Fitch walk off with the story, *with the woman,* but Louisa had been left with the story unfinished. She wanted to *know.*

Perhaps, she thought, Fitch would find something new. Or perhaps something would happen that would finish the story and explain everything. Perhaps, somehow, the murderer would reveal himself!

All prayers are answered, but not necessarily in the form that we prayed for.

CHAPTER 6

BOWERY BUTCHER SLAYS AGAIN

Louisa stared at the morning's naked headline. It was right there on the front page, taking up the width of the newspaper. She felt as if she had been plunged underwater, realized she was holding her breath. What had she written to Arthur? That terror was exhilarating? But this was not exhilarating, it was exhausting and horrible, and yet she knew that what she felt was terror.

BOWERY BUTCHER SLAYS AGAIN
Second Victim's Body Found
'Revolting' – Murder Squad
*How Many More Will He Murder and Maim
Before Our Police Stop Him?*
By A. M. Fitch

This correspondent was on the scene when members of the Municipal Police removed the second butchered woman's body from a filthy alley in that notorious precinct, The

Bowery. Found in a noxious passageway between Hester and Canal Streets, the nude corpse had suffered the same egregiously horrific woundings as that of the red-haired beauty discovered five nights ago.

Members of the Murder Squad were present as the violated female remains were removed to the coroner's horse-van for transport to the City Mortuary. They would say only that they were pursuing every avenue of investigation and that their determination is absolute. 'We will rid the city of this fiend!' Commissioner Roosevelt assured the public.

To date, no hint has been given of any 'leads' in the first murder, although this correspondent has it on the authority of a reliable witness that the victim was seen in an uptown hotel only hours before her death. Up to the time of this writing, however, the police have remained silent as to what they know.

The second victim is believed to be another broken blossom of the heartless city streets. One 'copper' in fact declared that he recognized her as 'Lina,' an habituée of a corner not two blocks from where her stab-riddled body was discovered by a wakeful pavement-sleeper.

This writer was able to interview the discoverer, a man of no known address who called himself 'Tipple.' He was, he said, making his way along the aforesaid alley for purposes of nature when he stumbled and almost fell and found himself staring into the lifeless eyes of the murdered miss. 'My heart was in my mouth,' he said. 'She was a horrible sight. I've seen some things in my time, but this was the worst.'

Police arrested 'Tipple' on the spot because the skirts of his ragged coat were bloody, as were his shoes. We are told, however, that other pavement-sleepers of his acquaintance were able to support in Mulberry Street Police Court his contention that until the moment he had encountered the corpse, he was lying on a grating in Clinton Street and sharing a 'jug' with them. They had seen him make his way into the alley, and they had heard his scream of terror and alarm. Police are continuing to hold him in the Mulberry Street lockup, nonetheless, although the magistrate refused to allow a charge of murder to be placed. 'Tipple' is being held 'for his own protection,' said Lieutenant John Cleary of the Murder Squad.

If 'Tipple' is not the slayer of two women, who is? Who takes such vicious pleasure in disfiguring and mutilating women? And are only ladies of the night his targets, as were

185

those of the well-remembered Ripper of London?

The *Express* demands answers. In order to encourage those who have knowledge to come forward, this newspaper offers a reward of one thousand dollars to anyone who gives information that will aid us in bringing this madman to justice.

In the meantime, it is our understanding that the police are working on the case, under the direction of Detective-Sergeant Harry Dunne, in a very methodical fashion.

She skipped through it again. Minnie must have been up in the middle of the night to have been on the spot. Was it a sign, a gift, a curse, this second killing? Maybe the police would solve it at once; maybe there would be new evidence, some lucky happenstance that would put him into their hands.

'I must get up!'

'You haven't had your breakfast.'

'Help me into the grey wool; I haven't time to bother with a corset – stockings, of course; they'll have to hold themselves up. Oh, damn the bodice! Not you, Ethel – well, fasten it any old way. Oh, hell! Why are women's clothes so *slow*! That'll do, that'll do, stop fussing. I'm only going downstairs for a moment and then I shall be back.'

'Mr Galt is coming at half-eight.'

'Is he? Oh, yes. Well, tell him to wait.'

She could maneuver a bit better on the crutches now, although as soon as she swung herself forward she felt the soreness in her upper back and her arms. *I shall turn into a strongman from it. Strongwoman.* She smiled at that, thought of herself pulling on Arthur's chest expander, lifting huge dumb-bells. *I should have to grow a moustache.*

She hobbled to Reception and asked to use the telephone.

'In Booth Two, please, Mrs Doyle. The number?'

'Oh – I don't know – it's the *Express* newspaper.'

'I can find that, thank you, ma'am.'

She backed herself into Booth Two and sat rather awkwardly on the triangular wooden seat fastened across a corner. There was hardly room for herself and the crutches, but she managed to close the door on all of them. The booth was made of a lovely dark wood, she thought mahogany, with an electric lamp that had a shade that was supposed to look, she supposed, like antique vellum and had tassels hanging from it. The telephone was an enormous, already antiquated thing that stuck its snout out of the wall like some sort of reptile. The earpiece was on a separate cord. She had used a telephone in London and so recognized the device's parts. Still, when she picked up the earpiece, she heard nothing; she blew into the reptile's circular snout and still heard nothing; she said, 'Hello?'

She waited. Then there was a pop and a sizzle and a male voice shouted, '*New York Express*, what can I do for you?'

'A. M. Fitch, please.'

'That's the newsroom.'

'Will you connect me, please?'

'There's a separate number; do you want that?'

'Can't you connect me?'

'Oh . . . I suppose, all right. Hold on . . .'

More sizzling sounds – electricity running through the wires, she thought – and another male voice, very young, 'Newsroom, whatcha want?'

One of the urchins, she thought. 'A. M. Fitch, please.'

The voice got faraway and muffled. *'Fitch! Fitch! You here?* She what?' His voice returned to normal. 'She ain't here. She was out on a story all night. Woman murdered in the Bowery. Read it on page one.'

'When will I be able to find her there, please?'

'Try 'er after two.' The line went dead. Not even a sizzle. Louisa looked at the earpiece, sighed, hung it up. Back at Reception, she said, 'Could you put my telephone call on the bill, please?'

'Sure can, Mrs Doyle.'

She felt deflated. Was it only not being able to get Minnie Fitch? No, much more – she wanted to get *on* with the . . . was it a story? An experience? How horrible, to turn another woman's death into an 'experience.' Something to tell, a creepy tale. No, it wasn't that. It was that she wanted to take part in helping to avenge the dead women. And surely telling their story was helping? 'Live to tell my tale aright.' She envied Minnie

Fitch her privileged place in it, able to see the scene of the crime, even the corpse itself. Or had she made all that up?

If I don't learn more about it soon, I shall scream! And what good would that do?

Back in her room, Louisa read the article twice more with even hungrier haste than she was downing pieces of cinnamon toast. Sitting up in bed, the newspapers around her like carelessly dealt cards, she took in Minnie Fitch's words as if they were a new gospel. When she reached for her teacup, she didn't take her eyes off the page; when she set the cup down, she missed the saucer and the cup fell to the carpet.

'Oh, madame.' Ethel was sponging up the spilled tea with a towel.

'Oh – I'm so sorry – oh, Ethel, leave it – it isn't your job . . .'

'It's somebody's, madame.'

Louisa let Ethel's annoyance wash over her and recede. Ethel was right, of course. Louisa poured herself more tea and reached for another piece of toast.

Who was this 'reliable witness' of Fitch's? It must be Louisa herself – or had Fitch moved so fast that she'd found somebody else? She certainly had 'made tracks,' as Louisa had heard somebody say yesterday in the lobby. And how had she managed to be on the spot when the body was found? Well, not when it was found, but soon after. A third, more careful reading of the article suggested that

189

Fitch had got there after the first policemen and after the Murder Squad (who were, she gathered, some sort of separate entity). Did this mean that Fitch bribed somebody at police headquarters? Probably so, if what Manion had said about police venality was true.

The article also seemed to hint that Fitch knew more than she was telling. Again, whatever she knew was probably what she had got from Louisa, but suppose she had tracked down the identity of the first victim? *Oh, Minnie, why don't you telephone me? Or come to see me because you can't wait to tell me everything?*

Louisa started to jump out of bed but got only as far as touching her injured foot to the floor.

'Agh!'

Ethel appeared in the bathroom door. 'Madame?' The tone meant, 'What now?'

'I'm sorry, Ethel. I was thoughtless.'

Ethel disappeared back into the bathroom, where she was wringing out the tea-stained towel. Had Louisa heard a grunt – the kind that meant 'Of course you were thoughtless'? She would have to placate Ethel somehow. How? Perhaps give her the tickets to the Wild West. But whom would she go with?

'Ethel.'

'Madame?' Same tone.

'Ethel, do you remember that Colonel Cody gave me tickets to his show last night after dinner?'

'Yes, madame.'

'Would you like to have them? I'm sure you must have friends upstairs you could enjoy them with.'

Ethel was holding the stained towel across her arms as if she were performing some rite that had perhaps involved animal sacrifice. She looked rather ecclesiastical, Louisa thought, although not at all Christian. To her surprise, Ethel said, 'If they're included in the offer, I'd rather have the other ones, madame.'

'Sir Henry Irving's?'

'It's only that I saw the Wild West in London, and I've never seen Sir Henry.'

'Well – of course. I suppose.' That left her with the tickets to the Wild West, and of course no one to go with her, as it didn't seem now that Ethel would go unless ordered. 'And you have somebody else who would like to see Irving?'

'I think I could hunt somebody up, madame. Thank you for your very kind offer.' Ethel reached behind herself and hung the towel in the bathroom. 'More tea? More toast?' She began to straighten the newspapers, her good humour (or whatever that was) apparently restored.

'I'd like the grey silk today, Ethel, without the bustle because it gets in the way of my ankle. And lay out my waterproof cloak, which of course isn't waterproof, is it? I may go out and I see rain on the window.'

'Madame, you can't.'

'I can and I will. Just so you'll know, Ethel, I went out yesterday.'

'So I heard, madame.' Ethel sounded severe again.

'Did you! From whom?'

'The doorman, madame. He says you arrived in a *motorcar.*'

Louisa was instantly angry, turned herself into a woman she didn't like: 'I didn't realize that I was the subject of gossip among the hotel servants, Ethel. I am disappointed in you.'

'Madame, I discourage gossip at every opportunity. I do not engage in gossip. But everyone has heard of your accident – some witnessed it – and they are concerned about you. The doorman wanted me particularly to tell you that he thought your recovery was "real brave." I don't believe that that can be called gossip, madame.'

Louisa said nothing but regretted the coin she had given the doorman. The busybody. Then it occurred to her that he must have seen the murdered woman come into the hotel, *and* the man with her. If he was such a busybody, perhaps he would tell her what he remembered. And, now she thought of it, *when* the woman had left the hotel and with whom, because that might give them (she meant herself and Minnie Fitch, not the police) something useful to go on with.

It occurred to her, too, rather astonishingly, that she hadn't really thought so far about who had killed the women. If it had been the good-looking young man, why had he done it? A lover's quarrel? But in that case, wouldn't he have done some violence to her in the hotel? And if he had killed her there – meaning, perhaps, only a blow struck in anger to hurt, not to kill, although so much more had been done to the poor woman than a single blow – then how had he got her body out of the hotel? She had a mental picture of him, carrying the body through the lobby. Ridiculous. And colourful as imaginative stratagems were (putting the body in a laundry hamper; holding the body upright and walking it out to the street as if alive; putting it in a trunk and taking it down in the freight lift), they were the stuff of fiction and not of life.

As she dressed, she thought about Minnie Fitch. She realized that she liked her – no, that was the wrong word; *was attracted to* her – and then she remembered that she had been dreaming just before she woke, dreaming about something that had put Minnie's name in her mouth when she swam up out of sleep. (Like a trout? To capture what fly on the surface of wakefulness?) She couldn't remember what she had dreamed. Yes – no; it was gone. Something pleasant. Like – like *being young*. Whatever that meant.

I want a woman friend, she thought. Perhaps that was all the dream had meant – having a friend, as she'd had Tenny when she'd been very young. The only other possibility at hand was Marie Corelli, and she seemed rather too formidable to become a friend.

Ethel was fastening her in back. Ethel, of course,

could not really be a friend: rather sad for both of them. Louisa missed women she knew in England, missed that intimacy, different from what she had with Arthur. She needed, wanted, both, she thought. She said, 'Do you have friends here, Ethel?'

'Not as to say *friends*, madame. You don't make friends so quick, do you? Acquaintances, more like. But people come and go so fast in a hotel, don't they.'

'Do you miss your friends at home?'

'I do, yes, I do.' Ethel finished doing her up and said, 'Mr Galt is coming by just at any minute, remember.'

'Is he? Oh, drat, I'd forgotten again.' With that, there was a knock on the door.

Galt looked at her ankle and watched her use the crutches and said she was making wonderful progress. He showed Ethel how to wrap an X of bandage around the ankle to hold it in what he called its natural position. Ethel seemed flustered; after watching her make a hash of it, Louisa said, 'I can surely do that for myself.'

'I don't at all mind, madame.' Ethel sounded hurt.

'The thing,' Galt said, 'is to get it right but not too tight. If you can get a finger under the bandage, it's too loose – loose as a goose, they say where I was born – but if you feel your toes numbing up, it's too tight.'

'Will I be able to walk on it?'

'Not yet, you won't, but when you can, that bandage'll help.'

'I'm sick of hobbling around, Mr Galt. I want to be *well*.'

'I think that's something you have to discuss with the Man Upstairs, Mrs Doyle.'

She thought he meant old Mr Carver but then realized he meant God. She didn't chat with God much and she didn't believe at all in divine intervention, so she supposed what Galt meant was she should grin and bear it. Or perhaps he was a religious man. She hoped not; religious people always wanted to lecture one.

After he was gone, she tried the X-shaped wrap again. 'I think I've got it, Ethel.'

Ethel said, 'May I tell you something, madame?'

'Please do.'

'Mr Galt has asked me to walk out with him.'

Galt? And Ethel? 'What did you tell him?'

'That I'd ask you, madame.'

Louisa was astonished. But rather pleased. She didn't think of either of them as a catch, but a friend would be good for Ethel. Of course, it couldn't go too far: after all, they wouldn't be in New York a great while longer. She said, 'Are you asking for my approval, Ethel?'

'For your permission, madame.'

'Well, you may certainly have that. But you must be careful, you know . . .'

'I am very careful when it comes to men, madame.'

'That's wise.'

'And I am not a babe in the woods.'

Louisa met Ethel's eyes. They were direct, almost challenging. Did Ethel have a past? A past with a man, *men*, in it? How surprising people were. 'You will be careful, nonetheless, Ethel. Remember, anything you do could reflect on Mr Doyle.'

Ethel said nothing, but busied herself with bits of lint and invisible specks on the carpet. Bent over, her voice muffled, she said, 'I thought that Mr Galt and I might go to see the play.'

Good heavens, it isn't Galt who's asked her to walk out, it's Ethel who's asked him! 'Is that wise?'

'He's a perfect gentleman. He understood about me asking you first.' She pushed herself upright. 'If you disapprove, I won't do it.'

Louisa dodged the implied accusation. 'You'll need to alter that dress you mentioned. We shall have to get the ribbon and lace today. In fact, why don't you do that now? And a small bustle with some sort of train; I'm sure the shops will have something in black.' She pulled a Liberty shawl over her shoulders. 'I'll just slip downstairs to see if there's any mail.'

She had barely emerged from the elevator and was gathering herself and the crutches together when she saw an arm waving at her from the lobby. It was Mrs Simmons, covered again in cascades of lace. She was actually calling, 'Yoo-hoo.'

Louisa hoisted herself on the crutches and launched herself into the lobby.

196

'Look at you, you poor thing! But you get along real good on those contraptions. I'd be scared to death to try them, and I've got two good feet! How are you today? I hear you were out on the town yesterday and came back in a horseless carriage with *Sir* Henry Irving. I'm sure he's the nay plus ultra of respectability, but a girl can't be too careful. Sit, sit, take a load off your feet, I'll get the girl for coffee. My, that's some eye you've got.'

Louisa had forgotten to powder her bruises. She collapsed into a chair, grateful to sit, if not to have to listen to Mrs Simmons. 'I was out on business yesterday – which *everybody* seems to know about, I must say.'

'Oh, honey, a hotel's like a small town, everybody sees everything that goes on. You couldn't keep a secret here if you were Bluebeard the Pirate.' She was looking for more ice cream in her glass, which had nothing left in it but streaks that her spoon wouldn't pick up. 'I'll have another of those, and some cookies,' she said to the waitress who had appeared. 'And coffee for my friend here.'

'Oh, I have to go back upstairs.'

'You got time for a coffee.' The old woman waved the waitress away. 'And what's to go back upstairs for? It does get dull, doesn't it, being kind of a prisoner in a hotel? I'm not really a prisoner, but it gets harder and harder for me to go out, and I must say it can't be easy for you, either, horseless carriage or no. There are days when if it wasn't

197

for Fannie, I declare I'd go right off my noggin. Fannie's company, you know.' Louisa had no idea who Fannie was. 'That odious Carver can complain about her, but I *like* her to bark.' Then she knew who Fannie was. 'It's another voice. It just picks me up. Have you ever had a dog?'

'When I was little, I wasn't allowed.' When she was a child on an impoverished island in Scotland, she meant, but she didn't tell people that.

'Well, then you can't know what a comfort they are. When I first had her, she just barked and barked and barked. People were livid!' She shrieked with laughter. 'There was one part of my sitting room, all Fannie had to do was *look* at it, and she'd start barking. She'd sniff and back away and sniff and back away and then she'd just bark her sweet little head off. If I was feeling blue, I'd just point her at that wall, and she'd bark and cheer me up. How's your ankle?'

'Oh, better, I think, but I'm still not able to walk on it.'

'Of course you're not! It'll be weeks yet. I had a friend who sprained her wrist, and it was three years before she was normal, and even to this day, it gives her pain when it rains. You take cream or sugar? Have a cookie.' She took two for herself. 'Of course, Fannie *always* barks at men. She pretty much hates the entire species. I've always liked men, myself, but dogs are very sensitive. What I figure is, there was some man in a past life who was mean to her. That Carver, now, she goes after

198

him like she means to tear his pantlegs off, which I think shows good judgement on her part. And that house detective, too.' Mrs Simmons looked across the lobby at where Manion was sitting. Although he was too far away to hear her, she lowered her voice. 'Fannie barks at him like she's one of the geese saving Rome.' She lowered her voice even farther. 'He's a bad actor.'

'How so?'

'I'm sure he has a past.' Her voice changed. 'There's that nephew of mine.' She bit into a cookie, waved at the approaching Newcome, and sipped her coffee. She said to Louisa *sotto voce*, 'He was out till all hours again and looks it.' With satisfaction, she said, 'Fannie barks at him until the cows come home.'

Newcome looked perfectly healthy to Louisa, although when he came closer she saw that he had a bruise high on his left cheek, and perhaps he looked a little pale. They went through the formalities and Louisa said she had to go; Mrs Simmons shouted that she'd just got there; Newcome murmured something about the pleasure of seeing her up and about. He sounded as he always did, she supposed, rather British and proper and a bit wispy, or perhaps bloodless was more accurate. She found herself looking at him and remembering that her first response to him had been the word 'safe.' Now she wondered why. He didn't seem safe to her now; perhaps it was the bruise, which suggested violence, another aspect of him. He was, she thought, one of those men who didn't love women (she skirted whether he was one of those men who loved other men, about which she was mostly ignorant and not very curious), but such men were surely not necessarily then *safe*. Might not a man who didn't love women then *hate* women?

What odd things I am thinking. I am being unfair to Mr Newcome because he disappointed me.

Newcome had appropriated an orange from the fruit basket and now took something from a pocket that abruptly grew a shiny blade as long as his fingers. He cut a perfect circle around the stem end of the orange and then two circles around the entire fruit like lines of longitude. He put a thumb in the top circle of the ring and began to pry it off. He smiled at Louisa. 'You are admiring my *coltello*, Mrs Doyle.'

'I was admiring your technique with the orange, actually.'

He held the knife up. It was quite elegant, with a mother-of-pearl handle and an engraved silver bolster. He said, 'I bought it in Italy last year.' He folded the blade into the handle with a click. 'It's the knife with which the bravos of Sicily fight what they call their duels of honour. I limit my duels to oranges.' He pressed a button, and the blade flashed out. He closed it again with a titter. 'My honour is too limited to mention.'

Louisa found herself repelled by him, by his knife. Rising and supporting herself on the back of her chair, she said, 'I had thought to accept your offer of your friend's carriage yesterday, Mr Newcome, but you were not to be found.'

His face went blank. 'I'm so sorry.' He flushed. 'I didn't realize you'd need me so quickly.'

'One should never depend on others, should one. It's always helpful to be reminded of that.' She went off on her awkward way, hearing Mrs Simmons asking her nephew what *that* was about.

Stillman Hotel
Cleveland, Ohio

Mr dearest, darlingest Touie:
 It is not the way I would have done it, and I think perhaps premature, but you must accept whatever has been put before you.

Whatever was he talking about?

The application of ice

Oh, that's it – my ankle.

is I should think less indicated than a good hot-water bottle that is hot but not torrid to the touch, perhaps wrapped in a towel for safety's sake. I think you are alarmist to question morphine for another three days; it is a benign anodyne, though overuse can induce a habituation akin to dependence.
 The audience for my lectures to date have

consisted almost entirely of women, perhaps because they have been held at hours when sensible men are working (perhaps to escape from the women, who are, insofar as I have been forced to commune with them, philistine, overbearing and benighted).

Oh, Arthur, somebody is *killing* women here.

I am now inured to questions about Holmes's most trivial details, and what I cannot recall from the stories, I simply make up. I told some harpy yesterday that Holmes's mother was an authoress who had taught Watson how to write the stories. She seemed delighted and said roguishly, 'I knew there was a woman in the case!' I could cheerfully have murdered her.

Oh, Arthur! Oh, don't.

I have been trying to gauge the intellectual level of my audiences – which have been gratifyingly large in terms of quantity, if only the quality were better – and have so far failed abjectly to get responses to Queen Cophetua, King Log, Boadicea, or Gog and Magog, although they do seem to respond to such sentimental slush as the two little princes in the Tower. Any reference to Shakespeare or the Bible is readily understood. Any reference to Shakespeare's contemporaries or the Apocrypha are treated as if I were mentioning works unfit for the ears of ladies. In general, I would say that they are less interesting than a mob of fourth-formers on a drowsy afternoon.

When will you be able to join me? I do miss you so, Touie. I realize that I am lonely, although I am surrounded by people much of the day. Travel without you is excruciating, for I am doomed on the trains to the company of men, not the good fellowship of men like myself, but drummers and back-slapping businessmen, who sit in the 'smoking cars' and tell salacious stories or Munchausenesque lies by the hour. The only thing that will silence them is my telling them I am an author, which causes sudden palls to descend, and thereafter I am eyed shiftily, perhaps as a threat to public safety.

Will you be well enough to come to Milwaukee, at least? You know that thereafter I shall be getting so close to the time that I shall be back in the East that it would hardly be worthwhile to travel to somewhere like St Louis instead of waiting a few days and meeting me in Philadelphia.

Oh, my dear, pity your poor husband, alone and footloose in the wilds of America! This is a country of savages – well-fed, pink, buxom, brainless savages! I fear I shall be thrust into a pot and boiled, to be served up for what they call 'Sunday dinner'. Boiled Author with Mashed Ideas and Brainless Salad!

Your loving, lonely, going-mad
Arthur
P.S. Where are the drawers you promised? If
they have not reached me by Chicago, send
others to St Louis. A.

She had written to Arthur every day, sometimes
even twice a day. Now she saw the problem that
the great distances of the country created: he
replied so long after she had written a letter that
she lost all sense of connection, and his letters
arrived so much later than that, that she couldn't
remember what she had written. It was like playing
tennis with the players over the horizon from each
other.

She sat down with letter-paper and pen, determined to write to him that very moment – but
only things that could stand by themselves, that
would be timeless, without referrents. *And that*
would not cause him to write terrible things about
women. Her health, Ethel, the murders – no, not
those. He had shut himself off from those. *The*
murders were hers.

She stared at the wall. What did she mean by
that, the murders were hers? It was what Minnie
Fitch had said, too. People said 'his murder' when
they meant somebody had done a murder, or 'his
death' when somebody had died. They weren't her
murders, then – yet she felt proprietary. Should
she write that to Arthur?

No, best to write about him, not herself. Should

she start with the under-drawers, which had already been sent to Chicago? Or perhaps the shirts. What she wished she could write about were things that made her blush even to think about. How was it that what was the most astonishing and delightful part of being man and wife was the part one couldn't mention?

She looked at the clock. It was only half past ten. Where was Minnie Fitch?

Lieutenant Cleary had had the on-duty members of the Murder Squad on the scene of the second Butcher murder as soon as word of it had reached Mulberry Street. The immediate investigation belonged to the precinct, but he knew that the powers that be would kick it up to him as soon as the newspapers got their teeth into it. That was no problem; what was a problem was that if there really was a Bowery Butcher, investigating this new murder might turn up something about the first one, and then there'd be trouble from Roosevelt because of Harding, and just a whole lot of shit he didn't want to think about. He had to put the kibosh on it *now*.

'Get Dunne in here.'

Grady made a motion that might have been a salute, if salutes could have ended at the waist; thirty seconds later, he was back and holding the door open. Dunne, wearing one of his signature hairy suits, came in. Seeing him come through a doorway and sit in a chair was like watching a steamship dock.

'Yeah?'

'What's new on the first Butcher murder?'

'Nothing. Like you wanted.'

'Where's the fucking paperwork?'

'Just coming back from the literary piano.'

Cleary frowned. He didn't like having to figure out what people meant. 'Literary piano?' The typewriter, for God's sake! 'Jeez, Dunne, how can you take so long on this simple shit? No wonder you're where you're at.'

'I had it typed for your signature – right?'

'Jesus H. Christ, no! For *your* signature, you mullet-head!'

'You were the investigating officer.'

'I wasn't! I was acting in my capacity as commander. I told you, the precinct had it. You wanta get them to sign off on it, do that, but if you been doing the work, sign it yourself.'

'I'll have to send it back to be typewritten again.'

'Well, fuck, how long can that take?'

Dunne sighed. 'I'm not a priority for the typewriters, Lieutenant.'

Cleary wiped his hand across his face to show that he thought that Dunne would be the death of him, and he said, 'You seen there's a new murdered woman?'

'I read the morning paper.'

'We'll get it. It's at the Eleventh just now, but we'll get it. I want you to take it. You and Cassidy and Finn. And the Wop.'

Dunne blinked but didn't otherwise react.

Cleary didn't have time to fart around while Dunne looked at him. He said, 'I don't want it to slop over into the first murder. Get it?'

'Newspapers say it already has. "Bowery Butcher Strikes Again."'

'Fuck the newspapers. You start over with this one and treat it like it's bran' new. Wind up the paperwork on number one and sign it and give it to me. Then work on number two as a completely separate case. I don't wanta hear you're making a connection with the first one – no interviewing witnesses connected with the first murder for this one. Don't make *any* connections. Get me?' He made a helpless gesture with his hands. 'This isn't me talking, Dunne, it's upstairs. Teddy's guy.'

'If it's the same killer, then there's the connection.'

'Don't tell me shit like that! Don't think that way! Solve this one, and if by some chance it turns out it's the same loony, then we'll deal with that when we get to it. You see how I want this done or don't you?'

'I see how you want it done; I don't see how I'm gonna do it. But I'll try.' Dunne put on a Buddha face, waited long seconds, and at last said, 'I guess you don't want me to ignore the evidence.'

'What evidence?'

'Whatever there is. You don't want me to do bad police work, I mean.'

'Well, of course not! Jesus H. Christ, what do you think we're here for?'

'I just wanted to be clear on that point.' He stared at Cleary.

Cleary said, 'Okay, that's all.'

Buddha nodded. He got up and sailed slowly through the door. He continued most of the way across the squad room and came to anchor at a littered desk. He looked at Cassidy, who had followed him. 'No connection to the first murder,' he said.

'Cleary's losing his buttons. What's he think we are, loony?'

'No, he thinks we're stupid, because anybody who isn't on the take is stupid. But you're right, he's crazy to think that whatever graft he got on the first killing won't come out.' Dunne puffed out his cheeks and blew out air. 'He said that it all came from upstairs. From Teddy. Now, you know Teddy wouldn't be in on a scam. He's a blowhard, but he's straight. On the other hand, Cleary wouldn't say it came from him if Roosevelt hadn't put his oar in somehow.' Dunne tapped a lapel of Cassidy's shiny blue suit. 'Tell you what I'd like you to do, Cassidy: how good do you get along with TR's Hahvahd errand boy?'

'Can't hardly say I ever breathed the same air as him.'

'Good. What you do is, you go upstairs and have a talk with him. You ask him if he ever carried a message from the commish down to Cleary, and if he did, what it said. And then ask him what he thinks we ought to do about it.'

'And you think he'll tell me? Now you're the one's loony.'

'No, he will. Because you're gonna be nice to him and tell him there's nobody else we can talk to. He'd give a nut, maybe both, to be a real cop, y'see? And here you come, a real cop, to ask for advice.'

'What he'll say is, ask Cleary.'

'And what you'll say is, between us coppers, Cleary thinks he's protecting the commissioner, and all we want to know is if there's anything he needs to be protected about. Eh?' Dunne lowered his considerable bulk into his desk chair. 'Take him out for coffee at Canelli's. He'll love you for it; it's the filthiest cop's nest in New York.'

'It'd be better coming from you.'

'Nope. You have a face that expresses infinite innocence. Mine makes people think of sin and damnation. It's why I didn't last in the seminary.' He smiled. 'Go.'

Louisa went downstairs again at noon with some thought of having luncheon in the restaurant instead of in her room. Ethel was still out shopping; Louisa could hardly begrudge her that after the spilled tea. Anyway, Ethel would have her evening out at the theatre, and perhaps she'd feel less put upon.

She crossed the lobby, avoiding the carpet on which she'd had her fall, and made for the doors. She had no hat on and wasn't dressed for the

209

outdoors; still, one of the boys ran to open the doors for her. 'I only want to talk to the doorman. If you'd ask him to step in?' She produced a nickel coin.

'Got it!'

The doorman said straight off that he couldn't stay inside, missus, his job was in the street.

'I shan't keep you. I only wanted to say that I am not pleased to learn that you gossiped about me to my maid.'

'I never!'

'Whom else did you tell I'd arrived in a motorcar yesterday?'

'I didn't. Only that it was an event, and I thought made you, because of your injury, a very, mmm, great—'

'A very great fool, I suppose. If I find you've talked about me to anyone in future, I shall speak to the management.'

'Now, ma'am, just let me—'

'I'll let you do nothing. What I want you to do is answer a question. Five days ago, as you must know, a woman was murdered down in the Bowery. She had been in this hotel – you held the door for her, in fact. She was a very pretty woman, with lovely copper-red hair. Do you remember her?'

'Can't say I do, ma'am.' He had got very stiff.

'Or did Mr Manion tell you to say that when he shared his bribe with you?'

'Now, now—'

'Do you remember her or don't you?'

'Well, maybe I do.'

'Then I want to know this: when did she leave the hotel?'

'Wouldn't that be gossip, if I told you, madame?' His beefy face, which usually carried a broad smile for hotel guests, had only a smirk.

Louisa flushed. 'You are impertinent.' She wanted to say something about the fifty-cent piece she had given him yesterday but couldn't think how to put it without seeming miserly. She also wanted to say something about 'if my husband were here,' but of course that was already the point: if Arthur had been there, the man would never have dared say such a thing. She tried to draw herself up, found it impossible on crutches, and said, 'See here, Mr . . . ?'

'Gerrigan.'

'Mr Gerrigan, I haven't harmed you and I haven't done badly by you. It's you who've done something to me, and you ought to face up to it like the man I think you are. Now, this matter of the woman is important to me, and I'd rather you didn't smirk or dance around it. Did you see when she left the hotel, or didn't you?'

He had his chin out, and he was looking down at her from his great height. He said, 'I didn't, then!' as if she'd asked if he'd killed the woman himself.

'You're sure?'

'I seen her come in all right. That wasn't Manion's doing, and I don't know nothing about bribes. But

211

I didn't see her go out. I'm off duty at six, so maybe the night man was on. But *I didn't see her*!'

'Could you ask the night man?'

'Well, now, there we go with gossip again.'

'Mr Gerrigan!'

He sighed theatrically. 'All right, I'll ast him. But I don't promise he seen her, either!' He was worked up now; he might have said more – and regretted it – but an annoyed man in a silk hat came through the doors and said *would* the doorman of this place please do his job and *would* he please see that his grips were carried in!

'Yes, sir, right, sir, only helping this lady – had an accident, very sad business . . .'

They were gone. Disgusted, Louisa turned away. She looked for Manion in vain but saw Dr Strauss in his usual place and smiled. She started for the restaurant but saw a boy from the desk at Reception hurry towards her. There was no question but that it was her he wanted: he held up a finger, then a brown envelope in his other hand. He even managed to sound as if he were breathing hard when he reached her. 'Packet for you, *special* messenger, just came! Run as fast as I was able. Glad you hadn't gone any farther away, ha-ha-ha-ha.'

She looked at the envelope without taking it. It said only, 'Mrs Doyle.' No room number. It had to be from Minnie Fitch.

She produced a coin; the boy handed over the prize. She tried to open it as she made her way to the restaurant, of course couldn't because of the crutches, finally found herself a chair in the lobby and tore the envelope apart as if it held the secrets of the pyramids.

Inside was a curt note:

Got these last night. Thought you'd want them. George Manion.

'These' were two handwritten pages that looked as if they'd been balled up, pitched into a grate, and fished out again – the draft report of the policeman who'd found the first body. Louisa blinked, looked again at Manion's note, then at the pencilled, much-crossed-out pages. *He certainly moved quickly after he got McClurg's sketches. Or had he already got them before I saw McClurg?*

She read the draft report:

January 1896
Per standing orders I was walking my beet which is Bowery 5, namely Elizabeth and Mott Streets and the streets alleys and etc. crosswise up to Broome from Divission. I turned into Elizabeth from Broome Street at 1 A.M. per orders of Comm Roseveldt on time and come down Elizabeth heading South. All I seen for two blocks was two gents of the sidewalk wich is to say vaggrents wich I didn't disturb as they was causing no trouble, they was drunk asleep. I checked windows and doors per orders found all locked and etc.

I come to Hester Street and crossed it and proceded forwards until I come to the alley by Bickner's Office and Claculating which is a dead end. I flashed my dark lantren into the foresaid alley as per orders and seen something wich was not clear to me, I thought a human legg or arm but thought I hadn't seen it, so I proceeded into the ally with my night-stick drawn and reddy and the lantren in my other hand and I seen it.

What I had seen was a human legg in fact, it was sticking out stiff and no clothes on. I flashed my lite and seen a site I hope never to see again, though twenty years on the Municipal Police, it was horrable. What I seen when I looked was a nood woman with no clothes and she had been cut up terrible. I seen stabs in both her bosoms, which was nine in one bosom and fourteen in the other, not that I counted then but later. She had also had her nose cut off and her mouth and her eyes was missing. When I moved my light down I seen a terrble woond on her belly wich was a cut all around to make a circle and things removed because the caviddy had been stuffd with horse manoor on wich was her mouth nose and eyes in form of a face. She was siting or had been purched on a trash can with legs and arms out straight, her body was stiff, she looked like jumping.

214

This was the most horble thing I ever seen. I saw no blood anywheres that I could see.

I at onst blew my whissle and removed to Elizabeth Street to prevent anybody from seeing this site until Officer Flynn # 3167 from the next beet come running, I sent him to the station for help and call the Murder Squad in Mulberry Street. Then I wated until they come and others with the doctor and others and until they removed the body and I resumed my beet, which was done for that nite as it was past four o'clock.
James Malone Number 3492

She thought she would be sick again, but she got through it and made herself think, *think*, about what she had read. McClurg had prepared her for the disfigurement but not for the 'mutilation,' which she now understood too well. The horse manure was shocking and at first like something that might have been done as what men called a 'practical' joke, though she couldn't see what was practical about them. But as she forced herself to think she realized what had been done: the murderer had cut into the abdomen and removed enough to make room for the manure; what he had removed was probably the womb (the source of female hysteria, *hysterectomy*, yes) and replaced it with manure. *Shit*. She knew the word;

215

everybody did. And she knew how men used it, to mean both nonsense and something loathsome.

But the face made on the manure with the lips and nose and eyes? What did the murderer mean – that this was the face of woman? This was the real face of the womb? Or was it simply that he had cut off what made her pretty and desirable and put those things where they were most alien, and so most loathsome?

It wasn't, she thought, something that an angry lover would have done. It was too cruel, too horrible – and in a dreadful way too poetic – to be explained so. Or did she not understand the force of male rage? Arthur was never truly angry with her; he could be irritated, petulant, even loud, but he could never be like this. But could other men?

He hates women. What did that remind her of? Something in the lobby. Yes, sitting with Newcome and Mrs Simmons and thinking that there was something different about him, and she had wondered why she had first thought that he was 'safe.' And then she had wondered whether only a man could have committed the first murder (because she hadn't known about the second one then), and if so did that mean any man, all men – even Alexander Newcome? He had had a bruise on his face, which had suggested violence to her: gentlemanly as he seemed, even neurasthenic, was he capable of ripping out a woman's uterus and filling the cavity with shit?

And was no woman? Could a woman do it? She thought the idea was unthinkable but realized that she was thinking it. Could it have been another woman, one who hated the copper-haired woman, perhaps because she had stolen the good-looking young man?

I haven't lived enough.

She read the policeman's report through again and was struck by how strange he had made it all seem – how strange it had been to him. As if he had rounded a corner and found himself in a different world. As in a dream, perhaps. And having fenced in his experience with this idea of strangeness, he had left himself and anybody reading his report with a conviction of unreality, of uniqueness. And so the conclusion might well be that this was the unique work of a madman. (Or woman, she forced herself to think.)

And no blood. Not even on her? Did it mean she had been washed? And where did you wash a human body – in a bathtub? Few enough living places had a bathtub, let alone the means to get a dead body into it and drain off the blood and leave no sign. Perhaps something like that could be done in some sort of factory? Something with vats? Or a commercial laundry? *Or a hotel?*

She shuddered.

She went to Reception and asked for Manion but was told it was his day off. She left a note, thanking him. She wanted to ask him to visit her, but that would be improper. She wanted to try

217

telephoning Minnie Fitch again but made herself walk away from the booths. She would make herself wait until two o'clock.

It seemed too early for lunch, but eating was a way to pass the time. She wandered to the door of the restaurant and looked in, but as she had expected, almost nobody was there.

'Luncheon for one, ma'am?'

'Oh, no, I – oh . . .' A hand was waving from a distant table. She made out two women, both wearing hats, realized that one of them was waving at her. The waiter said, 'Will you join them, ma'am?'

'Well, I hadn't . . .' At that point, the woman who was waving got up and came charging across the big room. Louisa knew from the walk and the look of iron-bound corsetry that it was Marie Corelli. Before she even got to Louisa, she was saying, 'There's somebody you *must* meet, *cara.*' She took Louisa's free hand. 'Come along – you'll like her – a remarkable woman – a *serious* woman . . .'

'It's so early, and I don't like to interrupt—'

'You're not interrupting; I'm inviting you!' She pulled Louisa forward.

The other woman, who had turned to look at them, seemed somewhat desiccated – what Louisa thought was *used up* – by both time and trial. She was too thin, older, her face made severe by much frowning. She didn't get up.

'And *this*,' Marie said, 'is Victoria Woodhull!'

The woman smiled, the smile not a great success. She said in a nasal American voice, 'And Mrs Doyle is asking herself, "Who is Victoria Woodhull?"' She laughed with her mouth closed; the laughter came out as a series of small coughs, mm-hmp, mm-hmp, mm-hmp.

They sat, Louisa already embarrassed because she was supposed to know who the woman was. Perhaps understanding this, Marie said, 'Mrs Woodhull has been a valiant campaigner for women for many years.' She glanced at the other woman and smiled. 'You won't remember, because you're English, but Victoria ran for the presidency of the United States twenty-five years ago.'

Louisa stared. 'But women can't vote!'

Mrs Woodhull laughed again. 'Of course not! That's why I ran!' She was picking at some sort of soufflé. 'I ran on the Free Love platform. "I shall love whom I want, when I want, where I want."' She smiled at Louisa. 'And I have, though I've been married three times.'

Marie babbled something about being so glad she could bring them together; it seemed that she knew Mrs Woodhull in England, where she lived now. Marie said to her, 'Louisa is very upset about some murders of women here.'

'I'm not upset—'

'You *should* be very upset,' Mrs Woodhull said in that unpleasant voice. 'We should all be very upset. I saw the morning papers. We should be picketing police stations and smashing windows

219

until they find the killer. But of course they won't.'

'They *will* – in time.'

'They won't – they're men.'

'Forgive me, but I think that's unfair.'

Mrs Woodhull looked up at her, fork halfway to mouth. 'Men hate women,' she said crisply, then put the food between her jaws and chomped.

It made Louisa laugh. 'Not *all* men, surely.'

'All men. All women. Some of them handle it better than others. *Contain* it better may be the apter word.' She was working on her plate again, cut something and speared it and said, 'You learn the real truth when they're angry. Or scared. Then the language shows the real man. When I ran for president I received lots of letters that called me dirty names and threatened to kill me. Men.'

She made Louisa angry – it seemed so unfair to Arthur and all the nice men. She said, 'Perhaps you generalize because of that bad experience.'

Mrs Woodhull gave her a shrewd look. 'You're married to Conan Doyle the author, aren't you. Treat you well? Not a brute? So he's the other sort – treats you like a child, probably. Has a pet name for you – something small and soft and cuddly? One of my husbands called me "Bunnikins." What does yours call you when he's being nice?'

'It would hardly mean he hates me, Mrs Woodhull.'

'No. It would mean he's one of the better sort, not like the one who's committing these murders.

220

On the other hand, it means you're his little play-toy and everything you have is through his largesse, meaning you'd better toe up. Does he give you your own money?'

'Do forgive me, but I think that's insulting.'

'Of course it's insulting; everything that men do to women is insulting. Or worse. And forgive *me*, Mrs Doyle; I do tend to go too far. Have you seen Ibsen's play about the doll's house?'

'Oh – no – Ibsen is . . . My husband doesn't approve of Ibsen.'

Mrs Woodhull laughed, a full laugh this time, mouth open to show her false teeth. 'I rest my case, m'lud.'

Marie said, 'I saw it in London. *Epouvantable.* You're not eating, *ma chère.*' This to Louisa.

Louisa had ordered the *table d'hôte* luncheon and had simply looked at it and listened. The truth was, Mrs Woodhull annoyed her, more for Arthur's sake than her own. She said, 'Just because there is a man who is murdering women doesn't mean all men are evil. The murderer is a monster!'

'On the contrary, my dear.' Mrs Woodhull smiled at her around a piece of lettuce. 'He is the perfect man – from a man's point of view, I mean. The *beau idéal.* He is doing what they'd all like to do.'

'I think that's nonsense.'

'*Do* you? Well, you got spunk, anyway.'

They finished eating; the others ordered dessert; Louisa wondered how she was to get away. The conversation turned to other things – cooking, shops, British politics – and suddenly Mrs Woodhull was getting ready to leave. She muttered something about the convention of the International Society of Women's Clubs and got out of her chair. She said to Louisa, 'Are you personally frightened of this murderer?'

'I hardly think in a city of this size he will pick me out, if that's what you mean.'

'No, it isn't what I mean. Does his *existence* frighten you?'

Louisa had thought about that. 'Because of what he is – yes.'

Mrs Woodhull nodded. 'Get yourself a gun. I always carry one. They supposedly called the Colt revolver "the equalizer" in the West; they meant for men, but it works for women, too. Go buy a gun. And if the perfect man shows up, start shooting.'

When she was gone, Marie apologized to Louisa. 'I didn't know she was going to pick on you so, *chère*. She's very clever, you know.'

'She has somewhat peculiar ideas.'

Marie made a very French-looking moue. 'It depends on which end of the street you look at things from, perhaps.'

'What'd he say?'

Cassidy was standing over Dunne with a smug look on his face, rare for him. He said, 'You were right. Like always.'

'He told you?'

Cassidy nodded. He pulled another chair close so

they couldn't be overheard. 'At first he was real stuck up and Hahvahd, but oncet he saw I was the honest skinny, he came around. We went out to Doheny's; I hate Canelli's.' This was pretty daring of him to say, because Canelli's was where Dunne always took him. 'He told me his troubles. In a nutshell, the rank and file don't like him. I made like that was all news to me. He isn't such a bad kid, actually.'

'Only stuck up and rich.'

'Yeah, and a snob. But I gave him some pointers on being more like the rest of us, starting with those collars he wears. He was grateful.'

'And he told you?'

'He did and he didn't. He wanted to tell me the whole kaboodle, but like I say, he's a good kid: He thinks he owes Roosevelt loyalty. So what he told me was, Roosevelt got a letter from some woman who was staying at an uptown hotel and she said she saw the murdered whore – the first one, not the new one – there in the hotel the day before her body was found. Roosevelt told Hahvahd to tell Cleary to deal with it.'

'"Deal with it." That's what he said?'

'His very words.'

'He didn't say what hotel?'

'I think what he said was "a very good uptown hotel."' He made himself sound like the Harvard man.

'Well, there's only about a dozen of those. Cripes.' Dunne gnawed on a finger. 'What'd he say about the woman that sent the letter?'

'Something like she's the wife of somebody. No, wait – "the wife of a visiting author."'

'What the hell is a *visiting* author? Somebody from out of town? Well, of course, if he's staying in a hotel, he's visiting.' Dunne heaved his body out of the chair. 'You a member of the Authors Club, by any chance?'

'Ha-ha.'

'Your big moment has come. Follow me.'

Forty-five minutes later, they were walking out of the Authors Club on West Twenty-fourth Street with smiles on their faces.

At ten minutes after one, a boy came up with the message that Miz Doyle had a telephone call in Booth One. Ethel was home by then, very proud of the bargains she had found at Mr Stern's emporium on Sixth Avenue. Louisa, sure she would miss the call because she was so slow, sent Ethel down to hold the caller until Louisa could get there. Ethel was unhappy about talking to a stranger but dutifully went off; she would do it, Louisa knew, on manner – the voice of the perfect servant, even if she was seething inside.

When Louisa finally hobbled to the telephone booth, Ethel jumped out, handed over the earpiece, saw Louisa safely seated, and bolted back to her dry goods. Louisa put the device to her ear and leaned into the horn and said, 'This is Louisa Doyle speaking. Whom have I the pleasure of addressing?'

'Wow, that "whom" really knocks me over.'

'Miss Fitch!'

'Whom else would it be?'

'I've been thinking of you so much, it's as if I know you. About the murders, I mean. Oh, Miss Fitch, I read your—'

'Look, Miz Doyle – I'm in a telephone exchange; time is money. Can I come to see you?'

'Now?'

'Not tomorrow.'

'I thought you're due at the paper at two.'

'Sure, sure, but they know I'm on a story. Can you see me?'

'Yes! The New Britannic.'

'Tell them I'm coming, but don't tell them I'm a reporter or they'll throw me out.'

Louisa left the booth, her face flushed, a feeling that she had to call excitement making her feel light headed. *Something was happening!* Well, she hoped it was that. And perhaps the prospect of a female friend.

'Ethel, I shall have a lady calling shortly, a Miss Fitch.'

'Was she the one on the telephone, madame?' Ethel looked severe. 'She tried to pump me.'

'*Did* she? About what?'

'About you, madame. And the hotel. I hope she is not a particular friend, madame, because I found her presumptuous.'

'Oh.' Louisa thought it was rather bad of Minnie Fitch. But it was her profession, after all. 'What did she ask about me?'

225

'It wasn't quite *asking*, Mrs Doyle. After I identified myself, she said things like, "I suppose Mrs Doyle is easy to work for," and "I suppose Mrs Doyle has a great many friends." I said I was sure I didn't know.'

'What did she ask about the hotel?'

'If I'd heard "things" from the other servants. I wasn't hardly about to pass on gossip, even if I had heard things! Which I haven't.' She pressed her hands together. 'Much.'

'I shall tell her that she presumed, Ethel. She's American, after all – we shouldn't expect too much.'

'I like Americans. But sometimes they carry friendliness too far, don't they. Shall I order tea for the two of you?'

'Yes, please.' Louisa's pleasant bubble of excitement had been pricked. Minnie was vulgar, she had to admit she had thought that yesterday. Now Minnie had behaved vulgarly to Ethel. It really was too bad of her.

Yet when Minnie Fitch came into her sitting room, it was Louisa who was beaming, and Louisa who embraced her guest, not the other way round. Minnie looked rather startled and settled her hat as if she thought it had been knocked loose.

'Oh, do take off your hat Miss Fitch.'

'I can't stay. And call me Minnie.'

'And you must call me Louisa. Oh, please stay. I've ordered tea. I'm dying for company. And for information about this second horror.'

Minnie Fitch looked her over, then began pulling out hatpins. 'I was up all night,' she said. She handed the hat to Ethel, then her coat. She was wearing a rather mannish wool jacket over another white shirtwaist and a bustled navy-blue skirt, this time without a necktie but with a flouncy jabot instead. She looked rather smarter, and in fact close to pretty. She fell into a chair with a loud groan. 'This second murder is a beaut.'

'How did you know about it?'

'Money. There's a sort of slush fund in the news-room for snitches and cops. I've got a guy at Mulberry Street.'

'You said you haven't a telephone.'

'He sends a beat cop to bang on my door. The cop gets a cut, too.' She put her head back and squeezed her temples with both hands. 'My God, I'm tired!'

'Was it awful?'

'It was mysterious, was what it was. They wouldn't let us near the body. It was in an alley again, Clinton Street, a lot of similarities to last time. But differences too. Blood, for one thing. There was gallons of it. You could see the cops wiping it off their feet when they came out. So she'd been killed in there, which is different.'

Shyly, because she was proud of herself, Louisa said, 'I have the policeman's report on the first one.'

'Yeah, I had it, too, but I couldn't use it, so what good is it?'

'Oh, Minnie! And I thought I'd done so well! However did you get it?'

Minnie, still not looking at her, held out a hand and rubbed the thumb and fingers together, the old sign for lucre. She said, 'This place is really nice. It must cost tons.'

'Minnie! I want information! Don't talk to me about my rooms.'

'Oh? Oh. Well, what can I tell you?'

'Was she disfigured? Was she – oh.'

It was a boy with the tea. He trundled in a mahogany tea cart and made a lot of useless to-do about what had hot water and what had tea, and he whisked a white cloth off a plate of biscuits as if he meant to produce a rabbit. Louisa got a coin from her dwindling stock and sent him on his way.

Minnie said, 'This one had the eyes done the same, only they were done differently with. I can't put this in the paper, and I didn't see it myself, so it isn't gospel, Louisa. But my source said – this is nasty, so stop me if it's too much for you – the eyes were in a paper sack that had been wet somehow so that the eyes, you know, hung down, and it looked like – you know, like a man's *pair*. You know?'

'Why?'

Minnie sighed. She took the tea that Louisa handed across and said, 'Do you know what a belaying pin is? It's a wooden thing that sailors use to tie off ropes to, and it's got a shape that's like a man's – you know? So what this maniac had done was put a belaying pin up . . . inside her, so it stuck down, and then he tied the sack with her eyes in it just where, you know, men's onions—'

'He turned her into a man!'

'There's more. Can you take it?'

'Tell me!'

'He cut her bosoms off. They haven't found them. He did the same damage to her abdomen as the first one.'

'Cut her womb out.'

'That's what he did.'

'Was it there?'

'No.'

Louisa looked at the biscuit she'd picked off the plate and put it down. Bile was rising in her throat, yet she felt mentally calm, in fact quite focused. 'That would be to turn her into a man, too. Had he cut her hair?'

'Not that I was told.'

'So she was superficially a woman, and that was the joke.'

'Jeez, Louisa, some joke!'

'I meant in a grisly way. Not a ha-ha joke, but a horrifying joke that shows how much he disdains the things we usually associate with death. Or with women, for that matter.' Absent-mindedly, she picked up the biscuit again and bit into it. 'Tell me what you know about the woman who was called "Shakespeare".'

'That was years ago.'

'Tell me about it.'

'Oh, Cripes – what do I know? She was a prostitute who was murdered five-six years ago, name of Carrie Brown. She was old for the trade. There was a detective named Byrnes, he sent up the guy he collared for it. Called "Frenchie," although he was African or something. What the talk is now is that Frenchie didn't do it and Byrnes framed him to get a conviction.'

'Were the injuries at all the same?'

'I think she was just stabbed. A lot.'

Louisa frowned and took another bite of biscuit. 'Is this Byrnes with the Murder Squad now?'

'Nah, Byrnes's gone; he was a hell of a cop in his way, but he got too big for his britches. The Lexow Commission was all over him last year – by then he was Chief of Police, worth half a million, they say, on a cop's salary, ha-ha – and Roosevelt gave him the boot first chance he got.' She reached for the biscuits, stopped. 'Hey! That's an angle! I was going to tell you, the reason I telephoned, I'm working on what you gave me about the two cops in the Murder Squad coming here and trying to push you around. You thought they maybe got money from the hotel to keep quiet about you seeing the woman here. Well, maybe I could tie that into Byrnes and jake-legging the evidence to get a conviction on "Shakespeare." Whadya think?'

'But one's corruption and the other's something different. If there's a connection with "Shakespeare" it's—'

'They're both corruption. One for money, one

230

for fame. I can make that work, trust me. Hey, I like it. I'm trying to get a line on how much moolah Cleary and Grady got socked away. They don't use banks much, cops – they've invested in whorehouses and saloons all over the city, real estate – Byrnes had some big mansion upstate. Could be Cleary and Grady are doing stuff on their own, so they might have put money where it'll show up under their own names – real estate, maybe. I want to do a search at City Hall, which is a bugger, but a guy down there will do some of it for me. Want to help?'

Louisa frowned. 'I'm interested in the women victims, not the police.'

'Louisa, it's sitting-down work; you go through property records. It's dirty and it's dusty and it's boring as pig dirt, but I need the help!'

'I have trouble getting about.'

'I'll get you there and back, and there's only a few stairs. All you'll be doing is sitting! Louisa, please!' She frowned. 'How come I get to call you Louisa?'

'I call you Minnie, don't I? I want a friend!'

'How about doing this work for me, then, *friend*?'

Minnie was so earnest that she had taken Louisa's hand. But what Louisa said was, smiling to soften the words, 'I'll trade you for the medical reports on both women.'

'I don't have 'em. What good would they be to me – my editor won't print that stuff!'

'Get them. You can, Minnie, I know you can. Can't you?'

Minnie began to smile back. 'You look like butter wouldn't melt in your mouth, but you're a dinger, you are!' She still had hold of Louisa's hand. The smiles widened; the eyes locked. They squeezed each other's hand. 'I'll have a cab waiting outside the hotel at eight a.m. tomorrow morning. Okay?'

She was going out of the hotel next morning as Manion was coming in. Seeing him, she backed clumsily into the lobby and shook her head at the doorman, who was gesturing for her to come through. She was afraid she was blushing again.

'Mr Manion.'

'Yeah, good morning. You're looking lots better.'

'I wanted to thank you for the papers you sent me. And to apologize – I thought you'd given me – it – up.'

He shrugged. He had taken off his soft hat. He always wore rather good clothes, she thought, dressed this morning in a dark brown, double-breasted suit with a faint stripe, a wool overcoat worn open. He looked respectable, she thought. He said, 'I thought it was important to you.'

'However did you get the report?'

'I told you, beat cops need cash.'

She reached towards her handbag, thinking that she would have to give him money and she would soon run out. 'How much was it?'

He touched her arm to stop her. 'Forget it. I used the two sawbucks those coppers gave me. Glad to get rid of them. My treat.'

She looked at him, moved her hand away from her bag; he took his hand away from her arm. There was a silence. She said, 'You know there's been another murder.'

'Hard not to know. It takes the load off the hotel, anyway.'

'What "load"?'

'You seeing her here, if that got out. Carver was sweating bricks about it. Now it's out there.' He waved vaguely to include all of the city.

A question roamed around her brain but wouldn't settle – something about whether the second murder had been committed to take attention away from the hotel. But that would mean that the hotel was involved . . . She dismissed it, said, 'Whoever did it is very dangerous, Mr Manion.'

'A real lunatic. You going out?'

'I have an appointment.' She started to turn away, thought better of it. 'Mr Manion, while I have you here – the first murder victim, the woman with the copper-coloured hair – you said you saw the man leave the hotel, but not her. Is it possible that she never left the hotel?'

'Judas Priest, don't say a thing like that! Carver'd split his britches!'

'I think an objective person ought to consider every possibility.'

'That's all we'd need, for one of the papers to get hold of that idea.'

'"We"? I suppose you mean you and Mr Carver. I hardly think that's worthy of you, Mr Manion,'

She sounded severe because she was disappointed in him and because – she had to admit it – he flustered her. She made her voice pleasant. 'Good morning, Mr Manion.'

She moved; he jumped to the doors to open them for her.

Detective-Sergeant Dunne got down from the El at Twenty-third Street and tumbled down the stairs and waited for the cross-town horse-tram. He hardly noticed the scene around him, although he saw it all and in fact would have been able to describe it if a crime had been committed. He was thinking, however – thinking about the small irony of finding that the wife of an author of detective stories was a possible witness in a murder investigation. Dunne didn't read mystery stories – didn't read much of anything except police news, in fact – but he knew what they were.

He had learned at the Authors Club that Arthur Conan Doyle had been staying in the city on the day before the first Bowery murder, and that he had been staying at the New Britannic Hotel. Presumably he had a wife and it had been the wife who had written to Roosevelt. To Dunne, this meant one of two things: because well-off people (all authors were well off) didn't usually involve themselves in murder cases, the wife had written to Roosevelt either because her husband wanted some publicity or she thought of herself as Roosevelt's social equal and was writing to him as a class thing.

Dunne wasn't a class warrior, but he knew that America had classes and he mostly disliked the fact, as he disliked Roosevelt's Harvard-bred assistant and as he'd have admitted, if driven to the wall, that he disliked Roosevelt. Dunne didn't like it that some people started the hundred-yard dash fifty yards ahead of the rest.

He got down at Fifth Avenue and stood there and looked across the avenue and Twenty-third Street at the New Britannic Hotel. Five storeys and a penthouse, mostly brick with some nice stonework here and there; a wide entrance with bronze doors and a canopy of black metal and brass; three marble steps up from the street and a uniformed doorman who looked like something out of an operetta.

There's my man.

Dunne crossed Fifth, then crossed Twenty-third and watched the doorman for some seconds. He was tall, beefy, tougher than the uniform suggested. He got three tips while Dunne watched. Not bad.

Dunne walked up the steps and waited for the doorman to climb to his level, when he said, 'Hey, Gerrigan.'

Gerrigan looked him over with the acute, quick stare of experience, dismissed him but said, 'Sir?' just in case Dunne was more than he looked.

'You want to have a little talk with me.'

'Sir?'

'Dunne, Detective-Sergeant.' Dunne held his card in the palm of his hand so that nobody could see it but Gerrigan. 'You're Fred Gerrigan, two to five for assault in Attica, three for statutory rape, New Jersey State pen. Don't fuck with me, you understand?'

Gerrigan had got red in the face, then pale. Somebody came out of the hotel and he hurried to get the door, then hurried down the steps to wave in a hack. When he'd pocketed his tip he looked up at Dunne and then came more slowly up to him. 'I don't want no trouble.'

'Neither do I. They know about you here? No? No reason they need to, so long as you're square with me. What I want to know is—'

A cab stopped and Gerrigan ran down to get the door and help a couple down; then he strode ahead of them to open one of the bronze doors and then pocket his tip. He came back, and Dunne said, 'There was a woman's body found in the Bowery a few days ago. You ever see her here?'

'I wouldn't know if I did.'

'Her picture was in the paper.'

'You think I got time for the papers? You seen how they run me ragged?'

'I think you'd remember this one. Red hair, a lot of it. A looker.'

'No idea.'

But Dunne thought he was lying, so he said, 'You want me to take you down to Mulberry Street? You want me to turn you over to a couple of Clubber Williams's old boys to work on you?

You know, you lie to the police, that's a third conviction – Sing-Sing this time.'

'For sweet Christ's sake! Okay, maybe I saw her. So what?' His Irish accent had got thicker.

'How come you remember her?'

'You just asked me, for Christ's sake, like I *should* remember!'

'But you see all sorts of people. How come you remember her?'

Gerrigan let more people into the hotel and more out, and he came back and he said, 'The hotel detective told me they were coming, now, didn't he?'

'They?'

'Her and a fella.'

'A matinee.'

'Yeah, something on the order of that.'

'The detective was on the take.'

'I suppose he was, indeed.'

'What'd he give you?'

'Couple bucks.'

'So you saw her go in. Did you see her come out?'

'She musta come out after I went off duty, like. Six o'clock and it's me for home.'

'The guy?'

'Indeed, I saw him come out. Half-past five, something like that. I remember my feet were killing me, I saw him and I thought, "You sure had a better afternoon than I did, me boy."'

'Describe him.'

'Shorter than me, good-looking if you like that type – smooth, you know? Little moustache like you drew it on with a fountain pen. Nice clothes, a little too sharp, not what you'd usually see here – good but a little, you know, extreme. Could have been a Jew or a Dago, a little dark, y'know, dark eyes like women go nuts over. Maybe thirty.'

Dunne was writing in a notebook. Gerrigan ran back and forth a couple of times and asked when Dunne was going to finish, because people would notice and think he was talking to a newspaperman and there'd be a stink. Dunne said, 'You had a Mrs Conan Doyle staying here that same day.'

'Yeah, Mrs Doyle, lady on crutches; she's still here. Jeez, funny you should ask about her; *she* was after me about the woman and the guy she was with.'

'*Was* she. Well, well.' Dunne put away his notebook and pencil. 'I'll just step inside and have a look-see. What's the house D's name?'

'Manion.'

Dunne nodded and pursed his lips as if to whistle but made no sound. He stood in front of the bronze doors, and when Gerrigan didn't move he said, 'Well, *open* them.'

Dunne didn't think much of hotel detectives. In his view, they weren't detectives at all; worse, they were mostly as crooked as a dog's hind leg. Even if they'd once been cops. Maybe *more so* if they'd been cops, but at least if they'd been cops he usually knew them. But this Manion was different

238

– nobody he knew. And his first glance at Manion across the lobby told Dunne that he didn't like him.

Dunne had him pointed out by the swell at Reception, who raised his eyes to heaven when he saw Dunne's police card. Dunne expected to be told to wipe his feet, or maybe change his clothes, but the swell only pointed and sniffed. Dunne went over to where the house detective sat in a leather chair and pulled another, less comfortable chair close and sat in it. Leaning close to Manion, he held up his card and said, 'Cop.'

'I saw.'

Dunne disliked him even more close up – the moustache was too thin, the suit too tight. The guy looked like an actor playing an Irish crook who's made it. 'Your name's Manion.'

'So?'

'So we don't know each other, so I just want you to know that if you're not square with me I'll take it amiss. Get me?' When Manion said nothing but then shrugged, Dunne smiled. Manion, he thought, was afraid of him. That was a good start. 'Okay. So tell me about a red-haired woman who passed through the lobby the day before the first Bowery Butcher murder.'

Manion frowned. Dunne knew the frown: he'd said something surprising. Why was it surprising? Usually, that kind of surprise meant somebody had been found out and hadn't expected to be. Dunne said, 'It was fixed?'

'What?'

'Her and the lady killer she was with. You got a little what they call a "lagniappe"?'

Manion sighed and told him that there had been an arrangement, yes; he'd seen the woman and the man, yes; he'd seen the man leave but not the woman.

'That's it?'

'That's it.'

'You don't want to shit me.'

'That's all of it.'

Dunne watched him, decided he was being truthful. He said, 'A woman named Doyle.'

Manion almost jumped. This time he was *really* surprised. Dunne liked the effect, but he, too, was surprised: why the reaction? Because a man like Manion, who was only one step up from a gigolo himself, had been turning the charm on for this Doyle woman? He let Manion dangle there while he thought about it, and then he said, 'Mrs Doyle is one of the guests. She got some particular importance to you, you seem to recognize the name right off?'

'She's been here a while. Fell and hurt herself.' Now Manion set his jaw, as if to tell himself too late that he wasn't going to be pushed around by some cop.

Dunne smiled. 'Nice woman?'

'I suppose.'

'You suppose. What's her connection with the woman I asked you about first – the woman was here with the gigolo?'

Manion shrugged. 'No connection at all, that I know about.'

Dunne leaned in. 'We were getting along so fine, you and me. Now you're stringing me. You don't want to do that more than once.' His voice changed. 'What's her connection with the woman?'

Manion looked him in the eye. He'd decided to take a grip on his balls. 'Why don't you ask her?'

Dunne snorted. 'How'd you come to be a so-called detective?'

'Pinkerton. I was a Pinkerton.'

'Beating up strikers? Shooting organizers in the back?'

'I thought that's what cops do.'

'Not as easy as sitting on your arse in a hotel lobby, what cops do.' Dunne put his face close to Manion's; Manion pulled his head back and swiveled his eyes around the lobby. Dunne growled, 'Don't let me ever hear you say anything against cops again. Hear me?' He punched a stiff index finger into Manion's collarbone. 'I know your type inside out. You're not a cop; you couldn't *be* a cop. Because you got no guts. Am I right? You're all show. You sit on your arse, scare the drawers off kids, and try to get off with the lady guests, am I right? And take a few bucks from tinhorns who want a nice spot to bring their girl friends to, am I right?' He punched the collarbone again with the finger. 'Well, I'll tell you something – I think your spine is made of baby-turds. You want to argue with that? Come on down to Mulberry

241

Street, I'll lock the two of us in a room, they can come in in fifteen minutes and scrape you off the walls.' Dunne sat back. 'As you say, I'll ask the lady. Of course, you don't know her room number, do you? Of course not.' He stood over Manion, his coat billowing out like a cloak. 'I don't want to take you down to Mulberry Street, but I will if I have to. You haven't told me everything you know yet, but you will. *Everything*. Mr Detective.' He snorted and turned away.

New York's City Hall looked to Louisa rather like a railway hotel in some aggressive but lesser city such as Birmingham. She first saw it when she was wondering if she was being taken on some wild goose chase so that the cab driver could charge a huge fare because she was a foreigner and virtually helpless. The ride had gone on for far too long, she thought, to get from Twenty-third Street to the bottom of the island. And when she did see City Hall in all its overdone assertiveness, it seemed to her that there were still miles of New York beyond it, because all she could see were more buildings and more streets. Where was the water? Where was the statue of Liberty Enlightening the World?

But Minnie was there to meet her, although in a bad mood because Louisa was late. Minnie muttered, 'I ought to be sleeping right now, you know,' and led her impatiently to the building, not the main entrance but one far around to the side and much less elegant, with an iron railing that led down, not up. Minnie sent in a message; somebody came out to meet them, and Minnie hurried away.

Louisa's guide was a youngish man with dandruff on his alpaca jacket and spectacles on his nose; behind them, he seemed a reasonably good-looking man, if a little short on chin and, she thought, intelligence. 'My name's Cullum.'

'I'm Mrs Doyle.' She had decided not to use Arthur's name, proud as she was of it. She was, she thought rather thrillingly, 'under cover.' 'I'm to look at property records.'

'Oh, sure, Fitch told me all about it. You in the newspaper game, too?'

'In a manner of speaking.'

'Pay pretty good, does it?'

'Enough to live.'

He was trying to hurry; she was hobbling on the crutches. He was nice enough about it, but it was clear he had other things to do. She was aware of his giving her several appraising looks – hat, bodice, gown – and, although she'd dressed conservatively on purpose, she thought he disapproved. She had the feeling he had totted her up and found her too well dressed. She saw a few other women in the corridor and an office; they were all in shirtwaists and skirts. It was true, next to them her grey cashmere with the beaded bodice looked ostentatious.

Tomorrow, I shall borrow something from Ethel. She couldn't afford to buy anything, certainly.

She was put at a table at the far end of a basement area as big as a ballroom, though with a far lower ceiling, where rank after rank of shelves held records in accordion files that were tied with faded tape; sometimes, frustration with the knots had caused the tapes to be cut or broken, and the ends hung limp and chewed-looking.

Cullum pointed at a wooden thing like a tea cart, but with smaller wheels. 'Fitch said property records for Manhattan. Brooklyn stuff isn't here; you got to go to Brooklyn for that. Different city. These here are Manhattan Ward One. Put them back on the cart when they're done. When you've done them all, put them back on the shelf.' He explained notations. 'Mind you don't mix them up. Upstairs really hates it when they're mixed up, and then *I* catch it. I'll be back in to check, but I can't stay.' He told her where the ladies' convenience was, apparently most of a city block away, but at least in the basement. 'Sorry I can't give you a hand with these things, you being crippled and all, but that's life.'

She was appalled by the quantity of material. What could Minnie have been thinking of? Then she realized that a very young man working at another table a dozen feet away seemed to be doing the same thing. When he saw her looking, he came over. 'Name's Rogers. You Miz Doyle? Pleased t'meetcha. Minnie said you'd be in. You get the dope on the layout? It ain't as bad as it seems. My advice, you can go through Ward One like a dose of salts; it ain't a likely ward. Where we wanna look is from Five Pernts north, mostly east, all the way uptown 'cause that's where the cheap properties are, you follow me? It's a matter of logic, am I right?' She thought he might be all of twenty years old.

'Do you work for the *Express*, too?'

'Nah, I'm what you call a title searcher by trade, but I know Minnie personal, so she come to me as an expert. Anything you want to know about propitty, ast me. As a favour 'cause you're lame, I'll push the carts back and get you new ones, that way you won't make collywobbles of the files. First name's Leonard, you can call me that. No food or drinks on the table, by the way, and if you brought your lunch, push yourself off from the table when you eat. Anything else?'

'Where do I hang my coat?'

'Over the back of the chair. We ain't supposed to be here, that's the pernt, get it? Minnie greased Cullum, so it's kosher, but it's like we ain't here. Cheers.'

Cheers, indeed. A less cheerful place would have been hard for her to imagine. The walls were grey-green, the ceiling grey-tan and discoloured with stains; the floor was oiled wood, blackened with dirt. Such light as there was came from windows high in the walls – she could see pairs of legs walking past several of them – and from electric bulbs with inadequate shades high against the ceiling.

She sighed and set to work.

She had brought pencils and two fountain pens and a pad of lined paper that Ethel had bought for her at the news-stand, whose operator had reportedly greeted her with, 'Hey, Limey!', a familiarity that had caused Ethel to growl, 'I'll Limey him!'

She opened the first file. Inside were papers tied in bundles with more faded and rotted tape. Presumably, the bundles held the same sort of documents, each bundle having to do with a property that (she didn't need to know this, but Cullum had told it to her rather breathlessly because he was in a hurry) could be located on a plat map in the Hall of Records, which was in another building. But what she wanted was the name of the most recent owner of each property, and that would be – presumably meaning in the ideal case – towards the bottom of each bundle. She put the first bundle in front of her and pulled on the tape knot to untie it.

'Don't do that!'

Startled, she looked up. It was Leonard. He bent over her and tied the bundle tight again. 'We did that, we'd have a fine mess, wouldn't we! Someplace in each file, there's an index. *That's* what you want.'

'Nobody told me.'

'Cullum's too thick to look through a ladder. He don't understand what people who don't do this twelve hours a day don't know. He thinks everybody walkin' up and down the streets off City Hall Park awready knows there's an index. Here.' He

246

flicked through the bundles and extracted a sheet of paper. 'This is an index. Sometimes they's two, even three sheets – depends how often the propitty's been sold. So on the left, see, there's the propitty numbers that tell you what plat map to look on. Then there's a colyumn gives the street address. Then there's this last, big colyumn where the propitty owner's name is. The current owner is always the *last* name. They don't cross nothing out, that's strictly ta-boo. So you get all these names sometimes, and they really cram them in, sometimes they draw arrows and put more down at the bottom of the colyumns; I've seen them continue on the *back* of the page, which is really stupid because they're so easy to miss. Anyway, that's it. Find the index, look at the *last* name for each propitty and check it against the list Minnie gave you. Minnie gave you a list, right? Oney thirteen names on it, so it's a piece of cake, goes like lightning. Mostly.' He grinned. 'You'll catch on, smart girl like you.'

Minnie had indeed given her a list of names – Cleary's and Grady's, their wives' maiden names, and the names of several brothers and some married sisters. By the time she had finished the first cartload of files, she knew the names by heart. She hadn't found any of them in the indexes, but checking, even futilely, had taught them to her.

'Leonard!' All she had to do was call his name, and he would jump up, usually laughing, and run to get her cart. He loved this work, she realized;

when they took a break at his insistence, he told her that doing anything having to do with real estate was 'my kind of work,' that he learned from everything. 'I'm gonna know more about who owns what and how and when and for how much than anybody else in the city.'

'And then what?'

'And then I'm gonna do deals and rake in the shekels.'

They were smoking two of Leonard's cigarettes in a part of the basement that had a curled and faded No Smoking sign high on the wall. Louisa was both worried and excited to be doing something illicit. She had at first objected, then joined in; Leonard had said that she was 'a girl with grit.'

'I'm hardly a girl, Leonard.'

'Manner of speaking. M'father always calls my ma "the old girl." How'd you get that black eye?'

It was much faded but still visible. She thought he was hoping for a tale of wife-beating, but tripping on a carpet seemed good enough.

'I bet you're a peach when you're all in one piece,' he said. It made her laugh. She said, 'An old peach, young man.'

'Yeah, well . . .' He dropped his cigarette on the floor and ground it out with his heel. 'I'm old for my years, everybody says so.'

By noon, her fingers felt dusty and she had dust in her nose and even, perhaps, her lungs. She took the long walk to the ladies' convenience and washed her hands and face and thought how terrible it would be to do this all day, five and a half days a week, and then remembered her mother and was ashamed.

Minnie was waiting for her in the street. 'Lunch is a pushcart in the park. It's a warm day.' Louisa had been looking forward to a pot of tea and perhaps a nice tray of sandwiches. Instead, they sat on a bench with white mugs of scalding coffee (five cents deposit on the mug, redeemable when it came back to the kiosk) and a kind of sandwich bought from a pushcart – some sort of unidentifiable sausage with a heap of sauerkraut on it, the whole mess mashed between two halves of a long, soft roll.

'It tastes rather good,' she said.

'Seasoned with hunger. I live on these things. This is people's food, Louisa – news to you, right?'

'I don't like you saying that, Minnie. I don't advertise it, but I haven't always been well off.'

'I thought you were a lady. Ain't you?'

'Of course I'm a lady, but that isn't only a matter of money. I think I've always been . . . My mother always wanted me to be a lady. Kept telling me I had to be one.'

'Hard on you, huh? Pushed you.' Minnie was chewing the sausage and sauerkraut with enthusiasm.

'No. She was the gentlest person I've ever known.' She was looking out over the park, the people moving in twos and small groups, a great many men in tall hats. It could have been London, except for the pushcarts selling food. Without realizing quite what she was going to do, Louisa began to tell Minnie what she had come from. 'My father was a clergyman and a very bad one – he thought he was better than his parishioners and far better than his wife. And his daughters. All he really cared about was fishing. He drowned when I was eight. My mother moved us to Glasgow, where she had family; we lived in a tenement, with my grandmother down the stairs and a married aunt up. I had older sisters and an older brother and a little brother. One sister, older than I, died of diphtheria the first year. My older brother ran off two years later. My other sister married and moved away. My little brother and I were all my mother had left.'

'She worked, did she?'

'My mother sewed kilts for the British army in an attic workshop with some other women. Soldiers said the wool was so coarse it wore the skin off their knees. I've seen my mother come home with her fingers bleeding, trying to force the needles through four layers of it. By the time I was ten, I knew that I should be helping her. But she said I had to stay in school. I wasn't going to end up like her. If I heard her say that once, I heard it a hundred times.'

'You're not so different from me, you mean.' Minnie finished her sausage, licked her fingers. She eyed Louisa. 'I grew up on a farm. Until I was fifteen. I'm like your brother – I ran off. It

250

was a miserable place. They were hard people with hard lives and hard ideas. I couldn't take it. You want some fried dough?'

'Good heavens, no. I didn't know there was such stuff.'

'Oh, get off it, Louisa! You probably got the same thing in England only they call it Spots and Blotches or something.'

'I'd rather eat library paste.'

'You're the limit.' Minnie went off and came back with a round, brown thing that looked like a large muffin dusted with castor sugar. She insisted that it was deep-fried dough. 'Italian,' she said. She lifted it as if in a toast. 'At least the Italians brought good food when they came over. What'd the Irish bring us? Boiled potatoes and cabbage.'

'How are you coming on the medical reports on the two murders?'

'It's on my list.'

'What does that mean?'

'It means I'm a busy working girl and I have to make a list.'

'Is that a way of saying I'm not a working girl?'

'It's a way of saying you have to wait your turn.'

'Minnie, I'm going through those wretched files for you!'

'There's a lot going on right now, Louisa.'

'Minnie, you promised!'

'It's on my list, I told you!' She finished the fried dough and licked her fingers. 'I'll get to it, I really will.'

'When?'

Minnie shrugged. Louisa let a breath hiss out. She told herself that she liked Minnie but thought that she was selfish and a user of other people. 'Really, Minnie,' she said.

'What? You going to get the galloping peedoodles and stop working in City Hall because I haven't brought you some damned useless medical report?'

Louisa struggled into her crutches. 'No, I'm not. I *keep* my promises.'

Leonard found the first property that afternoon, a tenement on Water Street whose owner was one of Lieutenant Cleary's brothers.

'It could be legitimate,' Louisa said. 'His brother could be in that business.'

'Yeah, yeah, could be. My ma says, "If could be was feathers, we'd all sleep in feather beds." We'll see.'

Louisa finished her third ward, Twenty-three, and Leonard brought a cart loaded with files of properties east of Bowery and north of Canal Street, which he told her was an immigrant area and likelier than the ones she had been working on. He smacked the cart of new files. 'Most of N' Yawk's immigrant, let's face it, but these streets're where they come first crack outa the box – they used to be Irish, then German, now they're Jews and some Italians. It's the story o' New Yawk – it's history in buildings! Isn't that great?'

She found her first match almost at once, this

252

time between one of Cleary's sisters and a tenement on Broome Street. She called Leonard; he looked over her shoulder (his face too close to her hair, one hand on her chair so that his fingers touched her back) and said, 'That's a double-decker. That means it's one a the old style – two buildings on the same lot, catwalks that go from one to the other on the sixth floor, I ain't joking, they're something! Cellars under them, too, people crammed inta them like matches in a box. They're something. Okay, you're doing good.' He patted her shoulder. She thought Leonard entirely lacked respect for either age or gender.

They had found three more between them before she left at four o'clock. He offered to walk with her 'someplace,' even asked her whether she didn't want to 'catch a show and maybe a bite to eat.'

'Leonard, I am a married woman, and I don't go out to shows or restaurants with men, even if they're far younger than I.'

'What, you don't like me?'

'It has nothing to do with liking; it's a matter of what's proper.'

'Proper's just a word for losing time! We're young; we gotta grab hold of life while we can. Your husband waiting for you at home?'

'No, he's . . . traveling.'

'So, you're married to a traveling man, you think he's being proper out on the road? Come on, live a little!'

'Leonard, someone is waiting for me,' she lied.

'Oh, but you're husband's traveling. I get it!' He laughed. He was enormously good-natured, she thought. 'Okay, sweetheart, I see what's going on. Why didn't you say you're way ahead of me?'

She found a cab, for which Minnie had given her the fare; still, she wished she had the courage to try the Elevated Railway; it would be so much faster. As it was, the journey up the island at the busiest time of day took almost an hour.

Two letters from Arthur were waiting for her at Reception along with a telegram that said WIRING TEN POUNDS BANK TODAY STOP PLEASE BE FRUGAL STOP PLEASE STOP ARTHUR.

Ten pounds! She'd asked for a hundred.

But she tamped down her anger. Something was better than nothing. *Still* . . .

'Oh, madame, Galt was here to do your ankle but he's had to go again.'

'Oh dear. Well, it doesn't matter, Ethel.' She looked at her maid. 'Or does it? Have you and Mr Galt walked out yet?'

'We had a stroll down Fifth Avenue this afternoon, madame, as he had a few minutes while the doctor was with old Mr Carver, and I had no duties. I was sure you wouldn't—'

'No, Ethel, not at all.' She took off her hat and gloves.

'In fact, if it's all right, we hoped to go to see the play this evening, as it's Mr Galt's evening off. If I could change my usual day—'

'Yes, yes, do go. I shall simply go to bed, anyway.

I find I'm tired. I suppose it's being ill, or injured, at any rate.' She was about to say that she wanted Ethel to help her into a bath, but there was a knock at the door; Ethel answered it, said something Louisa didn't hear, and then turned to Louisa with a frightened face. 'It's another policeman, ma'am. He's downstairs and he wants to know if he can come up.'

'Oh, damn! No, tell him – oh, tell him yes, but how thoughtless, how . . . Damn!'

She wanted a bath but she knew she hadn't time, so she settled for bathing her face and washing her hands and arms really well. Then she removed her stockings and debated changing into a dressing gown, but that seemed more intimate than she wanted to be with a policeman. And then it was time to face him.

Detective-Sergeant Dunne had been up to the Doyle woman's floor that morning, but she hadn't been there. Now he was tired and cranky and wanted to see his wife and his kids, and here he was, trudging down the corridors of a fancy hotel instead. This time, the door was opened by a homely maid with no bosoms and a black dress that would have been just right in a convent. Dunne took his hat off and held up his card. 'Detective-Sergeant Dunne of the New York Municipal Police to see Mrs Doyle.'

Mrs Doyle had been injured for sure. She was doing her best to stand very straight on a crutch, but she was hurting, he thought. Her face looked as if somebody had pounded it with a mallet. Still, Dunne liked what he saw. He identified himself, told her he was looking into the murder of a woman whose body had been found in the Bowery: could he ask a few questions?

He sat where she pointed. She sat on a little sofa that cost more than he made in a couple of months, he supposed. She said, 'Did Lieutenant Cleary send you?' She didn't sound friendly. In fact, a definite frost.

'No, ma'am. I doubt that Lieutenant Cleary knows I'm here. Do you know the lieutenant?'

'To my regret.'

Well, well. Dunne asked her whether he might slip off his coat.

He asked a question about how she knew the lieutenant. She told a surprising tale of a visit from Cleary and Grady. She accused them of being threatening and rude. Of calling her 'nuts.'

'I do apologize, ma'am. In the name of the police, I mean. And this was in connection with you seeing a lady downstairs in the lobby, was it?'

Then it all came out, as if she'd been waiting to talk to somebody who'd listen. She finished by saying she'd written to Commissioner Roosevelt, and the result was that Cleary 'and his toady' had shown up.

'I didn't know it was like that, Miz Doyle, I truly didn't. How you must feel! Cheated, I mean. And badly used.' He put on his innocent face and his innocent voice. 'Did you think to discuss it with the hotel detective?'

Her momentary pause told him that she had, and that, as well, the hotel detective meant something to her. Oddly, he felt a twinge of – was that jealousy? No, probably not, except it was of Manion, and he didn't like Manion. But she had recovered, and she said that she had talked to the hotel detective, yes, and she had asked the doorman, too, and it was her belief that perhaps the poor woman had never left the New Britannic. Alive.

'Miz Doyle, are you saying that you think she was murdered *here*?'

'Well, no – but isn't it a possibility? We should consider every possibility, shouldn't we?'

'I see, yes, a possibility.' He was thinking of the Wop's map and the sightings of old men in wagons. None this far uptown, though.

He was impressed. She seemed to him to have a lot in the upper storey, and she was determined. And the way she talked about the dead woman suggested some special urge in her – something about the woman *because* she was a woman. What his wife called 'feeling sisterly.'

Tea appeared; the maid passed him a tray of little sandwiches and cookies and things. Suddenly he'd been there an hour, and he'd thought it would be a difficult ten minutes. Now she was telling him about a woman at a newspaper and a sketch artist and how she'd known the woman she'd seen in the lobby was the victim.

'You should be on the police force. You're very thorough,' he said. He had devoured the sandwiches, now was working on some small chocolate things. His wife would scold him.

'Somebody has to be,' she said. He was to understand that she meant that the police work so far had been less than thorough. All he could do was nod and drink his tea; he didn't dare tell her that the police work was non-existent because of orders. He thought of asking her whether her interest came from her husband's being the one who wrote about Sherlock Holmes, but he didn't think he should ask that. It would be like saying she was only an idiot female, and she wasn't. Then she was telling him about forcing the hotel detective to help her get the patrolman's draft report on the first murder.

'Didn't take so much force, I guess.' He smiled, but he was mentally damning Jimmie Malone for being on the take.

She looked at him without a smile. 'I don't understand you, Detective-Sergeant.'

'Hotel detectives like to help the ladies, I meant.' He got up. 'Except their own wives.' He smiled to show her that that had been a kind of joke, although he'd said it to plant the idea that Manion was married. *Maybe that* had *been jealousy he'd felt.* 'You've been very helpful, Miz Doyle.' He was brushing crumbs from his lap. 'I could only wish half the public was so helpful.'

'I want you to catch whoever did it, Detective-Sergeant!'

'Yes, well – New York is a big place, ma'am.'

'Does that mean you're sweeping her under the carpet?'

'It does not! It means that I'm a slow and careful man. In the force they call me "Never." Never Dunne, y' see? But I do get done finally, though not at a time that pleases the great ones.'

She was giving him a shrewd look, both hopeful and sceptical. She said, 'Do you work for Lieutenant Cleary?'

'Ah . . . in the formal sense, yes, ma'am.'

'Are you working for him at this moment?'

'Lieutenant Cleary isn't aware that I'm here, if that's your question.'

'Will he be?'

'Ah . . . not by me telling him, ma'am. Sometimes, what we don't say . . .'

'You mean you'd prefer that I not say anything, too.' She had a nice smile. Quite lively, maybe a bit of mischief around the edges.

Dunne struggled into his huge coat. 'You've a good head, Miz Doyle.' He settled the coat on his shoulders and then took one of his cards and handed it to her. 'Anything you think of or remember, I'd like you to let me know. I don't have my own telephone – we're not that wealthy in the police – but there's a number there for my squad's room.' He grinned. 'And I'd like an excuse to come back for more of those sandwiches.'

He looked around the lobby for the detective but he wasn't there; he asked at Reception and found that Manion had an office on the mezzanine. Dunne went up there and collared Manion again and learned everything else he thought the man had to tell him. He also gave Manion what-for about having bought a patrolman's notes for Mrs Doyle, and he threatened Manion again, not this time with the basement of 300 Mulberry but with arrest for bribing a policeman. To himself, he admitted that he wouldn't do such a thing because he would protect Malone, the patrolman, because he was an old friend, and then he thought, *And that's corruption. Now I'm in it, too.* Manion, however, seemed convinced. Apparently he had decided that Dunne was right about what his spine was made of.

Dunne kept his hat in his hand until he was heading out the hotel's front door. He kept the thought of Louisa Doyle much longer than that.

Louisa was relieved when he was gone, yet pleased because he was the first *nice* policeman she'd met. Had she told him anything she shouldn't have? She didn't think so; she'd tried not to tell him anything that would steal Minnie's thunder. No, she had done well, and it was even better because she had liked the detective. But what had he meant about hotel detectives' wives? Or was that simply a way of telling her that Manion was married?

Heavens, was he?

She went into the bedroom and started to read one of Arthur's letters, which she found annoyed her because of the complaining, and she put it aside, then felt guilty. She wanted a bath, but she couldn't bathe yet because Galt was coming. She looked at her watch; it was late: if Galt and Ethel were going to the theatre, they'd have to dress quite soon.

I mustn't be annoyed with my husband's letters. It's something that's wrong with me, not with his letter – am I exhausted? irritable? unhappy? Well, I've every right to be unhappy, being marooned here with almost no money and no friends and no husband, but the fact is I don't think I'm unhappy! Guiltily, she added, *Though I do miss my babies. And my husband.*

She was contemplating what was meant by being happy when Ethel announced Galt, and she turned her attention to her ankle. He told her what she already knew, that the colour was much better but there was still some swelling; had she been on it a good deal? If her progress continued, he thought she could exchange the crutches for a cane in a day or two.

A cane! That would be a blessed release – and rather fashionable, too. How many women got to use canes, when men used them all the time? She said, 'A cane would be most welcome.'

'Not tomorrow. Maybe the day after, just for trying, and of course we'd have to get doctor's permission. Then in a couple o' days . . . You'll be up and dancing the hornpipe!'

They all three laughed.

And Louisa realized she had started to menstruate.

She excused herself, and Galt took this as a signal he should leave, as he did after a significant exchange of looks with Ethel. She, colouring, asked whether she could go now to get ready for the evening. Louisa, thinking more of the dampness between her thighs than of Ethel, let her go, with an inner smile that Ethel could be anxious about a man at her age.

She went into the bedroom, closed the door, and stripped. Garments fell around her like leaves from a dying tree. As she suspected, her drawers were stained. They were her oldest pair, and she had taken mostly to wearing combinations; had she known she was about to start? She didn't think so; certainly she'd made no other preparations. But it was a relief to know that her irritability hadn't really been because of Arthur; it was the curse.

She pulled off the drawers and threw them a couple of feet from the other clothes, then went into the bathroom and started herself a bath. Surely one of the luxuries of a good American hotel was this bath right en suite with one's bedroom; so many places made you trudge down the corridor, towel and soap in hand, to a bath somewhere at the far end of the building.

Where, she wondered, had Ethel put the German pads and their truss-like harness? They traveled in the smallest of the hand luggage; good heavens, could they have gone off with Arthur? More for him to complain about. *Oh, that's unfair. That's the curse speaking again*. The little valise was in the first place she looked, the big steamer trunk, otherwise empty and resting against a wall. She should have had it carried to the cellar or wherever they stored things for the guests, but then what a pickle she'd have been in!

She emptied the valise and put it back, then put most of the pads in a drawer with her underwear, keeping one pad and the harness for now. She carried them into the bathroom, set them down on the porcelain sink, and let herself into the bathwater with the care of somebody trying to sit naked on a block of ice: she sat first on the wooden lip of the long tub, then put her good foot into the water and got her weight on the toes; then she raised her injured leg, balanced, and slowly sank back into the hot water, only at the last letting her ankle get wet.

It was delicious. Doing a day's work, or at least a day's activities, had truly wearied her. Arthur would say she had lost muscle tone lying in bed. Or that being ill 'took it out of one.' She could agree with that. Now, however, the hot water was like a reward, a prize at the end of the day. And she had not done so badly: they had found three properties that might be outlets for Cleary's illicit money, and she had had what turned out to be a pleasant visit from a policeman, and—

She heard a sound, a sort of thump from her bedroom, as if a cat had jumped down from a chair. No, it must have been something in the street. Quiet the hotel certainly was, but it couldn't have been expected to block out every bang and knock.

She tried to give herself again to the water, but she had a little frown between her eyebrows; she could feel it; and she couldn't relax because she was listening.

Damn the noise!

Then there was . . . something. Another sound, unidentifiable.

'Ethel?'

It was as if somebody were standing just on the other side of the door – not making sounds, but *being there* because of making no sound. As if the room and the door and she were all holding their breath.

'Ethel?'

Nothing. But a nothing into which the ordinary ticks and purrs and clicks of life poured, filling it and becoming normal again. There was nobody out there, of course. It was all in her head, or perhaps her womb. Hysteria. She said aloud, 'Nonsense.'

She began to wash herself, soaping between her legs as if something evil lived there. It was the fear of the smell, which she knew Arthur disliked and which she tried always to save him from. Arthur wouldn't make love to her when she had her period, not that anything had ever been said, but he simply didn't. Nor had he when she had been pregnant, as if the only woman he wanted to do it with was the pristine bride he'd married.

An odd squeamishness, for a doctor. It was only blood, after all. And she thought of the two women who had bled to death.

She soaped herself one more time and balanced again on her good foot and, by pushing up with one hand and reaching high to the towel bar with the other, was able to stand, her bad leg bent to keep weight off the ankle, so that she looked like a nymph in a bad painting; she'd have needed only to put a hand over her pubis and an arm across her breasts to look really revolting.

'Psyche Surprised by Bad Taste,' she said aloud.

She toweled her upper body, then sat and pivoted her legs over the side of the tub and struggled to stand again and dried her legs and the rest of her, leaving pink smudges on the towel. 'Can't be helped.' The water had run out of the tub, leaving bubbles and a faint ring. Ethel or the hotel chambermaid would clean it in the morning. She felt a pang of guilt but knew she didn't want to get down and up again so as to clean it.

She got herself into the pad and the harness, had a look at herself in the bathroom mirror. The effect was decidedly erotic – straps around each thigh, the pad barely visible, pubic hair very much on display. What a glorious thing was the female body! She thought so, at least, but the thought reminded her again of the slaughtered women, and she shook her head to get rid of them.

When she went to open the door, the fear – yes, she admitted it, it had been fear – she had felt

265

when she had heard the noise came back. What if she opened the door and there was somebody standing out there? She looked around for a weapon, thinking herself a fool, doing it anyway, found the scissors with which she trimmed the ends of her hair. She held them in her left hand and turned the knob with her right.

Nobody there, of course. Her heart pounded anyway. She felt as she had in the sanatorium in Davos, weak all over. She took two very deep breaths (deep breathing very much part of the Davos cure, the Swiss mountain air like a knife) and stepped into the room. There was the bed, the trunk, her clothes. God was in his heaven; all was right with the world.

She put the chemise in the hamper for the hotel laundry and hung up the petticoat, the bodice, and the skirt, then rolled the corset and put it in a long drawer with her other corsets. Bending to do so, she caught herself in another mirror, felt a stab of desire. For herself? Was that what the badly painted nymph always showed, self-desire – self-admiration?

She pulled a clean chemise over her head and got out a clean pair of drawers and remembered the bloodied ones she had tossed to the floor.

Where they no longer lay.

She felt breathless again, weak. She had thrown them right there, just off the corner of the bed. Had she picked them up with the other things and forgotten she'd done so? Was she that exhausted?

She looked in the hamper: no. In the dresser: no. In the trunk, for no sane reason, and in the little valise: no.

What had she done with them?

She had thrown them on the floor; that was all that she had done with them.

She got on her knees and looked under the bed: no.

It must have been Ethel. She must have come back for some reason and saw the drawers and knew I was having a visit and took them away to rinse them out. That's all it can be. I'm sure it was Ethel.

Which gave her no comfort but did give her an idea, by way of a tortuous chain of associations that led from her missing and bloodied drawers to the bloodied women to the details of what had been done to them, to Minnie Fitch's failure to get her the medical reports as she'd promised. The medical reports were important, she wasn't sure why. The horrid details would tell her something. Or they would make her feel something, some affinity. Sisterhood. Like nuns sharing secrets.

That was idiotic.

She was dressing, looking over her shoulder, listening for sounds; she was like a dog that had heard distant thunder. She was pulling on stockings.

How do I get the medical reports if Minnie won't get them?

Or how do I could get a look at the bodies? That made her feel nauseated again.

She selected a tailored jacket that fastened down the front, because it was easier when she had nobody to help. It wasn't really proper for evening, but she was going only to the hotel restaurant, and she'd be early, so perhaps it wouldn't yet really be evening.

She looked at herself. She thought of the nymph. She wanted Arthur.

In the lift, the descent did something to her insides that felt a little like the effect of lovemaking, at which she giggled. The boy on duty looked at her as he might have looked at a cow, the most idle kind of curiosity.

'Thank you.'

She was a woman alone, normally a most unwelcome diner, but they knew her and the waiter looked impassive when she said her maid had the evening off. He led her to a table for one that was mostly hidden from the rest of the room. She ate what was put before her, kept thinking about the dead women, tried not to think about her missing drawers and the noise while she was in the bath.

She was barely finished with her hors d'oeuvres when Henry Irving came in. He bowed to her, smiled, then walked over but didn't sit down. 'I daren't ask to join you, Mrs Doyle; it would be too much for the hotel's sensibilities after we appeared together in that motorcar.'

'I shall forgive you, Sir Henry. They're terrible gossips.'

He laughed. 'Actually, I've put some new

business into the play and I need to review it in my head as I eat. Please do forgive me.'

'I do, as I have things to think about, too.'

He strode to his own single table. Her eyes stayed on him, not a difficult thing as he was a commanding man despite his age; he gave a sense of controlled power, although she believed he was in fact quite mild-mannered. Tall, not particularly good-looking, he was yet so overpowering on a stage that some actors were afraid to work with him.

Something from the conversation at the dinner they had shared before Arthur left came back to her. He and Arthur had been talking theatre talk, Arthur allowed to do so because he had written plays; Irving had said something about the absolute need for the artist to seek out reality.

'Whatever we're doing, it's reality; we don't have to seek it out,' Arthur had said.

'Yes, but that everyday reality gets stale, and it's incredibly dull. I mean reality's extremes, Doyle!' He had told them he was visiting Sing-Sing prison the next day, something about soaking up the reality of 'violent men condemned to live in silence.' Arthur had said that that sounded like a hard school, and Irving had said, 'We have to inure ourselves to it, Doyle. We need to know the mad, the condemned, the dead, the dying, the despairing . . .' It had been a long list.

Yes, the dead. That was why she wanted to know about the women – to understand the reality of them: not her responses of nausea and horror, not what *she* felt, but what they *were*.

Louisa watched Irving. She signaled to the waiter. 'Might I have a piece of notepaper and a pen, please.' They came with her main course. She wrote, 'Sir Henry, will you do me the favour of stopping at my table before you go? I have something to ask.' She wrote 'Sir Henry Irving' on the other side and folded the paper and called the waiter again. 'Please take this to Sir Henry Irving. You may read it, as it isn't sealed.'

He didn't read it, of course. Irving did, looked at her, raised his eyebrows, smiled. A fast eater, he was standing by her as she picked through a too-sweet dessert. He said, 'By the time Arthur reads of this in a Midwestern newspaper, they'll have us eloping to some such exotic spot as Jersey City.'

'Oh, surely not.'

'Newark, then. What can I do for you, Mrs Doyle?'

'You said to my husband when we dined together that you look for the extremes of life's experiences. For reality.' His expression said that he was surprised that she remembered. She went on, 'I'd like to look at a corpse. With you.'

'I've seen corpses, I'm afraid.'

'Two murdered women, their insides cut out. "Ripp'd untimely from my mother's womb" – wouldn't that give more meaning to the lines? And their eyes removed, too – like poor Gloucester.'

'I'd never play Gloucester, Mrs Doyle, and I feel

I do the Scotsman pretty well as it is. But you have something else on your mind, I think.'

'I want to see these women who were murdered. It is important to me, Sir Henry. I can't get permission on my own; you know why. I think you can.'

He looked down at her, serious but a little amused. 'I know the right people?'

'You got into Sing-Sing without committing a crime, didn't you?'

'Yes, and out again, thank God. Well . . .' He stood looking away from her. He jingled something in his trouser pocket. 'I suppose I could ask the mayor. I'd have to say you were my assistant, or something of that sort; would that offend you? Although I might say it was for a play Arthur was writing about Sherlock Holmes. No, that makes too much of it and drags Arthur in; let's say simply my assistant, Mrs Doyle. Hmp?' He looked down at her. 'These women were *murdered*?'

'Very much so.'

'Would Arthur object?'

'Arthur isn't here.'

'But I don't want to offend him. I wouldn't want him to think I'd encouraged you in something improper.'

'I think it's for me to decide what's improper.'

'Yes, dear lady, but you can't decide for Arthur. I tell you what; if you'll get him to telegraph me that it's all right with him, I'll do it. If not . . . Please do forgive me, but it simply wouldn't be right.' He gave her a fatherly, perhaps condescending smile. She

271

said that of course she understood, but what she was thinking was that men stood together to . . . to do what? Keep women proper? Keep women pure? Keep women . . . *in their place*? Damn Victoria Woodhull for giving her such ideas, anyway!

She went up to her room and searched all over again for her missing drawers. Before she climbed into bed, she checked the lock on the sitting-room door, then closed and locked the bedroom door and put a chair under the knob. Nonetheless, she spent a bad night.

CHAPTER 7

Anote from Irving was waiting in her pigeon-hole behind Reception just before eight next morning. It was over-polite and too apologetic about his refusal, but he looked forward to Arthur's telegram, so the refusal remained a refusal.

Rubbish!

But it was something to think about instead of her missing underwear, which seemed half-comic to her now, or did until Ethel told her this morning that she hadn't been in the bedroom and hadn't picked up the drawers. Pleased by her evening out with Galt, she had seemed offended by the idea that she might have come back into Louisa's rooms without telling her. Louisa had had to say, 'It's nothing,' although she believed it was in fact some-thing. But what?

To placate Ethel she had said, 'I hope you had a nice time last night, Ethel.'

'*Very* nice. Supper after the theatre at Planabo's restaurant, which is just up the street and quite fairly priced. Mr Galt knew all about it and was very good and sensible about us sharing the cost.'

'The play was good?'

'Sir Henry is a wonderful actor. Seeing him downstairs, I was hardly prepared for what came out of his mouth. I said to Mr Galt, "He's a wonder of nature," and he is.'

Louisa was on the pavement at two minutes to eight, in time to see a cab drive up with Minnie Fitch behind the driver. She jumped down before Louisa could hobble to her. When they were close enough, Minnie handed her an envelope and said, 'I keep my promises, too.'

'Oh, Minnie—'

'Oh, Minnie, yourself!' She stalked off. The doorman helped her up into the cab, although either she was learning to do it or the ankle was really better, because it seemed to go much quicker and she did much of it herself. The doorman tried to tell the driver where to take her, but the driver sneered, 'I awready been told, Bismarck! And I been paid, so cut dirt.' He touched the horse with a whip, turned to say to Louisa, 'Dresses like a general in a operetta, thinks he can tell me my business. Stupid Mick.' As they made their way into the Fifth Avenue traffic, he said, 'This is a grand ride for me, lady, but yous could do it in half the time on the El. *Less* than half the time. *Lots* less.'

She was trying the read the sheets in the envelope that Minnie had given her, but all she could read was Minnie's card, *A .M. Fitch, The New York Express,* and scribbled on it in pencil, 'With my compliments'. She murmured to the driver, 'I can't climb the stairs.'

'Sure you can.'

Exasperated, she gave up trying to read and folded the papers. As she pushed them into her handbag, she half-listened to the driver. He seemed to live in a world of his own insistence: what he asserted, was. He distracted her from the drawers for a while: he told her his idiosyncratic convictions about baseball, the Irish, blacks, the Catholic Church, New York itself. When she asked, he diverted to Bowery and took her down to City Hall that way. She wanted to see the Bowery's gaudy shoddiness as it woke but found that the saloons were already open, the pavements crowded. Bowery was flashy and cheap; it abounded in signs with garish colours and crass, empty promises – Best 25-cent Dinner in New York! Prettiest Girls This Side of Broadway! 3-Cent Beer Lavish Free Lunch! Games of Skill and Chance – Every Man a Winner! Gent's Hotel Permanent Transient Cheap! She shuddered.

Above the ground floors, the buildings mostly turned into tenements; life was already awake there, too. She looked at a woman who was leaning out a window, her arms clasped over her breasts as if she were cold (and she probably was; it was a bright but nippy morning); the woman looked back at her, and they watched each other as the cab moved past. The woman gave her a small wave; Louisa waved back. It was a sign that there was normal life here among the cheap hotels and saloons and erotic shows. That pleased her, she didn't know why.

Before nine o'clock, she was at the basement entrance to City Hall. Leonard was already there and at work. 'They let me in early,' he said with a wave that was too familiar for Louisa's liking. 'How ya doin' this mawning?'

She bent over the files but spread in front of her the pages that Minnie had given her. They were typewritten – the two medical reports on the dead women. No real autopsy had been done, but somebody with medical knowledge had examined the bodies with some care. The language of the reports was clinical, often technical; she wished she had some of Arthur's medical books, which had taught her so much about many things, including her own body and Arthur's. Still, she could follow the words well enough to guess at the Latin terms and make some sense of them.

One of the oddities was, as she had once speculated, that the first body had been washed. It was empty of blood and had no dirt or bloodstains on it. The eyes had been gouged out with a human thumb, not with a tool; some of the wounds had been made with a 'very sharp instrument, perhaps a scalpel,' but others with a 'common knife' to a depth of four inches. Bruises around some of the wounds might have been made by a handle or guard.

The descriptions of the wounding of the lips and

nose were sickening to her, the more so because they were so emotionless. The upper lips had been removed almost to the (Latin term that she took to mean the line of the roots of the upper teeth), the lower to the point where the chin projected. Only the flesh of the nose had been cut off, leaving the septum and bone. All this horror appeared to have been done with the same scalpel-like instrument.

The incision in the abdomen, on the other hand, had been made with the cruder, knife-like instrument, whose blade was estimated to have a thickness of an eighth of an inch. The incision was 'ragged,' the cuts so deep that they had penetrated and even severed the intestines. The womb and ovaries had been cut out along with something named in Latin that she didn't understand; the upper part of the vagina had also been cut.

The examiner had done no speculating about the murderer.

The second body had been 'exsanguinated *in situ*' but was bloody and unwashed; dirt from the alley clung to its underside. As with the first corpse, the eyes had been gouged out with a thumb; the examiner posited that the killer had used the right thumb for the left eye, the left thumb for the right, starting each time at the inner corner of the eye. The breasts had been removed by cuts made by a blade seven-eighths of an inch wide and approximately an eighth of an inch thick along its backbone. These wounds, like the eyes, had bled. The breasts had not been found.

The mouth contained 'one common tennis ball and a gentleman's handkerchief, the latter pushed down the throat.'

The incision in the abdomen had been made 'crudely' by the same instrument, which had penetrated at times four inches and had perforated the intestines. The womb and ovaries had been removed ('forcefully'). The upper vagina had been touched randomly by the blade, but most damage to it had been done by the insertion of a 'tapered wooden cylinder with lower protrusion, not unlike a common nautical pin.' This damage was described at some length using terms Louisa didn't know.

'The eyes were located outside the body but contiguous to it in a paper sack suspended from the pubic synthesis by a "safety" pin under the wooden cylinder described above. The arrangement may have been intended to imitate the male external sexual organs.'

When she was done reading, tears were running down along her nose. One dripped on the page. She fumbled in her sleeve for her handkerchief, blotted her eyes and blew her nose. The handkerchief was ridiculously small and lacy for the job; why couldn't she carry a good, big piece of cloth like a man's?

'You all right there, Miz D?'

'Thank you, Leonard, it's the dust.'

'Right, yeah, gets in your nose.'

She folded the reports and put them in her bag. The second woman had been brutalized while she had still been alive – she knew that now. And the first one? There was no reason to think it had been any different. She had been alive – *alive* – while he had cut off her lips and nose, *alive* while he had hacked into her abdomen, *alive* while he—

She put her hand over her mouth, She couldn't possibly get to the ladies' convenience in time. She made herself stop gagging. She tasted what wanted to come up, fought it, felt it in her nose, forced it down. When she had won, she put her head back and took deep breaths.

'You sure yer okay, Miz Doyle?'

She waved a hand. Oddly, he didn't come over. Leonard had a surprising tactfulness.

She forced herself to work. The women and the reports kept lurching into her mind; she pushed them aside, concentrated on the files. A disgusting taste filled her mouth; her nose and throat stung; her eyes burned. She read, read, read.

'Got one!' Leonard sang out at a little after ten.

'Good for you.'

'We oughta go out and celebrate, Miz D. How about a little lunch at Delmonico? They know me there.'

'Thank you, Leonard, but no.'

The first woman must have been killed where the murderer had facilities. All that blood, but he had washed it away somehow and he had washed the body. *Washed it!* She shuddered. To do such things, and then to wash it the way a mother washes an infant. *Lovingly? Is that what he felt, washing his work*

– *some perverted kind of love?* And he had had a scalpel there as well as a knife, but for the second one he had had only the knife. And he had put a ball and a handkerchief into her mouth to gag her, so that her screams . . .

Louisa closed her eyes, thinking about the screams that couldn't get out.

So the two murders were different. The knife was probably the same, but the killings were different. Why? Because the location was different? Was that all? Or could the second one have been an imitation, done by a different madman? Or done by the same man, but for a different reason? The first victim had been a woman who had visited an uptown hotel; the second had been a common prostitute who had probably never been near an uptown hotel in her life. What was their connection?

Of course, what connected them was their murderer. But did he simply choose at random, killing one day because he saw a woman in a hotel, killing next miles away because he saw a woman in the street? What drove him – an urge, an obsession, a cold calculation? And why need he ever have been in the New Britannic at all? Couldn't he have seen the first victim on Fifth Avenue? Or could he have passed her on the street as she made her way somewhere else?

Louisa could be stubborn. She was stubborn now about what she saw as a possible connection with the hotel, although in fact the only *known* connection was her own sighting of the woman. (Sherlock Holmes would have been contemptuous of this circularity.) The only argument she could make, and it was a feeble one, was that it would probably have been easier for the killer to kidnap a woman in a hotel (mostly empty corridors, many nooks and crannies) than on the street.

Except that clearly he had taken his second victim from the street.

Minnie Fitch was waiting in the corridor when she came out at noon. Louisa was pleased to see her, in fact delighted, but she said severely, 'You were rude to me this morning, Minnie.'

'I meant to be.' She was leading the way up the corridor.

'I have to go to the convenience.'

'Oh, for God's sake, say *toilet*. I hate words like that. Well, go!'

Louisa wanted sympathy because she was menstruating and because of the dead women and because of her missing drawers, but she clumped away on her crutches and clumped back again, and Minnie said, 'You're getting better on those things. Come on.'

When they reached the street, Minnie said, 'All right, I apologize. I was sore this morning. It's over.'

Louisa thought of climbing on her own high horse but grinned instead and burbled, 'I'm glad! And it was my fault, Minnie, partly my fault, because I was a prig. And I have a guest in the house; it makes me cranky. Are we friends again?'

They went into the park and sat on the same bench, but Minnie had brought sandwiches from the bakery where they'd had tea. The sandwiches were miles beyond the sausage things of yesterday, freshly baked bread with crisp lettuce and hard-boiled eggs and bits of pickle and mayonnaise, and others with slices of chicken, and sweet biscuits that Minnie called cookies, like Mrs Simmons.

'Coffee?'

'Can't they make tea?'

'No. N-O. This isn't Blighty. Coffee or GW.'

Louisa looked at her without understanding.

'Go Without.'

'Oh. Well, I'll have the coffee.'

'You're a real sport.'

They talked as they ate – the reports, the second murder, the properties that Leonard and Louisa were finding in the files. 'We have five. They're all in the slums, Leonard says. What do those places cost?'

'Maybe twenty-five thousand each. Four of 'em, that's a lot of moola for a lieutenant.'

'But none for Grady.'

'Maybe Grady spends his on women. Or gambling. Or maybe he doesn't get as big a share. I'll tell you what I think: Cleary is in The Club, which is upper-level cops at Mulberry Street; Grady's not. So Grady gets crumbs. Maybe when it's just him and Cleary, they split even, but

282

Cleary's getting a lot more the other place.' She brushed crumbs off her lap and glared at half a dozen pigeons. 'I hate those things. Rats with feathers.' She sat back and folded her arms. 'Anyway, it doesn't matter. You found enough I can write the story.'

'You won't use my name!'

'How many times I gotta tell you? Monday, I'll aim for Monday. This is gonna be big, Louisa. It's gonna be a scoop, and I'm gonna fly to the moon on it.'

'What about the murdered women?'

'Them, too. I'm gonna tie it all together. It'll be sensational.'

'Are you going to catch the murderer?'

'Don't I wish! No, but you know, I might give him a little dig. Flush him out, maybe. Like the paper knows more than they're telling. Yeah, that's a nice angle.'

'But you don't know.'

Minnie waggled a hand back and forth. They both watched the people in the park. It was a crisp day, the sky starting to turn grey; it felt as if it might snow later. Still, it was better outdoors than working in a basement. Abruptly, she told Minnie about the missing drawers.

'Hey, that's funny. You got a dog? Or a cat? Jeez, I can see the headline, "EVIDENCE OF RATS IN SWANK HOTEL." I'm kidding, Louisa.'

'There are no rats, Minnie. The walls are made of brick, and they're two feet thick.'

'Okay, ghosts. Ghosts are always good copy. A ghost that steals drawers when girls got the monthlies. How about we headline it, "GHOST WITH THE CURSE"?'

'Do be serious.'

'Well, how can I be serious? How likely is it that somebody came in and stole your pants? They didn't steal your pocketbook? Your jewelry? A pair of *underpants*? Sure, there's bums'll do that, loonies, perverts, but Louisa – in the New Britannie? Come on! You kicked 'em under the bed or you threw them in the wastebasket or you stuck them in a drawer.' She grinned. 'Or, you got a ghost pervert.' She jumped up. 'I gotta get to the paper.'

'You're so full of energy.'

'It's this story. I can't wait, you know? I got a couple more pieces to put together, but when I get those, I'm gonna fly! You and Leonard finish up this aft, then Leonard'll bring me what you find and I'll take it from there.'

'Leonard's rather a prize.'

'Has he tried to get into your unmentionables yet, speaking of drawers? Leonard's a poon hound.'

'I think he's rather sweet, in a vulgar way.'

'Between us girls, Leonard would, as they say down South, jump a rock in case there was a snake under it, but he works hard and he really knows the city records.'

'Has he tried his charms on you?'

'Every time I see him. He thinks "No" means "Keep trying."'

Before they separated at the City Hall door, Louisa told her about the tickets that Colonel Cody had given her to the Wild West. Would Minnie like to go?

'Why me?'

Louisa was set back a little. 'Because I want you to.'

'Oh.' Minnie looked suddenly shy. 'Well, sure, okay. You sure you wouldn't rather take Leonard?'

'Saturday evening? Surely you'll have finished your story by then.'

'Well, ye-e-e-s, I guess. Okay, sure. Yeah. All dolled up, a nice supper? Wow, a night on the town. All we need is two men.'

'It was very nice meeting you, Leonard.'

It was twenty minutes to two. They had found five of Cleary's properties. They would never, she was sure, see each other again.

'You ain't leaving!'

'I have an appointment.' She was pulling on her gloves. She didn't have an appointment, but she had made a decision.

'You're supposed to stay until four.'

'I have something more important to do.' She had decided to go to the city morgue, Irving or no Irving – and of course there would be no Irving, because she knew what Arthur would say if she asked him.

'Hey! You can't go outa my life just like that!'

'Leonard, you're a very impertinent young man. I was never "in" your life. I am a married woman.'

'So? You said your old man's a drummer. What could be better?'

'Now you are being offensive.'

'It's love.'

'Goodbye, Leonard. Be sure to take the list to Miss Fitch.'

'You and me coulda made beautiful music together, Miz Doyle!'

'The only music you should be hearing is the wedding march. Find yourself some nice young woman and marry her.'

'Oh, no!' He put his hands on his head and mimed going crazy, then ran around the big space moaning and screaming and shouting, 'No – no, no, anything but that!' And laughing.

She shook her head, but as she went out the door she was laughing, too.

She had to take a cab to the Tombs, where the morgue was, but she managed to get herself in and out by putting some of her weight on the bad ankle; it hurt, but not as much as yesterday. Galt had told her to test it, after all. Well, it was tested, and it had more or less passed.

The Tombs was a prison and a police court. Her guidebook had told her that the building housed 'murderers, incendiaries, burglars, thieves, and all their horrid crew.' But the city's mortuary was down a gloomy, stone-walled corridor below the prison, so that the murderers and incendiaries were pacing the cells over her head as she was led to the proper door. The smell beyond it told her everything.

286

A sceptical-looking young man met her at a battered oak counter, a kind of parody of the New Britannic's Reception and its Cerberus. He was wearing a long cotton coat, perhaps once white, now the colour called Isabella. He looked at her, frowned to show that he disapproved, and then said, 'Can't be done. No visitors.'

'But of course there must be visitors! These are the dead!'

She had no idea how many people died every day in New York, or how many of those found their way to the city morgue, but she thought that there must be hundreds beyond the metal door the young man was guarding. Surely they couldn't be just left here, ignored, forgotten! She said, 'I demand to see these unfortunate women. I wish to pay my respects.'

One side of his mouth curled up. 'Respects, is it. You a professional girl too, that it?'

Louisa fell back on her training in a teachers' college. Her voice was frigid. 'Do I look it?'

He looked at her, flushed, shrugged. 'Anyway, can't be done. No visitors.'

'Why?'

'This is the city morgue! It ain't the Toole and Hanrahan Undertaking Parlour! We don't do viewings!'

'I want to see the two women who were murdered in the Bowery, young man. If I don't, Commissioner Roosevelt will hear of it!'

'Commissioner Roosevelt, oh, la-di-da. What you

think he's got to do with the morgue, for Cripes' sake? He's the *police*! Anyway, there's only one woman murdered in the Bowery here now; the other one's gone.'

She was dumbfounded. 'Where?'

'Family.'

'What *family*?'

'I got no idea. Somebody came and identified her and claimed her. She's probably in the ground by now. Go pay your respects there.' He laughed, enjoying his own joke. She wanted to hit him, thought she very well might, but then the metal door behind him opened and things changed, because Detective-Sergeant Dunne came through.

Dunne looked at her; his mouth opened and a frown formed as if he were trying to remember how he knew her, and he said, 'Miz Doyle!' Behind him, a smaller man came out and looked at her as if he recognized the name that Dunne had just pronounced.

'Detective-Sergeant Dunne.' Louisa tamped down her anger at the young man. She smiled – she knew her smile had worked on the detective before. 'What a happy coincidence! Would you *please* tell this young man to allow me to see the latest victim of this butcher!'

'*See* her. You don't want to see her, Miz Doyle. I just came from seeing her, and I've seen a lot, but . . .' He shook his head, looked as if for support at the smaller man, who nodded as if to say that it really was whatever the detective-sergeant hadn't managed to say. Dunne murmured, 'This is Detective Cassidy. Miz Doyle, Cassidy.'

'I want to see her.'

'Why?' Dunne scowled. '*Why?*'

'You know why. You understood when we talked. This maniac is murdering women!'

'And so you want to *see* her? Isn't that a little morbid, Miz Doyle?'

'What are you suggesting?'

'It isn't normal for a nice woman to go looking at corpses, now, is it?'

'Normal! No, it isn't *normal*. Are you like all the rest, Detective-Sergeant? You want me to be a good little woman and go back into the box like a dolly when I'm threatening you with not being what you call "nice?" All right, I'm not *nice*. I want to see her.'

'Well, you can't.'

'Give me one reason.'

'There's a law. No unauthorized persons viewing deceased or injured or sick persons in city facilities.' He looked at the young man. 'Right?'

The young man was delighted. 'Exactly what I tole her.'

'You didn't, you fool; you accused me first of being a prostitute and then you said "la-di-da."' She turned on Dunne. 'I'll go to Commissioner Roosevelt if I have to!'

Dunne sighed and took her arm. 'Let's go to the out-of-doors; I'm sick of smelling death.' He started her away from the desk and the young man, and she tried to object, but he kept hold of her arm and made little sounds of the sort he might have made to a stray dog or a horse – 'Now, now, now, there,' and 'It's fine, you'll be fine . . .' until he had her out in the silvery light. Then he released her and faced her and said, 'You really must not go in there, Miz Doyle. It's too horrible for the likes of you.'

She returned his look. She felt no fear of him. Cleary and Grady had flummoxed her, but a great deal had happened since then, and anyway she had liked this one. Up until now. She said, 'You're just like all the rest.'

He sighed again. He chewed his lower lip, said suddenly, 'Cassidy!'

'Right.' The detective had come up behind them.

'Can you walk back to Three Hundred?'

'Well, if I have to . . .'

Dunne nodded. 'Off you go.' He faced Louisa again. 'I've got a carriage. I'll take you back to your hotel, and we'll have a little talk, you and me.'

'I can get myself back to my hotel, thank you!'

'You can, but a policeman is *telling* you that you're going in a police carriage. Now look here, Miz Doyle, I'll put it straight before you – you charmed the daylights out of me yesterday, but this time I see I should have been tougher on you. You're just too close to these murders. You see? I can't let it go like that. You see a victim in the hotel; you get visited by Cleary; you've got

290

something going with that hotel detective about the murders. Now you want to see a mutilated body! It won't do! I can't let it go! You're coming with me in the carriage.'

'Or else what?'

Dunne sighed again, a long, theatrical sigh this time. 'You'd tire out a steam engine! Or else you'll spend a few hours at Three Hundred with people who aren't as pleasant company as I am. Oh, come on, ma'am!' He led her to the kerb. He had had the wisdom not to take her arm this time, not to seem to force her. She followed him. His threat was perhaps real enough, but what really took her after him was his seeming to *suspect* her.

The 'carriage' was really a kind of buggy, barely big enough for two. She saw why Cassidy had been made to walk. 'Up you go.' Dunne held out his hand for one of hers.

She looked dubiously at the narrow step. 'I'm not sure I can do this . . .'

'Sure you can!' Without warning, he picked her up under the arms and raised her so high that she was able to find the buggy's floor with her good foot, first yelping and then saying, 'Detective-Sergeant!' and then letting herself down on the buggy seat so that the vehicle swayed. 'Detective-Sergeant Dunne!'

'Short way round Robin Hood's barn.' He took her crutches and pushed them under the seat, cross-wise of the buggy, then ran around and climbed up on the outside. The horse, blindered and bored, turned its head but wasn't able to see what was going on; it didn't seem to care, dropped a load of manure on the street, and then moved out in a leisurely way as Dunne flicked a rein over its back.

'I don't like to be manhandled in the public street, sir.' She heard what she'd said, added, 'Or anywhere else.'

He looked at her, chuckled. 'You're a dinger, you are.'

'What are your suspicions of me?'

'I didn't say I had suspicions.'

'You as much as did. Get on with it!'

He shook his head, urged the horse into a near-trot. He seemed at home with reins in his big hands. 'I thought I'd show you a bit of New York as we go, do you mind? We'd go up to Mulberry Street and maybe go by where the murders were found.'

'I'm surprised you don't find such a thing too morbid for me.'

They rode in silence for a hundred feet. He said, 'Now, where we are right now is Park Row, heading sort of east. See, this corner here is Bowery.' He pointed at a congested opening between the buildings; down the centre of it ran a girdered construction that seemed to suck all the light from the street below. 'That's the elevated railway, what we call the El.'

'I have been on the Bowery, and I know what the Elevated is.'

'The Bowery's got more life than a trunkful of monkeys.'

He touched the reins to the horse's back to move it along. At the foot of Bowery, they went back into Park Row and then left into a broad road that was filled with vehicles. He said, 'I'll show you the eighth wonder of the world if you don't mind taking the time.'

'If I say no, will you arrest me?'

'Not if you behave yourself.'

He urged the horse into the fastest line of traffic, but they were all fast. She sensed hurry, tension here, as she had not in the other streets. They were going up a long approach; on each side, the second storeys of tenements were on their level, then the third storeys as they climbed. Ahead, two enormous arches appeared. He said, 'Know what it is?' She knew, but she shook her head.

'The East River Bridge. The Brooklyn Bridge, most of us call it. It's really something.'

She asked him where her hotel was and he pointed behind them and to the left, told her how many miles away it was. She said, 'We shall be hours!'

'Nah.' He maneuvered the carriage to the middle of the roadway just before they reached a line of toll booths. He stopped, causing other drivers to shout and curse. He held up a wooden sign from the dash that said 'POLICE.'

'Isn't that about the grandest thing you ever saw?'

The view downtown was spectacular, the first lights coming on along both banks of the great river, the sun down but its pinks and greens in the sky and reflected in the water below. Despite her annoyance, she was moved: natural landscape was sublime, she had been taught, but so was this, surely – a human landscape made sublime by the moment and the light and the great bridge whose cables soared up in great arcs like hope itself.

Dunne began to recite:

'Flow on, river! flow with the flood-tide, and ebb with the ebb-tide!
Frolic on, crested and scallop-edg'd waves!
Gorgeous clouds of the sunset! drench with your splendour me, or the men and women generations after me!
Cross over from shore to shore, countless crowds of passengers!
Stand up, tall masts of Manhattan! stand up, beautiful hills of Brooklyn!'

He looked at Louisa and grinned. 'Whitman.'

'You astonish me.'

'I learned it so's I'd know it if I ever took a girl for a ride across the bridge.'

'And did you?'

'I did, but I couldn't recite it. I was too embarrassed. She married me anyway.'

He moved the carriage across into the lines of traffic heading back to Manhattan, and they started down again. 'Now you've seen the Brooklyn Bridge,' he said.

When they came off the approach to the bridge, he turned right and then partly right again as the street made a bend. 'Now we're in Mulberry Street.' He sounded pleased.

She saw tenements rising on each side like cliffs; many had decorated façades all the way to the top, where stone faces looked down. Inexplicable names – Barbara, Halston, Meyerbeer, Grace – were carved in large letters. Dunne said, 'Don't be fooled by the fronts. Inside, it's a half-dozen families to a floor and one convenience per storey if they're lucky. If they're double-deckers, there's no windows in the middle flats. The weather's good, they live in the street.' Late in the day as it was, pushcarts lined both sides of the street, and women with baskets pressed themselves against them. They were dark, often tough-looking women, some with the popping eyes and almond-shaped faces of Renaissance paintings, others with aggressive noses and shrewd, hard eyes.

'They must be difficult customers,' she said as she watched a woman lift, appraise, and put down an apple. 'You grew up here?'

He shook his head. 'I'm Irish. These are all Dagos now.'

'But you're a New Yorker.'

'Born and bred. All Irish then; not so much now. People move uptown when they get some money. Now this is Little Italy – one of the Little Italies.'

In the fading light, people were leaning from windows and iron fire escapes; chairs were out on

295

the pavement despite the chill, leaving hardly room for a single line of pedestrians between them and the pushcarts.

She said, 'I never see any coloured people.'

'We drove them out. We used to have gang fights with them when I was a kid. The coloureds lost, so they moved way over west and uptown – the forties. Now we're up there and moving them out again.'

'Why?'

'Because if you're Irish, you got to show you're better than somebody.' He smiled. 'And the coloured aren't better than anybody.' The smile took up only one side of his mouth.

They jogged along. People were calling in a foreign language; shirtsleeved men and boys were playing a card game on the pavement. She heard music, a singing voice, a sentimental melody. She was aware of cooking smells, baking bread, the usual city stench of horses and dust and people and the rivers.

'There are so many of them,' she said.

'Isn't London the same?'

'Parts of it, but it isn't the same. We don't have so many Italians, for one thing. Perhaps the truth is I don't go into those parts of the city.'

'Same thing here. Most New York people never come down here. These are the slums. This is just a place you try to get out of.'

'As you did?'

He nodded. 'As I did.'

He jerked his head towards a big, once-white building. 'Police headquarters. There's Cassidy, just walking in.' He laughed. 'He must have stopped for a pailfull someplace.'

He turned the carriage to the right. 'Here we are in Bowery again. Not "the Bowery," but Bowery, which is a street. "The Bowery" is a state of mind, meaning cheap everything, crooked everything, sleazy everything, the last resort of the down-and-out, a place to get fleeced, a place to get chloral in your drink, a place to get rolled, taken, flim-flammed, killed.'

'I can't imagine living here.'

'You'd do all right.'

He turned again and went to the next street and turned down it. 'This is Elizabeth. You want to see where the first woman was found?' He went another street and pointed at a dark opening between buildings. 'In there.'

She looked in. Its ordinariness frightened her. In there, a man had posed a dead woman, arranged parts of her face on a pile of manure where her womb had been. She shuddered. 'How did he do it?'

'Without getting caught, you mean? This place is dead at night. Until midnight, one in the morning, it's alive; then everything closes up, they lock all the doors and put out the lights. You could do anything in an alley like that, three in the morning.'

'But he had to bring her here.'

'Maybe not. Maybe he killed her in a flat upstairs, dumped her out the window.'

'You know he didn't.'

'Wasn't it you told me to consider every possibility?'

'Nobody mentioned any marks of the kind she'd have had if she'd been dropped. And there's been nothing about the buildings here, people hearing or seeing anything.'

'People around here don't hear or see things – even when they hear and see things.'

She sat up as tall as she could and looked back up the street, then down, then again into the alley. 'You can't just carry a dead woman on your shoulder, Detective-Sergeant. And the policeman said her legs were stiff. Could you move a stiff body in a pushcart?'

'You can move a lot in a pushcart. Though I wouldn't want to do it for much distance, I can say.'

'Or a wagon! A horse and wagon could carry a lot.'

He started their horse going again. 'You use a wagon, you gotta own a wagon. Or steal one. A lot easier to steal a pushcart – you come down here after dark, you see pushcarts chained to lamp-posts and things all over the place. You steal one, though, you better know what you're doing, because the owner'll kill you.'

He showed her where the second body had been found; there was little to see there, little enough where the first had been.

He crossed on Canal to Broadway and turned up.

She said, 'I thought you were going to question me.'

'I just wanted to get to know you.'

'I'm no longer improper for wanting to see the bodies?'

'That still bothers me.'

'What did that oaf at the morgue mean by saying that the first victim's body had been identified and taken away?'

'Just what it sounds like.'

'Did you know about it?'

He didn't answer, seemed to concentrate more on the horse.

'Detective-Sergeant Dunne, did you know that the body had been taken away?'

'I can't discuss police business.'

'So you didn't! What kind of police do you have here? I thought you were in charge of the investigation!'

He made some movement with his shoulders, perhaps a shrug. 'There's layers upon layers.'

'Of what – lies? If the body has been taken away and buried, and you don't know about it, then who identified her? And who *was* she?'

He flicked the horse and sighed. 'I don't know.'

That silenced both of them.

It was past the time when she wanted to be at the hotel, but she said nothing: what good would it do? The horse and the traffic were moving as fast as they could. She found herself almost asleep, then abruptly awake as the brightly lighted mass of Madison Square Garden appeared, a huge sign for the Wild West across its façade, and Dunne turned left into Twenty-third Street and they were at her hotel. 'I've made you late,' he said.

The doorman had appeared to help her down. Had she a coin?

Dunne jumped down. 'I'll help the lady.' He made a sign towards the doorman as if he were wielding a small broom and the doorman were dust. He reached up for her. She hesitated, then leaned down, allowed his hands to grip her under her arms, aware of his hands so close to her breasts, and her good foot was on the pavement and she was steadying herself on his shoulder. 'I wonder what gossip the doorman will spread about *that*,' she said.

'Nothing, or he knows I'll have him for breakfast.' Dunne retrieved her crutches. 'And I hope you enjoyed the Municipal Police deluxe tour.'

She thanked him quite formally. Her annoyance with him had dissipated, but she felt disappointed in him because of the first woman's having been taken from the morgue and his apparently knowing nothing about it.

She went up the steps and looked back as Gerrigan opened the doors for her. Dunne was still in the carriage, looking at her. She gave him a little gesture and a smile despite herself.

In the hotel, she went straight to Reception and then the telephone booth and left a message for Minnie at the *Express* to say that the first victim

300

had been identified and the body taken away, but it was all very fishy and she thought something was being hushed up.

She lay down on her bed still dressed. It amused her that Dunne had been flirting with her (what else could the poetry have been?), then annoyed that he had been doing it so as to 'know' her – meaning to satisfy his suspicions of her. Why couldn't he understand that she wanted to see the corpses *because* of the horror of them, because of the awfulness that he seemed to think was improper for her? Did he think the horror was improper for the two victims? For the next victim?

What was there to be done? Except for Dunne, the police seemed to be doing nothing: the newspapers had reported nothing that suggested progress, except that the vagrant who had been held 'for his own protection' had now been charged with the second murder. Everybody must have known he hadn't done it, couldn't have done it, but he was charged anyway and the police said that they had a confession. Beaten out of him, she supposed. But they hadn't found a knife, and he couldn't have done the first murder because at that time he'd been in the city jail in Jersey City, just across the North River. Hopeless. A dead end. A very dead end.

She sat up. She would look at the railway schedules and consider joining Arthur. He was still in the Midwest; she could be with him late tomorrow. It was foolish of her to go on in New York. She could get about on the foot now. She would be walking on a cane in a few days. What had she been thinking of – that she would find the murderer herself? Avenge the women?

Then she heard the sound.

'It was a kind of click, Ethel – like the closing of a wooden box.'

'I can't imagine, madame.' It was the next morning, and Ethel was still reliving her evening out.

'I told you about the other sound. While I was in the bath.'

'Well, old buildings are full of funny sounds.'

'This is hardly an old building.'

'It could have been the wind. Or a bird hitting the window.'

'No, it didn't sound like that. It was a *click*.'

'Well, madame, those women upstairs hear all sorts of things.' The women upstairs were the other personal servants. 'You'd think they've nothing to do but frighten themselves with hearing things and chattering about it. I had a good laugh at them with Mr Galt, I must say.' Ethel was going over Louisa's clothes to see what needed pressing or laundering, as she did once a week.

But Louisa was thinking again about the noise, which had so frightened her that she had slept on a sofa in the sitting room with the bedroom door locked, although the night before, she'd slept in the bedroom and locked herself in against the sitting room. *I'm being very silly*, she thought, and she said, 'I'm thinking of joining Mr Doyle.'

There was a moment, but only a moment, of silence, then, 'Leaving New York, you mean, madame?'

'I'm thinking about it.'

'Then I oughtn't send out the clothes, ought I.'

'It isn't certain yet, Ethel.'

'We wouldn't want to leave anything behind.' Though what she seemed to be saying, except for that instant's hesitation, was that she would be leaving Galt behind, but that was life. She went on taking clothes out of the cupboard and the drawers, holding them up, smoothing them, putting some back in and laying others in two piles on the bed.

After several minutes, Louisa said, 'What do the women upstairs think they hear?'

'Oh, madame! They say they hear ghosts.' She sounded scornful.

'What ghosts?'

'Oh, they're full of tales. "Full of wind and whiskers, like a barber's cat," my Aunt Emmeline used to say. The ones of them that have been here the longest, that work for ladies who live here, I mean, tell a great tale they've made up of a male and a female ghost, and they don't like each other, and so you can hear the female one running. It's quite ridiculous.' She held up the grey silk dress and turned it to look at the other side, found something she didn't like and took a pin from her bodice and pinned it into the dress. 'You've put a little tear into your grey silk.'

'Have I?'

'I'll mend it when I have a bit of time. How those busybodies upstairs ever get any work done, I don't know. *Some* of us don't have time for ghosts.'

'Who are they the ghosts of – I mean, who were they? Do they say?'

'One, the male one, is supposed to be the architect of this place; they say he killed himself by jumping off the roof. For all I know, that's a true piece of history, but it could be just another tale for all of me. The woman ghost is a French lady's maid.'

'Heavens.'

'Well, there really was such a person, madame. I asked Miss Castle, who is old Mrs Simmons's maid, and she's been here as long as Mrs Simmons has, and she says that there truly was a French lady's maid who disappeared two years ago and has never been found. Miss Castle is too sensible to believe in ghosts, but she says there *was* something strange; the woman simply vanished, and her employers, who were French themselves, didn't change their plans but went back to France and that was that.'

'Surely she was looked for.'

'I suppose she was, although Miss Castle says the hotel was very stiff about telling things to the press.'

'Perhaps she ran off with somebody.'

'Well, madame . . .' Ethel hung a dress back up in the cupboard and lowered her voice. 'According to Miss Castle, the lady's maid was, you should pardon the expression, *carrying on* with the monsyoor.'

'Oh – you mean her employer.'

'Well, she was the wife's maid, but it was with the husband she was . . . you know.'

Louisa did know, but she was thinking about something else. Only two years ago. That was not such a long time. And somebody had told her something else that had happened two years ago in the hotel. What was it? It flitted in and out of her head like an evening bat. It was no good. She couldn't get it. She realized Ethel had asked her a question. 'I'm sorry, Ethel; I was wool-gathering.'

'Do you want me to hold off sending the clothes out, or are we staying?'

'I don't know; I don't know. Just leave them as they are today. I'll . . . think about it.'

She was hobbling on one crutch now, able to maneuver pretty well. She now and then forgot and put her right foot down. It hurt, no question of that, but the pain didn't seem to last, and the swelling was partly gone. The foot and ankle were still rather lurid, although faded; her face was much better, in fact almost normal. Or at least not so bad as it had been. She said to Ethel, 'I think I want a cane.'

'Oh, isn't it too soon, madame?'

'That remains to be seen. I shall also need a shoe, as I can't possibly get my own shoe on that foot, not to mention the bandage that Galt insists I wear.' She'd been wearing both of a pair of heavy black stockings on her right leg the last two days, with no shoe. 'I can't go limping about on a stockinged foot for ever.' She thought about the cost of buying shoes so as to have a right shoe in a size that would go over the foot and the bandage. Money thrown away, because the shoe would be useless once the foot was normal again, not to mention the left one, unworn. 'I'm going downstairs, Ethel.'

'Yes, madame.'

She limped out on the single crutch, feeling like Tiny Tim without the cheerfulness. The elevator operator, now a familiar, nodded and didn't bother to call out the floors. She went at once to Reception and asked to speak to the housekeeper but was told that Mrs Wayne was on three seeing to a conversion, whatever that was. Not a religious one, she supposed. Told that the woman would be down 'shortly,' she said she would wait in the lobby.

Mrs Simmons was not yet at her table, but Manion was already in his chair against the far wall. His eyes locked into hers. To her surprise, he looked away.

Her foot hurt, but she went to him and she sat down in an armchair next to him. He said in a sour voice, 'I got a going-over from a cop. Twice.' He looked away again, then back at her, his eyes miserable. 'You told him about me getting the cop's draft report on the first murder for you.' He allowed anger to show.

'Was it Detective-Sergeant Dunne? I didn't know it would make a difference, I'm sorry.' She said, 'Do you know anything about a lady's maid who disappeared two years ago? French.'

He pushed himself deeper into his chair as if to get away from her, frowning. 'The Frenchwoman. That one? Yeah, I know something. Between keeping the cops quiet about her and trying to find out what happened to her, I was busier'n a dog with six legs and fleas.' He laughed too loud, too fast. Then, a silence.

She filled it with 'What happened?'

'She disappeared. Like that, pouf. One day she was here, then she wasn't.' He was scowling, his voice almost bitter – still, she thought, because of Dunne. 'Who told you about her?'

'There's talk among the servants. She's a ghost now, it seems.'

'Oh, the ghost. Yeah, yeah.' He waved the idea away with a gesture, gave a kind of shrug as if to get rid of whatever was tormenting him. 'Well, to be a ghost she'd have to be dead, and I could never find that she was dead.'

'The police?'

'Oh, the wonderful "New Yawk" police! Yeah. But Carver wanted it kept quiet, so the cops backed off and took some cash and I did the work. And came up empty.'

'Carver paid them?'

'*I* paid them. I mean, I was the middleman.'

'Cleary and Grady?'

'Nah, this was Missing Persons, not Murder. What're you after this time?' He sounded hostile.

She hadn't really put it into words before. 'The French maid would be another woman from the hotel. The first chronologically.'

'Oh, your hobby-horse.' He shook his head. 'But the French maid wasn't murdered. It doesn't fit. Anyway, it isn't your business.'

'Why not!'

He leaned towards her, his frown ferocious, his voice punishing. 'You know why? Do you know how many people die in this city every day? You know how many die and nobody cares? People die here in rented rooms and they don't find them for a week! People die in the gutters, they sweep the dirt right over them! We look the other way here. It's how we get by. Leave it!'

She leaned away from him. 'Then shame on you.' She stood. Over his shoulder, she saw Mrs Simmons making her way to her table. Part of her brain registered how well the old woman did with her canes, what care she took to place them, the way she lifted her heavy body on them. She murmured, 'I have to go. I'm sorry if I got you into trouble with Detective-Sergeant Dunne.' Then she said, remembering something that Dunne had told her, 'Are you married, Mr Manion?'

Manion looked at her with angry, defeated eyes.

'What if I am?' He shrugged. He said, 'If you get any more notions about that Frenchwoman, leave me out of it.'

She limped across the lobby to Mrs Simmons. 'Might I sit down for a moment?'

'Oh, hon, do that! I'm dying for company. If that Carver would let me have Fannie down here I'd be all right, but I just hate being alone. You look better, but I'd use a little powder if I was you, not that you want to look made up. How's that ankle? One crutch is better than two, I guess!'

'I wanted to ask you about canes.'

'Oh, I hate 'em.'

'It would be like matriculating if I could move up to a cane, Mrs Simmons.'

'Oh, well, you, yes. You're young and it's only an ankle. With me it's hips, both of 'em, they hurt like knives are being stuck into me, and it's either the canes or crawling. I look like a wounded duck with them, I know I do, but I dare say you'd look pretty smart.'

'I thought it might cheer me up if I got myself a nice cane.'

'There's no such thing as a nice cane, dearie. It's like saying "nice artificial leg."'

'How about "walking-stick," then? Men's walking-sticks are quite handsome.'

'Yes, but try hoisting yourself around on one! You need a handle to lean on. But if you want walking sticks, ask my nephew. He knows where every smart thing in New York is sold. He's kind of a Beau Brummel, if you take my meaning – very big on piling on the lugs.'

But Louisa was off somewhere else – back, in fact, in her conversation with Manion. 'Do you remember a French maid who disappeared two years ago, Mrs Simmons?'

'Oh, that was terrible!' She leaned close, dropped her voice. 'There was scandal.' She straightened. 'They shouldn't allow foreigners into a hotel of this quality. Not French foreigners, I mean; of course, English people are just like us, but the French, well, really.'

'A young woman disappeared.'

'She surely did. She couldn't have disappeared more completely if she'd been a soap bubble somebody had stuck a red-hot needle into.'

'They say her ghost haunts the hotel.'

'Who does? What an idea! Ghost, indeed – I've said it before, ghosts don't haunt, they *inhabit*. And the last place she'd want to inhabit is this hotel, I can tell you, from the way she carried on. Her and her so-called employer. While his wife was doing the stores. It was a scandal.' She leaned forward again, lowered her voice, and tapped the table for emphasis. 'If you ask me, if she *inhabits* anything, it's some sporting house in one of the bad parts of town, because that's where she belonged!' She sat back. 'I take the wife's side.'

Louisa hadn't paid much attention to this. She'd been thinking. *The copper-haired woman comes here for an assignation and is murdered. The French maid has an affair with her employer and disappears.* She said very slowly, because she remembered now what it was she had been told, 'Mrs Simmons . . . You told me . . . that Fannie . . . barked at something in your rooms a year or two ago.'

'Oh, she did. It was terrible. I love her dearly, but I thought the first time she did it, if that dog don't shut up, I'll give her a licking. That's what I thought, poor dear little thing. Now I'm used to it. *Like* it.'

'So it was when you first had her?'

'Yes, I hadn't had her, oh, long enough to know when she had to do her business, you know, and what toys she liked, but not *too* long. I suppose it was a couple of months.'

'When was that?'

'Well – Fannie just had her third birthday three weeks ago; I know that because we had a party for her. I didn't have any other dogs; she hates other dogs; but I had some people. I'd have had *you* if you'd been here, but you hadn't got here yet. It was really nice, even with Fannie barking at everybody.'

Louisa felt let down. 'So her barking came before the French maid disappeared.'

'Oh, she was always barking. Oh, but you mean at my fireplace. Well, no. After, really. You see, Fannie was a year old and a bit when I got her, because she'd belonged to my youngest daughter, who's married to a fairly nice lawyer in New Jersey, but they couldn't stand the noise, so I took her. It was a love match. Sweet little thing.'

Mrs Simmons went on with the details of the birthday party. Louisa smiled and nodded but was thinking about what it meant that the dog had barked at the wall after the French maid had disappeared.

Then the hotel housekeeper showed up.

As she had expected, the hotel had a Valley of Lost Things, actually a boxroom far in the back. Louisa found a pair of shoes with a label, '#244 1887 Hochausen.' The shoes – boots, really – were indeed years out of style but just what she wanted, coming well above her ankle and tied with laces so she could pull the right one tight for support. 'I'll take this one, if I may, and of course I'll return it.'

'You needn't return it, ma'am, it's been so long. And take both.'

'I need only the one, thank you so much.' It was a hideous thing, but it was several sizes too big for her normal foot, and so she could wear it over the swelling and the bandage. And walk! After a fashion.

Coming out of what the housekeeper had called the 'left-behind room,' Louisa almost ran into a hurrying man who turned out to be Alexander Newcome. He was dressed to go out in a very tight overcoat and a rather narrow hat with brims so tightly curled they looked like tubes. He stopped, apologized, doffed the hat, and stood there in what she had heard Arthur call 'an agony of embarrassment.'

'I'm thoroughly ashamed of myself, Mrs Doyle. I disappointed you.'

'Of a carriage ride? Hardly a major tragedy, Mr Newcome.'

'How can I make it up to you? Please.'

His pain was so evident that she smiled. Was he so refined that social pain was the only sort he felt? She said, 'You could take me somewhere to buy a walking-stick like yours, if you like.' Today's stick was quite handsome, ebony with a handle that went out at right angles and would give the support that Mrs Simmons had said was needed.

'I know just the place – quite antique and I think a bit fusty, but they have the best sticks in New York.'

'That would be lovely.'

He insisted that he take her to lunch, as well – tomorrow? And a ride in Central Park? And he would show her a remarkable block of French flats called the Dakota. And the millionaires' castles on Fifth Avenue. And—

'Enough, enough! We'd need a week, not an afternoon, and I must be back to dress to go out.' She would be meeting Minnie to go to the Wild West. And of course she *would* meet Minnie, so of course she wasn't packing up to go and meet Arthur. What had she been thinking of?

Of course.

When had she made that decision? Perhaps when she was talking with Mrs Simmons. The French maid, the dog. Manion's saying, *It isn't your business*. Meaning that it wasn't his, either, because she saw that Dunne had unmanned him somehow. What had he said? *Leave me out of it*. She felt a niggling disappointment. And he was married.

She picked up her letters at Reception and went up in the lift, leaning on her crutch and sorting through them. Two from Arthur, one mailed in Minneapolis and one on the train. Oh, dear, he must be beyond Chicago already; how had she lost track? She knew, of course: the missing garment, the noises, her fears, working for Minnie at City Hall.

Under the letters was an envelope from the hotel. From another guest? She started to open it, found that she had reached her floor, and so clumped out. It was hardly correct to read it in the corridor, so she went on to her rooms and let herself in. Ethel was in the bedroom, sewing.

'I've decided not to leave New York just yet, Ethel.'

'Yes, madame.'

'Mr Doyle is all the way beyond Chicago; it's no good our going to the expense to travel all that way, as he's coming back quite close – Philadelphia – rather soon.' It was an aspect of the tour he'd objected to, and she agreed that it was foolish – both inconvenient and inefficient: he went to Chicago and then backtracked to several other cities, then south to St Louis and so east again from there. Louisa thought that Marie Corelli's plan of going out from and back to New York was a much better one, but of course she wouldn't say that to Arthur. So now she said to Ethel, 'Perhaps we'll leave in a few days and meet him in Pittsburgh, Pennsylvania.'

'Of course, madame.'

Louisa went back into the sitting room and fell into a sofa and opened the hotel envelope. She expected a personal note from some new acquaintance; instead, there was a bill. It was dated the day before and covered the time since Arthur had left.

Only a formality, I suppose.

But her eyes went to the bottom, where it said 'Balance' and 'Payable upon receipt,' and there was a figure that made her heart pump – a hundred and seventy-seven dollars and eleven cents!

Of course, it had to be a mistake.

But the mistake was hers. She had been eating all her meals in the hotel, and so had Ethel; she had had meals sent up when she wanted. She had bought things for the children every day on the mezzanine and charged them to her room. She had sent telegrams. She had sent boys off with packages to be mailed to England.

And she had been charged for three visits by the doctor and five by Galt!

And two dollars a night for Ethel's room upstairs!

She knew she was blushing, and she knew why: she was angry, and she was ashamed. She had assumed that all the bills would wait until Arthur returned to pay them.

I was leaving it to him. Leaving it to the man to fix. Only a woman . . .

She jumped up and cried out when she landed on her ankle. Well, all right, she'd been a weak-minded fool; she'd been *stupid*. She'd fix that. But it was beyond bearing that she had been charged for Ethel's room when Ethel was there only because she, Louisa, had tripped on their damned carpet! And that she should be charged for the doctor! And for Galt!

'I shall be downstairs, Ethel.'

'Yes, madame.'

She marched into Carver's office and put the bill down on his desk and said, 'I demand an explanation for these charges.'

Carver looked more like a reptile than ever. She expected a red, forked tongue to slip out between his lips and flicker towards her. He ignored her obvious anger, however, and purred, 'The charges are quite usual, Mrs Doyle.'

'You said my stay here would be without charge until my ankle was better.'

'And you have not been charged for your suite – one of our better suites, in fact.'

'But you have charged me for my maid's room.'

'Your maid wasn't in the arrangement.'

'Did you think I was going to stay here with a bad ankle and no maid?'

'That was quite up to you, of course, Mrs Doyle.'

'And the doctor! Four visits at two dollars per visit!'

'Perfectly normal.'

'But . . . but . . . and then Galt! A dollar a visit by Galt. Nothing was said about Galt costing me.'

'It wasn't part of his usual duties, Mrs Doyle. I couldn't ask him to do it for free, could I?' His hands had come up into Uriah Heep pose.

'I was going to give him something when I left – when Mr Doyle returned.'

Carver looked shocked, actually got a little pale. 'You weren't, surely, planning to stay until Mr Doyle gets back!'

'What about it?'

'Mr Doyle is to be gone for a month! You can't, I mean you mustn't think, you shouldn't assume . . . Mrs Doyle, our arrangement was that you were welcome here *at no cost for your personal living space* until you could get around on your foot, and I've been watching you, and you're getting around.'

'Where? When? I'm on crutches, Mr Carver!'

'One crutch. Both yesterday and the day before, you got into a cab that was to take you to City Hall. Yesterday, I'm told, you went for a carriage ride with a policeman! I've seen you myself, Mrs Doyle, walking around the lobby.'

'That Irish toady at the door – I suppose he told you about the carriage.' She drew herself up. She knew that that was what she should do; she had read the very expression in any number of books. 'Very well. I will leave the hotel.'

He started to look delighted, then looked wary. 'I didn't say you had to do that.'

'You can hardly want a crippled woman taking up "one of your better suites" when you could be getting *money* for it, Mr Carver. No, I shall find another place, *with* my maid, and of course without the expensive medical services this place offers! Naturally, I shall see my lawyers about recovering my exorbitant costs here. And damages, as well.' She didn't have lawyers, of course, but Arthur's publisher did.

'Oh, that isn't wise.'

'I've held off suing you until I saw how matters turned out. Now I've seen. You're a money-grubbing snake, and the only thing you'll feel is the weight of the law. So be it.' Should she turn about and march out now? She wanted an exit with some drama to it. How would Irving do it?

But Carver was wringing his hands and whining: the gist of it was that she'd misunderstood him.

'Oh?'

'I didn't mean for you to *go*. It wouldn't look, it wouldn't be nice, for a guest to leave in, um, anger. I see now that the charges for the doctor and the other one must have come as a surprise; of course, we can make an adjustment. Let's say – half?'

'Let's say none.'

'Oh, well, really—'

'Did I send for the doctor? Never! Did I ask for Galt? I did not. I thought you were sending them both out of the goodness of your hard little heart, or at least because you thought you wanted to be

318

seen to do the right thing. And now you want *me* to pay for it! Really, Mr Carver, you have the gall of a vendor of patent medicines. No, I shall sue.'

'Wait!' She had started away; *I shall sue* had seemed a good exit line. Nonetheless, she turned back. Carver said, 'Let me make you a proposition.' He smiled – a terrible mistake. 'The hotel will, mmm, *absorb* the medical expenses, if you'll agree that from now on, you'll pay for Galt and Dr Strauss at the usual rates. All rightee?'

'And?'

'And, ah, if you will go on the American plan for your meals, meaning you will accept the table d'hote, including the dessert of the day; then we'll charge you only for that and make it, mm, retro-active to your accident.' He hurried on. 'But the maid either goes on the American plan, too, and you pay for her, or she eats upstairs in the employees' dining room with the other servants!'

'I need my maid to help me to the restaurant! Or would you prefer that I not eat?'

'You did need her, yes, you certainly did, of course, but *you don't need her now*. You're getting around real good!'

She tried to draw herself up again, but her ankle hurt. She settled for lifting her chin (about which she'd also read) and said, 'What, then, would be the amount I would owe you?'

'Well, well – let's see . . .' He sat, mumbled some sort of apology and asked her to sit – she did not – and began to scribble on her bill with a pencil.

'Well – we can make the dining-room bills . . . mmm . . . three times nine – twenty-seven dollars. And take off for the doctor and Galt – that's . . . eight plus five is thirteen – um, that's forty dollars off.' He looked up, cringing and threatening at the same time. 'I can't reduce what you spent on the mezzanine for clothes and toys and things.'

'Nor would I expect you to.'

'Hmp. Well, then – how does a hundred and thirty-seven sound?'

'Ridiculously high.'

'Mrs Doyle!'

'I will not pay for my maid's lodging! She was as essential to my recovery as . . . as . . . as your useless doctor.'

'But Mrs Doyle, when you think of what it's costing me for your suite . . . !' Something happened to his face – the arrival of an idea – and he smiled and looked like a crocodile. 'I'll make a deal with you.'

'I think not.'

'We've got some very nice single rooms in the annex. If you move to one of those, I'll throw in lodging *and* meals for your maid for gratis. How about it?'

'What is the annex?'

'Next to the hotel. It's part of the hotel; there's connecting doors. We bought it eight years ago because we had so many clients. It's every bit as fine as the hotel itself.'

She knew that that couldn't be true. She was

vaguely aware of a door on the mezzanine through which she'd seen people coming and going. She knew instinctively that the annex would be a come-down from the hotel. The idea of going there rather hurt her feelings. At the same time, if she could save the entire cost of Ethel . . .

'*En suite*?' she said.

'The convenience is right there off the room. The bath is just down the hall a few steps.'

Just down the hall! She pictured herself walking down a corridor in her dressing gown. And she remembered how she'd grown up, in a tiny house with six other people and a privy out behind.

What came out of her mouth was not anything about the bath, however; it was one of those seemingly random cannons that ricochet off the birth of an idea. She said, 'Have you ever had a guest complain about noises in the rooms, Mr Carver?'

'Noises? This is the quietest hotel in New York.'

'I've heard that people hear noises.'

'Our walls are two feet thick.' He was looking in a drawer for something. 'This hotel was designed along the most modern lines to provide—ah . . .' He pulled out one of the brochures they'd been given when they arrived. 'It's all in there.'

She ignored the brochure. 'People hear ghosts.'

'That's ridiculous.'

'I see by your face that it isn't ridiculous at all, Mr Carver. What your face tells me is that you have had people complain, and you're terrified. What is it – rats?'

'The New Britannic does not have rats! Don't even whisper the word. Do you know what a first-class hotel would suffer if somebody said there were *rats*?' He put his head on his hand; for a moment, looking down at his thinning hair and scabby scalp, Louisa felt sorry for him. He said, 'There can't possibly be rats. Or anything else!'

'People hear things. *I* heard things.'

He looked up quickly. 'You did? What?'

'A kind of click. And one day when I was in the bath, I heard . . . a sort of thump.' She reddened, dug with the toe of her crutch at his carpet, said, 'A piece of my clothing was stolen, too.'

Now he looked truly pale. He swallowed. 'We'll pay you what it cost.'

'It isn't that. It's the *mysteriousness* of it!'

'It isn't rats. We don't have rats.' He stood, but he didn't look at her; he fidgeted, rattled something in his pocket, licked his hips. 'It's hard to get good help. Our housemaids, they stay a long time but they die and so on, we have to find new ones, there's always a bad apple. You know, pilfering. We always make good on that. Just scribble it on a piece of paper so I have a record; we'll reimburse you at once. Cash. You don't need to say what garment it was.' He said that as if he already knew.

But she was thinking about the annex. Did people hear noises in the annex? She was going to ask him, but then she was sure he'd lie to her, so she said instead, 'What was the annex before it became the annex?'

'A private house. Very elegant. Absolutely up to the highest standard. Completely refurbished before we offered it to the traveling public – electricity, hot water, central heat . . .' He petered out, as if his own boiler had grown cold.

'I'll take your offer, including the annex, if you'll reduce my bill to an even hundred dollars.' A hundred dollars was about all she had left, even with the money – such as it was – that Arthur had wired. She felt her heart beating very fast. She'd never bargained for anything before. 'I deserve some reduction for having to stay here in the first place, with the noises and the pilfering and . . . all.'

He moved his lower jaw to one side and stared at her, his head twisted so that he was looking upward at her out of the corners of his eyes. He looked sinister and shifty. 'You won't say anything about hearing noises or losing clothing, will you?'

'You mean, will I sell my silence for thirty-seven dollars? Hardly.'

'People hear talk like that, they get ideas.'

'I am always discreet, Mr Carver. However, I won't stoop to promising silence on a matter of . . . of *public health*.'

He stared down at the floor, then the desk. She was surprised to see that he was trembling. He took a pen and drew a somewhat shaky line through the bill's total and wrote '$100.' He handed it to her, the paper vibrating in his fingers. 'Payable today at the cashier.'

'Of course.'

'And you're moving to the annex, you understand.'

'I hope I shall have the help of the hotel staff to do the move.'

'Of course, of course, yes, naturally, yes . . .' He seemed disoriented. She left him without saying anything more, leaving him staring at his office floor.

'We're moving, Ethel.'

'Oh, madame!'

'Only next door into the annex. Do you know the annex? It's quite part of the hotel.' The truth was, she knew she was taking a step down – after all, what did 'annex' mean? And what would Arthur say about it? But she was saving money. Surely he would understand.

Hearing nothing from Ethel, she put her head into the bedroom and said, '*Do* you know the annex, Ethel?'

Ethel looked severe. 'The people who stay in the annex rarely have servants, madame, so I wouldn't hear. I believe it's patronized mostly by the better sort of traveling men.'

'Oh.' That complicated the problems of the bath.

Ethel said, 'The rooms over there don't have bells to call the servants, even. You'd have to go to Reception to have them ring for me.' The words seemed to give her perverse satisfaction.

'Oh. Oh, dear.' She hadn't thought to ask about

a bell. What else would she find in the annex? She hadn't demanded a room in the front, but surely Carver would give her one because she was in a front room now. She pictured herself huddling in some back attic like a despised relative.

'I'm sure it will be quite satisfactory, Ethel.'

And how bad can it be?

The question that answers itself.

Dunne was sitting in a dive called Shankey's with a schooner of beer in front of him that, except for some collapsed foam, held precisely what it had held when it had been brought to him an hour before. Shankey's tolerated cops so long as they ordered – and paid for – a drink. Cops used the place as a sanctuary; it was tucked in behind the House for the Detention of Witnesses at 203 Mulberry and was the Tenth Precinct's refuge from wives, senior brass, and creditors. Dunne used it to think and to make notes where neither Cleary nor Finn could see what he was doing: Finn, who had also been using it as a refuge, had cleared out when Dunne had come in.

At the moment, Dunne had his street directory on the table in front of him with the map pulled out and unfolded so that the city, from Central Park south to the Battery, was displayed. The map was the one that everybody used, Mitchell's map first drawn in 1853 and constantly updated. The island of Manhattan looked in it like a thick penis about to penetrate the New Jersey Bay, which rather tickled Dunne; at the moment, however, he had the map placed vertically so that the penis seemed too flaccid to penetrate anything.

Dunne had had the Wop mark up the map with his researches – the locations of the two 'Bowery Butcher' murders; possible sightings of old men in wagons (not necessarily Jewish) within an hour of the times of discovery; and, a small inspiration of Cassidy's, the locations of the theft of horse-drawn wagons that had been reported to the police on the nights of the murders. Lots of men who could afford a scrawny horse to draw a wagon around New York could not afford a stable, so they left horse and wagon in the street, tied to a weight or a lamp-post. It wasn't strictly legal, but it was cheap; to balance that benefit, there were a lot of thefts. And a lot of those never got reported: the wagons were usually old and rotten; the horses were headed for the glue works. But maybe, if somebody had stolen a horse and wagon to carry a corpse, luck would smile and the theft had been reported.

Dunne found the marks on his map intriguing. They didn't yet form a pattern, nor could he say that they gave him a theory. At best, they gave him a notion, really something more like the kind of images that flow through the mind just before sleep. What his mind imagined now was a man stealing a horse and wagon somewhere uptown to carry a woman's body somewhere downtown. That was all. Not even an old man; not even a Jew. Perhaps not even a man.

326

Cassidy stopped at the bar and got the necessary beer and took a curving path to Dunne that had something to do with not spilling the beer.

Dunne, although he had seemed to be asleep, said, 'Well?'

'Can I drink some of this? I'm perishing.'

'You can as far as I'm concerned. Don't let Teddy see you.'

Cassidy drank deep, holding the back of his head with his free hand as if he thought it might come off as he tipped back. 'Aaaahh.'

'That doesn't tell me much about the matter at hand.'

Cassidy put his beer down and turned an expression of resigned patience to Dunne. 'You're a hard man.' He wiped foam from his sandy moustache. 'I found him.'

'I'm glad to hear that.'

Cassidy opened a small notebook flat on the table. 'Name of Carnahan, William, Number 3077. Walked the beat up in the Sixteenth on the night of the first murder. The only thing he put in his book was meeting Roosevelt.'

'Did he indeed! Teddy vetting the foot soldiers. Admirable. What time?'

'Bit after eleven. But he has no memory of anybody with a horse and wagon.'

'Wouldn't you know.'

'Well, he didn't. We had one stolen from Twenty-eighth west of Ninth Avenue sometime after ten, but if it went by Carnahan, it was invisible.'

'You mean he was too busy having a quick one or he was trading tales with some pal. All right, it was worth a try; you did the best you could.' Dunne looked at his map. '*Maybe* we have him – or her – traveling south on Broadway below Nineteenth Street at eleven-fifteen or thereabouts.' He tossed his pencil down on the map. 'We've done all the connecting precincts down to the Bowery. It's a sad fact, Cassidy, but we're stymied.'

'Until he murders somebody again.'

'You always see the bit of blue in the grey sky.'

The room was smaller than the bedroom she had had in the hotel proper, and of course there was no sitting room. Her trunk and several pieces of luggage would have to go into a boxroom.

She and Ethel spent part of the afternoon sorting her clothes and packing the trunk with things she could live without. Louisa was left with only one evening dress, and she felt rather proud, in a puritanical sort of way, for thus denying herself. She kept one traveling outfit for when she would go to meet Arthur, and her cashmere cloak and her best London waterproof, which wasn't really waterproof but was made of two layers of wool and would be useful in the New York cold. Five day dresses filled the new room's tiny clothes cupboard, and there was space on its shelf for only three hats.

'Well, shoes aren't a problem, at any rate.' She was trying to cheer Ethel, who was suffering pangs of loss of status. 'I have to have room for only one shoe of each pair.'

'Madame means to wear that black boot with every shoe she owns?'

'Only the black ones; the coloured shoes will go into the trunk. For later. We must be practical, Ethel.' She'd broken the news to Ethel that she was to eat in the employees' and servants' dining room; the reaction had been stoic, and for all Louisa knew, Ethel preferred things that way. Still, she said very little all afternoon and oversaw the move to the annex with the resignation of a saint moving to Alaska.

Louisa had determined to see the move as an opportunity, not a bad turn, and as soon as she was in the room alone she sat at the minuscule desk and made herself a budget. She would be ruthless. She wrote 'Budget' at the top of a sheet of hotel paper, then drew lines with pen and the edge of a book and made three columns, 'Item,' 'Proposed,' and 'Actual.' She went back to the top and wrote in the date. The budget would be for the week; next week, she would make a new one.

She began to write down the items – Food, Transportation, Gratuities, Gifts – and bit the end of the pen and then added Postage, Telegrams and Miscellaneous.

The difficult part was filling in 'Proposed.' The truth was, she had very little idea how much she had been spending – on cabs, for example, or on gratuities to the boys and the doorman and cab drivers. In the end, she added up the little money she had on hand and added two hundred dollars as the money Arthur would wire when he got the telegram she had sent earlier:

MOVING SMALLER ACCOMMODATION HOTEL STOP LESS EXPENSE STOP PLEASE WIRE FORTY POUNDS FOR REMAINDER STAY HERE AND RAILWAY TICKETS TO MEET YOU SHORTLY STOP LOVING LOUISA

She made a guess at how long the money would have to last, than pro-rated the total for a week, and wrote that amount at the bottom of the Proposed column. Then she parceled the amount out into the other columns. Food was easy; she knew exactly what the hotel would charge her for its American plan, two dollars and sixty-five cents a day. Transportation was a poser, however. Need she go anywhere? Newcome was going to give her a tour in his friend's carriage; that would be free. She wouldn't have to go to City Hall again, nor down to Minnie's newspaper. And she could walk on her own now, more or less. Surely she could walk to the Madison Square Garden tomorrow night to see the Wild West.

She put a zero in the Proposed column for transportation.

The rest of it was painful: one gift a week for the children, postage reduced accordingly; telegraphic costs that would allow only one telegram a week, and she'd already sent that to ask for more money. Nothing for clothes or small treats for herself.

She liked the feeling that gave her: *Nothing for myself.*

Gratuities. She would have to give less, and less often. She had probably been giving too much, anyway. Whom could she ask? Mrs Simmons, who would undoubtedly set the amounts too low; Louisa had seen one of the boys scowl at her. And she would ask Newcome, whom she had forgiven for offering the carriage when he hadn't meant it, and who was a man of the world.

For Miscellaneous, she allowed herself three dollars a week. She had no idea what it would include.

On the back of her budget she made vertical columns where she could keep a running tally of each category day by day. When she was done, she felt better about everything. Even the smallness of the room comforted her, gave a kind of blessing to her self-denial.

It was not, in fact, a bad room at all. The bed was quite pretty, the furniture good. The walls had been papered in a tasteful pale blue and pink that made it seem larger. To be sure, the room was in the back of the annex, but she had a window that got the afternoon sun (at an angle) and looked out on the blank wall of the hotel itself, so that nobody could look in. She was on the first floor (second floor to Americans) and could see, if she put her forehead against the glass and looked down, the door through which the kitchen workers went into the hotel. She supposed the ones who got the breakfasts came quite early. She hoped they would be quiet. Being the annex and not the hotel proper, there were no two-foot-thick walls to keep out the noise.

She sighed. Arthur would be nearing Milwaukee, and the telegram would meet him there. Then he would go to St Louis and turn east again. She would meet him in Pittsburgh or Philadelphia, depending on the cost of the tickets.

She reread his two letters. One was beginning-to-end complaints, and she skimmed it and put it back into its envelope and into her letter-carrier. Couldn't he understand that she, too, needed something to cheer her up? But that was unfair.

The other letter was a bit more like it, and a good deal better than that in its early part:

My darling little wife, How I miss you, especially in the nights! I miss your dear corporeal self, which I long to hold and kiss and – but you will know what I long to do, as I hope you do, too. This separation seems to me more wearing than the months when you were in Switzerland, because I am doing something I dislike and most days I don't dare have even the comfort of looking forward to a letter. The post here is so unpredictable that I am sure that letters have piled up at hotels I have already left, and there they will lie, the corpses of affection, for years!

I had for a change a jolly evening yesterday at what they called the University Club of Chicago, which is a club for any varsity man who cares to pay the fee. For once, the majority of the audience were male, some wives scattered about but not too many, and all were most appreciative. After dinner, I did have a run-in or two with fellows who rather badgered me (being, I think, the worse for American whiskey), but even these didn't spoil the evening. One of them chastised me for killing Holmes and went on at great length about how I could resurrect him and make the whole business of the Reichenbach Falls – which as you know I worked very hard to make perfect! – a trick of Holmes's, who is really alive and has been haring off after criminals all over the world while poor Watson sits grieving for him. The other chap, who I think was 'in cahoots' with the first, told me rather boozily that I was a genius but not in the way I thought, because anybody could have created Holmes, but the genius lay in creating Watson!

I don't know what one can do with such people. Sober them up, I suppose.

I pray for you daily, my only love, and I wait with the impatience of a Dartmoor prisoner for the time when we shall be together again, and we shall be with our dear children and I shall *have the reality of you in my bed again! Your own loving, lonely, yearning Arthur*

She sat at her window, the letter in her hand, and stared at the dark bricks of the wall opposite. A slow, sleety rain was falling. For no good reason she could think of, she began to cry.

In the evening, Arthur Newcome went through the unpretentious front door of a Sixth Avenue saloon and found himself facing a large man in a boiled shirt who asked if he had a connection. Newcome was prepared; he mentioned a name, offered a card. The boiled shirt open another door, and Newcome entered Paresis Hall.

That wasn't its real name; it had had several names, but Paresis Hall was what everybody who went there called it, or simply 'The Hall.' It was a large room with a bar along the far end, the walls matchboarded up to the height of a chairback, above that a powdery blue-green, with framed paintings and photographs at eye level, most of them of men with not too many clothes on.

A piano and a violin and a viola, or maybe two violins, were playing off to one side. People were waltzing in an open area. Some of them were men dancing with other men, some men dancing with girls who were also other men, but the newcomer had to guess about that. Some of the guessing was difficult.

Elsewhere in the room, men sat at round tables,

some alone, some in twos or threes or fours. A couple of the girls trotted from table to table, where they were mostly tolerated, smiled at, sometimes laughed at, once goosed.

'Best beer,' Newcome said at the bar.

The barman could have fitted into any saloon in the city; he had a moustache, a white apron, a toupee, a white collar and shirt, a narrow necktie and sleeve garters. He pushed a respectably large glass of beer across, took Newcome's money and said, 'New here?'

'Very.'

'Looking for somebody?'

'Ah, let's say "getting the lay of the land."'

'Rooms upstairs if you decide. Bit quiet just now.'

'That suits me.'

He sat at a table by himself, feeling eyes on him, a necessary examination: was he a cop? was he a pigeon? was he a find? One of the girls trotted over and sat down and said his name was Anna May and wouldn't he like a companion?

'I wouldn't, really, but I don't object to buying you a drink.'

'Oh, I don't come here to *drink!*' Anna May laughed. He had a pleasant, soft voice, a manner more deliberately feminine than was quite convincing. His dress was surprisingly tasteful, a reserved dark blue with a wine-coloured bustle. He referred to the other girls as 'she' and said that they were a darling lot, and wouldn't he like to dance?

335

'The only dance I know is the gavotte.'

Anna May giggled. 'Do you really want to be alone?'

'I do.'

Anna May gave a theatrical sigh and a flounce and trotted away to gather with two of the other girls and look at Newcome. He turned away from them to watch the dancing. It was not particularly graceful; two middle-aged men in tweed suits were dancing together and looked to him rather like two bears pushing each other slowly around the room. An older man in a black frock coat was dancing with a younger man, almost a boy, who was wearing a working-man's unpressed trousers and mismatched jacket, no necktie. The man was talking into the young one's ear; he didn't dance well and seemed to be concentrating on keeping up.

Newcome looked around some more, thought it wasn't quite the Café Royal, but one didn't come to it for style or elegance. The Hall was famous. It was said to be the only place of its kind in New York; perhaps it was. It was said to be owned by a policeman, but it might have been only that it was protected by the police and paid accordingly. It was raided now and then, pro forma, but nobody important was ever arrested. It had been closed by the Lexow Commission, but here it was again. Still, once the fact of being there had registered and the glow of the new had worn off, Newcome thought that he wouldn't become a habitué. And the beer was too fizzy.

He glanced across the room and saw a tall man standing at the bar. He was about Newcome's age, well cared for, good-looking in an American way, whatever that meant. What did it mean? Newcome thought it had to do with the air of being well fed, on the edge of overfed; also a sense of self-confidence, even brashness.

The man looked at Newcome. He smiled. Newcome smiled back. The man raised his glass a couple of inches, inclined his head an inch to one side. He raised an eyebrow, raised his glass again. Newcome shook his head. The man detached himself from the bar and ambled over.

'Happy to buy you one,' he said as he got close.

'One's enough, I think. I'm used to English ale.'

'May I sit? Yes, one doesn't come here for the beer, does one.' The man looked around the saloon. 'My name's Frederick.' He looked at two of the girls who were now dancing together. 'I really hate fairies.'

'"Hate" is a strong word.'

'"Detest," then. They give us such a bad name.'

'I'm Alfred.'

'You're English.' Frederick – Newcome doubted that it was his real name – sipped his beer. 'How's the Wilde thing going in London?'

'Badly. It's one reason I'm here. Suddenly it's dangerous to be "so."'

'It's always dangerous. Damn Oscar anyway. He's as bad as those girls for what he does to the rest of us.'

Newcome didn't much care for the talk about 'us,' not because he didn't feel some solidarity but because he was above all himself and he didn't attach himself to groups or causes. They watched the other people dance for some seconds and Frederick said, 'What're your other reasons?' He looked at Newcome. 'For being here. You said Oscar was one.'

'Oh.' Newcome laughed. 'I've an aunt who's going to make me wealthy one day, and I like to keep an eye on her. Not that I mean her any ill; she's a good old trout, but she likes a certain amount of attention.'

'Is that what you do? For a living, I mean. We Americans always want to know what people do for a living.'

Newcome laughed again. 'I *live* for a living. I suppose I'm like a character by Mr Henry James: the American who lives abroad, has no visible means of support, and has discreet but illicit liaisons. We're supposedly spoiled by European immorality, but in fact we thrive on it. Perhaps we even cause it.'

'How did you find The Hall?'

'Drawn by its magnetic properties.'

'Not very magnetic right now.'

'Quite dull, in fact.'

Frederick finished his beer. 'I belong to a club that meets once a week in a Turkish baths after they close to the public. It's quite amusing, really. There are several members who always bring some new lads from downtown. Would you like to go?'

'Tonight's the night?'

'As it happens.'

'My lucky day.'

'Luckier than The Hall, I suspect.'

'Now?'

Frederick looked at his watch. 'If we leave now, we'll be early but not outrageous.'

Newcome looked at him, gauging how likely it was that the man really belonged to such a club. Newcome had had a good deal of experience, some of it bad, in sizing up offers. He said, 'I don't mind.'

CHAPTER 8

Next day, Saturday, Alexander Newcome sent up the message that he had the carriage at the hotel door, and Louisa hurried down, at least insofar as she could hurry. She wasn't accustomed yet to navigating her way out of the annex; there had been a moment when she had turned the wrong way – the old way – to take the lift. She was still taking the lift, even though it was only one floor now; she wasn't about to risk going down the stone steps from the mezzanine, which was what her own floor in the annex communicated with. In fact, if she'd been well, she could have done it in a moment; the short passage into the hotel was only a few feet from her own door. But she had to go the other way, halfway across the annex and then to the rear where the lone lift was, and so down. And then all the way back, to enter the hotel almost directly below her own window.

'I'm so sorry I was so long,' she said when Newcome rose from one of the lobby chairs.

'Not at all.' He was, as always, beautifully dressed, but he looked weary, in fact older. A bad night?

She let him help her to the carriage step by holding her hand and lifting a good deal of her weight; she was able from there to lift her right foot and then pivot and pull herself to the seat. The carriage was open but had a tonneau that could be pulled up against rain. She had expected that Newcome would drive, but there was a top-hatted driver.

'This is so very kind of you, Mr Newcome.'

He began a kind of travelogue of the city as they rode. He pointed out several Fifth Avenue houses and hotels that she had already seen on the motorcar ride, although she didn't mention that. She was really thinking of the telegram she had had from Arthur that morning, cruel in its curtness:

FORTY POUNDS OUT OF QUESTION STOP YOU HAVE SHOWN SELF INCAPABLE FRUGALITY STOP TEN POUNDS FOLLOWS STOP ARTHUR

It had seemed wantonly unkind. In her anger, she had torn up her budget, which was useless, anyway, as she had based it on the certainty of having forty pounds. How did he think she was to live?

A second telegram had come just before noon:

WILL SEND TEN POUND INCREMENTS AS NEEDED STOP IF RAILWAY TICKETS REQUIRED I WILL BUY STOP ARTHUR

She had started to send him a telegram saying that she could not live like a beggar, but she saw the futility of a husband-wife spat at long distance. But she was hurt and disappointed in him.

Newcome showed her Union Square, which would have been pleasanter had the leaves been out; as it was, it seemed to her commercial and rather stark, although Newcome seemed delighted with the permanent reviewing platform for parades.

When there was a lull, she said, 'I have moved to the hotel annex, you know.' She waited for some sign of what a come-down this would be to him; surprisingly, he said only, 'Oh? It was quite a nice private house when I was a boy. I used to visit my aunt's family – where the hotel is now, you know – and I played with the children where the annex now is. They were nobodies, but the house was quite fine.' He seemed little interested. 'And here we are.'

At the walking-stick shop, he meant. It proved exactly what he had said, rather fusty and dark, the mullioned window dirty. The sticks, however, were works of art, or at least of artisanship. She passed over an Irish blackthorn, although she liked its heft and the impression it gave of the country, but Newcome whispered in her ear that they had better ones in London, and this wouldn't do, simply wouldn't do for a lady. In the end, she selected a polished ebony with an ivory handle like a hunting crop's.

'It must bear all my weight,' she said to the stooped old man who was tending to them.

'That stick would hold up this gentleman and more.' But he insisted on measuring the height of her hand from the floor; he pronounced it all right, then went into the back somewhere and came out after several minutes with a new horn tip on the stick.

'If ever there's anything not right, you bring it back. No matter how long.'

She had barely enough money for it. Arthur's ten pounds – *Ten miserly pounds!* – wouldn't arrive until Monday. Could she afford to take Minnie to supper?

Newcome put her crutch cross-wise of the carriage. She rode with one hand on her new stick, admiring it. Even on that cold, damp day she felt better with it in her hand, riding in a carriage up Fifth Avenue and looking, she thought, rather nice in her grey and her velvet hat. It was not, however, compensation for Arthur's telegrams and a growing distaste for the hotel, which she blamed on her move to the annex.

She wanted not to be staying there, if she was honest about it. If she had had the money, she'd have moved to another hotel until she had to join Arthur. Not merely because she was in the annex, but Carver and the noises, and the stories, and . . .

She reminded herself that that evening she would be with Minnie, and they would see the Wild West.

Newcome gave her a choice of Clark's for

343

luncheon or Dorlon's Oyster Saloon, the first on the same block of West Twenty-third Street as the hotel, the other on Madison Square. 'Clark's is generally preferred by ladies.'

'In that case the other one, by all means.' She didn't know what she meant by that, the more so as she disliked oysters. But his tone had been so knowing, as if he could predict what she would say, that she chose the other.

The truth was, Alexander Newcome irritated her, now that she had spent a little time with him. He was too clever, too negative, too bored, too *civilized*; she compared him with Detective-Sergeant Dunne – but why was she doing that? – and surprised herself by thinking that Dunne had been a pleasanter guide.

Nonetheless, the afternoon was not painful, particularly as the evening was there to be looked forward to. They cut across Twenty-third Street to Dorlon's, then resumed the tour up Fifth Avenue. Newcome mostly sneered at what he saw but seemed to love the older brownstones because they were unpretentious but 'honest,' the houses of his childhood. Of the grand ones built more recently, he was contemptuous – the block between Fiftieth and Fifty-first, for example, was 'infested with the bad taste of the Vanderbilts,' who had built four houses there. 'Some people should never be allowed to have money,' he droned. 'Or they should put it in trust for the second, perhaps even the third, generation, when taste seems to develop.'

Louisa mostly stopped listening. She enjoyed the smoothness of the rubber-wheeled carriage on Fifth Avenue's well-paved length, a contrast to the streets she had ridden with Dunne; in fact, between bad paving, tramcar rails, and holes, most New York streets were dreadful – certainly worse than London's.

Newcome pointed out the beginnings of Central Park but told the driver to continue up Fifth so that she could see 'vulgarity immortalized in stone.' There were more millionaires' houses, most not yet completed: chateaux, castles, palaces. It was true that the total effect was rather flashy, the competition among them both clear and crass. She didn't tell him, however, that she agreed with him. His perpetual denigration of everything American was wearying.

They turned into the park near the Metropolitan Museum of Art, at which Newcome waved a hand. 'You don't want to go in. You've seen *the real thing* in London and the Continent, without doubt.' They went on across the park and he showed her the huge and elegant block of flats called the Dakota, situated so far uptown that most of the streets around it had been laid out but not paved, most of them without townhouses or other proper buildings. Instead, there were wooden shacks and shanties, hardly houses at all, some seeming to decline into the mud around them. Newcome gave one of his smiles and said, 'The Irish. Hibernian *nostalgie de la boue*.'

She heard the names of landmarks in Central Park – the Ramble, the Mall, the Lake – and looked at those things and found herself not thrilled but not bored, either, a kind of bearable lack of pain. Still, she was pleased, in a muted sort of way, to see people of all sorts in the park, as if they really did enjoy it and really had made it their own.

They passed a statue that he said was Garibaldi, the liberator of Italy, 'insisted on by the resident Dagos; they've put one of Columbus somewhere, too.' Then they started down Sixth Avenue. He offered afternoon tea at the New Netherland but she refused. Back at the New Britannic, she tried to manufacture enthusiasm for the afternoon. He seemed satisfied, perhaps took her muted tone to be an imitation of his own. They parted, both having done their duty.

She went in and started for her old rooms. When she remembered her new room in the annex, she felt her soul sag. *Cheer* up, *Louisa!* She tried to stand very straight and walk gracefully, but it wasn't yet possible with the cane. She realized as she reached the corridor to the annex that she'd left her crutch on the floor of the carriage. *Oh, dammit!* Her ankle hurt from the weight she had to put on it with the cane. Before she passed into the annex, she waved one of the boys over to her and asked him to have Reception ring for Ethel and tell her to bring ice. She gave him five cents. He looked severe.

The ice helped. So did having Ethel there.

But she wanted – what? She wanted to be some-where else; she wanted to be taken care of, protected, *understood*; she wanted to be well away from murders and noises and money worries. She wanted life to be a quiet, pleasant journey that stretched into a quite distant future without bumps or horrors.

She slept.

The Wild West was enchantment. It pulled her out of herself and out of her doldrums, and she applauded with gloved hands and grabbed Minnie's hand right at the opening, when Cody and the entire cast of Indians and cowboys and pistoleros came riding into the arena at the gallop and pulled up within inches of the barricade that separated them from the audience. She gasped, too, when the Indians threatened the settler's cabin, and she laughed and shrieked when the Deadwood Stage was held up.

'I loved it!' she said to Minnie afterward.

'It's bunkum, but I liked it, too.'

Thrilling. Yes, decidedly thrilling.

'But taffy,' Minnie said as they walked across Madison Square, Minnie holding Louisa's hand to help her.

'Don't spoil it for me, Minnie.'

'I don't mean to spoil it; I just mean that the West wasn't like that, and the men didn't dress up like grand opera.'

'It's the way it should have been, then.'

'Well – you're English.'

'Allow me a little romance, Minnie.'

They walked to Clark's –'preferred by ladies' – and had supper. Clark's didn't bother Louisa now; to the contrary, without Newcome's snide comments, the company of women was pleasant, even soothing.

Minnie said, 'I've got an announcement.'

'Oh, Minnie – you're not marrying!'

'No, Louisa! This is serious!' She lowered her voice. 'I'm getting the front page on Monday, and I'm going to tear the Murder Squad to pieces!'

'Oh.' Louisa had pretty much forgotten that part of the last week. 'Did what Leonard and I found help?'

'Help! It's the foundation, the core, the, the . . . *pedestal*.' Minnie held up a fork loaded with veal. 'I've got the dead wood on Cleary. I've got that flannel-mouth at your hotel, too – Carver?'

'You talked to him? At the hotel?' She felt neglected.

'Sure, that's what reporters do. I asked him how much he'd had to give Cleary and Grady to shut them up. I thought he was going to pass out. He's a pill, that one. But I got him.'

'He admitted paying them?'

'He threatened me with the police. That'll go great in the story.'

'And the women?'

'The women. You mean the murders? Yeah, that's in there, too – I tied it all together in a neat little bundle. Murder Squad, murders they aren't investigating, dirty money, Cleary's tenements – it's all there. *And* the identity of the first victim!' Minnie gave Louisa's hand a little slap. 'You really struck gold on that, hon! I'm really, *really* grateful.' Minnie lowered her voice, actually looked around for eaves-droppers. 'Roscoe G. Harding! Whaddayou think of them apples?'

'I don't know him.'

'No, hon, o' course you don't. Harding's a big noise in coal. Millionaire. He just happens to be the husband of the first victim.'

'The woman I saw in the hotel?' Louisa was dumbfounded, and obscurely disappointed, too. But why? She said, 'How do you know that?'

Minnie made the universal sign for baksheesh, fingers and thumb rubbed together. 'A sawbuck to the night guard at the morgue to tell me which mortician had picked up the body; another sawbuck to the mortician's driver to say where the body went next; two sawbucks to a so-called reporter in Mount Kisco to find out who was buried in a private plot up there – Mrs Roscoe G. Harding!'

'But Minnie – at the hotel, she was—'

'That's where it all started. It's beautiful! My article goes from there to Cleary to Carver and Harding, and then I ask the questions: why didn't the police investigate this foul crime? Why has Roscoe G. Harding buried his beautiful wife without a public funeral? What are they hiding at the New Britannic Hotel?'

'Are they hiding something?'

349

'Louisa! You're the one that told me about it. Carver paid off Grady!'

'Only to keep them from mentioning the hotel in the newspapers.'

'Yeah, well, now they're gonna be *featured* in the newspapers. Or in one newspaper, and *I scooped the* World!'

'But what about the second murder?'

'All in good time. That veal was great.' Minnie pushed her plate a half-inch away. 'Vegetables, no. I ate enough vegetables when I was a kid to last me. You ever eat ramps? Ramps and potatoes, ramps and potatoes . . . I want dessert.'

'What does "all in good time" mean?'

Minnie put her elbows on the table and leaned forward. 'It means that on Monday we scoop the other papers. Then they'll start to scramble: they'll be all over your hotel, the cops, Harding – all of it. So we have to keep something for Tuesday, see? So what I do for Monday is ask questions; it's a tease. Then on Tuesday, when the other rags are coming out with their versions of what we've already given, we keep the bulge on them – exclusive interviews with high police officials, a statement from Carver – oh, yeah, he'll be dying to give me one by then – and probably something from Roosevelt, because he's gonna get on his horse the instant he reads the Monday paper! Terrible Teddy will draw his anti-corruption six-shooter, and it'll be better than the Wild West.'

'Minnie – what about the *murders?*'

'They'll be in there. They're the hook, for God's sake!'

'But what's being *done* about them?'

Minnie shrugged. 'Cops've got nothing, because they haven't done anything. That's the guts of the story – Cleary's too busy taking bribes to do the business of the Murder Squad.'

'Is that really true?'

Minnie opened her eyes very wide and spread her hands. 'It sells newspapers.'

'But the head of the investigation is Detective-Sergeant Dunne.'

'But it's Cleary I'm after!'

'Minnie – dear Minnie – there's somebody out there who is murdering *women*. *That's* the gist of your story.'

Minnie shook her head. 'That's old. I mean, I'll go over it again, but you can't trick the same dog twice, or whatever that saying is. If we had another murder, sure. But the two we got were days and days ago. In the newspaper trade, that's a lifetime.'

Minnie had her dessert. Louisa felt her doldrums returning. She had expected to have some kind of woman-to-woman talk with Minnie, something confidential and perhaps whispered, something in which they would share Louisa's fears and talk about the murders. She admitted to herself that she had fears now; why couldn't Minnie sense them?

Walking back to the hotel in the bright glow of

West Twenty-third Street's shops, the two of them hand in hand, she said, 'Could you find a newspaper story from the past for me?'

'Louisa, please! I already spent time on the "Shakespeare" thing; that didn't pan out very good. I used it, but there's really nothing there.'

'This is something else to do with the hotel.'

'That's better, anyway; that's a tie-in. What?'

Louisa told her about the French maid. Minnie said, 'It might do for a para. I don't see a story in it.'

'Minnie, forget your stories! I'm talking about the murders! Here's another instance of a woman who may have been . . . I don't know what, but it was probably something dreadful – and again it comes back to the hotel!'

'You say "again," but the only "again" is that you saw the first victim in the lobby. I'm gonna put that in print – leaving you out, leaving you out, I know – but it's thin, Louisa. It's suggestive; it's innuendo; it ain't facts. So you got a sighting of a victim and you got somebody two years ago who disappeared – this is a pattern? Give me the facts – that's what my editor's always saying. Give me the facts. Louisa, what you got is *notions*.'

'It could be the same madman.'

'I'd love to be able to say it is. Maybe I'll drop a hint that it is on Tuesday, how's that? But what's really the same? A woman disappears, but nobody saw her, no body's turned up, no this, no that. Then you see a woman in the lobby and she gets croaked, only it's two years later and nothing connects either one with you or the hotel.' Minnie squeezed her hand. 'Sherlock Holmes you ain't.'

Louisa wanted to tell her again about the noises, about Mrs Simmons's dog, about the 'ghosts.' About her fears. About her disappointment in Arthur.

About her self-pity?

But she was spoiling the evening, and she didn't want to do that, so she laughed and squeezed Minnie's hand and said, 'So I'm seeing things and jumping at shadows and leaping at conclusions. It's quite athletic!'

'You just need your husband back. You need a good . . . you know.'

'Minnie!'

'Don't deny it, Louisa.'

'Minnie, that's what *men* say – "She just needs a good . . ." mmp-mmp-mmp.'

'Well, I wouldn't mind a good mmp-mmp-mmp myself.'

They began to laugh. *Like a couple of schoolgirls*, Louisa thought. She giggled, and when Minnie tickled her ribs she screamed all the louder. When they stopped in front of the New Britannic, tears were running down their faces. Somewhat sobered by the stares from the night doorman, they subsided. Louisa blotted her face with a small handkerchief and passed it to Minnie.

'Anyway,' she said, 'could you look up the missing French maid in your archive?'

'Our what? We call it the morgue, sweetie. Hon, I'm not gonna have the time. I'm just not.' She grabbed Louisa's other hand, now held both of them. 'Louisa, if I do this right, I'm made. I'll be able to write my own ticket. I'm going to get a job on the *World* if it hare-lips me!' She was suddenly serious; the tears were real now, for some vision of herself, of her future. 'See?'

Louisa, who thought that stopping the murders was the only thing that mattered, didn't see but said she did. She kissed Minnie's cheek. 'You'll be a star.'

They held each other's hands for several seconds, then let them go, suddenly embarrassed. Minnie said, 'I'll tell you what. I have to go in tomorrow even though it's Sunday. We're planning the whole week. If I get a few minutes, I'll send one of the kids down to see what he can find – because I really do owe you for Roscoe G. Harding. Okay? I don't promise anything. Frenchwoman, disappeared two years ago, the hotel – right? Boy, it isn't much.'

'Stop by tomorrow if you can.'

'I can't. Well, maybe late, late afternoon.'

'Tea?'

'Oh, God, you're so English! If I can, hon, if I can – I gotta go . . .' She was backing along the pavement. Louisa watched her go, waited while she walked to the corner of Fifth Avenue, where she turned and waved. Louisa waved, then turned towards the hotel and let the night doorman open the doors for her. She didn't tip him.

★   ★   ★

354

In the morning, she went to St Bartholomew's Church. She chose it because it was in her guidebook and was described as having 'a sumptuous richness' and because the cab would cost the same to take her there as to Trinity Chapel, which was much closer but hardly described at all. She was able to limp along on the cane from hotel to cab and cab to church. (The crutch had appeared at her door that morning in the hands of one of the boys, with an apologetic note from Newcome.) The ice had helped the ankle, whose swelling was no worse and whose pain was now bearable – mostly. And she wanted now to triumph over the ankle, as if it were standing in for things she couldn't put ice on or ignore – Arthur, the murders, the hotel.

The service at St Bartholomew's was very like home, the music splendid, the sermon rather flashy and superficial. It wasn't a high church, but quite a fashionable one. The parishioners could also have been described as showing a sumptuous richness. The dresses were good, men's silk hats and frock coats abundant. Private carriages lined the street when she limped out.

The comforts of religion. She had sought them but not found them this morning. She had prayed, *Almighty God, take away my fears, take away my loneliness,* but she came out of the church unaware that anything had been lifted from her shoulders. Her churchgoing that morning, she thought, was religion as tourism, not very comforting but a pleasant part of the New York tour. She thought that if she were in New York another Sunday, she would go to one of the old churches, St Mark's or Trinity; but the idea of being in the city for another week saddened her and seemed to make her ankle hurt more.

Ethel had Sunday morning off. Mrs Simmons spent Sundays with relatives; Newcome was God knows where. Marie Corelli was away again. She'd have welcomed seeing even the austere and over-powering Victoria Woodhull, but she had gone back to England, according to Marie. Louisa ate a solitary lunch and lay down, couldn't sleep, went to the hotel's reading room and looked for a book and found nothing she could keep her mind on. Several of Arthur's books were there on a shelf labeled 'adventure,' although looking over the other authors' titles she couldn't understand why Arthur's had been set apart.

She went back to her room and sat at her window. She watched the clock, hoping Minnie would come. A pigeon landed on her windowsill, cheering her, then flew off, saddening her. She thought of ordering more ice but realized she would have to pay the boy and so didn't.

When Minnie came at five, Louisa threw her arms around her and pecked her cheek.

'My Lord, Louisa, you saw me just last night!'

'I'm dying of boredom.'

'Lucky you. I've been on my feet for hours. But – guess what?'

'I can't.'

'I got a raise! My editor came in – on a *Sunday*! – to work on my story and he gave me a raise! And we're talking about giving me a regular feature on crime, mostly the unsolved ones. And you know why? Because he's afraid I'll jump to someplace better. And I will!' She had taken her hat off and now threw it in the air. 'The world's my oyster!' She sat on the sofa next to Louisa. 'You look glum.'

'Sunday. I'm Scottish.'

'You're lonesome, I can tell. You need your man. Nice to have around sometimes, men.'

'*You* need to fall in love.'

'I used to do that a lot; it isn't what it's cracked up to be. You fall in love with what's-his-name, Arthur?'

'Well . . .' Louisa was embarrassed but wanted to tell her. 'I certainly set my cap for him.'

'Oh, it was that way!'

They both laughed. 'Not quite what you think. I told you that my mother worked but made me go to school; I stayed two years past the mandatory age, and then I was given a scholarship to a teacher-training college, which was supposed to train girls to go to the outer islands to start schools. My mother was failing by then, and I had an appointment to go to Lewis – that's an island far away from the mainland – at the end of the summer. I thought it would be just me and my mother, and that would be my life. Then we went to the English coast because I got a temporary job there, and my little brother fell ill and Arthur – he was a doctor, you know – came to tend him, and . . . one thing led to another.'

'Louisa! How far did it lead?'

She blushed and laughed. 'Not as far as I wanted it to.' They both giggled. 'He was a doctor – I could see myself married to him, my mother living with us . . . And then I fell in love with him.'

'And he fell in love with you.'

Louisa looked out her sooty window. 'Arthur is a good man. He has a profound sense of duty.' She smiled quickly. 'Now, you mustn't ever tell anybody I said that. I've never said it before.' She frowned. 'Perhaps I've never thought it before.'

'Not wildly romantic, huh?'

'We're all different, Minnie.' She took one of Minnie's hands, became a bit brittle. 'Now you tell me your secrets! Tell me about all these men you were in love with.'

So they sat on the sofa like two much younger women, sharing confidences and giggling. Minnie did most of the telling: she wasn't a virgin; she'd ducked out of an engagement twice; the men she made a fool of herself over were never the kind you take home to mother. 'If I'd had a mother.' She had a tough exterior, but inside was a lot of hurt and a lot of disappointment. She turned over her left hand and showed Louisa a scar the size and shape of an oak leaf on the palm, the skin shiny, slightly puckered. 'My mother did that when I was seven. She pressed my hand on the woodstove.

To punish me. God, I hated her. I left when I was fifteen, just *left*. And never been back.' Then she went back to telling racy stories of her adventures with men.

Louisa held her hand and smiled and laughed and said, 'Oh, Minnie,' from time to time, loving the softer Minnie that was emerging, glad of this woman friend she had found, and as the dusk fell outside it seemed the most natural thing in the world after one of Minnie's confessions to kiss her lightly, really as one child might have kissed another. Minnie, rather red from her tales and her giggles, looked surprised, then gave Louisa a small kiss back, which Louisa returned; and then Louisa was astonished that Minnie was kissing her, *really* kissing her, a kiss that lasted, became a firm pressing together of mouths, and then the tip of Minnie's tongue's first probing.

And then Minnie pushed herself back and said, 'Oh my God!' She jumped up. 'Omigod, omigod—!'

'Minnie—!'

But she was out the door, and the door slammed and Louisa was alone. She struggled up, had to look for her cane, then limped to the door and opened it, but the corridor – the still-strange corridor of the annex – was empty.

'Minnie?'

She went the slow route to the lift and down to the ground floor. She walked through the lobby, looking in the deep chairs as if Minnie might have decided to sit and rest in one.

'My friend,' she said to the doorman, 'did she go out? A young lady.'

'Young lady came through a few minutes ago. Brown coat, little brown hat?'

Louisa went out and stood on the hotel step – the one she'd tripped on after buying the *Police Gazette*; it seemed like years ago – but Minnie was gone.

How very peculiar. She will think the wrong thing about me. Or about herself? What did she think? No, she didn't think at all. Surely she did what she wanted to do. To kiss me that way. It wasn't as if we were . . .

Were what?

We weren't going to do anything.

But Minnie had been frightened. Perhaps they were going to do something.

Louisa shrugged and went back inside. It was cold out there. She pictured Minnie's heading home on one of the tramcars, looking out through a dirty window but seeing not the street but Louisa's hotel room, two women on a sofa.

Louisa sighed. *I prayed to have my loneliness lifted from me. Well?*

CHAPTER 9

CORRUPTION IN POLICE 'MURDER SQUAD'
How Far Does It Go?
Witnesses Suppressed, Bribes Taken
ARE THE BOWERY BUTCHER MURDERS PART OF IT?
by
A. M. Fitch

The Municipal Police have a 'Murder Squad' of supposedly crack detectives whose job it is to solve the often grisly murders that afflict this great city. Of late, we have seen two particularly horrific examples of same, namely those committed by the so-called 'Bowery Butcher.' Those crimes remain unsolved by the 'crack' Murder Squad. Recent discoveries by this reporter, which we will reveal today and in subsequent days, demand answers to urgent and vital questions about these 'stars' of our Municipal Police.

We have learned that a witness made

herself known to the police immediately after the first of these gruesome killings, telling the 'coppers' that she had *seen the victim* in the New Britannic Hotel in the company of a 'good-looking young man.' Did the New York Police applaud her willingness to help them? They did not! What they did was send two officers of the Murder Squad, Lieutenant John Cleary and Sergeant Thomas Grady, to visit the witness in order to intimidate and humiliate her!

Did Cleary and Grady use the witness's information to look for the 'good-looking young man'? They did not! They were too busy hunting down the victim's husband to fish for a 'reward' for keeping his name and his wife's identity out of the newspapers and off the police blotter.

It can now be told that the husband of the first victim, who was mistakenly identified *by the police* as a 'lady of the night' – an allegation that the police have never retracted – is in fact the wealthy industrialist Roscoe G. Harding, whose Murray Hill townhouse is one of the show-places of that part of the city. Interviewed by this reporter, Harding admitted that he paid Sergeant Grady one thousand dollars to hide the fact, attested to by a reliable witness, that his lovely young second wife had been in the New Britannic Hotel with another man.

As if this was not enough, Cleary and Brady also visited the manager of the New Britannic Hotel and received money from him to keep the hotel's name out of the investigation of the Bowery Butcher murders, even as a witness was connecting the first victim of those murders to his hotel.

Lieutenant Cleary may be too busy with managing his properties in New York to bother unduly with the cases of the Murder Squad. This reporter has uncovered at least five tenements in the names of Cleary's wife and his two brothers, not to mention Cleary's own handsome brownstone dwelling in Brooklyn Heights and a summer 'cottage' in Far Rockaway that we are told rivals some of our better uptown villas in its palatial accoutrements. The estimated value of these properties – not to speculate about others that may yet be found scattered around Manhattan and Brooklyn – is more than two hundred thousand dollars. Where, Lieutenant Cleary, does an honest policeman find that kind of money on a detective's salary?

In tomorrow's edition, we will look deeper into the methods of crooked cops. We will show the brazenness with which Grady demanded money of tycoon Harding. We will quote the manager of the New Britannic Hotel directly to reveal how threatened he felt when Cleary and Grady held him up for an additional five hundred dollars. We will look into a mysterious entity within the police called 'The Club' to see how, and how far, corruption has spread through certain offices of 300 Mulberry Street despite the recent Lexow Commission report on cleaning up this malodorous piece of moldy cheese.

And we will ask – and answer – other questions: How close is the connection between the New Britannic Hotel and the Bowery Butcher's murders? Is it because the murderer himself is so close to the hotel that the manager has tried to conceal its association with the crimes? (Remember: the first murder was not committed in the Bowery! The body was carried there from another place. Could that place be a certain hotel? Remember that the first victim's body was washed! Where better to wash a corpse than the farther recesses of a metropolitan hotel?)

What do the police know that they are not telling us, and why? What do they know about certain organs that were missing from both victims? What have they learned from the murderer's grisly clues – especially the victims' eyes? Or are they not investigating these murders at all, for reasons of their own?

Read about it tomorrow.

Louisa folded her hands on the newspaper. Minnie had indeed triumphed – the story on the front page, the headline 'above the fold,' which Minnie had told her was the preferred spot. But had she gone too far in suggesting so strongly a connection between the murderer and the hotel? In accusing Cleary and Grady by name?

Oh, Minnie, Minnie.

She went to the lift and downstairs and put herself into one of the telephone closets while Reception connected her with the *Express* switchboard. When she reached the newsroom, she said, 'A. M. Fitch, please.'

'Not here. Too early.'

'Can I reach her at—' But he had already rung off. And of course she couldn't reach Minnie where she lived, because Minnie had said that she didn't have a telephone. And Louisa didn't even know where Minnie lived.

She called again and asked the newspaper switchboard to leave a message on Minnie's desk to call Mrs Doyle as soon as possible.

Louisa pushed herself up and opened the door and found Manion standing there. They looked at each other; he looked away, back. He said, 'I saw you come down.'

'Yes, good morning.'

'You seen the papers?'

'Of course.'

He shuffled, seemed unsure of himself. 'How have you been?'

'I've been fine, Mr Manion.'

'Using the cane now.'

'Yes.'

'Nice cane.'

She waited, out of politeness, then said, 'I have to go.'

'Oh, for God's sake!' He turned away and vanished into the lobby. She went back to her room in the annex, the ankle as painful again as if it had been kicked.

'Who the fuck is A. M. Fitch? I'll fucking kill him!'

'It's a girl, Jack.'

'A *girl*! What the fuck!' Cleary picked up a brass ashtray with a brass-plated female nude on it and threw it against his office wall. 'How did she find out this shit? Who talked?'

'I dunno, Jack, I dunno—'

'It's all about me! Not you; she didn't touch you! For Christ's sake, Grady, she's put a hot poker up my arse. Jesus H. Christ. I'll fucking kill her, I mean it.'

'Jack, Jack, you gotta think. It's in the paper; they can't take it back. It's too late for all that.'

'Some cunt ramrods me, and I'm supposed to sit on my thumb?'

'It's Roosevelt we gotta worry about. We gotta have a story for him.'

'Story, shit! She's got my tenements in there, my house, the place in Rockaway! I told that shyster we oughta put them in phoney names, he says, oh no, that's trouble down the road. I'll bet everything I got that that cunt was into the records, looking for my family's names. How come she didn't find anything a yours?'

'I put it where they can't find it.'

'Where's that, between your buns? Well, they'll find it there soon enough, Roosevelt'll have you bend over while he shines a dark lantern up your hole. Jesus!'

'Jack, we gotta have a story.'

'Yeah, great. So make up a story.' Cleary threw himself into his desk chair. 'What are those fucks out in the office doing, laughing at me? They better not. I'll have their nuts.'

'I thought if we said we took the money from Harding and Carver because we were trying to see who was bribing cops—'

'We gotta find a way to make that rag retract the whole thing. The *New York Express!* Who ever heard a them doing a story like this? Who d'they think they are, fucking Joseph Pulitzer? Somebody must have something on them – or maybe on this cunt, what's her name? Fitch. Jesus. I want her fired. I want every word taken back. You got me? You got what I want?'

'Jack, Jack—'

'Tell ya what. I'll go to Byrnes. He's tight with Tammany. They know all the dirt. What we'll do is—'

There was a knock on the door. Through the frosted glass, they could see the pink blur of a face, the dark column of a suit. Cleary and Grady looked at each other. Cleary shouted, 'Not now! Later!'

The knock came again. 'You stupid shit, I said not now!'

The door opened. The young Harvard graduate who served Roosevelt stood in the doorway. 'Commissioner Roosevelt wants to see you.'

'Hey, ah, I didn't know it was you. Sorry. We were—'

'*Now.*'

Cleary looked at him as if he were readying himself to kill him. Then he tightened the knot of his tie and pulled back his shoulders. 'Sure. Come on, Grady.'

Detective-Sergeant Dunne came out of the City Mortuary and stood on the pavement to wait for Cassidy, who was always behind. When Cassidy had joined him, Dunne said, 'I don't like to be told by a flunky to get a warrant. Especially a flunky who works for the same City of New York that I do.'

'Can we get a warrant?'

Dunne pulled deeper into his overcoat. 'Maybe. If that newspaper isn't lying, Harding must have been here to identify her, so his name should be on the release certificate. But they won't let us see the certificate, or the visitors' book, or the death certificate. How do you suppose that newspaperman – Fitch? – got his information? Or is it all lies to sell newspapers?'

'I hope you noticed that threatening the flunky that you'd tell Roosevelt didn't exactly make him shit himself.'

'More like he knows something about Roosevelt that I don't. He *laughed*!'

'So what d'we do?'

'We get a warrant. Then we go ask Harding himself.'

An hour later, Dunne walked down the brownstone steps of Roscoe G. Harding's house on Thirty-fourth Street. Cassidy was leaning against the police carriage. He looked up, his face asking the question for him.

Dunne said, 'I didn't even get in the front door. Roscoe G. "isn't in to the police." Make an appointment, was the word.' Dunne's jaw came out. 'I don't like to be stiffed, Cassidy.'

'So what do we do?'

Dunne sighed. 'Find ourselves a crapper and have a think.'

Terrible Teddy was in full enraged-bull fettle. His eyes were wide, his pince-nez flashing; he smelled of sweat and testosterone. His high voice was, at its quietest, a bark, at its loudest a roar. His office was a jungle, and he was the king.

'Corruption!' He smacked his fist into a palm. 'You stink of corruption! I have made fighting corruption the hallmark of my time in this office, and you *stink* of it! A lieutenant! A man with the responsibility of an entire squad on his shoulders

369

– a man who should be an example, a model, a *paragon*! And you sink to the level of the lowest patrolman in the poorest ward in this corruption-riddled city! I could have found a more honest man among the vagrants of Chatham Square!

'And you, Grady. A sergeant. Eighteen years on the Metropolitan Police. How many of those years have you had your palm out for the bribe? How many years have you held the bag open so they could pour the money in? Thieves, both of you! Crooks! *Criminals!* You are worse than the malefactors you are paid to pursue. A hundred times worse. A thousand! Because you are paid to be *honest*. A word, I am sure, that has no meaning for you.

'Well? Well? Speak up. Tell me how you came to this desperate place.'

Cleary made a sound in his throat like the wheezing of a frightened deer. His eyes met Roosevelt's dead on, as if he were the most honest man in the world and had nothing to hide. He made his voice strong as he said, 'Mr Roosevelt, it was this way. It's all lies.'

Roosevelt had his thumbs in his waistcoat pockets. His belly rounded a little as he leaned backwards. 'What's all lies?'

'The newspapers. They'll print anything. The *Express* is the worst of the bunch. That's how she got away with it – they'll print anything.'

'Who is "she"?'

Cleary made the sound in his throat again. 'That

370

was a woman wrote those lies, sir. Her name is Fitch. She uses initials – what are they again, Grady?'

'A. M.'

'Anne-Marie. Yes. Annie Fitch. Now, I have a confession to make, Mr Roosevelt, but I ask that it never leave this room.'

Roosevelt simply stared at him.

'The way it is, Mr Roosevelt, me and Annie Fitch had a . . . well, you know, people being what they are, we had a—'

'Are you trying to hint at an illicit liaison, Cleary?'

'The very words, sir. Yessir, and I made a fool of myself over her, and then we had a falling-out, y'see, and she swore vengeance. And you see it in this morning's newspapers.'

'Are you saying that a hundred and fifty years ago, Peter Zenger went to trial so that your paramour could print lies about you, Cleary?'

'I don't know Zenger, sir, but I know she printed lies, yessir.'

Roosevelt looked at Grady. 'How about you? Did you have an affair with this woman, too?'

'Uh, no, sir. But she musta just drug me in for ballast, like. For the weight.'

'Weight! There isn't a moral balance in the world that you'd tip down a fraction of a degree!' Roosevelt went behind his desk. He stood looking down on them, his thumbs now in the armholes of his vest. He said, 'You are both suspended without pay effective this morning at eight o'clock. This has already been cleared with the Chief of Police. You will both consider yourselves under house arrest while a thorough investigation is made of everything that was printed in the *Express* newspaper. Until I learn otherwise, I will continue to think that you are both a disgrace to the Municipal Police. Now get out of my sight.'

Cleary's face worked its way through several expressions and settled into one of hurt dignity. Grady bent his head as if he were afraid the Commissioner was about to hit him. They went out silently; as they did, the Harvard man caught the door and came in, closing it behind him.

'This morning,' Roosevelt intoned, 'I am ashamed to be associated with this police department.'

'But are they?'

'Of course they aren't!' Roosevelt sat in his desk chair and gnawed on his knuckles. 'Cleary gave me a cock-and-bull tale that wouldn't have fooled a three-year-old. What have you found?'

'I spoke with Roscoe Harding, who's rightfully enraged. He says that it's true that they asked for money to pay off journalists. I gather he didn't mind bribing people; it's not getting the result he wanted that's set him off. He's talking about a lawsuit.'

'Let him sue the newspaper. Cleary said, by the way, that the author of that wretchedly written piece is a woman. Can that be true?'

'Unlikely, Chief, but I'll check. We have a man

372

on his way to interview Carver of the New Britannic; I suppose it'll be the same story – gave money to pay off journalists, and so on. Concerned, like Harding, for his public reputation.'

'And apparently utterly unsurprised that two New York police detectives had their palms out.'

'Quite. I've sent a clerk down to City Hall to delve into the records and double-check what was in the newspaper. One of our colleagues in the Brooklyn force is going to have a look at Cleary's house; the address is apparently quite a good one. We'll have to check the Brooklyn real estate records, too.' He lit a cigarette, offered the open case to Roosevelt, who refused, and snapped it shut. 'It's all quite damning, Chief. Do you want to turn it over to the Ethical Squad?'

'Not yet. I wish to know first whether we have an argument with the newspapers. We must be absolutely sure that we aren't skating on the thin ice of journalistic fiction.'

'You can't make this stuff up, Chief.'

Roosevelt gave a kind of snort. 'All right, get me the head of Ethical; tell him I want to discuss charges. Then get me the department legal brains. And somebody who knows the banks and real estate. We need to put our heads together to see how we follow the money, and how far.' He folded his hands in front of him. 'So far, you know, this is "peanuts," as the saying is. That is its charm. Its routineness, its common vulgarity. I suppose that we have here two policemen who have spent their lives taking bribes. Are they the end of the yarn that will pull the whole ball apart, or are they simply a thread that will unravel a bit of the skein and leave the rest intact? That is a mixed metaphor, although the general field of subject matter is the same, namely that of women's work – knitting and sewing. I wouldn't do it if I were writing.' He pushed out his moustached lip. 'If it's only the two of them, then they'll serve as an example to all the other sergeants and lieutenants who are "on the take." I cannot presume to put the fear of God into them, but I can certainly put in the fear of Roosevelt!'

Louisa had tried twice more to call Minnie at the newspaper. The first time, a bored male voice had said that she wasn't in; the second time, a different male voice asked who it was, meaning that Minnie *was* in. He'd gone off, presumably to tell her, and when he came back, all he said was, 'She isn't here.' And he had rung off.

She won't talk to me. She was there and when she knew who was calling, she refused to talk to me.

Louisa went up to her room. She hadn't expected Minnie to reject her like that. She had thought that they would both treat what had happened as a bit of foolishness, a reversion to girlhood. A 'crush.' She took hotel notepaper from the pigeonhole in the desk and wrote: '*Dear Minnie, I hope you feel as silly as I do at this moment. I think we've stumbled over a pebble on the path to friendship. We shouldn't* take it seriously. I do want to see you and talk this out thoroughly and finally so that we can go on being real friends. Yours sincerely, Louisa (Doyle)'

She had to take it down to Reception to have it mailed, for the annex lacked the rather clever mail chutes that allowed guests in the hotel proper simply to drop their letters through a slot. The chutes had glass fronts; it was rather amusing to wait by the elevator and see several envelopes plummet past, headed one couldn't guess where.

Minnie would have the note tomorrow. Then she would telephone or come by. Nonetheless, Louisa was upset. Worried, saddened, deflated: she couldn't describe her condition. *As if I were feeling a bit ill and were waiting to be very ill. Or as if I were waiting for something terrible to happen.* She paced back and forth in her small bedroom, then a little after five could stand it no more and went downstairs yet again. She gave Reception the number of the *Express*; she corraled one of the boys and led him to the telephone closet. She gave him a coin.

'Here is what I want you to do. When you get the switchboard at the number that will be called, tell them you want the newsroom. When you get the newsroom, ask to speak to A. M. Fitch. If they ask who's calling, tell them you have some information. Understand? "I have some information." Then, when Miss Fitch – it's a woman – comes to the telephone, hand the earpiece to me and leave the closet. Do you understand?'

She thought that his male voice would keep

Minnie from knowing who was calling. And that, in fact, was what happened: the boy did as he had been told; he handed her the earpiece; Louisa, face red and heart pounding, had leaned close to the mouthpiece and had said, 'Minnie, it's Louisa.'

And the call had ended as Minnie had rung off.

She hates me. She corrected herself: *She fears me.* She corrected herself again. *Or herself.*

At nine o'clock that night, Minnie Fitch was reading over the proofreader's corrections on the next day's article, nodding her head and making almost no marks on the typeset copy. She thought it was good, awfully, awfully good. She had had to dance very fast over things she hadn't been able to learn, most of all how well or badly the Murder Squad had done in finding the Butcher, but the piece was intriguing and rather racy, as she had intended. Her editor had said, 'It'll sell papers.' From him, that was high praise.

She tried not to think of Louisa, because to think of Louisa was to think of The Moment. The Moment of The Kiss. Every time she thought of it, it was as if she'd been hit with something. How had such a thing happened? How could she?

She sent the pages back to composition and looked around to see what things she wanted to take home with her.

'*Fitch!*'

She turned. 'What?'

One of the older reporters was standing at the

far end where the telephones were. 'It's for you, *again*!' They were all pissed at her because most of the calls had been for her that day – cranks, admirers, a few threats, doubtless from cops. And calls from Louisa.

'Man or woman?'

'A man. Your heart's desire.'

She wound her way among the desks. None of the usual remarks came her way. That's what a move above the fold did for you – respect, some real, some fake, a lot of envy, but an improvement either way.

'Fitch here.' She was prepared for Louisa's voice again, ready to hang up.

'Ah, it's a female you are!' It was a good voice, a little hearty, certainly Irish, apparently good humoured.

'I'm sorry, I'm busy; we're putting out a newspaper. What is it you want?'

'Oh, darlin', if I went into that, we'd be all night. It's not what I want, it's what I'm offering, y'see.'

'Okay, what're you offering?' Her heart was beating too fast because of fear that it had been Louisa. She tried to take a deep breath.

'It'd be in the way of information, love. Ye do *pay* for information, now, don't ye?'

She became cautious. 'Sometimes. Depends.'

'On the quality, I hope, because what I've got is the best, the very best.'

'About what?'

'What would it be, darlin', but the coppers and that hotel ye wrote about.'

377

'How come you have that kind of information?' Louisa had been driven out of her head; she was thinking *another scoop, above the fold, a move up* . . .

'Amn't I what you'd call close to them, dear.'

'You a cop?'

He laughed. 'That would be telling.'

'And the hotel?'

'I don't want to say too much without I'm paid, y'see? I've awready had an offer from the *World*; they come to me, not me to them, but as I thought ye'd broke the thing, I'd give you first crack. Fer a consideration, as it were.'

'Come to the *Express* newsroom. I'll wait until ten.'

'Aw, no, darlin', I wasn't born yesterday, as the saying is. Ye got to come to me. Alone. I don't want to find meself with five lawyers and two tough boys instead of a dear woman, as I know you are.'

'Where?'

'Ye know the fountain in Bowling Green?'

She thought of the place: the very foot of Manhattan, all commercial buildings now, the fountain derelict. But well lighted at night. She hesitated – the caller could be a crank, a hoodlum, a cop wanting to take revenge for Cleary and Grady. Even a cop sent by Cleary and Grady. That worried her: how far would somebody like Cleary go to get revenge?

She said, 'People will know where I'm going, get me? Just so you won't try to get cute.'

'I'm never cute, darlin', as you'll see when you get a look at me mug. The fountain at ten o'clock?'

She didn't like it. Yet she knew she had to do it; it was part of the business. Still . . . She said, 'Give me a detail that'll convince me. Give me a reason for trusting you enough to go out.'

There was a silence. Then he said, 'The doorman at the New Britannic. He knows more than he lets on. *Lots* more. And that's all I'll say until I see some silverbacks.'

'What's he know?'

'That would be tellin' without bein' paid, darlin'. Will ye meet me, yes or no?'

In for a penny, in for a pound. 'Ten o'clock at the fountain.'

She rang off. Ten minutes to get over there, spend an hour with him, that would be eleven; then back if he gave her anything good – could she get it into the later editions tomorrow? Only if it was something big. What? Maybe what he'd said – things the doorman knew. Maybe about the French maid who'd disappeared, maybe more than that. Like what? *Good Christ, could he have meant the doorman was* him? *Was she about to get the whole thing?* Her heart thumped.

When she left the building, she had told nobody anything. She was going home, she had said. She was afraid they would steal her scoop.

Alexander Newcome was in a dive called The Golden Pit on MacDougal Street. He was still more or less sober but on his way to being good and drunk. He intended to be *very* good and drunk. And he wanted to do something for which being good and drunk was the best state.

The Golden Pit was a low place reached by a flight of stone steps down from the street. The patrons were men, a lot of them badly dressed and not too clean, but some of them were like Newcome, older and well turned out. The spiffy ones didn't have much to do with each other; the poorer, younger ones did. A few of both sorts sat at tables, but there were only three tables in the whole place, and everybody else either stood or they sat on benches like church pews that ran around the walls. A bar took up one side of the room; the other walls – there were only two, the room triangular – except for scuffed wainscoting and a few cheap engravings, were bare.

Newcome was on his feet. He moved slowly around the room, a glass in his hand, because if you went to the Pit, you had to buy a drink. You didn't have to drink it, however; Newcome had been advised not to, as the drinks were said to contain things like benzene and turpentine and shoe dye for colour. So Newcome circulated slowly, as most of the well-dressed men did. When he had made a complete circle and come back to the bar he rested his back against it and put his glass down.

'Another?' a barman said at once.

'Not yet.'

'You've held on to that one pretty long.'

Newcome thought he'd rather gag down the

380

contents of the spittoon than drink what was in the glass, but he didn't say so. He wanted to get drunk, but not here, and he wanted to get drunk, but not alone.

He looked around the walls. On his right, below an engraving of the Colosseum, was a face he hadn't noticed before, probably a new arrival. Newcome, who was wearing a silk hat and a cashmere overcoat and who had a silver-topped stick in his right hand, cocked an eyebrow.

The young tough by the wall looked back with rather a sneer.

Newcome tipped his head back as a summons.

The young man looked at him, his face sullen, his arms crossed, then shrugged and came slowly towards Newcome, weaving around other men who were in his way.

'Yeah?'

'I thought you looked as if you needed a drink.'

'Not the shit they serve here.'

'I was thinking of moving on to more salubrious climes.'

'Where's that at?'

'I was thinking of Street's, and then perhaps the Burnt Rag for some giggles. And then perhaps a Turkish bath to rid ourselves of the after-effects of what we've drunk, and then someplace private.'

'I wouldn't mind that.'

'Your enthusiasm is infectious.'

'Don't talk down to me, awright? You get snifty wit' me, I'll give you a couple good ones.'

'Only a couple? I'm disappointed in you.'

'My name's Phil.'

'Well, Phil, my dear, why don't we get out of this hole and find ourselves a spot where we can get beautifully drunk together and see what the night will bring.'

Phil looked around. He shrugged. 'Suits me.'

Newcome nodded slowly, as if Phil had confirmed something rather sad. He had a fleeting nostalgia for somebody nicer, younger, fresher. He smiled and nodded towards the door. Phil was what was on offer.

CHAPTER 10

A wagon pulled by a broken horse dragged out of an abandoned abattoir near the Produce Exchange and came up West Street, along the docks. It was the dead hour of the night, nearer three than two. The bustle of the docks hadn't begun yet; the fleets of wagons that would pick up goods from the warehouses that lined the river were still in their barns. West Street was an urban desert at this hour, only scraps of newspaper and even a few leaves from God knew what tree blowing along the cobbles and pavements like sad imitations of sagebrush. If there was another living human being out, the driver of the wagon certainly didn't know it: he was hunched down, as dispirited as his horse, the stub of pipe in his mouth as dead as the night, his lank white hair hanging around his face like a ripped curtain.

Opposite Pier Thirty-four, he lifted a weary rein and piloted the horse to their right into Spring Street, then left again into Washington, the dark shadows of the El at the end of the short block to his right silent and unpeopled. Ahead of the wagon now was a street lined with ancient

383

buildings turned into warehouses. Some had started as houses, put up so long ago that they were of frame construction; some had begun as shops and commission houses, when New York had grown only this far and was bustling with primitive trade. On the right was a strip of one-storey sheds, perhaps once carriage houses, now either crumbling storage or abandoned derelicts. Even so, there would be life here in two hours, chaos in three – cursing drivers and warehousemen, percussive iron wheels on cobble, slamming doors.

Now, nothing but the man and the wagon and the horse.

Beyond the wooden sheds was an old brick building three storeys tall, its false façade half a storey higher than what stood behind, its windows boarded over. Across the front, barely legible in the feeble lamplight, were old painted letters, once white and now almost the dirty brown of the brick: SAUSAGE.

The wagon turned into the open space next to the building and went halfway along and stopped. The driver got down. If he had looked up, he would have seen another sign, also painted long before on the brick, 'Baum's Sausage.' But he didn't look.

He pulled a heavy roll from the bed of the wagon and hoisted it on his shoulder with a grunt; he carried it to the foot of the building's wall and put it down by bending forward and flipping the thing so that half of it landed with a thump. He stood, put a hand on his back, stretched. Bent back like that, he could just make out 'Sausage,' and under it a row of meat hooks. Here, presumably, Baum had once had the deliveries of offal and bone scrapings hung.

He grabbed the sides of the canvas roll and pulled, and the cloth unrolled. He raised his arms as he pulled so that the thing inside the roll fell free almost at his feet. He dropped the canvas, got his hands under what lay there and raised it to his own height, then bent his knees and heaved upward, then upward again, and he slammed the thing over one of the meat hooks and let its own weight come on it, and it hung there.

Breathing hard now, he went back to his wagon. He was getting a second roll out when a voice said, 'Hey, you!'

A light shone on him. He peered into the light like a man with bad vision. His crumpled bowler hid the upper part of his face; his white hair obscured the rest. He said, 'I ain't got nuttink to steal, mister.'

'Who the hell are you and what're you doing here?' The light came forward; barely visible next to it were a hand and a cudgel that a trained eye would have seen was not a policeman's stick.

'Oi, Mister Policeman, you give me a scare. I t'ought you was one of those shicers robs old men. I'm only looking for bones, mister. I'm in the rag and bone trade.'

'You are, huh?' He sounded a cocky little bastard

385

– little, because the light and the stick were being carried low. He shone his lantern over the old man and the wagon and said, 'Stealing, are you, Yid?'

'Stealing never, I'm telling you! Only looking to pick t'ings up.'

'Yid, there haven't been bones around here in twenty years. Cripes, you do stink like it, though.' The guard blew out a breath, then turned and shone his light on the side of the building. It caught something pale, moved, and he said, 'Oh, Christ Jesus!'

But that was the last thing he would ever say. The old man had had his hand on a three-foot crowbar, and as soon as the guard had turned away he had swung it up and out of the wagon and two-handed it the way a baseball player swings a bat, and it hit the back of the guard's head with a sound like a coconut being broken with a hammer to get at the meat. The guard went down, his lamp bouncing once and going out. The old man never paused but swung again and hit the skull with another blow and then one more, then pushed the guard's body with a toe and waited for him to move.

After that, he moved quickly. He dropped the crowbar back into the wagon and got out the canvas-wrapped package he had been going for before, trotted with this to the wall and opened it the same way as the first. A terrible smell rolled out, excrement and garbage and death; he never hesitated but dipped into the mass that lay there and got some

386

of it into his hands and pulled it up and then turned to the hanging thing and began movements that were hard to decipher in the darkness – reaching up and spreading his arms, then reaching down and up, then circular motions with both arms, then a pulling again at the mass on the ground, as if he were making magical signs over the side of the building that said 'Sausage.' As if blessing it, the religion unclear.

Then from half a street away, another voice came: 'Herman! Hey, Herman!'

The old man stopped dead still. He bent, took the last of his load from the ground and disposed of it on the wall and wiped his fouled hands on the fallen guard's coat. He threw the canvas into the wagon.

'Hey, Herman! Where're you at?' Closer now.

He got up on the wagon seat and slapped the rein down on the horse's back to set it going. The wheels ground over the stones. The horse's hooves made sounds like wooden boxes being struck together. He made the horse go faster.

'Hey!'

He shot a look behind him to see the glow of another dark lantern almost at the corner of the building, then turned away and whipped the horse with the reins.

'What the hell? Hey, you – stop there, you sonofabitch! Herman, where the—? Oh, shit! Oh my God! Oh my God! Help! Help! Police!'

★ ★ ★

387

The wagon careened into Van Dam Street, actually up on two wheels as it took the corner, and rattled to Varick, the old horse at a gallop, and took the turn south at such a speed that it slid sideways on the cobbles and almost toppled over. The driver was using his whip now; the horse, frightened and pained, plunged ahead with whatever strength was left in it. As they crossed Canal, a police whistle sounded off to their right, then another from the left and somewhere behind them. The horse began to slow, but the driver whipped it on. Another whistle came, this one from up ahead, and the reins pulled and the whip fell and the wagon turned into Worth Street and clattered under the West Broadway El for a few heartbeats and then was out of that shadow, and they were pounding along between rows of tenements that rose into the blackness above.

They seemed to be free, and the horse was trying to rear, to give in to its fatigue, to stop, and the driver pulled up a little and let it fall into a trot, which it wanted to make a walk, but he touched it again with the whip. He half-stood in a crouch and looked around them, looked back, heard a whistle far behind and sat down, slumped, and slowed the horse to the walk it wanted. For one street, two, they were again the decrepit, dying pair they had seemed at first. They stopped being the hell-bound evil spirit of the night and became the first glimmer of the morning – the first slow outriders of the day's invasion.

They crossed Broadway at a walking man's pace. The driver glanced to his left and saw a moving light; then came the sound of galloping horses and a bell. *From the precinct building. Heading west.* They went another block and turned north into Elm, but up ahead another Black Maria was racing westward, and they turned right again and headed east, now like an animal that has lost the scent, trying this way and that, getting its nose into the wind to find the way – south, then east, more east, a jog to the north.

And then ahead, a police carriage with its lights bright, and policemen on the pavements and in the street with lanterns, one of them standing right in their path and waving the lantern back and forth like a trainman at a crossing.

He wheeled the wagon in the middle of the block and whipped the horse to a gallop again. Whistles and shouts rang out behind them; the police carriage backed and policemen piled into it.

The wagon raced north, then east again as he saw another barricade. Now he was approaching Mulberry Street, with police headquarters only a few blocks to the left. Behind them, the police carriage, pulled by two fresh, decently young horses, was gaining ground, and there were the sounds of other hooves. He looked back: policemen on horseback!

He flew into Mulberry Street with the whip falling on the nag. The inertia of the wagon almost pulled the poor beast down, but it recovered, its

389

iron shoes sliding and striking sparks. Behind, voices were shouting, 'It's the Butcher! In the wagon! The Butcher! Stop him!'

A stunned-looking beat cop stared at the wagon and too late ran into the street with a hand out. The whip lashed across his face; he staggered; the wagon was past him and a moment later was crossing Hester Street.

The driver rose in the seat again. He shouted, but gone was the Jewish accent of before. He seemed younger, stronger – and Irish. 'The cops is coming! Get out the bhoys! It's the cops! Git out the bhoys!'

It was an old cry, a cry from the days of the great Irish gangs. But it still worked. Lights came on. Men put their heads out of windows, ducked back. Women came out on fire escapes. Street-level doors flew open and men, young and old, poured out as the leading police in the pursuit flashed past – two cops on horseback, a running roundsman, now puffing and not long for the pace, a carriage.

Paying no attention to them, the men of Mulberry Street did what they always had done when that cry had come: they smashed the street lamps; they pulled up the manhole covers; and they raised the steel lids of the chutes that ran from the pavements down to the cellars. Within seconds, that whole block of Mulberry was gloomy, then dark as every apartment light went out. Iron clanged on stone. Feet scurried. Then a remarkable silence fell, with only the scuffle of a few feet. And then men and boys began to appear on the fire escapes to watch the show.

In the darkness, the next wave of police came riding and running and driving. A horse screamed as its leg went into a manhole and snapped; a running man swore and then cried out as he fell down a delivery chute. A carriage tried to veer out of the middle of the street, but the lead horse's rear foot went into a manhole, and although he recovered, the carriage swayed and pitched, and the driver lost his bearings in the dark and the horses went over the kerb, then swerved away from the dark mass of the tenements and tipped the carriage on its side.

It was pandemonium, with the residents of the street cheering like Milton's demons from the balconies. There was glorious laughter when a dazed policeman wandered away from the crash of the carriage and fell into an open manhole. Shouts for help were greeted with curses and jeers. 'Cry for your mama, copper! Come into the cellar, copper, we'll give ye what ye gave us at the station! Put your nightstick in your gob and bite it, copper!'

Far ahead, the wagon clattered along. The horse was failing. Its ears were back, its breathing labored, with a terrible rasp at the end of each breath. The two mounted policemen had tried shooting at the wagon, had of course hit nothing but the street and the tenements. Aware now of the tricks the gangs played with manhole covers, they were reluctant to gallop, the more so because the street was lined with empty pushcarts and they were forced to go right down the middle. The police carriage, which had lost ground at each turn, was again catching up, but only the driver could see ahead to what was happening. All in all, even with a nearly dead horse, the wagon was holding its own.

It took the shallow right into Centre Street. Behind it, the mounted cops had let the carriage catch up to them and were shouting to somebody inside. A word came out clearly – 'bridge.'

The bridge?

Ahead, at the end of Park Row, lay the approach to the Brooklyn Bridge. The approach was nearly a mile long but open. At its top were toll gates, then the mile of the bridge itself.

'Get people to the bridge, I said! You're fucking deaf, are you? Get on that horse and get to a fucking telephone and tell them to man the fucking toll gates! We'll stop him at the toll gates!'

One of the mounted cops saluted, and so the other one did, too. They looked at each other, looked around as if a telephone might appear in the opening into Centre Street, and then galloped back towards the red lights of the Tenth Precinct station. Meaning, of course, that they would have to get through the chaos of the still-dark block where men and horses were screaming.

The carriage started moving again. It turned into Centre, went one street, then a second. The wagon wasn't to be seen. The officer inside was pounding

392

on the ceiling and shouting, 'Park Row, you fools! Park Row!'

He was right. They found the wagon in Park Row. It was stopped pretty much in the middle of the street. The horse was down, its harness tangled, the wagon itself pulled partly over. All the cops got out of the carriage – there were four, with the officer – and looked around. One of them decided the horse was done for and shot it. Another walked in front of the wagon and found the body of a man in a cheap suit. His head had been beaten in.

'Christ in a crock, he won't go to the bridge now. Goddammit! He's on foot!'

'No, sir, I think, sir, he's stolen a hack.' The cop, young and still a probationer, pointed at a pile of horse dung. 'It's still warm, sir. I think the corpse was the driver, sir.'

They were in front of the *World* building. One of the cops muttered that he'd been hoping it was a reporter. The officer said, 'Oh, shit, reporters! Get us out of here before they see us. You – what's your name? – stay with the body. Don't answer any questions. Let's go!'

They got back into the carriage and left the very young cop to his corpse.

The stolen hack was on the approach road to the bridge, going at a good clip but not one that would draw attention. A clock said not quite three, although a few bells were suggesting it was. The traffic was thin. The cab was a one-horse hansom, light and maneuverable, but the horse was another spavined plug, for which the climb up to the bridge was labour. On and on it went, nonetheless; it wouldn't collapse if it could keep the pace down. Ahead, the toll gates appeared. Only one was open, this side of it a line of half a dozen carriages, as if, as the traffic declined, gates were closed to guarantee that there would always be a delay getting through.

Behind the hack by half a mile, lights, movement, confusion: three Black Marias and five mounted police.

The hack driver looked back. His white hair was wild, his crumpled hat askew. He was coming up to the end of the line for the toll gate. He glanced back again, could see that the horses back there were galloping.

He brought the hack to the end of the line and dropped the reins; in two seconds, he was on the ground. He trotted forward on the side away from the toll operator. As he ran along the line, sleepy drivers looked down at him but said nothing. He kept going, ducked under a closed gate, and stood motionless.

The active gate opened and a milk wagon went through.

The old man jumped on the running board of the milk wagon as it moved forward.

'I need a ride, darlin'.'

'Company rules.' The milkman was short and thin, wearing a white duster and a cloth cap.

'Ah, what a pity, sweetheart.' The old man drove a knife into the driver's side, took the reins and urged the horse forward.

Behind them, the police were galloping towards the closed gates.

The milk wagon had a high dash like a carriage, and a roof that came out a little forward of the driver. There was a kind of bench to lean back on, although the driver stood to drive because he was in and out of the wagon constantly, making deliveries. Now the old man leaned on the bench as the driver collapsed on the floor, gasping and bleeding.

'You just stay down there, darlin'; I'll have you to the doctor-man in a jiffy. It was unkind of me, it was, sticking you, but I meant no harm. It'll all turn out well, you'll see.'

They were on the bridge proper by then. A huge stone support was just passing underneath them; above, miles and miles of wire soared into a sky without stars or moon or first daylight. On their left was the pedestrian railway track – three cents a crossing; above and beyond it was the raised pedestrian walkway.

'The best view in New York,' the old man said. He put his head out the side of the closed wagon and looked back. There seemed to be a lot of confusion at the toll gates. He slapped the reins on the horse's back, but they had no effect on the horse. He had one gait, and this was it. The old man looked back again. He looked up at the walkway, then ahead. The bridge was almost empty.

'Time to take care of you, then,' he said. He steered the milk wagon to the side and stopped.

At the toll gates, they had had to move the waiting carriages out of line so the police vehicles could go through. That hadn't gone down well, and a lot of surly suggestions had been made to the police. There was a view that they could wait their turn, or they could get somebody to open another gate. A cop saw that that was probably a good idea, and the one operator on duty was made to open the gate next to his own, although he complained that he lacked the authority and it was on their heads.

When he opened the gate, the civilian carriages waiting in line tried to go through.

Everybody cursed.

Then a cop who'd been standing off to the side shouted, 'He's jumped! The Butcher's jumped off the damned bridge!' He didn't say that he'd seen a hat lined with white hair sail after, because he didn't see it, nor did he see the hat float on the wind like a gull to the water, sit briefly there, and sink.

They all piled into the Black Marias and raced towards the distant milk wagon.

Louisa had spent a bad night, was still spending a bad night. Outside her window, it was as dark as at midnight. Light might have been showing in the sky, but she couldn't see it; down where she was near the bottom of the cleft between the hotel and its annex, it was dead dark.

She had tried to lie still in the bed but had made a tangle of the sheets. She had got up and drunk water, got up and paced. Now she sat in a hard chair by the window in the dark and waited for day to come. Below her was a kind of narrow alley on her right – the very bottom of the divide between the two buildings – that ended in a wall on her left, behind which were the corridors between the annex and the New Britannic. Opposite her window at ground level was, she knew, a door, and she knew what the door was for: it was an entrance for the kitchen workers. She thought that the first of the breakfast cooks would come in about five-thirty; now, with nothing to do, sleepless, the bird of fatigue a weight on her shoulders, she was waiting for the cooks' human presence.

She had spent the night in a tangle of thoughts as soiled and wrinkled as the sheets on her bed: now Arthur and regret for a letter she had written him the day before; now Minnie and regret for the kiss; now the annex and regret for having taken Carver's 'deal.' She had got nowhere with any of them: regret is regret, unrepairable.

Money. Why didn't she have any money? Why couldn't she get any? Part of the night had been spent thinking of who would give or lend her money. She had thought of two sources, Arthur's American editor and his bank. But would they? Banks were very strict. And she didn't know Arthur's editor. But there must be money due Arthur; his American sales were excellent. Could she go begging in her husband's name?

But why did she need to beg?

And dreams. She had got up once because she had found herself thinking of a dream and so arousing herself. Maybe she had been dreaming of Arthur; certainly she had woken feeling that she wanted sex. That had made her get up and drink water and walk around the little room. *I won't touch myself. I won't.* It would be too bad of her. Marriage was supposed to relieve this desire. But she hadn't desired the figure in her dream; it was simply there unbidden, like a dream shape between her legs. Not really Arthur, not recognizably Arthur. Minnie? But a Minnie with a penis? And there had been some sense of threat, of . . . fear? Was it Manion? What had she to fear from Manion?

She sighed. Where was the morning?

A sound came from below. Down here, the city's sounds were muffled, but the scrape of a footstep in the alley was clear. She put her forehead against the windowpane and looked down. A shape, black against black, moved up the alley. Then there was a different sound, rat-like, furtive. A bit of metal. A key in a lock?

The door opened to make a widening wedge of pale light. She drew back without thought. What would it matter if she were seen? But it did matter, and she knew why: her fears.

Below her was a foreshortened figure, really little more than the top of a head in a cloth cap and the shoulders of a dark coat. Painted on the pavement was his pale shadow: long overcoat, head cut off by her window and the wall it stood in. She supposed it was one of the breakfast cooks; good, it must be later than she thought. Day was coming.

The wedge of light started to narrow; the black figure moved into the doorway, moved inside, stopped. The top of the head was not so black in the light there, really brown, the brown of the cap. At the same time, she heard another sound from the alley – laughter. Male, slightly high pitched. And the scrape of shoes on pavement.

The door opened a crack more. He must have heard the sound, too. She could see his silhouette as he leaned out again and looked up the alley. Abruptly, he drew back and the door almost closed and she could see only a sliver of light, as if the man was still trying to see out.

Two figures moved into the near-blackness below her. One of them giggled and pointed at the door. Cooks? Something was going on; she pressed her forehead to the glass again and could just make out the two below her. Silence. Then words she couldn't make out, another giggle. Were they kissing? One must be a woman, then. Or—

Metal on metal. *Another key*. The door opening again, the wedge of light, and she saw the two as she had seen the other one – the top of a silk hat this time, shoulders, and the top of another head, male, no hat, the forehead pale. Not female.

The one in the hat almost fell against the partly opened door. He caught himself and looked inside, then said something that sounded to her ironic, jocular – had he seen the first man, who was already inside? Greeted him, perhaps? She heard his laugh as he turned his face back and up, and she recognized both the laugh and the face. Alexander Newcome.

He pushed the door all the way open and the bare-headed man went in, then Newcome, who grabbed him and pulled him towards himself as the door swung closed.

She knew what she had seen. *Safe*. Arthur Newcome didn't look very safe to her right then. Drunk, foolish. Bringing a young man into the hotel, just like the good-looking young man who had brought the copper-haired woman, but why through this back door? She found she didn't care about Newcome's kissing and fondling another man; she supposed she had always known that; what troubled her was his using this door. What was he doing at this hour of the morning, coming in a back door for which, surely, he wasn't supposed to have a key?

Only after she had twisted and turned in that tangle for a while did she think of the first figure who had gone through the door. Who was he, then? A cook, she had thought. But nobody else had come. Was he somebody who had had to come in early? But Newcome had seemed to know him – or had he?

She sat for three-quarters of an hour. When the breakfast cooks came, they came in a silent group, five of them, and then a dribble of waiters and dishwashers and boys who did she didn't know what.

She went back to bed and slept this time and dreamed of being on a beach with somebody and looking for a place where they could be alone, where they could make love, and there was nothing, only sand and wind and rock and the smell of salt water, and she woke from it exhausted.

POLICE PURSUE BOWERY BUTCHER THROUGH STREETS
Another Horrendous Murder Committed
Butcher Leaps from Brooklyn Bridge
Is he Drowned?

Louisa looked in vain for Minnie's name on the article, but it was anonymous. It seemed a bit scatty to her – there were several grammatical errors – and she supposed it had been written in the heat to get it into the breakfast edition. Minnie's second piece about the police and the murders was in the paper as promised, but relegated to an inside page, kicked there doubtless by this new excitement. How angry Minnie must be!

Louisa grieved for yet another woman murdered

401

and mutilated and, according to the *Express*, as yet unidentified. 'Rendered unidentifiable,' had been the *Express*'s murky way of putting it. *Why couldn't they say what they meant?* 'Mutilated in a particularly horrific and fiendish manner.' *Oh, really! You're not writing for children, after all.*

The Butcher had been interrupted at his ghastly work. *(Or is it play?)* 'I heard a wagon where a wagon oughtn't to have been,' said Richard Hoffman, private guard for the West Street Association, 'and I was looking for my pal, Hermie (Herman) Steinhoffer, so I turned into this kind of alley, and I saw him and his wagon just wheeling into the next street like the devil himself was behind him. Then I shined my light around and I saw what he'd been up to, and I knew it was the Butcher.'

The police had 'made a valiant effort' to capture the murderer, but he had 'used a vile stratagem on Mulberry Street that turned the residents of that decayed quarter into his fellow-conspirators as they poured from their tenements to smash lamp globes and tear up the covers of underground holes, with the result that two officers suffered broken limbs, three horses had to be destroyed, and a carriage was overturned with resulting damages of more than a hundred dollars.' The chase had continued on to the Brooklyn Bridge after the Butcher had murdered a hack driver and stolen his hansom. 'An unfortunate misunderstanding by the employees of the bridge authority held the police back at the toll gates for several valuable minutes.' The Butcher had then apparently commandeered another vehicle – the *World* made it a milk-wagon, the *Express* 'a conveyor of beef carcasses to the Jewish trade' – but, whatever the means, he got partway up the bridge and disappeared. 'Eyewitnesses assure us that the Butcher dove from the very middle of the bridge's mile-long span into the icy waters of the East River almost a hundred and fifty feet below. "No normal man could survive that fall in this season of the year," a police spokesman was quoted as saying.

'But are we dealing with a normal man?'

Louisa was experienced enough at reading between the lines to suspect that the police had had some share in their own failure. Perhaps it was remarkable that they had been able to assemble any pursuit at all. But the effect of the articles was to give the Butcher a morbidly heroic stature, one that was only increased by suggesting that he was supernormal. And therefore superhuman?

She had heard of Nietzsche's superman. Was this what the world got when the superman did whatever he wanted – mutilated and murdered women? Was he the 'perfect man'? *Damn Victoria Woodhull.*

Commissioner Roosevelt had been woken at home before the chase had ended, but not soon enough for him to take part. He had got his revolver, and he had had his carriage brought out, but he had been too late. He said to himself now that he should have had a horse saddled – the picture of himself riding in the chase, gun in hand, was too good to resist – but of course he had no charger at his house on Madison Avenue.

But he had been in plenty of time to learn that the Butcher had got away. That the Butcher had jumped to his death in the East River seemed an unsatisfying cheat; Roosevelt was actually relieved, then pained, when he learned in mid-morning that it looked as if the body that had gone off the bridge had been that of a milkman named Finter.

'We can't tell a milkman from a fiend?' It was after ten. He was in his office at 300 Mulberry Street with seven other men – the Chief of Police, two deputy chiefs, two of his fellow commissioners, the night's watch commander, and the acting head of the Murder Squad.

'We didn't know about the milkman at once, sir.' Deputy Chief Halloran was a smoother of feathers, a calmer, a soft-soaper. He had a lovely, soft voice that could become an Irish lyric tenor when he sang; now, he was purring for Roosevelt's benefit.

'How the devil did they think a milk wagon got on the Brooklyn Bridge without a driver?'

'I think it didn't occur to the boys at the time, sir. They were all keyed up, you know, just raring to go because of what that devil had done on Mulberry Street.'

'Within three blocks of this headquarters! Are we that hated that all he had to do was shout the word "cops" and the criminal residents of the tenements became an avenging army?'

Halloran looked deeply sympathetic and heaved a sigh. 'It's an old tradition on the street, and a very sad one.'

'I understand that we fired three rounds.'

'Oh, yes, indeed, the mounted patrol did their very best!'

'Oh, was that their very best? Not a one touched him, in fact. Galloping down a dark street, and they're firing pistols in a place that is surrounded by dwellings? I want those two mounted policemen demoted one rank and sent back to the foot patrol.'

'Oh, Mr Roosevelt, sir, that's harsh. They were doing their—'

Roosevelt leaned the tips of his fingers and the pads of his thumbs on his desk. He looked meaningfully at the other commissioners, then at the Chief of Police. 'I cannot demand, but I can recommend! I recommend that they be reduced in rank and sent back to foot patrol!'

'Ah, yes, yes, indeed, a fine idea, of course . . .' Halloran looked at the chief, who was scowling but who nodded.

'Where was the Murder Squad in all this?'

Many pairs of eyes turned on an aged lieutenant named Banks, known everywhere as Bangs because he was afraid of guns. He'd been brought in from Fraud and Confidence when Cleary had been suspended. Bangs fidgeted and cleared his throat. 'We weren't informed.'

'*What?*'

'Nobody told us.'

'Told you what?'

'Any of it. I didn't hear about the murder until I saw the morning paper, I swear. Sir.'

Roosevelt looked at the watch commander. 'You didn't tell the *Murder Squad* there'd been another murder?'

The man swallowed. 'In the confusion of the moment. No, sir.'

Roosevelt stared at him through his pince-nez. Suddenly he threw his head back and smacked a fist into a palm. 'Jehosephat! That's what they say in the West when men are unbelievably stupid – *jumping Jehosephat!*' His moustache worked up and down; his eyes bulged. He bent towards the chief, who was sitting next to where he stood. 'Chief! I can't tell you what to do, because I'm only a *civilian*. And I'm not *the* commissioner of police, but only one of five, although I am the president of those five.' He leaned still farther forward. 'But I tell you, if this police department doesn't pull up its socks and get itself together, I will make such a ruckus in this city as will make the Lexow Commission look like a ladies' tea party!' By the time he finished, he was bellowing. He could have filled the Metropolitan Opera with that voice. And they were in a rather small room. Several hardened policemen flinched.

Roosevelt stuck his thumbs into his waistcoat pockets. 'Now, I'm not going to take charge.' He was looking around at all of them. 'I'm not going to reach down into the ranks and tell individuals what to do. But by the Almighty, I expect there to be changes, and I expect there to be improvements! You *will* institute procedures that will have the watch commanders inform every pertinent squad when an event takes place! You *will* make sure that every such squad leader has a telephone connected directly to this building! You *will* learn from this debacle to organize a pursuit that could catch something more difficult than a child pulling a wooden toy! Do I make myself clear? Am I being understood?' His voice was thundering again.

Roosevelt in fact had no authority – except the authority of his presence. As one of the deputy chiefs had said of him a little after Roosevelt had arrived in office, 'If he's willing to cut the wood, he can build the fire,' and Roosevelt, they found, was always first in line with the axe. If he didn't actually run the police department, he certainly scared the daylights out of the men who did.

They filed out quietly, saving their curses and their jeers for their own offices. As the last one went out, the Harvard man slid in. 'Detective-Sergeant Dunne is waiting, Chief. You asked to see him.'

Roosevelt was staring at the American flag on the wall opposite his desk. 'This failure is a disgrace to the New York Municipal Police!'

'At the very least, sir.'

'A milkman! Probably in a white coat and

trousers. He threw a *milkman* over the bridge and they thought it was a killer they'd already seen wearing a long black coat and dark trousers! Are they blind as well as stupid?'

'The fog of war, sir.'

'What?'

'Clausewitz. You had me read him.'

Roosevelt folded his arms and stared down. He was still standing. 'This is not a job for a man who wants to focus on the larger questions.' He sighed. 'Send in this Dunne.'

Dunne came through the door seconds later. He was wearing another poorly pressed tweed suit; to English eyes he might have looked like a cattle auctioneer in some small market. Nonetheless, he carried with him that odd dignity of his: when he hove to, it was by a chair on whose back he rested a hand as if he were going to have his portrait painted.

'Sit down.' Roosevelt sat as he said it. Dunne waited until the great man's buttocks touched his own chair, then sat.

'You're the head of the investigation of these female atrocities, I'm told.'

'What they call the Bowery Butcher, yes, sir.' Dunne had missed the chase after the Butcher because he had no telephone, but he had been woken at four by a policeman sent specially by a pal at headquarters to take him to the scene of the latest murder. To Roosevelt, he seemed weary but alert – the sort of absolute professional who makes armies run, usually from the rank of sergeant major or below.

'You've been in charge for nearly two weeks now,' Roosevelt said.

'Yes, sir, but held back from doing much.'

Roosevelt pushed out his lips at that, then passed over it and said, 'Anything on this latest atrocity yet?'

'We have the wagon, sir. Blood in it, bloody canvas. Also a crowbar with blood on it – used to kill the private guard and also a hack driver, we think. They lost the man they think did it, as you know.'

'And the first two murders?'

'The fact is, we're still gathering clues and doing slog work.'

Roosevelt made a pained face. 'What progress?'

'Not much, sir.' Dunne got out his map and unfolded it, an operation that never went well because the map was on cheap paper and the folds had torn. Still, his circles and X's were clear enough. He said, 'That's about what we know, sir. Put together by one of our best men, Detective Forcella.'

Roosevelt liked maps. They seemed to him to smack of the military – artillery barrages, the use of technological gadgets like binoculars and calibrated compasses. He said almost cordially, 'Tell me what I see here.'

Dunne told him: sites of the murders, routes taken by the 'old man with a wagon,' who had now been seen before and after all three murders;

409

the place from which the second wagon had been stolen. 'We're not sure about where he got the wagon for the first murder. There were four thefts reported that night; one can't have been it because the wagon was all painted up – owner's Sicilian – and one was way uptown above the park. The other two . . .' He shrugged. 'And a lot of thefts aren't reported to us.'

'How can you know it was the same old man?'

'Timing and location, sir. And elimination – if it isn't any of the other possibilities, it's the one that's left.'

'Sherlock Holmes.' Roosevelt, a voracious reader, expected some agreement. Dunne's face might have been made of hardened clay. Roosevelt returned to the map. 'So what, taken altogether, does it mean?'

'It doesn't mean anything yet, sir. I may have a better idea when I interview everybody involved in last night's business. And we trace the wagon. Maybe it's significant he headed for the bridge; maybe it isn't. It may be only that he came down Mulberry because he knew he could play that trick of his, which, besides being clever, suggests that maybe he's an old New York bhoy from one of the gangs. Or maybe not.'

'You're very noncommittal.'

'Well, if you commit, then you're in it, sir. I'd rather get some facts first.'

'It's been *two weeks*, Dunne.' For the first time, Roosevelt's voice hardened.

'Aye, but I wasn't free to *work* until a few days ago. So what we did was pussyfoot about and do what we could on the sly. These little marks on this paper may not look like much, but they took hours and hours of work, every one of them. What they're going to tell us one day is where this devil is going and where he comes from. And then we'll have him.'

'If he commits enough murders, I suppose you mean.'

'As you say, sir. It's a sad fact.'

Roosevelt, who was still being astonishingly mild considering his thunderings at the high brass, said – and by saying so revealed why he hadn't lit into Dunne – 'What restrictions were put on your investigation by Lieutenant Cleary?'

Dunne frowned, put his tongue sideways between a couple of teeth, and with a questioning look that meant 'Is it all right?' began to fold his map. He spent several seconds folding the map just so, and when he spoke, it was very tentatively. 'I was told to do nothing that would bring in the, um, the private life of the young lady who was the first victim.'

'Lieutenant Cleary told you that?'

'From the highest level, he said.'

Roosevelt sat back. 'How did you interpret that instruction?'

'I took it to mean I was to do nothing, sir. I took it to mean that identifying her was off limits, sir, and so was the young man she was said to be seen

411

with. And so was the witness who saw her.' Dunne, who was fearless, although he didn't look it, stared right into Terrible Teddy's pince-nez. 'I believe it was you got a letter from that witness, sir, and passed it on to Cleary with the instruction to deal with her.'

'I didn't mean for him to silence her!'

'Well, the best-laid plans of mice and men, sir. So I didn't talk to her – I mean Mrs Doyle, which is the lady's name. Not then, I mean. And then when the second murder happened, I was told to keep the two deaths separate and not to connect one with the other.'

'With every newspaper in the city making them the work of the same madman!'

'Yes, sir.' He held up the now folded map. 'I exceeded Lieutenant Cleary's instructions, sir, and I won't disguise the fact.'

'Cleary's out of it, so forget about that!' Terrible Teddy lunged forward. 'All right, Dunne, here's what you're going to do. You appear to be the only competent man – maybe the only sane man – in this entire damned disaster! I want you to go full speed ahead, all stops out, to hell with the limits on boiler pressure! You understand me? The people of New York won't stand for more foot-dragging in these murders. *I* won't stand for more foot-dragging! Interview that woman who saw Mrs Harding in the hotel. Get a description of her paramour – he's your best bet for the killer, isn't he? Get to it! I want an arrest!'

'Does that include Roscoe Harding, sir?'

Roosevelt got very still. 'Harding's a very important man.'

'And as likely a suspect as the "good-looking young man" is.'

'I prefer you leave Harding out of it.'

'His name was in the *Express* yesterday. It was in all the afternoon papers.' The two men seemed to size each other up. Roosevelt, no mean judge of men, was surprised at the amount of spine he was facing. Before he could say anything, Dunne said, 'I was at the City Mortuary as soon as I read Harding's name yesterday. They didn't want to co-operate, so I've applied for a warrant. But one of them implied that you, sir, had something to do with Harding being able to take his wife's body away without signing or having his name appear in the book. As neither does yours.'

Roosevelt turned away and took a step towards a window, then back. He said, 'If you mean to try some sort of blackmail on me, Sergeant, I warn you—'

'I don't, and I'm surprised you'd say it. But I'll tell you this, Mr Roosevelt, if *you* mean to tell *me* not to investigate Harding now I know he's the woman's husband, then I'll say right off the reel, I'll quit the force and take it to the newspapers! It's one thing if a grafter like Cleary tries to get me to fudge an investigation, but you're a commissioner! You're *Theodore Roosevelt*!'

Roosevelt took off his eyeglasses, polished the

lenses carefully on a pocket handkerchief, returned them to his nose. He cleared his throat. 'You remind me of my responsibilities, Dunne. Good for you.' He cleared his throat again. 'Investigate Harding. The gloves are off there; it's common knowledge now that his wife was a fragile reed, so he can't demand we keep it quiet. Ask him for the names of her friends. Ask him about the man she was with. Maybe he knew all about him. Maybe he had a detective on them. Harding's a tough nut, so push him.' Roosevelt looked truculent but a but uncertain; abruptly, he changed his tone entirely. 'You're right – *I* took Harding to the morgue to identify his wife. I accepted his story about wanting his privacy protected, so I'm afraid I was guilty of warning Cleary off from investigating that side of things – although that was not my intention! You go ahead and investigate whatever you want!' He rapped his desk. 'If that leads you here, so be it!'

Dunne looked at him with what might have been cynical disbelief, or perhaps simply practiced blandness. 'I'm free to investigate *anything*, then?'

'Wherever the investigation leads you, I said.'

'Only that Harding's a friend of yours.'

'We belong to the same club, nothing more.'

They held each other's eyes for one, two, three seconds, and Roosevelt said, 'And keep up the good work on that map. That's the kind of police work I like to see – it shows hints that we might be an intelligent lot, after all. Then start to put things together. I want an arrest. Soon!'

'We have a man in custody for the second murder.' When Roosevelt looked blank, Dunne said, 'The pavement sleeper who found the body. We should let him go.'

'Did he do it?'

'He couldn't have. No way to move the body, no place to kill her – and we looked for one. Couldn't have lifted a grown woman off the ground by himself, that fella.'

They looked at each other again. Roosevelt took off his pince-nez again, remembered he'd polished them only seconds before, put them back. And took them off again. 'The newspapers will savage us if they hear we've released the only suspect.' He breathed on the lenses, putting them almost into his toothy mouth. 'Keep him in the Tombs for the time being.'

'In fairness, we ought to let him go.'

Roosevelt looked away from Dunne. He pulled a pile of paper towards himself over the desk's surface. 'Keep him in the Tombs until I tell you otherwise.'

As he got ready to leave, Dunne said, 'Oh, by the way, Commissioner.' Roosevelt looked up, met a rather steely look. 'On the night of the first woman's murder, you were walking the Sixteenth Precinct and ran into a patrolman. D'you remember?'

'If I looked in my notebook, I could be sure.'

'Well, the copper had it in his report that he met you, so it's certain. But what I was wondering, sir, was – when you were walking up to where you met him, did you happen to see anybody with a wagon? Anybody at all?'

Roosevelt frowned. 'Why in the world would you think I had?'

'Only the pattern I showed you on the map. Such a man was seen four blocks farther south. If you'd seen him, you see, then I could say he was that far uptown for sure.'

'I remember nothing of the kind. And I am not the sort of man who forgets what he sees!'

'Right, sir. I'll be on my way, then. But I'd be appreciative if you'd just have a look in your notebook, as you mentioned.' Dunne pocketed his map but turned back from the door. 'A detail, Commissioner. Cleary saddled me with a detective named Finn. Can I kick him off my investigation?'

'Is he a slacker?'

'He's a tale-bearer.'

'Get rid of him!'

An hour later, Dunne again came down the steps of Roscoe Harding's brownstone house and swung himself up into the police carriage that had brought him. Cassidy was waiting inside.

Dunne said, 'Harding knew.'

'About the wife?'

'And about the gigolo who was with her. He had a private D on her. The gigolo came to see Harding

416

the day before she was killed. He told Harding that for a thousand dollars he'd drop out of the wife's life and she'd never see him again.' Dunne smiled. 'And Harding told him he could keep her, as he'd rather have the thousand.'

'He give you a name?'

'He did. And an address.' He swung out to call up to the driver. 'Two-seventeen West Fifteenth Street.' He fell back into the carriage seat. 'Let's pick him up and sweat him.'

By noon, Louisa knew that Minnie wasn't ever going to telephone her. It might be that she'd yet stop at the hotel, but Louisa was clear eyed enough to see that Minnie had been changed by the kiss – that liking had probably turned to fear, even to hate.

'I'm going out,' she said to Ethel, who was doing some sewing in her annex room.

'Galt thinks you're doing too much on that ankle, if you care what Galt thinks.'

'I do care, but I don't agree. You're seeing a lot of him, Ethel?'

'We had a coffee together yesterday, if that's a lot.'

'I didn't mean to pry, Ethel.'

Louisa dressed, mostly without Ethel's help, although out of habit she asked for assistance getting her corset fastened. She wore the grey wool again, in which she felt inconspicuous, even invisible. She wanted now, without ever putting it into words for herself, to blend into the crowds of New York. The only consolation for her deep funk was that she had stopped menstruating: one less bit of bother.

Ethel told her that it was cold out again and that there might be snow. Louisa put on a rather wide winter hat and took her heavy coat from the cupboard. 'I intend to be back by supper. Don't wait for me.'

'It would be best if you tell me where you'll be, madame. Just in case.'

'I'm going to the *Express* offices in Printing House Square.'

Out on the street, she thought that Galt was probably right about the ankle. Still, she was getting along pretty well on the cane now, and she certainly didn't want to go back to the crutches.

She asked the doorman how to get to the Elevated, and he told her where to stand to get the cross-town tram going east. There was nothing to it, really, as she found when she'd done it – off the tram at Third Avenue, up the stairs with less fuss than she'd expected, drop a five-cent piece into a slot, and cross the platform. The little green station was made of wood, almost like a station-master's house in rural England, but without the flowers. She got on the steam train; a couple of men actually rose to offer her a seat – not what she'd expected of the completely democratic El.

And the El revived her: She saw ragamuffin boys, gentlemen in silk hats, Negroes, tired-looking working women heading home from the uptown sweat shops, a couple of tough-looking men in clothes too good for them – politicians? The car swayed as it went down the tracks, but she didn't care. The train was whizzing along the backsides of tenements. Few windows were open, but many were uncurtained. She saw a woman at an ironing board, a man sitting at a kitchen table, a man and woman arguing, a man and woman embracing: people living real lives within fifty feet of thousands who rattled past them every day. When the train made a slight bend, she knew (she'd looked it all up in her guide before she started) that Third Avenue had ended and they were now running down Bowery. She was delighted, as she had been on her first cab ride down the same street: here were those same buildings she had seen from below, seen a storey higher: now Bowery was a street of human beings, of homes, of kitchens and bedrooms and men in shirtsleeves and women in aprons and children coming in with books carried in a tightened strap. Maybe the men worked in the dime museums and the concert saloons; maybe the women did their work down on the street or in back rooms, but up here they were simply *people*, humanized and democratized by the Elevated Railway.

All this life! So many! How can we ever think we're special, even separate, when there are so many! We're not individuals; we're like herring coming in from the sea. But then she thought of the two murdered women and how individual they were. They had separate identities because they had been savaged. Because they had been picked out. *But how? And why?*

She had planned her route and so got down at Chatham Square and changed to the Second Avenue line – not half so bad as she'd feared – and took the short hop to City Hall. Coming down to street level was a disappointment. But again to her surprise, an overweight sort in a checked suit raised his hat and offered his arm to cross the whirling traffic of Park Row; he looked like a tout, but he certainly behaved like a gentleman.

Who was it who had toured America and been so sharp eyed? Mrs Trollope, of course, but she was more sharp tongued than eyed, much too harsh, in fact rude. No, the other one – Tocqueville, that one – he would have understood the man in the loud suit. He was the essence of America, both mannerly and mannerless, both tasteless and tactful. Perhaps she would write about him to Arthur, about the idea of capturing an essence in a single example. But of course, Arthur would think she was telling him how to write.

She went up to the *Express* offices in the grubby lift and went straight to the newsroom and this time didn't shilly-shally. She said to the first man who looked up at her, 'I'd like to see Miss Fitch, please.'

The man was working at a typewriting machine. He had on an eyeshade and had a pencil between his teeth, and he wasn't wearing his jacket, which was draped over the back of his straight chair. He looked up at her and said through his pencil, 'Isn't here.'

'She must be here. It's after three.'

'Hasn't been here all day. Out on a story, prob'ly.'

She tried one of the copy boys, got the same answer, so asked around with a pushiness that surprised her and got referred to an eminence called the city editor, who was perched in a tiny office that overlooked the newsroom as if he were a warder in some sort of institution.

'Excuse me?'

He looked up. '*What?*'

'I was told to ask you where Miss Fitch is.'

'Who the devil told you to ask me?'

'One of the men there.'

'Which one? I'll skin him alive!' He was a peppery little man of about sixty, and, she thought, more manner than substance, as if he'd read that newspaper editors were supposed to be tough and he was still trying to get it right.

She said again, 'I'd like to know where Miss Fitch is.'

'Wouldn't we all! Who the devil are you?'

'I am Mrs Arthur Conan Doyle, and Miss Fitch is a friend.'

'This isn't a tearoom. Help me out by not bothering those guys over there; it's hard enough to get any work out of them as it is. Nice to have met you.' He started to close his door.

421

'Have you heard from Miss Fitch today?'

'Would I look this worried if I had? She's got a deadline coming up on tomorrow's story and she hasn't filed and I haven't heard from her, and if you see her you can tell her from me that she's about one hour from being booted! Now go somewheres.'

She limped away to the newsroom entrance. As she got there, one of the copy boys shot out of the swinging wooden gate and stopped in front of her as if he were on skates, leaning back to keep his balance. He said, 'You the one's looking for Fitch?'

'Yes!'

'She ain't here and she ain't been here! Fer a dime I'll tell you something.'

Money, money. Louisa produced a dime. The boy said, his voice low and conspiratorial, 'Old Woebegone sent Jackson over to her place and she wasn't there and *hadn't been there all night* AND Woebegone's been tearing his hair out 'cause she's between the sheets someplace with some fella!' He laughed and fled.

What a vulgar child. What a terrible place for a child to be, all those rough men. And how terrible for Minnie. Of course, she didn't believe for a second that Minnie was with a man if she had a deadline and a story due, because Minnie lived for reporting, not romance. And this story was supposed to make her a star – her word.

She stopped at the elevator. While she waited,

she couldn't help reading the graffiti. She again read the one that said, 'Fitch eats the hairy banana.' Somebody had crossed out 'banana' and written 'muff' above it.

She could figure that out, too. She blushed. Had that been written because of something Minnie had done or said – was it the kiss? Or Louisa's telephone calls? She could imagine the jokes, made loud enough for Minnie to hear: 'Fitch's lady friend,' 'Fitch's girl.'

At least 'hairy muff' made more anatomical sense than 'hairy banana.'

But none of that was important. *Where was Minnie?*

She stared at that question. She heard the elevator crash its gates on the floor above. Minnie hadn't been home all night. Minnie hadn't telephoned in. The Butcher had murdered another woman.

She confronted a possibility.

She turned around and marched back to the newsroom and grabbed the arm of the first man who passed. 'Where is McClurg, the sketch artist?'

This one was pop-eyed and fortyish, not a reporter, she thought, but one of the copy-editors, unless she was confusing him with somebody else she'd seen up on the dais. He said, shaking off her hand, 'Look in the saloons, lady. Unless you're his wife.'

'Which saloon?'

She had moved around to block his progress.

He looked disgusted but shouted over her head at a boy, 'Hey, Gargan, where's McClurg at today?'

'The Seventy-seven! He's in the back polishing the sketch.'

'Where is the—'

But the man had pushed past her.

She went down and learned from Information where the Seventy-seven was – just along Park Row at number 77, of course. She set out on foot, her cane clicking on the pavement, her ankle hurting her from the first step.

Detective-Sergeant Dunne took the same low chair in front of Roosevelt's desk, wondering if the great man had deliberately made his own chair high and the visitor's chair low. It was the sort of thing a little man would do, Dunne thought.

'Well, do we have him?' Roosevelt bellowed.

'I went to talk to Harding. Harding's not a suspect any more: he was visiting one of his coal mines in Pennsylvania the day before his wife was murdered, that night, and part of the next day. His secretary was with him and vouched for him.' Dunne sighed. 'Unless Harding paid somebody to kill his wife.' He looked at Roosevelt, who was frowning and pursing his lips.

Dunne went on, 'We picked up a guy named Gerald Oppenheimer, not that that's necessarily his real name. It was the name Harding gave me. The one who was seen with his wife at the New Britannic, we hope.'

'Poor Harding – he knew all along. What sort of fellow is this Oppenheimer?'

'Ladies' man. A sort of gigolo, only he's a con man, too. His game is, he dances around some rich man's wife, makes her fall for him, gets her to give him presents, then he goes to the husband and says he'll stop for a chunk of money.'

'A complete blackguard, you mean.'

'Harding sent him packing. Which could be made to look to a jury like the gigolo's motive for murdering the wife.'

'I see, I see. Mm.'

Dunne was watching Roosevelt closely, probably more closely than Terrible Teddy understood. 'But no better than the motive Harding might have had for paying somebody to kill her.'

Roosevelt scowled at that. 'Men like Roscoe Harding don't have women chopped up.' He made a gesture with an index finger that meant 'Get on with it.'

'But neither one had a motive for murdering the other women, unless you want to say he did it to cover his tracks, but that's far fetched.'

Roosevelt frowned. 'What does this "gigolo" say?'

'He says he's got cover for the second killing: he was in a room at the Earle with a girl all that night. But so far we can't find the girl. This last killing, he's vague. He was maybe in his room all night, or maybe he was drunk in a concert saloon. He can't remember, is his tale. The first one, Harding's wife, he says he didn't do it.'

'Can he be broken?'

Dunne didn't like beating confessions out of people. It was his view that anybody could be taken to a precinct cellar and rubberhosed until he'd admit that he'd shot Lincoln. 'Is that what you want us to do?'

Roosevelt glanced at him and looked away as if he meant not to be there when the actual words were spoken. 'A man like that deserves no mercy.' He seemed to wait, perhaps for agreement from Dunne. When none came, he said as if to himself, 'Better that he hang for all three than that the police be punching-bags for the press.' He didn't look at Dunne, but concentrated on something on his desk. 'Get a confession from him by . . . customary methods. I want to have something for the newspapers by tomorrow at two p.m.'

Dunne got up and left.

The Seventy-seven could have been a saloon anywhere, although Louisa didn't know that because she'd never been in one before; it had matchboard walls and a few pictures and some men sitting where they didn't have to communicate with each other while they drank. She was frightened and disgusted, but what she wanted was too important to stop.

'No ladies allowed,' the barman said to her.

'Where's McClurg of the *Express*?'

'You his missus?'

'Do I look it? He's supposed to be in the back room. Where's the back room?'

The man glanced at a closed door and said, 'You can't go in there.'

'Oh, can't I!' She was already heading for the door. The barman came around the end of the bar and tried to head her off; she waved her cane and he ducked and backed, and somebody laughed. She put her hand on the knob and went through the door and closed it behind her.

McClurg was lying on a horsehair sofa with his coat off and a bottle and a glass on the floor beside him. He looked up but didn't move. 'I thought it was Attila the Hun,' he said.

'Where's Minnie Fitch?'

'The question of the hour. It redounds from house to rooftop to the mountains! Where is Minnie Fitch? Gone where the woodbine twineth, I hope *not*. Don't I know you?'

'You met me with Minnie in a bakery and did some drawings.'

'So I did.' He sighed, reached for his glass and drank, put it down. 'What now?'

'We have to go to the mortuary, Mr McClurg.'

'Oh my God, why?'

'Have you seen the Butcher's third victim yet?'

'No, and I ain't going to, because she's got no face to sketch. They already called and told us. Can't put a sketch of a woman with no face in the noospaper, m'dear, the kiddies would be shocked.'

No face. So that's why they can't identify her. She tried not to think of Minnie without a face. 'You said Minnie might be gone where the woodbine twineth, Mr McClurg.' Louisa tried to keep all feeling out of her voice. 'Well, maybe she has.' She plucked McClurg's coat from a brass hook on the wall and held it up. 'Come on. The City Morgue.'

He looked at her. 'Minnie?'

'Minnie's disappeared. In the mortuary there's a . . .' Her voice broke. 'A woman with no face. *Come on, you drunken sot!*'

'You can't talk to me like that.'

'Pretend I'm your wife. Come *on*!'

He sat up and took several breaths. 'You're too much like Minnie. *She* bosses me all over the place. Look, I told you, there's nothing at the morgue!'

'You mean you're afraid of what we'll find.'

'You've got a screw loose, lady.'

She advanced on him with the coat. 'It's Mrs Doyle. Put this coat on at once.'

She led him through the saloon to the jeers of several drinkers. Outside, she made him hail a cab because her ankle hurt too much to walk. At the morgue, a different man was on duty; he knew McClurg, hardly noticed when the artist said 'My assistant' and jerked a thumb towards Louisa. They went down into the depths, Louisa limping, and an attendant shook his head at McClurg and said, 'I told the papers, this one's got no face.'

McClurg said with drunken dignity, 'Orders are orders. Lead on.'

The attendant led them in and pulled out a slab. 'You really want to see this one?'

He pulled the sheet that covered the body; piling the cloth on the head so that the face couldn't be seen. What had been a grey mountain range became a wax-like female body. The colour had drained from it with the blood; now it was not much different from the shades of stone and dried concrete, slightly yellowed, of the walls.

Fortified, or at least forewarned, by the medical reports on the first two murders, Louisa was able to stand there. The smell was strong, repellent, but she stood there. She looked.

What was there to see? Only the pathos and the disgust of it. She had to steel herself to look at the rawness of the flesh where the breasts had been, now the colour of meat boiled too long in water; they were revolting, at the same time deeply touching. She thought of the pride she took in her own breasts; unconsciously, she put a hand on one, pressed it, felt her heart.

The doctor's wife in her looked and knew that everything from the stomach down had been removed. She said, 'Did you wash her?'

'First thing we did.'

'Was there blood?'

'Some. She'd bled out, but he'd cleaned her up some. Not like the first one, though.'

'And the . . . intestines, and so on?'

'Taken out, you know? When they brought her in, the guts were looped around her, wrapped up

429

her legs and all like that.' He was watching her. He was trying to make her faint or sick, she knew. 'He'd hung her on a meat hook under a sign that said "Sausages." Like her guts was sausages, get it?'

Louisa moved closer to the body.

'Don't touch it!'

'Hush.'

She reached to turn over the hand on which Minnie had shown her a burn scar.

'Don't touch it, I said!' The attendant's voice was brutal.

She made her own voice savage. 'She isn't an *it*! She's a woman!'

'I call all the stiffs "it."'

Louisa put her back to him and turned the hand over. He began to shout; she felt his hand on her shoulder, but she was looking at the shriveled skin in the yellowed palm, the scars of the childhood burning. She said, 'Oh, Minnie.'

Behind her, McClurg gagged, staggered, and vomited where he stood. The attendant swore. He let go of Louisa and roared at them to get out, look at the mess, now he had to clean it up!

Louisa heard him stamp away down the long room; there was the rattle of a metal bucket. She reached forward and jerked the cloth off the head.

The face had indeed been flayed. Her eyes went at once to what was left: the underlying muscles and tendons, half face, half skull in shape. The teeth were horrifyingly visible. The eyes were still there, now seeming huge. Louisa felt bile surge up her throat and into her mouth; she clenched her jaws, forced it down.

She gazed down at the terrible eyes, no more now like Minnie's eyes than they were like billiard balls on a table. She studied the browning facial muscles, the softness of what had been lips. She bent and kissed them.

'Hey, lady, Jesus!'

As if, with a kiss on the skinless lips, she could take away the kiss that had come between them. Or give it back in a different way.

He pulled her away. She smelled McClurg's vomit, smelled the corpse of her friend, which was only the smell of all corpses. McClurg was leaning on a wall, wiping his mouth with a handkerchief. His eyes were running tears. She said, 'You'd better tell them that it's Minnie.'

McClurg said, 'I'll do a sketch of her. I can do it from memory.' He began weeping.

The attendant held up a mop. 'Not till you clean up your mess on my floor, you don't!'

Louisa snatched the mop from him. 'I'll do it! You heartless, brainless dolt! You should be ashamed – you should be horse-whipped!' She began to scrub furiously. Most of what McClurg had thrown up was whiskey. It could have been much worse.

CHAPTER 11

When Louisa returned to the hotel, it was well past six o'clock. The police had kept her in an office at the morgue to question her about her identification of Minnie Fitch. Louisa had never been examined by the police before, so she wasn't prepared for what seemed to be their hostility. The hostility, she decided, was really a cynicism born of hearing a lot of lies for many years. Still, she felt more like a suspect than a witness. She became angry when the questioning was done all over again by a man who introduced himself as Detective Forcella from the Murder Squad.

'You *knew* it would be her, Mrs Doyle?'

'I thought it might be. I didn't say I *knew*.'

'Why'd you think it "might be"?'

'Because it was so unlike her not to have come to work.'

The detective looked at a policeman and squinched up his mouth and nose as if he'd smelled something bad. He was young and rather good looking in an Italian way. He said, 'Where were you last night, Mrs Doyle?'

She started to say angrily that that was none of his business, but she realized that she would only waste time if she did; she said, 'In my room at the New Britannic Hotel.'

A look she didn't understand passed between the two policemen, followed by some irrelevant-seeming questions about the New Britannic – how long had she been there, when had she left there today, where was her husband? Finally, they asked all the same questions again and then all three of them waited while her answers were written out in a fair copy by somebody else, and she was able to sign and leave.

'You stay where we can find you when we want you, please, Mrs Doyle.'

There was no proper answer to that, so she gave none. McClurg, who had also been questioned, had waited for her. He was soberer, but he still was grieving. He said, 'I couldn't believe it. I *can't* believe it. Why Minnie?'

'Because she wrote that article.'

'That's about the cops. You think a cop did this?'

'It wasn't just about the "cops." It was also about the murderer – and the hotel.'

'You knew before we went to the morgue, didn't you.'

'That's what the police asked. I didn't know; you can't *know*. But I was standing by the elevator, and I was thinking about her not coming in today and about what she was supposed to write next . . .'

McClurg shuddered. He took her arm. 'Don't you ever cry?'

'Often.'

'You ought to be in the newspaper business.' He had walked her to the street and got her a cab. 'We'll give her a big sendoff. The *Express* will want to make a big shindig out of it. Tell me you'll come.'

She had smiled. She took the cab only to the elevated station at Chatham Square to save herself changing trains there, and then she climbed the now-painful stairs to the platform and waited for the train. It was already half dark, lights coming on in the tenement windows. There was no joy in the trip this time, nor any of its interest in the life within the buildings. All she saw was Minnie, Minnie with and without a face.

Then she was back at the hotel, puzzled by a cluster of sour-looking men and women on the pavement, and two boys coming out the bronze doors with loads of luggage. It seemed to her an odd time to be leaving a hotel, but perhaps they had found something they couldn't bear about the New Britannic. She limped around them and was surprised to be stopped by a policeman. She tried to go around – she wanted a hot bath and her bed and a sleeping powder – and he held her arm.

'Only registered guests, lady.'

'I *am* a registered guest. What in the world is going on?'

'Name?'

She waited. She said, 'What has that to do with my going into my hotel?'

'You got a name, you're registered, you can go in.'

'I am Mrs Arthur Conan Doyle.'

'Room number?'

'Really, this is . . . !' She understood from his face that he was serious. He was young, too, and probably new, thus more truculent than he needed to be. Another, older cop was standing where the doorman should have been. He, too, was waiting for her answer: he had a sheet of paper and a pencil.

She said, 'Room 201, the annex.'

The older cop looked at his paper, drew a line, jerked his head. 'Let her in.'

The young one let go of her arm. The older one, to her relief, opened the heavy bronze door for her. She thought that she couldn't have done it herself, not with a weak ankle and the weight of Minnie.

The scene inside was astonishing. She saw at least five policemen. People she recognized as guests were seated in the front part of the lobby, cordoned off with brass standards and a velvet rope; other guests – she recognized Irving and Cody and a few others – were on the other side. They seemed more relaxed; several were smoking; one or two had drinks. Around the reception desk was a pile of luggage far too big to be for only one party; near it, three unhappy-looking souls were scowling at the world.

'What is going on?'

Another cop had appeared with another piece of paper. 'Name and room number?'

'I just gave that outside.'

'Makes no diff to me, lady; I need your name and room number.'

She sighed to show how abused she felt and muttered, 'Doyle, Annex 201.'

He made a mark on his paper and pulled one of the brass standards away from the wall. 'Wait in there.'

'For what?'

'I don't make the rules and I don't answer questions. I got my orders. Take a chair.'

She wanted to make herself regal, but she felt crumpled, sagging, round shouldered. She limped into the enclosure and let herself down into a leather chair. She recognized several of the people near by. When she met their eyes, they shook their heads or made faces. She said to a tall man in good clothes whom she had seen in the dining room, 'What in the world is going on?'

'Somebody's dead.'

'Who?'

'They won't tell us.'

She looked around, as if by elimination she might guess who it was; the fact was that in a hotel with two hundred rooms she could hardly know everyone by sight. She looked across to the other side of the lobby, met Irving's eyes. He smiled and bowed, said something to Cody, who then did the same.

Another cop appeared and called a name, and a man and a woman got up from her group and went away with him.

'What are they doing?'

'Asking questions.'

Death, police, questions. She had just left those things at the morgue. She had a momentary, disorienting idea that this was all about Minnie, was the same questioning, the same police, but she came to and realized it had to be different. But not usual, not merely a death; the police didn't appear by the dozen for a routine death.

Somebody was shouting at Reception. Carver was there, looking sweaty and harassed. The shouter and the others by the pile of luggage must be people who had reserved rooms and weren't being allowed to go beyond the lobby. And the people marching off with their luggage must be people who refused to wait and were going to another hotel.

She sank back into the embrace of the chair. A minute later, she was asleep.

'Doyle!'

Somebody was calling her, somebody with a telegram. No, no; that was a dream. She struggled towards the surface, remembered where she was. A policeman was shouting, 'Doyle! Doyle, you here?'

'Yes – over here – I'm so sorry . . .'

'Come on, come on!'

She followed the policeman out of the enclosure

and past Reception and into a corridor below the mezzanine where there were offices. He opened a door, shouted 'Doyle!' and all but pushed her in. Inside were a desk, several chairs, a plant that needed water, two men in suits.

'Sit down, please.'

'I wish to protest at the way I am being treated.'

'Write a letter to headquarters, 300 Mulberry Street, New York, New York.' His head was down, showing a balding spot. He was looking at more papers. The other man, sitting behind him, was stretching; he had papers, too. The balding one looked up. 'Please sit down, Mrs Doyle.'

'Why am I here?'

'We're questioning the guests and the staff. There's been a death in the hotel.'

'Who?'

'I'll ask the questions, please.' He was middle aged and looked tired; he was probably bored, she thought, and irritated with all these well-off people, a lot of them foreigners, who thought they were better than he was. If he really thought all that, he was nonetheless polite. 'I'm Detective Mercer of the Sixteenth Precinct, and behind me is Detective-Probationer Matthews. He's going to take down your answers. We can make this quick and short if you'll just answer what I ask.'

'Very well.' She was thinking that Minnie was dead; she had seen her corpse; she had mopped up vomit; why was she being questioned?

'Great. You just came into the hotel at . . .' He looked at a paper. 'Six thirty-seven, that right?'

'It sounds right; I didn't look at the time.'

'When did you leave the hotel?'

'About noon. A little after, I think.'

He made a notation. The other detective was writing. 'That your first time out of the hotel today?'

'Yes.'

'Did you see anything or anybody different from usual at any time you were in the hotel today?'

'No.' She wanted to say *Of course not*, but she was trying to be quick. She wanted to be alone; she wanted to grieve.

'Do you know a guest named Mr Alexander Newcome?'

'Is it he who's died?'

'Please let me ask the questions, Mrs Doyle. Do you know him?'

'Yes. To speak to. I know his aunt, Mrs Simmons, better. But we sit and chat sometimes.'

He looked at his papers. 'You've been in the hotel a couple of weeks, is that right?'

'More or less.'

'In that time, have you ever seen Mr Newcome with anybody who struck you in any way as unusual? Maybe somebody who didn't belong in this hotel, or somebody maybe not a guest?'

Should I tell him about what I saw this morning? No, it's trivial and it harms Newcome. But I should. It's only fact. If Newcome's dead, how can it harm him? She said, 'I believe I saw Mr Newcome with someone very early this morning. From my window.'

The detective seemed to quicken. 'What kind of person?'

'I don't know. A man, I think.'

'What time was this?'

'It was very early in the morning. About four? Perhaps some minutes before that.'

'*In* the hotel?'

'No – well, yes, in a way – my room is in the annex, you see.' She told him about the view from her window, the door, the figures she took for the breakfast cooks.

The detective seemed almost excited. 'You're sure it was Newcome?'

Sure. That was a hard absolute. Would she swear in a court that it had been Newcome? She thought of that face as it had looked up at her. 'Yes.'

The detective swung around and said to the younger man, 'Get that guy from the Murder Squad; tell him we got a break.' He turned back as the other man rushed out of the little room. 'Would you like some tea or coffee, Mrs Doyle? Happy to send for something.'

'I'd like to go to my room and lie down.'

'Ma'am, I'd love to be able to let you do that, and I promise we won't keep you a minute longer than we got to. But what you've told me is important. A cup of tea might help pass the time.'

It wouldn't pass the time. It would make it even

longer until she could be alone. Minnie had laughed at her for wanting tea instead of coffee in the park. 'Please. Tea.'

'You bet.' He went to the door and spoke to somebody there. When he was still standing there, closing the door, she said, 'Has Mr Newcome been killed?'

'What makes you think that?'

'Detective – I'm sorry, I've forgotten your name, it's very rude of me—'

'Mercer.'

'Detective Mercer, you wouldn't be here asking me questions if it weren't something bad. I don't think you'd be here for heart failure or a fall.' *And where were you when Minnie was being murdered?*

He looked as if he wanted to tell her something, but he said only, 'You'll know as soon as everybody else does, I promise.'

Her tea came, and very welcome it turned out to be, but it took another good quarter of an hour before the door opened and the wide body of Detective-Sergeant Dunne pushed in, his unbuttoned suit jacket billowing around him like a cape, making him seem all the bigger. He said to Mercer, 'Why don't you get yourself a bite, lad, put your feet up. They've laid on a feed for us in the kitchen. You, too.' This to the second detective.

She didn't like the idea of being alone with any man in a small room, but perhaps he didn't like it either, because he went to the door and spoke and another, quite small man sidled in and sat in

Matthews's chair. Dunne was going through the scribbled pages that Matthews had left behind. He was frowning and moving his lips. He looked up at her and said, 'We meet again, Mrs Doyle. I'll be with you in a minute.'

And that was about as much longer as he took. He sat in Mercer's chair and shuffled the papers and made a neat stack of them and then looked at her as if he meant to memorize every detail about her. He leaned back, hooked an arm over the back of the chair. 'You saw Newcome with another man at four this morning.'

'About four, yes.'

'Tell me the layout – where you were, where they were, where the light was coming from.'

She did it as well as she could, irritated that she was having to do it a second time, irritated with herself because she knew he had to do it this way. When she was done, he told it back to her in a shorter form that was accurate and crisp. He finished, 'So all the light came from the door, correct? If the door was closed, there was no light. Yes?' She nodded. 'How did Newcome and this other man behave?'

'They . . . giggled.'

He nodded as if that was something he heard all the time. 'What else?'

'I think that Mr Newcome had been drinking.' She tried to justify herself. 'He staggered once. And he giggled, which wasn't like him other times.'

'Did you see the other man's face?'

442

'No. Not well, I mean.'

'Did they seem friendly?'

'Well . . . They embraced.'

'Put their arms around each other? Or just an arm over the shoulders, like one of them helping the other one home? More like embracing when people kiss, would you say?'

'Yes, I think . . . in fact . . . I had the impression they were kissing.' *As I kissed Minnie and she me.*

That didn't seem any more or less interesting to Dunne than anything else he'd heard. He tipped his head back and looked at the ceiling and narrowed his eyes – was he seeing the scene? – and said, 'The other man. The first one you saw, I mean. What was he like?'

'I thought he was a breakfast cook. But they were too early to be the cooks, as it turned out; the real cooks came in later.'

'What was he like – young, old, tall, short . . . ?'

'I saw him only from above. He was wearing some sort of soft hat, but I couldn't see his face. I could see his shadow on the pavement when he opened the door; his coat looked quite long. That doesn't help much, does it.'

'He came along the alley first.'

'Well . . . I don't believe I was aware of him until I heard his keys. I suppose he did come along the alley, yes, but he was really directly below me when I first became aware of him. I heard his keys, and then the key in the lock, sort of a grating sound – I thought of rats, I remember – and then he opened the door and the light came out of the open door. In a kind of fan, you know.'

'Had the other two appeared by then?'

She tried to remember. 'I think . . . perhaps . . .'

'Could they see him?'

'I really don't know. They embraced and . . . kissed, I think, and then Newcome pulled the door open wider, and that's when he looked up and I recognized him. Oh, and then – I think it was then – he looked inside and . . . he might have said something, or . . . I remember thinking that maybe there was someone there he knew.'

Dunne sat back. He bit his lower lip and made small sucking noises. He studied her. 'And they both had keys.'

'The first man and Mr Newcome, yes.'

Dunne wiped his mouth, shifted his legs, and looked at the ceiling again. 'You've made a number of things clearer, Mrs Doyle. Much clearer. I think I'll let you go now, but I'm going to have a couple of fellas out in that alley below your window, so don't be surprised if you see them. And I'd like to come by in a bit to have a look from that window of yours myself. I'll bring you your statement to sign and save you waiting around.'

'I'd hoped to lie down.'

'And so you can, for at least a bit of time. Once I've seen what I need to see, I'll be out of your hair.' He stood and, to her surprise, held out his hand. 'You're a good witness.' He held on to her hand when she offered it. 'I think there are one or two

444

other things I'd like to talk to you about. Tomorrow? Not tonight, but certainly tomorrow. You're not leaving, I hope.'

'No. No. But I shall have things to do.' She didn't know why she said what she said next, but she did, responding, perhaps, to something warm in Dunne. 'I lost a very dear friend today.'

He looked solemn, then severe. 'So I heard. That's one of the things I want to talk about.' He went to the door. 'Thank you, Mrs Doyle. I'll see you in an hour.'

She was taken to her room in the annex by a policeman. When she closed her door, she saw a telegram on the floor. It would be from Arthur, of course. Had he relented?

YOU MUST LEARN ADULT RESTRAINT STOP NOT ANOTHER PENNY STOP OBEDIENCE YOUR DUTY STOP ARRIVE NEW YORK NOON DAY AFTER TOMORROW STOP DO NOTHING UNTIL ARRIVAL STOP ARTHUR

She threw it in the wastebasket.

Then she went into the WC and vomited.

She lay down on her bed and tried to sleep, thought instead of Minnie and now was able to cry. The terrible finality of death, the terrible chasm of loss. But in a way, weren't they really about oneself? Minnie no longer cared; Minnie didn't feel the horror or the finality. And although Louisa was revolted by the means of Minnie's death, that revulsion wasn't the worst of it. The worst of it was the complete loss of her. That Minnie had suffered pained her; she actually writhed on the bed, thinking of the wounds. But that was an essentially animal sympathy, woman for woman, creature for creature. No, what was worst was the hollow that had appeared in herself: the loss. *'The pity of it, oh, the pity!'* But wasn't it really self-pity?

Detective-Sergeant Dunne came back as he had said he would, but a good deal more than an hour later; she was asleep by then, red eyed, frowzy. He seemed hardly to look at her, but gave her two typewritten pages to read while he looked down from her window, then sat by it as she had sat before, then opened the window and gave some instructions to somebody out there. It was dark. Cold air flowed in the open window; he seemed not to notice. He was, she thought, restaging the scene. She even heard him say, 'Laugh,' then, 'A little closer in.' Light came on and went out in the alley – the opening and closing of the door? After ten minutes of this – what she had heard Irving call stage management – he closed the window and accepted the signed statement from her.

'I'll let you sleep now. But I do need to see you tomorrow.'

She said, 'It is Mr Newcome, isn't it?'

He nodded.

'How did he die?'

He shrugged. 'It'll be in the late papers anyway. He was beaten to death.'

She closed her eyes. 'In his room?'

'The housemaid found him about three this afternoon.'

Her eyes were still closed. Tears trickled down from beneath her eyelids. As if another voice were speaking through her, she said, 'This place is cursed.'

'That's the other thing I want to talk to you about tomorrow.' He had brought an overcoat that seemed to be made of many yards of hairy fabric. As he struggled into it, he said, 'And about you, Mrs Doyle. I'm a little worried about how you keep turning up in these matters.'

Roosevelt lived on Madison Avenue. Dunne was tired out and wanted to go home, but he'd had a message from the commissioner that said he wasn't to leave duty without reporting to him. The death of Newcome, Dunne thought, was somewhat like the death of Harding's wife – Roosevelt's kind of people. They mattered. He wondered if the deaths of people like this poor newspaper bitch who was the latest victim mattered to Roosevelt. Mattered in the way that a death of one of his own mattered.

He was shown in by a uniformed maid and led to a paneled, book-lined room that he supposed was called the study rather than the office. He'd kept his hat and coat, although the maid had wanted to take them; it would be more time lost, waiting for them, once Roosevelt was through with him.

'Aha, yes, well! Good of you to come.' Roosevelt was wearing short evening dress, a jacket instead of tails. His arse stuck out more than the tailor had meant it to. He rubbed his hands. 'Is it colder out?'

Weary now, Dunne was tempted to say, 'Colder than what?' but he nodded and said it was cold. 'I've just come from the New Britannic.'

'Yes, this chap Newcome. I think I went to school with one of his brothers. Well?'

'It looks like he was one of "those." A witness saw him bring another man into the hotel by a back door in the small hours. Saw them kissing, in fact.'

'Awh!' Roosevelt smacked a fist into a palm and turned away. 'How could he?'

'We think it's the usual story – he brings somebody back to his room, the other one beats him up and robs him.'

'Beats him to *death*?'

'It happens. If it's the usual type, some tough kid, they can carry a load of hate for what they have to do. It happens.'

'Will the family have to know?'

'The papers already got it. They'll be on the sex angle like flies on a mince pie.' Dunne picked up his hat as a sign that he was ready to leave. 'I've got people out looking for the suspect. There's a fairy saloon, the Golden Pit, down in the Village.'

He didn't whitewash it. He was tired, and tired of Roosevelt. 'Barman there saw the dead man with a kid named Philly Nugent. We should have him by morning.'

Roosevelt put his hands behind him. 'This city is a sinkhole.'

'Most cities are.' Dunne got into his overcoat and started away. 'By the way, the woman who saw Newcome and this kid, Nugent, at the New Britannic was the same woman who wrote you the letter about seeing Mrs Harding in the hotel with her gigolo.' He waited for a response, got only Roosevelt's frown. 'She seems to get around.' He went to the door, said, 'She's also the woman that identified the Butcher's third victim.'

Far uptown on the west side, in fact on the northern fringe of Yorktown, a closed carriage came slowly along a modest street, the driver slowing and peering at the houses to find a number. At last, he pulled to the kerb and said something to two men inside. One got out and went up the neat walk, the white-painted bricks on each side now smudges in the darkness. He rang, and eventually a light appeared in an upper window. After still more time, the front door opened; there was a murmur of voices, then another delay.

At last the first man came down the walk with Sergeant Grady, now under suspension from the Murder Squad. The first man opened the carriage door for him. Grady climbed in. The man called the driver down from the box and walked away with him up the street.

There was no light inside the carriage except for the dim glow from a street lamp a few yards away. Nonetheless, the man in the carriage said in a rich Irish voice, 'I guess you know who I am, Grady.'

'Yes, sir.' He'd have been a poor cop who didn't know Deputy Chief Francis Xavier Halloran, even in the dark. The rich voice, dripping sincerity and truth like slobber, filled the carriage.

'Well then, Grady, you can guess why I'm here. For the good of the department, man!'

'Yes, sir?' Grady was frightened, but he was thinking, *Here comes the shit.*

'Now, Grady, you're a man of sense and a man of great experience in the police. I'm sure you understand the seriousness of having a crooked cop in our midst. I'm referring to Lieutenant Cleary, your former boss, you know. It's a sad fact, Grady, but he's a dishonest man.'

'Yes, sir.'

'So I know you see as clear as I do that something must be done. Now, I've just come from a meeting of some of the senior fellas – I won't mention any names, but you know who I mean – and we all agreed that it's unfortunate that your name has been dragged into the mud with Cleary's. Now, you may know or you may not, that Cleary has offered to give evidence that you were the one behind the corruption that has so upset Commissioner Roosevelt. Did you know that, Grady?'

'No, sir! Nor will I believe it of him!'

'That's loyal of you, Grady; that's to your credit. Unfortunately, nonetheless, it's true. What Cleary is, besides being a skunk and a snitch, is a loose cannon. He'd tell anybody anything to save his own skin. I suppose he'd even tell Roosevelt it was me put him up to his shenanigans. He's a bad actor, Grady. You agree, don't you, Grady?'

After a second or two, Grady muttered, 'Yes, sir.'

'And so something has to be done about him, d'ye see that too, Grady?'

'I suppose so, sir.'

'And we think that you're the man to do it, Grady. And if you do, what we see is you being promoted, as you would have been years ago but for Cleary; and we believe we can see the way to improve your manner of living by putting you on to some fine investments, too. I guess your wife would like that, Grady?'

'I . . . suppose she would.'

'Everything can come clear once we've dealt with this villain in our midst. We'll have cleaned the barrel of the bad apple, and we'll be able to make a new life for you – promotion and a decent bit of money. D'you follow me, Grady? Are you with us? That's fine; that's excellent! Now, Grady, here's what you must do . . .'

CHAPTER 12

Louisa spent another bad night. Now it was Newcome as well as Minnie, appearing in dreams not as themselves but as cats and dogs and old patients of Arthur's, animals and humans she had somehow failed, losing them, trying to find her way back to them, running from somebody or something that took her farther and farther from them. Waking at midnight, she felt melancholy, futile; she dozed, twisted the bedcovers, dreamed through an agony of sex that never went anywhere, to wake and know the dream had been about Manion, although he hadn't been in it as himself. At three, she was sitting by the window again, shivering in a wrap. Nobody came down the alley until after five, and they were only the breakfast staff.

She felt little for Newcome himself. In the end, she hadn't liked him much. His aunt would be affected, she thought, but Mrs Simmons was probably tougher than her soft body and her laces suggested. And perhaps she hadn't liked Newcome much, either.

For Louisa, Minnie's death caused Newcome's to shrink to a dot.

Grief for Minnie had settled in as a kind of ache. She felt no pangs of the heart, no flashes of romantic loss, but the ache seemed always to be there. Grief, regret, loss. And anger, which did flash and thunder, anger not at Minnie for dying but at her murderer for killing her . . .

She wanted to lie in bed and sink back into sleep. She wanted to be numb. Instead, she dozed sitting up, then crawled into bed only to throw herself out of bed again at seven.

At ten, she was far downtown at Chase's Bank on Nassau Street. She asked there whether she could draw money on her husband's account, but no matter what documents she showed, they were terribly sorry, Mrs Doyle, but they would need permission from her husband and *his* signature. Couldn't he wire money to her?

She went back uptown to Union Square and found his publishers and then his editor, who was genial and gave her tea but couldn't advance her money from Arthur's royalties. He offered her a loan of twenty-five dollars of his own money; she refused, later regretted the refusal. He too suggested she wire Arthur; she murmured, 'Of course,' and went away.

Back at the hotel, she found a note from Detective-Sergeant Dunne asking to meet him at the hotel at one, no answer required if she agreed. *Why not?* she thought. What else had she to do?

The hotel had a stunned quiet to it, as if the building had itself suffered the death. The lobby was almost empty, the pile of luggage gone – most of it, one of the boys confided, to the Fifth Avenue Hotel. Not only had the new arrivals decamped, but also some of the residents. Newcome's death had been in the morning papers, grisly in the less staid ones, where 'inversion' was hinted at. The *Express* had it on an inner page, only a long paragraph; the first page carried a story about Minnie, who was called the *Express*'s 'star reporter' and 'the third victim of a crazed monster.' The article hinted darkly at a connection between her death and the piece she had written two days before but made no accusations – it seemed to have it both ways, that she had been 'fingered by Fate itself for so horrible an end,' but also that 'the explanation for the terrifying act may lie in her discoveries of only two days ago.' A separate box said that the newspaper would pay for 'the finest funeral New York can offer' as soon as her body was released by the coroner and the police.

But what difference will it make? What good will it do? Louisa remained a clergyman's daughter, for whom funerals were hollow rituals. She thought that Minnie would be forgotten as quickly as any other nine-days' wonder; memory of her wouldn't survive as long as the graffiti by the newsroom elevator, which might keep her name visible for another year or two.

Her ankle felt rather better. She sat in the empty lobby and drank tea and nursed her resentments: Arthur, the bank, the publisher. Money.

Well, I have to have some money. And I'm damned *if I'll ask Arthur again. I won't beg!* There would be a new bill from the hotel, certainly smaller than the last but payable on demand, regardless. There were Ethel's wages. There would be cabs, food, *things* until Arthur arrived, even if he did show up tomorrow as his telegram had said. She *wouldn't* let him ride in on his high horse and rescue her by paying all her bills: she wanted to pay them herself. *With his money?* a sneering inner voice whispered.

Then, she knew, there would be a major row, at first about the money, then about his having to return to New York when he hadn't planned to. It would be ugly. He was already angry; now so was she. They had had few real arguments, but she knew he feared her anger. Well, he had brought it on himself.

Money. How did people get money in a hurry?

She signaled to one of the boys.

'Where is the nearest pawn shop?'

He behaved as if guests asked him about pawn shops all the time. 'Closest one is Fine's Gold on Sixt', but don't go there; he's a crook. Go ta Friendly Pawn over on Sevent', couple blocks down – sout' a Twenny-foist.'

She went to Reception and asked for her jewel case from the safe, grateful that she had signed it in herself and had not had Arthur do it. The same panjandrum who had registered them was on duty; he said grandly that of course he would get it immediately. When he came back with it, he murmured, 'A very sad day at the New Britannic, Mrs Doyle.' He sounded to her like an undertaker.

'I suppose Mrs Simmons is in seclusion.'

'Dr Strauss was with her all last evening.' He lowered his voice. 'Mr Carver is in shock.'

She supposed she had some special status because she had been there for so long; otherwise, why would he have confided in her? She said, 'I don't see Mr Manion today.'

'He is helping the police, madame.'

She didn't see how Manion could help the police, especially as he had seemed so cowed since Dunne had questioned him, but she pictured his going over guest lists, perhaps letting the police into rooms. What could they be looking for now?

A cross-town horse tram took her west on Twenty-third Street, this time to Seventh Avenue. She got down and had to orient herself, then got in a queue for the downtown car of the Seventh Avenue Line. She left it at Twenty-first – it seemed ridiculous to her to take the car for so short a distance, but she was trying to save the ankle – and walked down, then back up, looking for the pawn shop, at last spotted it on the other side of the avenue.

Her mother had taught her that pawning was a sign of weakness, of failure, besides being low and common. Only people whose failures were their own fault were so morally low as to pawn.

But here she was.

She wondered if Minnie had ever had to pawn anything.

She walked past the shop three times before she could go in. The large window was filled with unrelated articles – musical instruments, clothes, suitcases, guns, fishing tackle, jewelry. She looked at the jewelry. It looked far inferior to her own. Surely they'd try to cheat her?

When she went in, a breezy-looking woman was just coming out. Her clothes were rather loud, her hair rather insistent; still, she sounded friendly as she held the door for Louisa and said, 'Don't let him Jew you, dearie.'

She found herself in a larger version of the window. The walls and even the ceiling were hung with other people's valuables. Banjos seemed to her to abound, also men's summer clothes. On the floor were three glass-topped cases and a pile of furniture, as if somebody were just moving in.

Nobody was in the place, or so she thought until she looked beyond the furniture and saw a barred window like a bank clerk's till, behind it a man. He had sparse hair, a seemingly emotion-proof face like the stone ones on the tenements. He was looking at her, apparently without interest, but she thought that if she tried to steal something, he'd be on her like a tiger.

She walked to the back.

'Whatcha got, dear?' His voice was harsh and

457

hard, somehow distant, as if he were really in another room.

'I, uh . . .'

'First time?'

'My first, yes, time to, uh . . .'

'I can always tell a first-timer. Knew it when you come through the door. In fact, when I saw you walking up and down. Whatcha got?'

She wanted to flee. 'Some jewelry.'

'We can't do business if I don't see it, can we, dear?'

She was carrying the jewelry case in a net shopping bag. She took it out and placed it on the ledge in front of his bars and pushed it a few inches towards him. He snatched it the rest of the way and had it open before she could have second thoughts.

In the case were her mother's diamond earrings, tiny bits of diamonds inherited from *her* mother; there was an opal necklace that Arthur had given her; some *pavé*; an emerald ring, also from Arthur; assorted jet and gold chains and bangles and pins.

The man had a loupe in one eye. He went through the jewels quickly, pushed the diamond earrings aside, then gathered all the gold pieces in his fingers and dropped them on a balance and began adding tiny weights to the other pan.

Louisa said, 'One of those chains was designed by Louis of Paris.'

'Don't make me no never-mind, dear; we pay

458

by the weight. Gold is gold.' He wrote something down, swept the gold out of the pan and dumped it next to the now empty case. 'A hunnert and sixty bucks, dear.'

'Oh, no.'

'Oh, yes.' He pushed the diamond earrings towards her. 'You can keep these.'

'Those are my mother's diamonds!'

'Paste, dear. If I had a dollar for every one of somebody's mother's pearls or diamonds that turned out to be paste, I wouldn't be sitting in this cage. Hunnert and sixty.'

'I must have two hundred dollars.' She didn't know why she chose that figure, but she thought that she was supposed to bargain.

'Give me more stuff, then, dear.'

'That sapphire ring alone is worth more!'

'It may be, dear, but we aren't *buying* your things; we're loaning you on them. They're collateral. If we forked over full value, we'd be broke in six months. A hunnert sixty.'

'And I can have them back?'

'Thirty days, total amount plus ten percent. You don't redeem or pay another ten percent in thirty days, we sell them.'

Ten percent would be sixteen dollars. A hundred and seventy-six dollars to pay back within thirty days! The money would have to come from Arthur. What a row *that* would be. She felt a glow of self-righteousness: he deserved it for being so miserly. It gave her a pleasurable pain to think that he had given her some of the things she would be pawning. *Serve him right if I didn't redeem them.*

But she was looking beyond the bars, beyond the man, at the wall behind him, where something that reminded her of Victoria Woodhull had caught her eye. She said, 'What is that little gun?'

'Which one, dear? This one? Oh, this.' He plucked it off the wall, constantly glancing back to make sure she wasn't covertly retrieving some of her own property. He held the gun, looked it over, looked at the tag on it. 'This is a Smith and Wesson .32 Double Action.'

'Double Action seems an odd name.'

'I didn't name it, dear. Ask the company. That's a very nice little revolver for a lady, fits her hand, not too much concussion of the fingers. You can have that gun for three dollars fifty.' He pushed it through to her.

She picked it up. 'It's very heavy!'

'It's steel, dear. You get used to it.'

She handled it as if it were an explosive. She knew nothing about guns, nor why she had fixed on this one, nor why any gun at all. She hadn't been thinking about guns. But she had been thinking about Minnie and Newcome and her fears, which, since Minnie's death, had seemed to come closer. Before, the deaths had been terrible but separate from her; no longer. 'Do you have bullets for it?'

'Of course, dear. Maybe partial boxes, you know, somebody buys the gun and shoots a few bullets

460

and decides he doesn't want it, but you get a bargain. That's a fine little gun, I assure you. Three dollars fifty.'

She put the gun down on the counter. 'I'll take your offer on my jewelry if you'll include the gun and some bullets.'

'That would be an extra five dollars, dear.'

'That's my offer.'

He actually laughed. 'I'm the one makes the offers.' He chuckled again. 'You got spunk. You're Scotch, am I right about that? You're not planning to shoot your husband, are you, dear? I see you got a wedding ring there. And a nice ruby; I'd give you another fifteen for the ruby ring, round it up to one seventy-five?'

'No, thank you.' She couldn't go so far as to do *that* to Arthur.

He smiled at her. He looked almost fatherly. 'Okay, dear, because you're a first-timer, and you got class, and you're the first one to say "no thank you" to me in about forty years. A hunnert and sixty and the gun and some ammunition.'

Her jewelry disappeared so fast she couldn't follow it; he seemed to have swept it into a drawer she could not see. However, he was doing something down there and writing on a cardboard ticket and then in a ledger, then scribbling on much smaller tags. As if he knew what she feared – and of course he knew exactly what she feared – he said, 'We tag everything with your number, which is the number of the ticket I'm gonna give you

461

with your money. Don't lose your ticket, dear; you can't redeem without it.' He went on writing, finished at last and pushed the ticket through to her. 'Read me the list on the back of the ticket and we'll compare.'

His writing was almost like a penmanship example, eminently legible. She read off the items, and with each one he picked it from somewhere out of sight and put it on the counter between them. He asked her twice if that was everything, was she satisfied? and then he had her sign the ticket and sign in the ledger in which he had listed everything.

'Louisa Doyle parentheses Mrs Arthur Conan Doyle. You related to the Sherlock Holmes writer? Are you really? Don't feel bad, dear, all kindsa people come in here and leave things. I had a duchess oncet. You'd be surprised at the politicians and their wives. Cops. Cops' wives. Everybody gets caught short now and then.' He was counting out paper money, US gold and silver certificates. He slid them under the grille. 'Count it, please.'

He opened a drawer to his left and took out two small boxes in bright blue and yellow and passed them to her. 'That's your ammunition. You notice I don't give it to you until the very last. That's so you won't use it to hold me up. I don't think you will, but we got a rule.'

'I shall need only one box, I think.'

'No, you need two. One's .32 shorts, one's .32 longs. The shorts you can use for practice and like that; the longs're for getting serious. They're more powerful. Neither box is chock full – there's four missing from one and six from the other – but those are boxes of fifty, so you can scare a lot of husbands before you run out.'

'That was generous, to give me both boxes. I wouldn't have known any better.'

'Believe it or not, we aren't hairy monsters with bad breath in this business. Just don't really shoot your husband, okay? It makes us look bad. And learn to use that gun. They're dangerous things.'

'Thank you.'

'Thirty days, dear. No exceptions.'

'You were really very good.'

'Don't spread it around town. Enjoy New York.'

Outside, she felt suddenly better, almost buoyant. A wintry sun had come out, and the avenue looked warmer and brighter. She was pleased with herself about the gun, which somehow was connected with Minnie. It felt dreadfully heavy in her handbag, and whatever would she do with it? She thought of what it would be like to walk along Seventh Avenue with a loaded revolver in her bag. No, no, that would be impossible. And pointless. Her fears had nothing to do with the daylight or the city; hers were night-time fears. And centred in the hotel.

Perhaps she could put the gun on her bedside table.

Or in a shoe pushed under the bed.

Arthur will be furious.

As soon as she was back in her room in the annex, she wrote a note to Colonel Cody: 'My dear Colonel Cody, I know it is an imposition but I must ask you for a favour. Is there anyone in your Wild West who could give me a few minutes to teach me to shoot a revolver? (I greatly prefer that it be a woman.) I feel so helpless because of my ankle, and this city is so dangerous. Yours sincerely, Louisa Doyle.'

Detective-Sergeant Dunne was there at exactly one, not in the same room as the evening before but in a small office at the back of the hotel. Louisa was led to it by one of the hotel employees, who told her somewhat dismissively that the office was 'old Mr Carver's,' as if old Mr Carver had disappeared a generation before and was not living five floors above them. The office was small, furnished with little more than a desk and two chairs and an oak filing cabinet, and it smelled of dust and being too long closed.

Dunne was standing at a window with his back to the door when she was shown in. The same plainclothes man she had seen at the mortuary was with him, already seated and going through the pages of a notebook; he jumped to his feet when he saw Louisa and said, 'Mrs Doyle!'

Dunne turned, looked at her, nodded several times as if her coming confirmed something. He and Louisa said, 'Please sit down,' at the same time, Dunne to Louisa, Louisa to Cassidy.

464

Dunne was still wearing his hairy overcoat, which seemed entirely wrong; the sun was pouring down outside. A hat, presumably his, lay on the empty desktop.

Dunne glanced back at the window, then around the room at framed photographs that hung at eye level, only a few inches apart, like a belt. He gestured. '*Please* sit down, Mrs Doyle.' He grasped the chair behind the desk, but instead of pulling it out so as to sit in it, he carried it around the desk and put it down facing hers so that they were a few feet apart and he could lean one arm on the desk. He pointed a finger at the other detective. 'That's Detective Cassidy. You met him at the Tombs.'

Cassidy gave her a quick smile and went back to his papers. Dunne sniffed and intertwined the fingers of his hands on his chest and looked at the floor. He said, 'I want to put some things in order, Mrs Doyle. It's the way I do some of my thinking. It doesn't always seem like a very good way to other people.' He went on studying the floor. 'Couple of weeks ago, you were just checking into the hotel and you saw a woman with a man, and you later identified the woman as the first victim of what they're calling the Bowery Butcher.' He raised his eyebrows. 'Identified her correctly, as it turned out.' He sniffed again. 'That got you a visit from two cops from the Murder Squad because you'd written to Commissioner Roosevelt about it.' He unwound his fingers and leaned his

465

elbows on his knees and grasped his right wrist with his left thumb and forefinger, still not looking at her. 'Then, I hear, you went to the morgue and tried to have a look at her there.' Now he looked up. His eyes were the pale blue of innocence, but they had finished with innocence a long time before.

'It isn't true that I tried to see the first victim at the morgue. I tried to see the *second* one. That's when you took me for the carriage ride.' She worked at making her voice bland. She looked at him and then away from him, settling on the oak filing cabinet behind him.

He said, 'Sorry I got that wrong. I know better. What you did was, you got the sketch artist to verify that that was her in the newspaper.' He looked up. 'One of my people talked to the sketch artist. Also the hotel Hawkshaw here, when he was telling me that he got the patrolman's notes for you. Which, by the way, was a crime – both you and him.'

'I didn't know that, and it seemed quite harmless.' Not quite true, of course.

'And then you managed to get into the morgue to look at the third victim. With the sketch artist again.' He waited. He said, 'Looking at a corpse didn't bother you?'

'To the contrary, it upset me a great deal. But I don't faint, if that's what you mean.' She made herself concentrate on the paper labels in narrow brass holders on the fronts of the oak drawers

– she thought that the top one, hard for her to read because of her eyesight, said 'Registers.' Something of that length, at any rate.

'So you didn't actually see the first corpse, but you did verify that the newspaper sketch was accurate. You went to Printing House Square to make sure the sketch was accurate, and that's how you got to know the Fitch girl – right?'

'Yes.'

'*Then* there was the second murder, and you tried to have a look at *her*. And I was there and took you for a carriage ride.'

'What are you getting at, Detective-Sergeant?' She looked back at him, allowing the look to be a challenge, then quickly swinging back to the filing cabinet. The second drawer was labeled 'Menus, [something] Dinners, [unreadable].'

'And then when Miz Fitch was murdered two days ago, you were the one who identified *her*.' He waited. He said, 'You *kissed* her.' He looked at her but seemed to expect no comment. He got up and put his hands behind him and paced towards the far wall, where he looked at a photograph and turned back. 'You were here to see the first victim; you try to see the second victim; you identify the third victim! Now, I have a question that you may find insulting, but I have to ask it. Does any of this have to do with your husband and the books he writes?'

It didn't insult her, because she believed he already knew that the answer would be no and would be truthful. She said, 'I think you know it didn't.' She looked again at the file cabinet and the third drawer, which was labeled 'History . . .' and narrowed her eyes and said to herself that she thought there was a dash and then 'Plans' and then something else.

He rubbed his chin, used an index fingernail to part the hairs at the middle of his moustache. He looked at another picture and said, 'You do admit that you seem to be at the centre of a lot of this.'

'I'm not at the centre of anything! I'm on the outside, trying to see in.'

'But you do understand that there aren't many women who will make two separate trips to look at pretty horrible corpses.'

'They were *women*. I wanted to know what had been done to them!'

'Why?'

'Why do you think? Why can't men understand that it's what this killer is doing to *women* that matters? He's debasing women, he's humiliating us, he's . . . he's . . . *erasing* us and turning us into something else. Sausages!'

'But what good does looking at the bodies do?'

She frowned. 'It helps me to . . . reach them.' She said, 'To understand what he represents.'

'What everybody says about this killer is that he's a maniac. He doesn't "represent" anything, does he?'

She didn't want to parrot Victoria Woodhull. She

wanted it in her own words. 'I want to understand whether he *represents* all of you.'

He frowned again. He looked at Cassidy. He looked back at Louisa. '*Men?*' He sounded astonished.

'You don't believe me.'

He didn't respond to that but sat again and put his elbow on the desk, the side of his head on that hand. 'You said last night that this hotel is cursed. What'd you mean by that?'

'I suppose I meant Mr Newcome's murder. Do you have a suspect yet?'

'We're looking.' He pursed his lips and stared at her. 'You know that Newcome was what's called an "invert."'

'I came to understand that, yes.'

'The likeliest explanation is that the fella he brought to the hotel killed him. It's pretty common. His pocketbook was gone, also the bureau drawers had been gone through, a box of cufflinks and studs.' He sighed as if it were depressing. To her surprise, he said, 'I don't care for coincidence.' She must have shown her surprise, because he added, 'You see a murder victim here; couple weeks later, man gets murdered here. Death's hotel, it sounds like.'

'And there's the French maid two years ago.'

'That was a disappearance.'

'So far as you know.'

'And not something that happened in the hotel.'

'So far as you know.'

'I remember that case. The doorman saw her leave the hotel; he never saw her go back in. Neither did anybody else.'

'The hotel's as porous as a colander, Detective-Sergeant. Look at Newcome and whoever it was who went in just before him. The French maid could have had a key to the workers' door, just like them.'

He nodded slowly. 'You've been thinking about this a lot, haven't you.'

'I don't like coincidence, either.'

'You think there's something in the hotel?'

'I think that perhaps Newcome . . . recognized somebody when he was in the alley – when he looked inside. I think that you should entertain the idea that he was killed because he recognized somebody. Or is that simply a hysterical woman's idea?' She shook her head. She told him then about the noises in her room before she'd moved to the annex; then she told him about the missing drawers, but she said 'garment.'

'By which I suppose you mean a lady's unmentionables, and if you didn't mean that, please correct me. No? Did you report it?'

'I mentioned it to somebody.'

'Who?'

'Mr Carver.'

Dunne snorted. 'He didn't do anything about it, did he? He wouldn't – he wouldn't want it to go anyplace. Well, I can see where a noise and a missing garment would worry you. Are you afraid here?'

She wanted to tell him that she was very afraid, that she was so frightened sometimes she couldn't sleep, but to do so would be to put herself with the believers in ghosts and Marie Corelli's archangels and Mrs Simmons and her dog. Instead, she found herself telling him about the noises that the servants said they heard and what they thought they were.

'Is that what you're afraid of? Ghosts?'

'Of course not! But there's something *wrong* with the hotel.'

'Two deaths and a disappearance. That's hardly a record for New York hotels.'

'Three deaths. The architect.'

'I missed that one.'

'He's supposed to have jumped off the roof. Before the hotel was finished.'

Dunne got up and walked to one of the photographs. He looked at it very closely. After several seconds, he turned to Louisa and beckoned. 'Look at this.'

She went to stand next to him. She could smell him, a mixture of tweed and man and a bit of pipe smoke. He said to her, 'What d'you make of these pictures?' as if they were continuing some conversation that had been interrupted.

'I haven't seen them before. Oh!' She was slightly near sighted but could read the white letters in the lower right corner of the closest of them, 'Carver Pittsburgh.' She stood, looked at several more. 'Oh, this one must be of the hotel when it was being built, don't you think? It says "Carver New York."'

'Most of them say that.' He was standing in front of one of the photographs signed 'Carver Pittsburgh,' this one of an austere woman in a black dress of twenty years before. She looked as if she had never smiled. 'His mother, d'you think?'

'I wonder which Carver it was who took them.'

'The old man. I asked.' Dunne looked at the hard-faced old woman. 'Tougher than tripe, that woman.'

He pressed a blunt fingertip against the glass of a photograph. She put her eye closer and saw, just above the fingertip, a star-shaped, grey something. He said, 'I didn't get it the first time I saw it. Not until you mentioned the architect taking a jump.'

She looked again, then put her head back to look at the whole photo. It took her seconds to make everything out – a view looking straight down, an avenue to the left, a jumble directly below with shapes she saw resolve themselves into wagons and horses seen from above, trees, clutter. And the star shape in the middle. 'It's the hotel. And that's a *man*.'

'The architect, maybe. How many jumpers have they had?' He tapped the glass again. In the lower right corner of the photograph it said 'Carver New York.'

'Ghoulish,' she said.

'Ghoulish to take it and then ghoulish to put it on the wall. Have you ever seen the old man?'

'Nobody has in years, they say. He lives upstairs with a male nurse. I suppose the doctor sees him. And his son.'

Dunne tipped his head back and looked along his nose at the photograph. He said, 'Maybe this place *is* cursed.' He put a knuckle between his teeth and chewed on it, then said suddenly, 'Tell me something.'

'Yes?'

'What *exactly* do you believe's going on in this hotel?'

'Something that frightens me.'

He leaned against the desk. 'What?'

'I don't know!' She sounded to herself like the archetypal hysterical woman – that is, like a man's idea of a hysterical woman. She added, 'That *he's* in the hotel – what else do you think?'

'The Butcher?' He frowned at that, looked at Cassidy, who was frowning, too. Dunne said, 'Anything else you haven't told me?'

'Mrs Simmons's dog.' She told him about the dog and the barking. He asked if she believed it was a ghost and she said she thought that was nonsense. 'But it *was* just after the French maid disappeared.'

He digested that. 'Was there any smell?'

'Mrs Simmons didn't say. But old people don't notice smells.'

'A corpse would smell.'

'I didn't say it was a corpse!'

'But it must be what you suspect – why else

would you put the dog and the disappearance together?'

'I don't know, I don't know! It's this damned place!'

He made a humming sound, then took a turn to the window and back. 'Mrs Simmons is Newcome's aunt.' He made it sound like *ant*. 'If it wasn't for his death, I'd march in and ask her about the dog. But you know, I'd never get a search warrant on anything that flimsy – we'd have to start taking the wall down, and there'd be a load of resistance from the hotel.'

'The walls are brick behind the wood paneling.'

'See? They'd never let me do it.' He sat and pulled his chair a few inches closer. 'Look, Mrs Doyle, I respect your feelings. You're a smart woman and you know what's what. But do you have anything – *anything* – that would kind of . . . *focus* your fears about the place? Anything?'

She shook her head. 'I think about it. I even dream about it. But it's all . . .' She shook her head again. 'I'm a foolish woman.'

'No, that you're not. But you're a puzzle, because you're connected to so many of the deaths. Connected by pretty thin threads, I admit – you saw somebody, you knew somebody, you went for a ride in the park with somebody – but you're connected.'

'What are you going to do?'

'I wish I knew.'

'You could look at the men in this cursed hotel,

474

then, if you've nothing better to do! Look in the register for starters, see who was staying here when the French maid disappeared and when Mrs Harding was murdered.'

'Mrs Doyle, time—'

'And look at all the male employees! How many men does this place employ? How many of them were here two years ago? And how many when "Shakespeare" was murdered five—'

'Mrs Doyle!'

She bent forward and hugged herself. 'Maybe I'm cursed, not the hotel.'

He shook his head at that. They both waited for something more to be said. When the silence had built for too long, he said, 'The idea that the Butcher is here is a pretty far reach.' Then he said he was done and she could leave. She got up and put her weight on her cane. She had been looking at the filing cabinet off and on and she was fairly sure that the third drawer said 'History – Plans, Construction.'

Put there by old Carver?

'Coming, Mrs Doyle?'

Sergeant Cassidy was holding the door for her. Dunne had already disappeared. She said, 'Oh – sorry.' She moved to go around him, but he stepped out into the corridor and stood with his right hand holding the door open for her, his back to the door. She put her left hand on the edge of it to steady herself and felt the side of her hand strike projecting metal. She felt down, found the shape of a big, old-fashioned key. She said to Cassidy, 'Should we lock up?'

'Yes, ma'am. Just waiting for you.' He showed her his key from Reception.

She didn't stop to think. She slid the inside key out of its socket and closed it into her hand. It was so big that the part that went into the lock stuck out between her thumb and her palm. She turned her fist and hid it in the folds of her skirt. 'Thank you so much. I'm so slow with this cane.'

'No trouble at all, ma'am. Take your time.' He was locking the door. She was limping up the corridor, wondering what she would do with the key. And wondering what doors it might open.

Dunne was just coming out of a booth where he'd written a telegram when Cassidy came into the lobby. Dunne handed the telegraph form in at Reception and showed his police card and said to the panjandrum, 'That's confidential police business. If you peach, I'll have you in the Tombs.'

The eminence behind the desk looked shocked. He said something about treating every message as confidential. Dunne went away grinning, muttered 'Oh, yeah' to Cassidy. When they were out on Twenty-third Street, he said, 'I wired Pittsburgh to find out what they've got on the Carvers out there. The old man took some of those pictures there.' He eyed the Irish doorman, who turned away. 'Did you see the old man when you were asking questions last night?'

'Saw him, yeah – asleep. That's all he does, is sleep.'

'Doctor with him?'

'No, some flunky. A nurse. A guy.'

'What's the old man look like?'

'White hair. Something wrong with his face – real red, a lot of bumps and things.'

Dunne pushed his fists into his huge overcoat. 'There's something fishy with the Carvers.'

'The nurse guy says you can talk to the old man sometimes, but he won't get it. He's off his nut.'

'That's what I'm maybe afraid of.' Dunne stared at the passers-by as if they were suspects. 'I want you and Forcella to go over all the hotel staff's statements we took yesterday about Newcome. I want to know how many men work for this hotel. Then I want to know how many of them have worked here for at least two years. If you can't get that from the statements, come back up here and get the information from that manager.'

'You really think there's something not kosher with the hotel?'

Dunne scowled at the street. 'I don't think Miz Doyle is loony, if that's what you mean.'

Louisa knew, of course, exactly what she was going to do with the key she'd stolen. She ate a small part of the table d'hote luncheon and instead of going back to her room went down the corridor that ran towards the back of the hotel from Reception. Anybody who saw her would think, if they thought at all, that she was going to the ladies' convenience back there (*Say toilet*, Minnie had said. *Oh, Minnie . . .*) She went on past the convenience, however, and put the key into the lock of old Mr Carver's office – it was her notion that if you did things confidently, nobody would ask questions – and slipped inside.

She went around the desk and leaned her walking-stick on it and sat on the edge of the chair that Dunne had used. She bent forward and read the labels on the filing drawers again. Yes, the third one said 'History – Plans, Construction.' She believed in history. It seemed to her to explain many aspects of life. Although not enough of them. Might it explain the New Britannic – and her fear?

The drawer was too full and opened grudgingly. Some of the papers were sticking up and caught on the top of the opening; all of them had been crammed and squeezed in so that she had to struggle to take any out.

There had once been order, she thought: gray card separators stood between inches-thick bundles of paper. She took out the entire first lot, releasing a smell of dust.

'History' meant mostly newspaper articles, along with an early version of the hotel brochure and some letters of congratulation on the hotel's opening. Many of the newspaper things were puff pieces – 'New Hotel to be Most Modern in This City,' and so on – but some were more like straightforward reporting on the building's progress. 'Cornerstone

Laid for New Hotel'; 'Twenty-third Street to be Beautified by Hotel Construction'; 'Centre of Fashionable Caravanserais Moves Uptown to Twenty-third.' She supposed that the impetus for most of them had come from the Carvers – young Carver, then only in his twenties, was quoted in a lot of them.

Some, nonetheless, had substance. Several focused on the unique construction: double-brick walls filled with 'crushed Italian volcanic stone.' That expression was used again and again; she guessed it had come from the Carvers, too. There was even a piece about the stone, 'Italian Isle of Stromboli's Volcano Erupts in New York,' which seemed to find newsworthy the purchase of seventy tons of 'porous, pumice-like Italian rock from a romantic Italian island.' The rock had come by steamship to a Brooklyn dock, then had been carried in 'a parade of more than a hundred wagons' to a crusher in the east Forties.

She moved to the second block of papers, the building plans. These were mostly no more help to her than hieroglyphics would have been. Most were highly detailed, therefore impossible for her to relate to the hotel as a whole. There were large drawings of a fireplace mantel to go into the bar (unseen by her, as she didn't go into the bar), of the lion-head bosses that were to decorate the front doors (still very much there), of the brass panels on the inside of the lifts (still on display). Many plans showed construction details she couldn't figure out – mortices, stone joints, brick-work patterns. She had had no idea that putting up a building required so much – even, in one case, specifications for the size nail and the kind of nail-head to be used.

Her eyes smarted after an hour of it, and her head was beginning to ache. Still, she didn't put on a light, afraid that it might call attention. She folded the papers and put them back into the pile with a sigh. Only towards the back of the drawer did she finally unfold plans that showed the entire hotel, one of them a 'typical floor plan' that at last gave her a grasp of how the rooms related to the famous rubble-filled brick walls.

It's like a giant centipede. What she meant was that the double-brick walls formed a kind of many-legged shape, the body a rectangle that ran around the outside of the principal corridors, the legs projections that ran from those corridors to the outer walls. These double walls were labeled 'sound-barrier walls' and in several places had instructions connected to them by beautifully curved arrows with delicate heads, such as '28" outer dimension' and 'stone fill between.'

But it was untrue that all the internal walls had these sound barriers. In fact, none of the walls within the centipede's body had them; in there, much of the space was taken up by two air shafts, much of the rest by the lifts and stairways and small rooms and cupboards labeled 'janitorial' and 'house-keeping.' The fact was, she saw, that if you stayed

480

in one of the New Britannic's few inner rooms, your view was of an air shaft, and your room was far from soundproof.

Outside the centipede's body, however, it was another story. The sound-barrier walls (the legs) ran between all adjoining suites and between most adjoining single rooms, although where single rooms opened on a short corridor that paralleled the centipede's legs, there was no double-brick wall. Sound barriers, the floor plan implied, were for those who could afford them.

The wintry light beyond the window told her it was mid-afternoon; she would have to finish soon. She turned back to something that had snagged her attention; she couldn't find it, then did, had to put her nose almost against the dust-smelling paper to read it: 'Deluxe closet.'

Closet means cupboard. She knew that because it was in a glossary of American terms in her guidebook. But what would a deluxe cupboard be? She followed the curving line down to the little arrow at its end; it pointed at – she had to go to the legend in a lower corner to find what the symbols meant – a fireplace. A gap of about eighteen inches seemed to have been left next to the fireplace for the deluxe cupboard. What would be deluxe about a cupboard only eighteen inches wide?

She pictured the sitting room in the suite she had had. There had been a fireplace. Next to it had been paneling. Were the panels eighteen inches wide? Only a foot and a half? Had their suite not been deluxe enough to have a cupboard?

Like one scene replacing another in a harlequinade, the mental picture of her former suite became one of Mrs Simmons's. It was exactly the same, except that there was a dog barking at the place where the deluxe cupboard should have been.

She peered again near-sightedly at the plan. Several suites had no deluxe cupboard, or at least the plan had no notation for one. But there was one with a cupboard where she thought Mrs Simmons's suite should be. And there was another! And another. And there was a pattern to them: they were evenly spaced around the legs of the centipede, six to a floor. Including the suite she'd occupied with Arthur.

It seemed odd to her, but odd was all it seemed just then. She sighed, stretched, looked at her watch. She hadn't even begun the final lot of papers.

Might as well be hanged for a sheep as a goat. She set the plan aside and put the final lot of papers on it, then scooped up the newspaper articles and the other plans and put them back into the drawer. Two minutes later, she opened the door and peeped out, then sidled into the corridor with the plan and the unread papers held against her as if they might have been a fat book she was carrying back to the annex from the reading room.

Three floors above, Marie Corelli in her own suite had just got back from Philadelphia and was dressing to go out. She had no lady's maid; when she needed help, she got somebody from the hotel. She didn't like spending money on what she called 'unnecessaries.' She was a lady novelist, true, but she wasn't rich.

Marie Corelli looked not at all Italian, was instead an English type – rounded, bosomy – that was often well upholstered by its forties, but she had remained slim waisted. Her face was what was called 'strong featured,' meaning she had a big nose; still, newspapers described her as 'striking,' and men might have been attracted to her if she'd let them.

She had got as far as undressing, which of course was the way to start dressing. She was walking around her sitting room wearing nothing but a filmy silk scarf that was big enough to cover a grand piano but hid nothing of her. She had a cigarette burning in an ashtray on the bedside table and a cold cup of tea on the mantel, and she was humming something that only she would have recognized as the Meditation from *Thaïs*, and now and then she whirled and let the scarf billow out around her. She was thinking of the climactic moment when Thaïs drops her veil and shows her naked body to drive the ascetic monk mad (on the stage, her body was always covered with a flesh-coloured union suit, not too ravishing on many overweight sopranos). She would love to sing Thaïs. Love to drop the veil and actually be naked!

But, of course, that would be improper.

She despised the improper.

Still . . .

The silk billowed and showed her naked from her ribcage down. She tried it again in front of the mirror, but if she turned enough to billow, she couldn't see the mirror. Anyway, she thought her pubic hair was too dark and really far too much of a good thing; you could hardly play Thais with something as obvious as that hanging out. Maybe she should colour it? Bleach it? Pluck it? She winced at the thought.

She hummed. She wrapped herself in the silk, then opened her arms wide, then dropped the silk to the floor.

And then she heard something. She knew it was something that was of the air, but it seemed to come from an upper corner of the room, right up against the ceiling, so she whirled, naked, and faced that corner. *'Azul?'*

'Ah – zool!' She sang the name, gave two notes to the final syllable. 'Come to me, Azul – manifest yourself! Oh, my guide, my angel – come to me.' She picked up the silk, held it as backdrop to her nudity. 'Here I am. For you, my dear one!' She pushed her pelvis forward. 'For you – for you . . .' She made kissing noises with her lips. 'Azul . . . !' This was not the relationship with Azul that she had described in her first book; that would hardly have been proper; but in the privacy of her room she could express what she thought of as the physical transcendence of the spiritual . . .

The sound from the corner was quite distinct. Marie threw her head back and shut her eyes. It was happening – actually happening! She had summoned Azul from the astral plane!

The sound changed to a bumping, coming not from the upper corner of the room now but from the fireplace. No, not the fireplace, the wall next to the fireplace. Marie opened her eyes and listened. Had the wall bulged a little? Had there really been the faintest of movements there? Was Azul about to step through the solid wall?

A monstrous oak library table stood against the wall there, its top piled with Marie's luggage and discarded clothing. She ran forward and leaned across the library table and her pile of junk and put her spread fingers against the wood. She could feel it quiver at her touch.

Maybe the table was too heavy for Azul to move. After another bump, the sounds ended and the wall stopped quivering.

'Oh, Azul, don't leave me!'

There was only silence.

'Oh, Azul, really!' Marie gathered up her silk shawl and went to draw herself a bath. 'Poo on you, my darling.'

Louisa spent two hours in her room going over the rest of the papers from old Carver's office. Some of them were incomprehensible – engineering requirements, 'load-bearing estimates,' invoices and receipts and letters to firms abroad that hired skilled workmen – all of which had to be read, understood so far as she could understand them. The exchanges of letters with the hiring agents taught her two things: that it was possible to contract for entire gangs of workmen abroad, including their housing in New York and their passage; and that the elder Carver had much preferred foreign workers. Puzzlingly, he had contracted for several construction crews in sequence, rather than together, the last arriving when the hotel had been mostly complete.

So no workman would know the whole story of the building?

At last, her eyes stinging and her back aching, she came on an invoice from an Italian building-materials company. She couldn't make out a lot of it, but she was sure that 'pietro' was stone, and Stromboli was the place from which the 'porous volcanic stone' had come, according to the newspapers. The invoice was for thirty-seven tons, *inglese* in parentheses; she had to go down to the restaurant and ask an Italian waiter what the word meant. 'Means English,' he said.

English tons, then.

She looked again at the newspaper articles. They all said seventy tons.

The large plan of the finished construction had pencil jottings in a margin. A calculation had been made, something about cubic feet, then a 'per ft^3'

figure, and a multiplication that reached '35.17 T.' Thirty-five tons and a bit? With some extra added to get thirty-seven? So that if the seventy-ton figure given the press had been the architect's figure to fill the gaps between the brick walls, then thirty-seven tons represented – what? For one thing, apparently, the actual tonnage bought.

She leafed through the bills again and found one from the firm that had crushed the rock after its arrival from Italy. It had billed for the crushing of thirty-eight tons.

She threw herself back in her chair. A strand of hair was hanging over her face, and she blew it away with a sigh.

About half the planned-for tonnage of rock had, apparently, actually been used. The amount given the newspapers, however, had stayed at seventy, so the actual thirty-five-plus had been kept secret.

Thirty-five to thirty-eight tons would have filled the walls about halfway.

She pictured what was left: a tunnel between brick walls less than two feet wide and perhaps five feet high. Crushed stone underfoot. Boards overhead? Some sort of flooring would have had to be put in on each storey – something strong enough to bear all that weight. And what would have happened to the supposed insulating property of the stone? Would a two-foot gap without stone itself have done the job of ensuring quiet? Or would old Carver have lined the exposed brick with something to deaden sound, thus further reducing the width of the gap?

The idea of it nauseated her: a hotel honey-combed with hidden passages. And an owner, now old, who had had it built that way in secret. To do what?

Should she tell Dunne? Should she risk another opportunity to be told she was hysterical? Another hint that she was part of too many 'coincidences'?

She went to her accustomed chair by the window and stared at the blank wall across the alley.

Late in the afternoon, there was a knock on Louisa's door, and a woman she didn't know said that Colonel Cody had sent her. She didn't seem very happy about it. 'About a gun,' she said when Louisa looked at her without understanding.

Then Louisa woke up. She let her in and explained about the little pistol, finding that she was embarrassed by the gun now that somebody was actually there about it. Louisa remembered the woman from the Wild West: her name was Marion McCousins and she was 'The Arkansas Rifle Girl' in the show. Louisa said, 'I loved your part of the Wild West. I saw it last week.' She showed her the pistol she'd got from the pawn shop.

'Well, this isn't much of a gun, is it.'

'Oh. I only wanted it . . . in case. You know.'

'I wouldn't shoot cockroaches with it, is the truth of it.' Miss McCousins took it and fitted her hand around it and aimed at a wall. 'Not enough barrel on it to push the pit out of a cherry.'

Louisa felt defensive of the gun. 'I was told it was right for a woman's hand.'

'Who told you that, some man? I bet. Well, the main thing is, don't shoot yourself with it.' She pushed a lever on the revolver and the barrel dropped and the rear of the cylinder appeared – holes spaced around the circle. She peered into it, then reversed the gun as if she were going to shoot herself and looked down the barrel. ''Bout shot out. You didn't look it over before you bought it?'

'I didn't know what to look for.'

Marion McCousins sighed. 'Well, a babe in arms, as they say. All right, hon, let's go through it.' They sat on the sofa and she showed Louisa how to open and close the revolver. She spun the cylinder and showed her how to load it, then how to eject the empty cartridges. She made Louisa do it and then do it again.

'All right, this here is the trigger. That's what you pull to make it go bang. This here is the hammer, which you can pull back to cock it, or you can just pull the trigger and that'll cock it, which is why it's called a double action.'

'Then what good is pulling the hammer back?'

'Well, if it had a decent barrel on it, you could shoot better single action – that is, without having to cock it with the trigger. Double action is faster, but most people jerk the trigger and the barrel goes all whopperjaw and the bullet hits somebody standing ten feet from where you thought you aimed.' She had warmed a little, either to Louisa or to the task, showed that she had by saying Louisa should call her Marion. 'Look, hon, this is a gun for scaring the galluses off people and hoping you never have to shoot, you understand me? The truth is, you couldn't hit a privy from inside with this gun. This is what we call a waving-around gun.'

'You mean it's worthless.'

'Well, no, I wouldn't go as far as that. If you were two feet away from somebody, you could probably hit him. Better still if you put the barrel right against his vest. Who you planning to shoot?'

'I just want to feel safe.'

'Well . . .' McCousins sighed again. 'I'd say what was *safe* would be to lock it in a drawer and carry a good sharp hatpin. However, if you're determined, then load it and carry it where it won't fall out on the floor and go off, and if you ever have to use it, try to do it in an elevator where you're sure to be up close.'

She had Louisa pull the trigger, a task that turned out to be harder than Louisa had expected. She tried sighting the gun, difficult because there were no sights.

'Just point it like you're pointing your finger.'

'I wish I could fire it.'

'Well, I don't recommend it in your hotel room, hon. You find yourself a shooting range someplace and shoot up a couple boxes, and you'll feel

490

comfortable with it, I guess. Just remember, guns make noise, and they kick, and if it's at night they put out enough flame so's you think a whole box of lucifers went off.'

'You make it sound quite daunting.'

'Naw, guns aren't nothing, really. But you got to shoot a lot to be comfortable with them. Oh, hell.' She got to her feet. 'Come on, I'll take you where you can shoot the damned thing.'

'Oh – that isn't necessary . . .'

'Bill said I was to see you're happy. Well, you don't look happy. Come on.'

She took Louisa to Madison Square Garden in a cab, then down into a warren of corridors under the vast building. Behind a door near the furnace rooms was a tunnel-like space with a chipped brick wall at the far end.

'This isn't much of a shooting gallery, but it's what they give us to use. We don't, much – it ain't much of a place.'

She set a metal dinner plate on a wooden chair halfway down the tunnel. The plate was battered and holed, and the chair had been splintered almost to smithereens.

Marion watched while Louisa, her hands shaking, loaded the cylinder with .32 shorts. Louisa held the loaded gun away from herself with her head turned the other way.

'It ain't gonna bite you. Just remember, don't ever point it at nobody unless you mean to shoot him. Now aim at the plate and shoot.'

491

Louisa put her hand out in front of her, closed her eyes, and tried to pull the trigger. For what seemed to be a very long time nothing happened, and then her wrist was thrown up as an explosion echoed in the confined space, and her ears rang. Acrid smoke from the black powder heaved in front of her.

'Well, you hit one of the side walls, and I guess you had to hit something eventually. Try it again.'

'I'd really rather not.'

'If you get afraid of that gun, you might as well throw it down the outhouse right now. Now you put that hand out and sight good on that plate and shoot.'

When she had shot the five cartridges and she couldn't hear and her wrist hurt and the tunnel was full of smoke – and she hadn't hit the plate, or even the chair – Marion took the gun, loaded a single round into it, and fired. The plate whanged and bounced. 'Well, it isn't as bad as it could be.' She took Louisa's wrist and swiveled it around and said 'That hurt?' and decided that Louisa should shoot with both hands. 'And try keeping your eyes open this time.'

The second five were not so bad as the first. The third five were better still, and she nicked the edge of the plate and felt very pleased with herself. Marion kept up a steady nagging – 'Don't hunch! Stop squinting! You flinched. You flinched again – what're you scared of? Don't point it at me!'

Halfway through the fourth five, Marion turned

the electric lights off and told Louisa to shoot. A blinding flare of light was added to the noise and the recoil. When the lights came on again, Marion said, 'Just in case you want to shoot in the dark, you know what to expect.'

'I still can't see.'

'You'll get over it. All right, shoot up that lot, then we'll try some longs.'

The longs proved to be not much worse than the shorts. Or was it that she was getting used to them? Then Marion said that was enough, and there was enough smoke in there to cure a ham with, and she had to go and get her dinner before the show, and let's get out of here.

Walking across Madison Square, as Louisa insisted on doing, Marion said, 'You going to carry that thing around with you?'

'Should I?'

'Well, it won't do any good in a drawer under your spare garters, will it.'

'A woman I met told me she always carries a gun.'

'Grand, if you know what you're doing. Fact is, I carry one myself sometimes, depending. Purse or pocket? That's the choice a woman's got. A man can carry a gun in a holster up under his arm, but women's clothes are too tight. Maybe in your handbag, hon.'

Louisa offered to pay her, but Marion McCousins declined. 'Men say, "professional courtesy." I say we're both women.'

Back in her room, Louisa tried putting the gun in one of her handbags, but her bags were all made of cloth and were small, and they sagged under the weight. She put her hand back into the pocket that each of her dresses had next to her bustle. A slit in the fabric gave access deep enough that her hand went in well above her wrist. She put the gun in, then walked around her room. She could feel the weight of it, both in the pull on her waist and in the swing of the skirt, but it was bearable. When she sat, she had to sit a little sideways so that she didn't sit right on the unyielding chunk of steel. But it was doable.

She cleaned the barrel and the cylinder as Marion had shown her, with a rod (actually a knitting needle) and a bit of rag and a viscous fluid that Marion had provided. Then, hesitatingly, she put a .32 long into each chamber and closed the gun and put it into her pocket. She thought of what would happen if it went off there.

I'd be limping for the rest of my life. Or worse.

But were her fears any less?

Her answer at that moment would have been no, but when she saw the afternoon papers, she felt a rush of relief that was like the sweetness of cold water on a hot day.

POLICE CAPTURE BOWERY BUTCHER
'We Have Our Man' – Roosevelt
Gigolo Confesses

494

Revenge on Women for Husband's Rejection of His Demands

That was the *Evening Sun*. The other papers had the same story, headlines more or less lurid, depending on their tastes. 'FEMALE MUTILATOR WITHOUT REMORSE AT CAPTURE,' 'LOVE TRIANGLE LED TO ATROCITIES,' 'MURDER SQUAD GRABS MANIAC – BUTCHER IN SHACKLES!' She went back to the *Evening Sun* for the details, feeling light headed, disoriented: could it really be true?

Detective-Sergeant F. B. Dunne apprehended Gerald Oppenheimer at his sordid room on the far West Side as the city finished its lunch hour and returned to work yesterday. Assisted by Detective L. Cassidy, Dunne, head of the Butcher investigation since the recent cataclysm in the Murder Squad, took along no uniformed police to make the nab.

'There was no resistance,' Dunne told us. 'He came along like a lamb.' Dunne said that the arrest was the product of weeks of detective work of the most careful and detailed kind. 'We mapped his movements, based on sightings before and after the murders. They led to Oppenheimer's room.'

The suspect is now in the lock-up at 300 Mulberry Street, where, we hear, the efforts of trained police interrogators have already produced a confession. One police source said they were sure of the first 'butcher' murder, that of Mrs Roscoe Harding, and were confident that the killer would confess to murders two and three within hours. Oppenheimer's connection with Mrs Harding has been confirmed by two witnesses, George Manion and Daniel Gerrigan, both of the New Britannic Hotel, where they saw the pair together.

There was a lot of speculation in all the papers about what sort of man Oppenheimer was and why he had committed the killings. 'Gigolo' was used almost universally; certainly it seemed that Oppenheimer, described by the *Times* as 'sleekly handsome in a reptilian fashion,' had made a profession of preying on women. To Louisa, there seemed a contradiction there (if he made money preying on women, why did he kill them?), but she wanted to believe that the killer had been caught. Arthur always made a good deal of what he called 'motive' in his stories, but the police didn't seem to care for it as much, because no motive was given. Perhaps that was the result of their experience of real criminals, as opposed to Arthur's imaginary ones. Perhaps real criminals didn't have motives. Or perhaps in real life motive was too obscure to unravel.

At any rate, it was over.

She could say that to herself, but the words didn't seem to get past her tongue. Her fears, she found, were still there. She kept the revolver in her pocket.

CHAPTER 13

That evening at her early dinner, Henry Irving stopped by her table and said, 'Several of us who have been here for a while are having a little memorial after the theatre for poor Newcome. Quite informal, and in no sense a *service*, but only something that can be reported to Mrs Simmons. I do hope you'll come, even though it will be late. In the music room. To please me?'

'Of course.'

The hotel seemed hushed at half past eleven; only a few people who had been to the theatre were in the lobby. Louisa took the lift to the mezzanine and made her way towards the back of the hotel along the far corridor. There were no shops there, but rather specialized rooms for the guests – the reading room, a writing room, a billiard room, a music room. Louisa heard the piano as she neared it.

Inside, Marie Corelli was playing a large Broadwood grand – English, not American, like so much else in the hotel – and Louisa went to her as soon as she stopped.

'I didn't know you were back!'

'Only today, *chérie*, and in a terrible rush at that. I'm off to Albany tomorrow. It's exhausting but it's necessary, yes? You look lovely.' Marie kissed her cheek. 'I'm here because of that poor Newcome; I only heard about it when I got back, who'd have expected such a thing? His aunt is a very strange person, though he seemed quite pleasant. Although his sort, you know, they do stupid things when they're on the prowl, if you follow my meaning. Are you here for the memorial? I've bought a mourning card for all of us to sign, and there are to be flowers. I think a contribution of twenty-five cents each would be more than generous; we don't want to look showy.'

'Sir Henry asked me to come.'

'I'm supposed to sing, though I don't know anything that suits the death of a man. I suppose Gluck. Will you come to a summoning in my room?'

'For Newcome?'

'No, no, my dear, for *Azul*. I have the most exciting things to tell you about Azul, who almost manifested himself in my room! I've thought and thought about it, and I decided that Azul is afraid of presenting his awesome countenance to only one person, and so perhaps the force of several of us would persuade him to show himself. I had wanted Mrs Simmons because she is *bien spirituelle*, although not of my persuasion, but it would be bad taste to ask her just now, no? One is never

499

sure in this debased age. Tomorrow at eleven, which I know is a brutal time, but it's the best I can manage because I have to be at the train at three. I think we'll be six, with you, so you *must* come. It will be a profoundly religious experience. Oh, there's Sir Henry.' She waved.

There were only a dozen people in all. Cody put his head in the door and signed the card and left a dollar but went away again. Marie sang Gluck's 'Cosa Faro Senza Euridice?', which was about a dead woman, not a man, but at least the grieving singer was always a soprano. She followed it with the Dead March from *Saul* on the piano. Louisa's thoughts were on the plans and notes and specifications she had read that afternoon: did they really add up to anything? Then Irving recited Tennyson's 'Crossing the Bar' and made it seem glorious, but of course Irving could have done the same for 'Baa-Baa Black Sheep.' Then an American intoned a dreadful poem called 'Thanatopsis,' with gestures, and Louisa went back to the murders and doubts of Dunne's story that the 'gigolo' had committed them. A woman from Irving's company recited the part of Ecclesiastes about there being a time for everything; and Irving ended it all with Jacques's 'seven ages of man' speech, and that was that.

Louisa limped back to her room and undressed and got into bed, but when she hadn't fallen asleep after half an hour of frightening herself with thoughts of crawling through the walls of the hotel

– there was a story about that, wasn't there? No, it was wallpaper, crawling through the pattern on wallpaper – she got up and decided to have a bath. It was after midnight; she was unlikely to meet anybody in the corridor, and the Butcher had been caught – hadn't he? She hid herself in her flannel robe and then pulled it tightly around herself and peeked into the corridor. It was empty and silent.

Towel over her arm and soap in hand, she tiptoed quickly down to the bathroom. Normally, it should have been Ethel who drew her baths, but of course she couldn't summon Ethel in the middle of the night. She knocked on the bathroom door, heard nothing, opened the door slowly; it was dark and silent and rather humid in there. The electric light made the wood-paneled room more cheerful. She locked and bolted the door and turned the taps.

Oceans of hot water, thank Heaven! One can't fault Carver for that.

The room grew steamy. She tested the water with a toe, shrugged herself out of the robe and sank into the blessed heat. Twenty minutes later, soaped, scrubbed, rinsed, glistening, she rose from the waves and toweled herself as the drain gurgled. It was all very comforting, rather homely. She ached to have her children in the next room to kiss.

The corridor seemed icy after the bathroom. She pulled the door closed behind her and turned towards her own room, thirty feet away. Moving towards it, she kept away from the doors as if she feared somebody's bolting out of them.

Still fearful, Touie. Still on edge. She reminded herself that the Butcher had been caught – it could be the good-looking young man, of course it could – as had Newcome's murderer. Dunne had performed splendidly. Even if the hotel were cursed, or at least unlucky, she had nothing to fear from it any more – she, after all, was now safe in the annex, which wasn't properly part of the centipede of possibly hollow walls at all. She thought of the hotel plan, the centipede, the tons of volcanic stone. Her interpretation of it seemed far fetched now – and, anyway, she was in a different building. She was *safe*.

But she didn't feel safe.

She had almost reached her room when the door from the annex into the hotel opened. It was only another ten feet along, at the end of the corridor. Louisa clutched the neck of her robe and tried to hurry to her door, her key out to go into the lock.

A strange figure lurched through the hotel door. One word rang through her head: *Man*. But what a man!

He was tall and stooped, visibly broad in the shoulders despite a greasy, billowing robe that was spotted with drippings of old meals. He wore some sort of pyjamas under the robe, the top and bottoms mismatched. His feet were bare and bulged with corns and bunions. His head was huge, ringed on the sides and back with white hair down to his jawline.

Yet it was his face that caused her to back against the wall. It was scarlet and it bulged with boil-like pustules; the nose was misshapen and swollen; the skin on the cheeks and forehead looked like badly ploughed red earth, scored with fissures in which old dirt had lodged. She thought *leprosy*, although she had never seen a leper.

He saw her. He smiled. The smile became a leer, showing yellow-brown teeth. He charged towards her, his balance bad, almost careering against a wall with a shoulder, then catching himself and reaching out towards her.

'Show me your titties!' He was whispering. 'I'll give you a nickel if you show me your titties! Let me see them—'

He was reaching for her. She cringed, fought him off with her left hand as she held the robe closed with her right. He was astonishingly strong for an old man; he held her wrist and twisted her arm away as the other hand reached for the top of her robe. She tried to hit him with her keys, struck his ear. She felt the fabric of the robe tear and then the front buttons popping.

'Tits! I see your tits!' He was still talking in an urgent, hoarse whisper.

She screamed.

He was trying to press himself against her. She thrust at him with her key, felt it contact flesh; she tried to kick him, aware of doors opening along the corridor, and she screamed again. He was trying to put a hand inside the robe to open it below her waist, and she tried to catch his hand and to twist away from him.

Then other people were around them. Two men in pyjamas were pulling at her attacker; she yanked the robe around herself, although they must have seen her, bare to the waist. Now the old man began to scream. It was a child's cry, high-pitched and terrified. He howled, 'She hurt me! She hurt me!'

The door to the hotel opened again. Louisa was trying to get her key into the lock of her own door, but her hands were shaking so that she couldn't do it. Galt came through, young Carver right behind him. Galt had a strait-waistcoat.

'Mr Carver! Mr Carver!' Galt pushed aside one of the men who had hold of the old man. 'Let me deal with him – please – Mr Carver! It's Galt – it's Galt, remember? Mr Carver? – Galt, your nurse?' He turned back to the younger Carver. 'Give me the gag.'

Old Carver was still keening, making a sound that Louisa knew a rabbit made when a dog got it. Galt snatched a canvas and leather thing like a brank from young Carver's fingers. He put it over the old man's head; there was a lot of twisting and screaming. Young Carver joined the guests in holding his father.

By now there were half a dozen people in night-clothes in the corridor. One of them was berating young Carver for the interruption of his sleep.

Galt got the thing on the old man's head and strapped it tight behind. It held his jaws clamped and allowed him to breathe only through his nose. As soon as it was on and tightened, the old man sagged into the arms of the men holding him, his weight so great that one of them almost let him go. Galt said, 'Hold him, I'll only be a moment now.' He slid a canvas sleeve up one of the old man's arms with the deftness of long practice. The old man's eyes went to Louisa. Was he smiling inside his mask?

Galt flipped the old man's arm behind him and pushed him face first into the wall and began to work the other sleeve up his right arm.

'You can all go to bed,' young Carver was saying. 'Please go to bed now. We do apologize for this unfortunate event. One of our guests from the hotel. A seizure. Of course, you won't be charged for tonight's stay. With the hotel's compliments – please – please return to your beds . . .'

Galt was panting. He had both of the old man's arms in the jacket now. He began to buckle straps that would hold the arms across the old man's back. Galt said, 'I'm so sorry, Mrs Doyle. I don't know how he got out. Please – when he's like this – I know it was horrible for you. It's my fault, of course it's my fault – he doesn't know what he's doing—'

She had managed to get her key into the lock at last. She opened her door and stumbled inside. She heard young Carver say, 'Mrs Doyle, please – this was a misunderstanding—!' Then she was slamming the door and bolting it, and she leaned against it and wept.

I'm so frightened. I'm such a coward. And then, *He* knew *me!*

She wanted to get back into her bath. She wanted to soap herself, to wash every part of her he'd touched, as if he carried some contagion. *That face.*

She lay down on her bed and wept. She wanted somebody to help her, to hold her, but nobody came. She thought she should call the police, but the telephones were in the lobby and she would have to go into the hotel, where *he* was.

Gradually, as the shock faded, her weeping stopped and she was able to sit up. She felt as weak as she had in Davos. Her knees felt too watery to hold her up. Her hands were still shaking. At last, she went into her water closet and threw up. She washed herself at the small sink. She put on a thick, warm nightgown and a different robe and sat by her window in the dark, trembling.

She thought of his whispered *I'll give you a nickel if you'll show me your titties.* Had he really said that to children? To young girls? Is that what he'd done in his hotel, too – spied on the female guests? Ever since it was built?

And *had* he known her – because he'd spied on her? *Stolen her soiled drawers?*

She thought of what she'd learned in his office that afternoon. None of it seemed ridiculous now. He must have planned the hollow walls from the beginning. The architect must never have understood what old Carver was really about. Not, at any rate, until the hotel had been half finished and they had poured the crushed rock.

And then, did Carver kill him? Push him off the roof at night? And take a photograph of the corpse in the morning?

She shuddered. Was there still more to it? Had the old man found murder to his liking? Had he watched the French maid making love to her mistress's husband and then killed her? Had he watched the copper-haired woman making love to her lover and then murdered her?

But what of the other killings? Suppose the young 'gigolo' hadn't committed them. Suppose . . .

A single figure walked along the pavement of one of the finer streets in Brooklyn Heights. He walked slowly, like a man with a burden, and when he came to his destination, he slowed, then stopped, might have been prepared to turn back, but after several seconds he went up the steps of a brownstone and rang the bell. Late as it was, there were footsteps in the house; an electric light went on over the door; the door opened.

'What the hell are you doing here?'

Grady tried to make his voice bright. 'Agh, I couldn't sleep, Jack, thinking of you and me. I thought I'd chew over our difficulties together. Brothers in arms, like.'

Cleary stared out at him. He needed a shave; he

wasn't wearing a necktie and his waistcoat was unbuttoned; he smelled of whiskey. Grady drew a pint from his pocket. 'I brought some of the Irish.'

'I got my own.' Nonetheless, Cleary held the door, and Grady went in. He followed his lieutenant along a corridor to the back of the house and into a sordid 'den' that needed cleaning. 'I've never been here before,' Grady said, as if he had just realized it.

'No reason to.' Cleary threw himself back into a chair. A mostly empty bottle and glass were at hand. 'Drink your own. Whaddayou want?'

'Just thought we could both use some cheering up.'

'Christ on a crutch, you think we'd come to each other for cheer?' Cleary poured from the bottle into his own glass. As if reminded, he said, 'Glasses in that tall thing against the wall.' He lit a cigarette. His hands were shaking. 'Not as if we was pals, Grady.'

'Comrades in arms.'

Cleary gave a derisive sound that might have been a cough.

Grady had one hand in his overcoat pocket. He was sweating like a coal-heaver; any second now, Cleary would smell it on him. Cleary was no fool. Better to get it over with. 'Well . . .' he said.

Cleary turned his head aside to tap cigarette ash into a dirty saucer. Grady pulled a revolver from his overcoat pocket. When he cocked the hammer, Cleary heard it and turned, an expression of astonishment on his face. But the chair was too deep for him to get out of quickly.

'I am very sorry, Mr Carver, but if you do not call the police, I will.'

'*Please*, Mrs Doyle! He's all right now; the doctor gave him—'

'I don't care what the doctor's done! Your father committed a horrible, a . . . a *despicable* act against me! Heaven knows how many other women he's done the same to or worse. Mr Carver, your father is *wicked*!'

'No, no—'

'What would you call him, then? *He ripped open my robe!*'

'He's old, Mrs Doyle. He's senile.' They were in young Carver's office. It was barely eight in the morning. Louisa, sleepless but determined to pull herself out of her funk by striking back, had put her loaded revolver in her rear pocket and marched down to beard Carver before she even had breakfast. Carver was almost in tears. 'He's *harmless*.'

Louisa, who had spent the night in tears herself and was now beyond them, looked down at him – she was standing, he was sitting – as the statue of Athena might have looked down on a particularly worthless Athenian. 'Harmless? Mr Carver, your father may be the Bowery Butcher.'

'NO! Oh, dear God, don't say such a thing! They've caught the Butcher; it's in all the papers. My father isn't like that. He just wants to . . . *look*

509

– do you understand? It's always been his . . .
failing. He had to leave Pittsburgh because of it.
When he came here, I thought he'd reform. He
threw himself into building the hotel. I thought
he'd turned over a new leaf.'

'And instead he was building a bespoke peep
show for himself.'

His mouth actually fell open, but at once his
eyes got shifty and she knew she'd said something
she shouldn't have. Yet she went on. 'And you
knew, didn't you? About the passages and the
"deluxe closets" that were really secret doors for
him to go into rooms and—'

'He hasn't done it in years! Please, please, don't
say it! It would ruin us. And I didn't know, not
for years and years—!'

'What do I care about you? What about me?
What about all the women he's spied on over the
years?'

'But it's only *looking*.'

Louisa dropped her voice. '"Only looking." Or
do you mean "Only women"?'

'I didn't mean that. I mean, looking is . . . is . . .
it isn't physical harm.'

'It's a crime.'

'Not a serious one.'

'But it is a crime! And that's why I intend to
telephone the police.'

'You can't!' He looked as if he would stop her
physically, then softened, cringed. 'You mustn't.
Look, Mrs Doyle, we'll come to an arrangement.

510

I'll pay you for your, what, suffering, and your . . . your embarrassment, your—'

'Try terror, Mr Carver.'

'Well, yes, I understand, of course. And you deserve compensation. Unquestionably. We can settle this between ourselves. Or between our lawyers; see? I'm entirely willing for you to bring in your lawyers.'

'I'm overcome by your generosity. Mr Carver, I have been *harmed*.'

'Well, in a manner of speaking, yes, but—'

'In the manner of speaking of the law, Mr Carver. That is the law's word, "harm." And the law's response to harm is to make whole. I was stripped naked to the waist by your father in front of not only him but at least six other men. Including you. What will make me whole is going to the police and seeing your father put where he can never harm a woman again.'

'You can't.'

'I can and will.'

Tears started running down Carver's face. 'Mrs Doyle – he's my *father*.'

Astonishingly to her, she was moved. She was sure she despised Carver; he was a snake and a coward and, for all she knew, he shared his father's vice. But in the way he had said 'father,' he had been sincere. She said, 'I'll give you until noon to find a private asylum that will lock him away.'

'He's locked away already.'

'And look what happened! Where was Galt?

511

Probably asleep – do you really think that one man could keep watch all the time? Your father is strong, Mr Carver. And I'm not entirely persuaded that he's senile. I am absolutely certain, however, that he is dangerous.' She pushed her walking-stick into the carpet and straightened. 'Twelve o'clock. If your father is not out of the hotel and locked up somewhere by then, I will call the police. Then I will go to my husband's lawyers and tell them to sue you for the value of the hotel.'

He was blubbering. 'They'll put him in Ward's Island!' To his credit, he for once didn't mention the hotel.

'I don't know what that may be, nor do I care. I dare say you can afford some private asylum.'

He moaned. 'We can't, we can't . . .' He actually wept. 'We're broke.'

She went straight to the restaurant and tried to eat her table d'hôte breakfast. The false energy of her confrontation with Carver quickly faded, however; she found she had no appetite. Her back ached between her shoulder blades; her whole body seemed to have a poor grasp of how to move, how to balance. Her head ached.

She drank tea and ate part of a single piece of dry toast.

Minutes later, she was in her room. She had asked Reception to ring for Ethel. The truth was, she didn't *need* Ethel: she *wanted* another human being.

Without beating about the bush, she said, 'What would you think, Ethel, of going back to England?'

'Oh, I'd be very pleased to, madame! But wouldn't Mr Doyle, mmm . . . ?'

'I would explain to Mr Doyle. The truth is, I think I've had enough of New York.' By which she meant *of this hotel*.

'Yes, madame. But isn't it quite expensive?' This was Ethel's way of saying that she knew that Louisa was out of money.

'I've taken care of that.'

'Well, then. You'd like to see your little ones, I dare say.' Ethel was looking into the bureau drawers – doing her job, in fact. 'I think if we're going anywhere, we should have our laundry done, madame.'

'Yes, that's a good idea.'

'And some pressing of our dresses. Should I tell them to bring the dresser trunk from the lumber room, madame?'

'Oh – it takes up so much space – still . . .' She thought that Ethel was rushing her fences a bit. 'Is something wrong, Ethel?'

'Not at all, madame. I simply thought that if we're going, there's a great deal to do.' She was piling dresses on the bed and starting to go over them for repairs. 'There is something I should tell you, I suppose.' She gave Louisa a quick look. 'I've given Mr Galt his walking papers.'

'Oh, dear, what happened?'

'He made advances.' She sniffed. 'He tried to put his arm around me when we were walking out.'

'Oh, I'm sorry, Ethel. But . . .' She thought of her own experience of the night. 'Putting an arm around you doesn't seem so very bad.'

'It's the thin end of the wedge, if you take my meaning. I told him I didn't put up with that sort of thing and I had no intention of it being that kind of arrangement. He was quite sheepish about it.' She said that with a good deal of satisfaction. At that moment, Ethel reminded Louisa of the women who had taught her at the teachers' training college. 'It would serve him right if I set sail for England.'

'Perhaps he'll apologize.'

'He already has. Very nicely, too. In writing.' She sounded more and more satisfied. Abruptly, she whisked some clothes off the bed. 'I'll just take these upstairs and mend them, if you don't mind. All my sewing things are up there, and there's no room here.'

And you have friends up there and human companionship, you lucky woman.

'Of course. Off you go, then.'

Louisa wandered out into the lobby. She thought she might find Mrs Simmons there, could say something sympathetic to the old woman about her nephew. She wasn't there, however. Manion was, sitting in his usual place; he gave her the look of a hurt cow; she tried the smallest smile she knew and turned away. She'd had enough of him and of men – especially men who exercised an attraction despite herself.

'Any messages for Doyle?'

'Nothing, sorry.'

One of the boys brought her the morning papers. Only a piece on an inside page cut through her funk:

Suicide of a Disgraced Policeman

Lieutenant John Cleary, recently of the Murder Squad of the Municipal Police, was found in his home last night, apparently dead by his own hand. With him was Sergeant Peter Grady, who found the body. 'I had just stepped out of the room. I heard the shot, and when I ran in, there he was on the floor.'

Cleary and Grady were both under suspension for suspicion of corruption. 'It must have been too much for him,' said Deputy Chief F. X. Halloran. 'The newspapers have hounded this poor officer to his death.'

Investigating officers of the Brooklyn Municipal Police say there is no question of foul play . . .

Louisa didn't finish reading. Cleary and Grady seemed unreal to her now.

At nine, Marie Corelli came down and headed straight for the restaurant. Louisa hobbled after her and asked if she could sit with her.

'Of course, my dear! Sit, do sit, you look simply

awful. I don't mean that; you look pretty, as always, but you look so *ravaged*. What has happened?'

She thought she would say, 'Nothing,' but instead poured out the story of the night's horror. It came in a gush, Marie wide-eyed opposite her, nibbling little bites of toast and nodding her head and saying things like, 'Ah, these men!' By the time she had finished, Louisa found that she, too, was eating toast. In fact, she was ravenous.

'He really said, "Show me your bosom"?'

'Well . . . He was more vulgar than that.'

'What did he say? Breasts? *Quel horreur*.' Marie finished the last of the jam on her plate, licking the spoon afterward. 'I, too, have had an adventure, as I hinted last night, though not one so *outré* as yours, poor thing.' She leaned across the table, whispered, 'Almost a visitation from Azul!' And with great excitement, she told Louisa about hearing sounds from the corner of her room, then the bumping next to the fireplace. 'It was he – Azul! But he did not quite break through the barrier.'

Louisa didn't have the heart to tell her it must have been old Carver. All she could say was, 'This is a terrible place.'

'Not at all! It is a *unique* place.' Marie dusted her fingers together to get rid of the crumbs. 'Come upstairs with me while I dress, why don't you? I will show you where it happened. You've had a fright; you need to talk. And do come to my summoning, won't you? I can feel that I'm very close now.'

516

Louisa still had more than two hours before her promise to Carver – an unwise one, she thought – ran out. Several men were standing at the desk; as she passed, she recognized two of them from the horror of the night before. She flushed and turned her head away: they had seen her breasts. She imagined jokes, nudges. But no, they were looking away from her.

'Do you like men?' she asked as they went up in the lift.

'Not a great deal.'

'But do you *like* them? As friends, I mean.'

'One cannot be friends with men.' Marie frowned at the boy who was piloting the lift. 'I have to agree with Mrs Woodhull on that score – for whom I perhaps owe you an apology, my dear. She was *very* harsh with you that day at lunch. I had hoped you would like each other.'

'I don't think it was a question of that.'

'Not that she and I "like" each other, either. I seldom see her; rather, we're epistolary friends. I think that one should have a *serious* correspondent or two, don't you? And she is serious! Perhaps too much so for you.' The lift stopped. 'At last.'

Marie's sitting room was chaos. The oak table that Marie had told her about had been pulled away from the wall, and luggage and books and the remains of a meal were piled on it. Every lamp had a silk scarf either draped over it or lying next to it. Clothes were everywhere.

'The *bonne* hasn't cleaned yet,' Marie said. An

understatement to Louisa, accustomed to Ethel's neatness. Marie turned on a lamp that had a scarf over it and said, 'What d'you think? The right effect? For the summoning, you know. It is all for the participants, not for Azul – what would Azul care about lights? Azul *is* light!'

'Oh, it's quite nice.'

Marie went around, unbuttoning the back of her dress and turning lights on and off. When she was down to one again, she said, 'One light? With the green scarf?' She picked up something from the oak table as if she meant to start cleaning, then dropped it. 'The housekeeper insists that they will have the room cleaned by half-ten. I sincerely hope so! I shall be out until then or a few minutes later, and the summoning is at eleven!'

Louisa was standing next to the fireplace. Now that the table had been moved, the wall there was accessible. 'Is this where you heard the noises?' She began to feel over the panel for a crack that would reveal a door. It had occurred to her that when she called the police, her story would be more believable if she could actually lead them to an entrance into the tunnels or passages or what-ever they were. If they existed.

Marie had gone into the bedroom, now put her head out the door but kept the rest of herself, except for one bare shoulder, out of sight. 'That's where I felt Azul's strength. As if he were *pushing* to make himself visible. It must be the devil's own fight, you know, breaking through the barrier from infinity into reality.'

Louisa felt all over that part of the wall but found nothing. It was paneled, like the same section on the other side of the fireplace and like the rest of the sitting room. The paneling was carved in rectangles made of simple bevels with a raised moulding around them. It was possible, she supposed, that the moulding hid the edges of an opening, but she couldn't get her fingernails under it to find out. Nothing felt loose; nothing gave when she pushed.

Marie came back wearing a silk kimono and smoking a cigarette. Louisa said, 'You felt you were being watched, you said.'

'I *knew* I was being watched, *chère*.' She pointed up into a corner of the room. 'Up there – I could feel rays of divinity coming from up there. Want a cigarette?'

'Oh, no, thanks. Yes! Yes, I will. For my nerves.' She went to the corner and looked up. A dentillated wood cornice ran all the way around the room. It all looked as solid as the trees it had come from. Still, she thought she might see something if she could get up there and really look.

Marie handed her a lighted cigarette. 'What are you looking at, my dear?'

'If I could stand on a chair, I might have a better look up there.'

'Stand on a chair – are you mad? You just broke your ankle! Come over here and sit down. Please, my dear. Stand on a chair, indeed!'

But Louisa wasn't listening. She was looking at Marie's room key, which she had tossed down on a table next to the chair in which she'd now seated Louisa. Marie went off to the bedroom again; Louisa puffed once on her cigarette, held it in her mouth, and whipped from her pocket the key that had opened Carver's office. She put it over Marie's key. They were identical in size, but the key from Carver's office had extra cuts and indentations in it.

Wasn't there something called a skeleton key?

It took her thirty seconds to find out.

There was.

'Not going, I hope, my dear.' Marie was back in the sitting room. 'I need you to help me get into a corset. Do you mind?'

Of course she didn't mind, but it occurred to her that it was time that Marie got herself a lady's maid. When she suggested it – Marie was displaying a formidable pair of breasts, holding up some flimsy French garment that would soon cover them – Marie said, 'In Paris, my companion dresses me. We are companions of many years.' Her eyes met Louisa's; Marie smiled, hesitated, said, '*Eh, bien,*' and turned away. 'The corset, if you please.'

In her own room again, Louisa thought about the skeleton key and Marie's wall. Marie was going to be out until almost eleven, she said, but of course she'd be later than that because she was always late. There would be time to go into her room and look at that wall again.

Louisa had convinced herself that she would have to have proof that passages ran through the walls of the hotel. Suppose, for example, the men who had seen old Carver attack her last night had all left the hotel, taken trains? Hadn't Ethel said they were mostly traveling men in the annex? Suppose young Carver had threatened Galt with something terrible unless he denied that any of it had happened? Suppose Louisa were to have no proof but what she could supply herself? She would most certainly call Detective-Sergeant Dunne at noon (or sooner), but Dunne would want facts. She didn't want him saying that she was again too much at the centre of things.

A knock sounded on her door. She felt a stab of fear, conquered it. 'Yes – who is it?'

'It's Galt, Mrs Doyle.'

She hesitated. At that moment, she didn't trust anyone – not any man, at any rate. And Ethel had given him his walking papers; might he be resentful? She said, 'What is it, Mr Galt?'

His voice was a little muffled by the door. 'I only wanted to say how sorry – how ashamed I am about last night.'

She made sure the gun was in her pocket and kept her hand on it as she opened the door. He moved back half a step and said, 'I won't come in. I just feel that what happened was terrible for you.'

'Mr Galt, will you tell that to the police if I call them?'

521

'Indeed I will! Though it was my fault, him getting out.'

She opened the door wider. 'I'm sure it wasn't. You can't be everywhere, and you have to have your sleep.' She lowered her voice. 'And I think old Mr Carver knows ways to get about the hotel that you don't.'

He stared at her rather stupidly. She said, 'He's been spying on at least one guest that I know of – Miss Corelli. I'm going to look in Miss Corelli's rooms to see how he does it.'

'I don't think he can be doing anything like that. It's just that last night, he got away from me.'

He was looking doubtful, maybe frightened. She said, 'I've told Mr Carver – the young one – I'd give him until noon before I call the police about last night. I mean to tell them everything.'

He backed away another half-step and held up a hand. 'I was hoping you might, well . . . You know Miss Grimstead's been walking out with me. I thought . . . as her and I had an unfortunate misunderstanding . . . you might, maybe, put in a word for me.' He got almost agitated and waved a hand as if shushing her. 'Nothing personal! Nothing I mean that she'd see as interfering, but only . . .' He looked helpless. 'I'm not such a bad fellow, Mrs Doyle.'

The triviality, the banality of it, made her impatient with him. She muttered, 'Of course. I'll see what I can do. Thank you for coming by, Mr Galt.' She closed the door.

She thought frankly that he had a lot of cheek – as if she would interfere in something going on between her maid and a man. But that was unimportant; what was important was getting facts before noon.

She made sure that she had the skeleton key, and she took the hotel's letter opener from the desk in case she found something she wanted to pry open. She would have forgotten the revolver, but it was already in her pocket, and she felt the weight of it as she went out. It seemed now ridiculous to her that she was carrying a gun, an actual gun. Marion McCousins had made it quite clear that she was all but useless in trying to shoot it. Still, it would be silly to own it and not carry it. The gun stayed in her pocket next to her bustle.

It was twenty minutes before eleven. In a little more than an hour, she would see to it that justice was done to old Carver.

She had crossed the lobby and got into the lift when she saw movement out among the leather chairs. It was Manion. He was getting out of his chair, looking at her, hesitating. Abruptly, he sat down again. The lift doors closed.

'*Third* floor watcher step *please*.'

She pushed herself forward on her stick, stepped out of the car on Marie's floor.

'*Going* down *please*.'

The gates clashed. She limped to her right. The corridor was much finer than the one in the annex;

here were good carpets, little lights in bronze sconces, vaguely good paintings and a statue or two. At the corner where she turned to get to Marie's room was a curtained alcove with two armchairs and a table in it, a little stage set that she supposed nobody used.

She limped to Marie's door. Her heart was beating too fast. She could feel weakness in her knees, like the weakness there of sex, like the weakness of the phthisis. And fear, now never far away.

She knocked, in case the maids were still cleaning. She put the skeleton key in the lock and it turned and the door fell open a few inches.

The room felt unsafe at first. There was no reason it should seem so except that the curtains were drawn and it was in semi-darkness. Marie's mess had disappeared from the heavy table. The odour of her cigarettes and her scent were still in the air. The odours of furniture polish and soap now lay over them.

Get it over with, Louisa. Do it and get out and call the police. And damn being frightened. And damn this place.

She opened the drapes; cold, silvery light poured in. That was better. She put on two of the electric lamps; the light got warmer, safer.

She felt around the moulding by the fireplace again and tried to slip the point of the letter opener under it, but it wouldn't go. If the moulding hid a door, it did so expertly, the work of a skilled craftsman.

She looked up into the corner where 'Azul' had first made his noises. A peephole up there? Perhaps hidden in one of the dentillations? She lifted one of the lamps to get more light, but she could still see nothing. She looked around for something to climb on and rejected the rather feminine gilt chairs because she was short and so were they. Even standing on one, she wouldn't have had her eyes level with the cornice.

Beyond the bedroom door was a slant-top desk with drawers below, rather narrow and quite delicate-looking. Still, when she rocked it, it felt sturdy. Could she move it? She could try.

After two pushes that moved it only a few inches over the carpet, she took out the drawers, lightening it. Then she pulled two prayer rugs out of the path and rolled the carpet – imitation Shiraz, but good – back and knelt so that she could lift the desk half an inch with one hand while she pulled the carpet from under the caster with the other. Another lift, another tug, and the left-hand casters were on bare wood floor. It was easy then to free the others and roll it across the room and position it in the corner, then little more effort to carry one of the gold chairs to set it with its back to the desk so that she had a kind of stair – chair seat, desk surface, top. But, easy as it might have been, she was breathing hard and, of all things, perspiring. *Ladies do not perspire. The teachers' college . . .*

She debated taking the letter opener. Falling off

the desk with it in her hand would be dangerous. Better to lay it on the top where she could get it if she needed it, although the idea of bending while standing up there, her front flat against the wall, was dizzying.

She placed the letter opener, then leaned her cane in the corner of the room.

She lifted her skirts and raised her right foot to the chair seat. The next movement, she knew, was going to hurt: she would have to put her weight on her bad ankle. She turned and tried to transfer some of the weight to her hands on the chairback; pain still shot through the ankle as she raised herself.

Dear heaven, it seemed a long way up! She could lean a knee against the chairback and put her left foot on the desk's surface, then lean still farther forward and grasp the extended edges of the top to pull herself up. But then the wall rose above her to the cornice like a cliff. She could look up into the dentillations but see no more than she had from the floor. The cornice was still two feet above her. The only thing for it was to step up to the top of the desk. Without anything to hold on to or take her weight.

She balanced with her fingertips on the top and then raised herself on her left foot. When she had to let go, she felt a momentary swaying backwards, then got her hands flat against the papered wall and clung there as if she had suction-cup fingers. Her heart was beating like a warning. But she had to go on, because her weight was on her bent left leg and the leg was starting to shake.

Up she went, feeling her left thigh muscles try to lock and refuse to go on; on she went until her left leg was straight and she could slide her right foot and stand there very straight, like a child learning posture, with her hands spread against the wall. Thinking, *How will I ever get down?*

The cornice was inches from her face. She tilted her head back without changing her balance, then slid her hands up the wall until they touched the dentillations and she could slowly, painfully, take a dentillation between each thumb and forefinger and so give herself the illusion of holding on.

At first she saw nothing. Then she saw, just above the complex moulding that formed the bottom of the cornice, a line. And then, she saw that the line, itself only a few inches long, finished at each end in a vertical line that ran up to the junction where a dentillation poked forward from the background.

A little flap. Or a tiny door.

Now that she had found it, she was sorry. Now she would have to go on.

She crawled her right hand to the left like a five-fingered spider, trying to hold a dentillation with the other hand as she did so, failing, pressing herself tight against the wall. The fingers reached the lines. She got her index and third fingers beyond the dentillation and pushed.

Her fingertips went in.

A section of wood as big as a matchbox swung up. She looked in.

And saw a pair of human eyes looking out.

She screamed, and then she was twisting and falling, and the weight came on her bad ankle and it collapsed and she was falling backwards, feeling her right thigh strike the chair, and then her head hit the floor and she felt the blow as a flash of light and a stopping of everything.

Sergeant Cassidy came towards Dunne's desk at Mulberry Street and waved a yellow envelope. 'You got a telegram.'

'Oh, Jeez, what now.' Dunne, his eyes baggy with fatigue, took it and rather expertly ripped off the end and extracted the message. He read it, grunted, looked up at Cassidy.

'The Doyle woman was right – it's the hotel.' He waved the telegram. 'From Pittsburgh. The old man – four complaints, one arrest. He's a Peeping Tom.' He got up and reached for his coat, then bent to take a revolver from a drawer. 'Let's go.'

'You want I should call a carriage?'

'I wanta get there today. We'll take the El.'

Louisa rolled on her back. She wanted somebody to help her up. Everything had been knocked out of her – her breath, her heartbeat, her vision. She had lost contact with the world. Where was she? And why—?

She looked up. Somebody was bending over her. He was whispering to her.

'You stupid cunt!'

It was Galt.

CHAPTER 14

She felt pressure on her left wrist and realized too late that he had closed a manacle on it. Seconds later, he closed another on her right wrist, then grabbed the chain that joined them and pulled her up. She shrieked.

'You make noise like that, I'll cut you!' She heard a click; a shiny blade appeared in front of her eyes. She tried to focus on it, recognized the engraved bolster: it was Newcome's Italian flick-knife. 'You give me trouble, I'll cut you right here. I'll put this knife up your hole and cut in circles, around and around.' He jerked her towards him with the chain. 'Say something.'

She tried, but no sound came out.

'Cat got your tongue? Not frightened of me, are you? Well, you should be, you sick bitch, you whore. I've seen you playing with yourself, sucking their cocks . . .' He jerked the chain again. 'Get in there!' He pulled her around so that she could see the opening behind him – next to the fireplace, as she had guessed, a whole section of the wall. Inside were wood and darkness. He gave her a push in the back. 'Get in there.'

She tried to struggle. He swung her around again, holding her at arm's length now by the chain, and hit her twice the way a man hits another man, low in the abdomen with a man's strength. All the air seemed to go out of her lungs. She vomited.

'I should make you lick that up, you stuck-up Brit cunt. Down on your knees, you'd like that, wouldn't you.' He pulled her close. She was weeping; she could hardly see. He said, his lips so close to hers she felt him form the words, 'Get inside when I tell you, or I'll cut you in the tit.'

He pulled on the chain to start her. She fell against the unfinished timber of the door frame, then fell forward, tripping over a sill at her ankle's height; she went down on her knees, her head crashing into a deal wall. He pulled her up by the back of her dress, pushed her to her right. 'Climb.'

She was at the bottom of a wooden shaft. A ladder of rough wood went up into darkness. She felt him close behind her in the confined space as he closed the door and the light faded and then disappeared. *'Climb!'*

She put her manacled hands on a rung at the level of her nose and raised her bad foot and put it on the lowest rung and went up. It didn't matter that the ankle screamed; it didn't matter that her abdomen had pains as if he'd broken something inside her. It didn't matter that she couldn't remember falling, that all she could remember was that she had recognized him and thought for a

531

fraction of a second that he was going to help her. What mattered was that it was Galt.

What mattered was that she was there and he was there, and he said he was going to kill her. Didn't that mean he was the Butcher?

The gun. I should use the gun. But the gun seemed abstract; the real was here in the dark, climbing this ladder that smelled of old wood.

He said, 'Put your hands out in front of you. You're at the top. Climb out and stand there. Or try to run away, if you want.' He tittered. 'Try it.'

She felt her hands on a flat surface that must be a floor; she could feel the roughness of the boards and the cracks between them, and she thought, *The crushed stone is under these boards.* Her feet had climbed only one rung of the ladder; the floor of the tunnel was no more than her head height above the floor of Marie's room. She climbed, her hands flat on the floor, then reaching out to her right as her feet came up, finding a wall and using it to stand. She took a step forward into the darkness, bumped her head, then stood there bent over as he came up. She tried to reach around with her manacled hands to find the pocket in her dress. The fingers of her right hand could touch the edge of the pocket, actually go in almost to the knuckles, but she couldn't reach the gun. She tried to twist herself and bend to the side.

'What the fuck are you doing?' Could he see in the dark? Or had he heard her, the whisper of her dress? He had a handful of her skirt in his hand;

he was close to the pocket and the gun. 'What're you up to?'

'I . . . please . . .'

'I'll give you "please."'

She heard a scrape, then the scratch of a match. The light seemed brilliant in the darkness; she thought of the flash of the gunshot in the tunnel under Madison Square Garden. There were more sounds, metallic, small, and the light grew and she realized that he had lit a lantern.

'All right. You're going to walk straight ahead until you come to the end. Then you'll turn left. If you don't, I'll cut you.'

She could feel the sting of the manacles on her wrists. His pulling must have broken the skin. Again, the pain was abstract. It was like a failure of belief: this was happening, but it couldn't be happening. It had happened to other women, but it couldn't happen to her. Surely?

She was shuffling, limping forward. She tried again to reach around to the pocket but couldn't do it. He would see. He had the lamp. She went on, following her own long shadow down the path of rough boards. Small as she was, she had to bend her head because of the low ceiling. On each side, bare vertical timbers ran up, and bare brick made diminishing lines like railroad tracks towards the end of the tunnel.

She reached another wall. Where was she now? She had been in Marie's room on the third floor. She must still be on the third floor. She looked left: blackness. Another tunnel. So had she come to the body of the centipede from one of its legs?

'I said go left, cunt.'

She turned and started into the dark. He turned into it behind her and his lantern again threw her shadow ahead. It was the same as before, verticals and horizontals and darkness, claustrophobic and terrifying. She thought of old Carver in these tunnels, bent because of his height, opening the peepholes to look at women. And there was a smell . . .

'You'll come to another ladder. Climb.'

That would be at an interior corner of the building, the corner of the centipede's body; on her right would be one of the air shafts, beyond it more walls of brick and stone.

Was she too terrified to be frightened? Like a small animal when it hears the owl's cry as the bird descends, when it is too late and shock strikes like early death to save the pathetic thing from pain?

I am not helpless. I am not an animal. This can't be happening.

She bumped into a ladder. Behind her, he laughed. 'You stupid twat. Walked right into it!' He spun her around and pinned her against the ladder; a rung pushed back at her shoulders, another at the top of her buttocks. She could feel the length of him from his chest down to his knees, pressing against her, forcing her into the ladder.

His face was close. 'You're stupid, you know that? Your brains are down between your legs. So high and mighty, not letting me touch you, laughing at me behind my back, and you thought I didn't know!'

She felt a fleck of spittle strike her face. He grabbed the chain of the manacles and bent to put the lantern on the floor, then put his hand under her skirts and stood, raising the front of her skirt and petticoat. She writhed, cried out.

'Go ahead and scream, bitch! Nobody can hear you here. The other one tried that. She screamed her head off, and I hadn't even cut her yet. Go ahead. You're afraid of me, aren't you. You're pissing yourself, aren't you. You're shitting yourself . . .' His hand was between her legs, feeling her through her drawers, then the fingers scrabbling at the fabric as he pulled the drawers down. She was moaning, 'No, don't, don't!' and trying to push his hand down, but he caught the manacles and raised them so that the chain was pressing into her mouth, and her words seemed to spur him on. She felt his hand go between her legs so that it could feel her buttocks, her anus, then it came forward again and fingers crawled into her vagina.

This can't be happening!

He put his thumb on her clitoris and began to press with his thumbnail. 'You like that, don't you. That's what you like, I know it is.' The pain was intense. His fingers were inside her. 'I'll show you some real stuff. I'll drive you crazy. You'll beg for it. You love it.' He began to whisper, the sound insistent, sometimes slurred, the words incoherent. His whole hand, his fist, was inside her. She screamed, not words but animal sounds: the owl was descending and all she felt was pain.

Then his hand came out and he was doing something between them. She wanted to faint, tried to faint, but she was awake, alive for the first time since she'd fallen. She knew suddenly that it was really happening to her; he had done these things and he was going to do worse. She screamed.

He was doing something between them. She could feel his hand moving, then a rhythmic beating against the tops of her legs.

'He's masturbating. He worked himself up and he's masturbating. Oh, God, oh Heavenly father, oh, please God, don't let this happen—

'You cunt, you bitch, you whore, you cocksucker.' He was panting. 'I'll give it to you. I'll have you raving. Now you'll see – you'll see . . .' He still had her skirts caught up between them. She felt something against her thighs, then his hand prying them apart, his knee, both knees, and something was pressing against her vagina.

'You're wet for me! You're fucking running with it . . .'

He was trying to put his penis into her, but it was soft. She could feel the hardness of the bones of his fingers, his knuckles, and this soft thing, this worm, this limp threat. He kept saying the same words over, *cunt, bitch, whore,* and she felt him harden as he tried to push it in with his fingers, and then she felt him soften and shrink again. He pulled himself away. 'You stinking diseased cunt! You did it! You shit-filled cunt!' He pulled her to him with the manacles and smashed her against the ladder. He was panting, raving, beating her with his free hand. 'It was your fault! You did it on purpose!' He hit her again in the abdomen. 'Climb! Climb or I'll cut your shitbags out and leave you here to die!'

She was moaning, weeping. She climbed as fast as she could. The air was dizzy with her pain. She sank again into disbelief, into surrender.

Yes, yes, kill me, just give me release. Yes, descend on me, kill me.

'Keep climbing!' She had reached another floor, had stopped, already trained. Her senses were closing down; existence was becoming internal; there was no seeing, no hearing, no touching. She kept climbing, up another floor, up, up, then up another; existence was only climbing, these pieces of wood in her hands, somebody moaning, somebody weeping . . .

'Stop!'

He stepped around her, did something. Light. He grabbed her manacles and pulled her forward. 'Stand there!'

She was in a room. It had no windows. It had a tile floor. It had two doors, both closed. In the middle, it had a double stone sink; on the sink was a wooden table. On the table, covered with a brown blanket and held down with leather straps, was Ethel.

Ethel's eyes flicked towards her. 'Help me.'

That was absurd. She couldn't help herself; what was Ethel thinking of?

The tunnel was behind her. She wondered if she could hide in the tunnels, like the rabbit hiding from the owl.

He slapped her. 'I said stand there!'

He had blown out his lantern. She looked at Ethel, but Ethel's eyes were closed now.

Under the sinks on which Ethel's table stood was a tube. It ran to a drain at the side of the room.

On the wall farthest from her was a shelf at head height. On it were bottles of several sizes. In the bottles was transparent fluid, and in the fluid were grey shapes like flukes or squids. In the one at the end of the row was a human face, twisted but still recognizable as a face because of the eyeholes. She thought, *Minnie*.

He stood in front of her. 'Like what you see?' He held her head and twisted it so that she had to turn all the way around, a full circle. What he was showing her was that the walls were covered with photographs of women. Women undressing, women dressing, women on the toilet, women making love to men, women making love to other women—

'You like that one?' He was holding her head so

that she had to look at a photograph of two women on a bed, each with her head between the other's legs.

'That's what I'm going to do with you and the very proper Miss Grimstead. I'm going to cut your tongues out last and then put you like that, and you'll bleed to death into each other's twats. And they'll find you like that. But they won't find your tongues. They'll go into my collection.' He started turning her head again. 'The old man took all these pictures. Years ago. He's a sick one.'

She had been moving her feet so he wouldn't twist her head off her shoulders. When she came around to face him again, he took hold of her chain. 'Shall we start? You two can watch each other. First a little of Ethel, then a little of Lady Uppity-cunt.' He pulled up on the chain. 'Upsy-daisy!'

Her arms were jerked upwards. He pulled her almost off her feet, tried again with both hands, but couldn't reach what he wanted, a two-inch pipe that ran the length of the wall. He cursed, let her down so that her heels touched the floor again, and reached into a pocket.

She had put herself into a place she didn't know existed, a place inside her where none of this could happen and all she had to do was wait. It was a safe place, if only she could keep the pain out of it.

He was putting a key into the right manacle. 'You try anything, and I'll cut you right now. I'll cut your mouth right off; see how you like sucking all those cocks then.'

Dimly, objectively, she saw what he meant to do: raise her left arm so that he could attach the open manacle to the pipe. That seemed a good solution to his problem.

Then she allowed herself to peek out of her safe place and see that her right hand was free.

He was reaching up, pulling on her left arm, his left hand reaching higher and higher towards the pipe.

She plunged her right hand into the pocket at the back of her skirt and felt the gun. It wasn't the way it should have been, upright and pointed so that all she would have had to do was close her hand around the grips; instead, it was upside down and backwards so that she got hold of the barrel when she tried to grasp it. He was trying to put the open manacle over the pipe; she jerked her left hand, tried to bend her weight towards the floor, her right hand feeling over the gun, feeling for the hard-rubber grips.

He pulled her up, having to use both hands. 'Bitch.' He pushed her face first into the wall and bent his knees and pressed his body against hers, lifting with his legs, trying to push her higher. His hands carried the manacle towards the pipe.

She found the handle of the gun. She found the trigger. She couldn't pull the gun out of the pocket because he was pressing against her too hard. She pulled the trigger with the gun still inside her pocket.

The sound was muffled, rather disappointing, but he screamed and moved so fast she almost fell coming away from the wall. He backed half a dozen feet away, screaming at her, bent, holding his right thigh.

She was out of her safe place now. There would be no going back. Now there was a great amount of pain. And the gun. And the smell of burned cloth.

She raised the gun. His face was contorted. He reached towards her and she fired again. She had forgotten the lesson in Madison Square Garden: she held the gun in only one hand; she fired at his head, not his body. The shot missed him and one of the bottles on the shelf exploded, and a putrid, penetrating stench gushed into the closed room. Galt turned, saw the smashed bottle, screamed again and went towards it in time to have something grey and soft slither off the shelf and fall on him. He screamed once more, and Louisa shot him in the back, recovering enough this time to aim at the mass of his jacket.

'You cheating shit! You cunt bitch!' He had hunched forward, his head turned towards her, but he was scuttling away towards one of the doors. His left hand was trying to reach over his right shoulder to get at his back. He got to the door and she thought with a surprising return of clarity that he was too far away now and the little bullets weren't doing enough damage. Still, she pointed the gun at him.

He screamed one more obscenity at her and went through the door. It slammed behind him and she heard a key turn in the lock. His shouts were muffled; then they diminished as if he were running away.

She was shaking again. Her teeth were chattering. She was talking to herself. 'Get away – must get away – must—' She limped to the door he had gone through and shot the bolt on her side.

'Help me.'

She whirled to look at Ethel. Her eyes were open again. 'Shut up, Ethel. I've got to get us out of here . . . get out . . . got to get out . . .' She began to totter around the room, looking for help, for succour, for escape.

She opened the room's other door. She screamed.

Old Mr Carver, or what was left of him, was sitting in his invalid's chair. The top of his head had been skinned, so he was hairless and bloody bone showed where his scalp had been. His diseased red face was pasty yellow and grey. His eyes were gone. His mouth was stuffed with something that Louisa realized was her stolen, soiled drawers.

She was sick.

She slammed the door and fell back against it. 'Help me.'

'Ethel, oh, Ethel . . .' She thought that Ethel wasn't showing any spine. Surely she must see what the situation was.

But it's up to me. She can't help me as she is. I must help her.

She staggered to the table and undid a leather belt. She went down to Ethel's feet and undid the buckle down there. She raised the brown blanket that covered Ethel.

'Oh, Ethel . . .' Blood had dried on Ethel's thighs. An oval cut had been made in her abdomen the size of a child's head, not deep enough to penetrate the abdominal wall but deep enough to show yellow-white fat. Her breasts had been stabbed half a dozen times. Ethel raised her arms like a child wanting an embrace.

Louisa cradled her head and thought of her own children. She whispered to her. She kissed her forehead. 'We must get ourselves out of here, Ethel. You must walk. Yes, yes, you must. If we don't get out, he will murder us.'

Ethel was weeping without making sound. She said in a numb voice, 'It's Mr Galt.'

'I know, dear. Now come along, I'm going to put your feet down and you're going to try to walk. Come on – a little more – Ethel, please, we must get out! Come – put your weight on my arm – good . . .' She draped the blanket over the naked woman and was encouraged when she saw Ethel automatically hold it closed at her throat.

Two things happened at once: Louisa heard Galt come back to the door, and Ethel saw the opening into the tunnels. Louisa turned back and pointed the gun; Ethel screamed.

'I can't go in there! I can't!'

'You must. It's the only way out.'

Galt was trying to push the door open. The bolt was holding, but Louisa could see its moorings in the door beginning to loosen.

'Ethel! Go through that opening!'

It was, Louisa thought, the greatest act of courage she would ever see. Ethel had been tortured; she had been dragged through those same tunnels to her torture. She had suffered worse than Louisa had, and she had had no revolver to give her hope. Yet Ethel did as she was told.

Louisa pushed into the tunnel behind her and put herself on Ethel's right so that she could take some of the weight on her good foot. It was black in there. All she could do was feel her way with her right hand. When she put her arm around Ethel, the woman said, 'I can't,' but she went on, and Louisa said, 'You can, dear; yes you can,' and it made it easier for her to have somebody else to think about.

They were, she knew, on the penthouse floor. Marie and her 'summoning' would be two floors below them. It was illogical of her to think of going back to Marie's, except that she knew that Marie's would have people in it – people to help Ethel, people to help her. *No, not people – women.* People to go for the police. Many rooms lay between them and Marie's, to be sure, but who was in them? How many people? And how would they react to two women coming out of the wall – if, indeed, Louisa could find the way through the wall? *And there would be men.*

And Marie, she thought, would fight for them.

They reached the first ladder; which Louisa felt not as a ladder but as the hole it stood in. She whispered, 'You must go down.'

'Oh, I can't!'

'You must. Galt's behind us now. He won't let us go if he can catch us. You must, Ethel – you must!'

'I shall fall.'

'I shall be right behind you. If he comes close, I shall shoot him.'

Still weeping, Ethel lowered herself into the darkness. When they reached the floor below, Louisa held her there, listened. Could she hear Galt? Or could she see a brightening of the dark from his lantern? She went back up far enough to put the top of her head above the floor; there, indeed, was the first glow of Galt's lantern, casting a faint shadow of a distant ladder as he came down. She ducked back and forced Ethel into the hole. 'We'll go down two floors. He'll think we've gone one.' She said that out of hope. Mad or not, Galt was no fool. And the tunnels were his warren. The thought led to one of old Carver; her stomach churned. Had Galt killed him simply for his scalp, or because he was sick of the old man, or was he now simply living to kill?

She let herself down to the rungs of the ladder and went down using her left foot and her arms. It was hard to say what part of her hurt most. Her abdomen, her vagina, her back . . .

Where were they now? They were crouching partway along a tunnel, listening for Galt. They should be on the fourth floor, she thought, almost to one of the corners where the legs of the centipede met the body. At the corner, there should be a ladder; they would go down and be on Marie's floor.

'Oh!' Ethel wept again. They had both heard it – a sound on the ladder they had just used, then hoarse breathing and a cough.

'Come on.'

Louisa pulled her maid down the tunnel. Once, she tripped, almost fell; feeling with a hand, she found the kind of trapdoor through which Galt had first forced her to climb from Marie's room. According to the hotel plan, there should be three of these on each side of the building for each floor. This would be the middle one – right above Marie's?

She looked back and saw the lantern's glow picking out the square hole where the ladder was.

They hurried on. Now, dimly, they could hear him coming down the ladder.

'Go down, Ethel.'

'No—'

'Go!'

Louisa lay on the floor on her belly, her toes over the edge of the hole. She had the gun in both hands, extended in front of her, her elbows steadied on the floor. When she could see Galt in the light of his own lantern, she would shoot him.

The light grew. She could see movement as he came down, the lantern on the floor above; then he must have reached up for it because suddenly she could see his head in the brightness of the light. Fear raced through her, trying to make her freeze, surrender.

It was an act of sheer will that made her wait there. At any time, he might catch the glint of the pistol or the pale smudge of her face. He would still be too far away, but she would have to shoot. If he came close and she missed, it would be over. She tensed. He had stopped. Was he looking into the darkness for something he thought he had seen? He bent forward, then coughed.

She fired. This time, the explosion seemed horrendous, and the flash of the gunshot lit up the tunnel for yards. She saw his face, contorted, enraged; she heard him curse and swing the light up; then she was gone down the hole.

He'll blow out his lantern because it makes him a target. I shot too soon.

She tripped over Ethel at the bottom. She was curled against the wall.

'I can't go any farther, madame.'

'It's only a little way now, dear. You must.' She felt with her left foot for the trapdoor that must be there; where was it? Ah, there. She pulled at Ethel and with main force got her away from the ladder and the trap. She had thought of the trick that Galt had played on the police on Mulberry Street, getting the men and boys to come out and open the manholes and the cellar doors. She could do the same.

She pulled at the trap and laid it back against the wall.

Above her, she heard a step on the ladder.

She gathered Ethel up and dragged her down the tunnel. Here, somewhere, somewhere near, must be Marie's room. Must be. *Must* be! Where, where – her foot found the trap. She yanked it open, pushed Ethel to it. 'Down, down!'

He was at the bottom of the ladder. She heard his step, then a cough and a thud and a curse; she could feel his fall in the boards under her feet. He had put out his lantern at the top of the ladder, and in the dark he had gone down the hole she had opened. She could picture it: one leg down all the way, the other caught behind him on the boards. Maybe he had broken something, a leg, an arm. The sound had been loud, complicated – limbs and head hitting wood.

If he scrambled out and came to her, she would shoot him. McCousins had said to put it against his vest and pull the trigger. She would do that. If he let her.

She dared to work her way along the low ceiling, fumbling for the spyhole that would look into Marie's room. She tried to picture its location in the corner: she remembered poking it open, then nothing. Where was it? Her fingers found a knob; she pulled. She looked through.

Marie Corelli was sitting at the far end of the

library table. Other women Louisa didn't know were sitting around it, their hands joined. Marie had her head back and her eyes closed and she was chanting in a sort of singer's moan, 'Azul! Come to us, Azul!'

Louisa stood on tiptoe and shouted. 'Marie! Help us! Marie!'

There was a flurry at the table. A woman's voice cried, 'An emanation!' Louisa heard Marie shout, 'Have I got through!'

'No, no – Marie – help us—!'

She heard the bang of a trap. Galt had picked himself out of the hole and was coming again.

Louisa scrambled to the trapdoor that led to Marie's room. Ethel was at the bottom of the ladder; all that Louisa knew of her was what she learned with her feet, a softness that must be Ethel's rounded back. Ethel was sobbing.

She slammed the trapdoor above them, dropped the gun into her pocket, then kept hold of the trap's curved metal handle above her. She tried to tell Ethel to push on the wall, but it was no good; Ethel was done. Louisa felt with her good foot over what she knew had to be the door into Marie's room. There had to be a lock or at least a latch that held it. All she could feel with her foot was smooth wood. She tried to raise her foot to feel along the top of the door, but then the trap above her began to lift.

She swung her left arm up wildly and caught the handle. The trap came down again. She heard Galt shout an obscenity. He started to lift again.

She swung her legs up and kicked out at what she hoped was the door into Marie's room. Nothing happened. The trap opened farther; she swung again, trying to pull it down and at the same time kick out at the door. A sliver of light appeared near where her feet struck, then closed, as if a door had briefly opened. She heard Galt's feet on the boards above as he tried to get better purchase. The trap opened more slowly this time but wider than before. She could picture Galt's straddling the trap, using his entire upper body to lift her weight. He coughed, went on coughing as he lifted.

She tried to make herself heavier, to hang dead, but the trap continued on up and she swung forward again and kicked, and the sliver of light opened and widened and there was a cracking sound, and she swung again and let go of the handle and flung her whole weight at the door, which flew open and dumped her into the room, Ethel rolling out of the 'deluxe closet' below her like a balled, hibernating animal.

Then Marie was running towards her, shouting, 'Louisa, *ma chère* – dear God, it's you!' A woman in a big hat was recoiling away from her. Two older women were leaning on each other and embracing. Another was trotting towards the room's outer door. Louisa screamed, 'It's the Butcher!' She turned and pushed the remains of the door closed on the ladder, seeing Galt's feet and legs as he came down.

'Help me!' she shouted at Marie. 'Help me keep him out! Marie—!'

Galt pushed on the door from the other side and forced her back. She leaned her shoulder on it and reached back for the gun. Behind her, Marie was shouting something – *'La table, la table!'* – and then Galt was pushing on the door and reaching through the opening, trying to find her with his hand. The hand touched her arm, clutched fabric; she recoiled, put her back against the door as her sleeve tore, and then she had the gun out and she put the gun forward until it was almost touching the groping hand and pulled the trigger.

Three women were carrying the library table towards her. They were all straining; the woman in the big hat had her eyebrows up and her eyes popping out, but it was she who panted, 'Only a few feet more, girls – keep going, keep going . . .' and Louisa ducked aside as they smashed the oak table into the door. She helped to push the door closed; they leaned into it and moved it a few inches more.

The woman in the hat was piling a chair on the table. 'Get the furniture – come on, girls, lend a hand!'

Marie bent over Louisa. 'How badly are you hurt?'

Louisa looked at her without understanding, then realized that she must look as ravaged as she felt. 'Get Ethel to a doctor. He stabbed her breasts.'

'Oh, *mon dieu.*'

Furniture was piling up on the table. Galt was still pushing at the door from the other side, and it bulged where Louisa had splintered it. She saw his bloody hand up there, and she pulled the trigger again, and then again and again, and at last she understood that the gun was empty and she had been hearing only metallic clicks, and she threw the gun at the door.

The woman in the hat had organized two of the women into a human bosun's chair by showing them how to hold on to each other's wrists and make a seat. They got Ethel on her feet and leaned her back into them, and that was the way Louisa saw her carried out, barely conscious between two women who were taking small steps and carrying all her weight.

'I need to get the police!'

'You need a doctor. What has he done to you?'

'Get *out* Marie! Send for the police—'

Marie and another woman had formed another bosun's chair and Louisa found herself leaning back into it, her cane in her hand. Marie, scuttling towards the door with her, panted, 'You left it somehow. I found it when I came in.' She raised her voice. 'Get the door, someone! And lock it behind us. Everybody out! We have a murderer here!'

Louisa heard the door slam, and they carried her along the corridor to the lift. 'Put me down, please.'

'You are hurt and exhausted, my dear.'

'The fire alarm!'

Next to every one of the hotel's elevators was a red box with a glass front and the legend 'Break glass to warn of fire.' Louisa swung her cane. The glass broke with a satisfying noise, and she pulled down the lever inside. At once, bells began to clang. The other women looked startled, then disapproving. One of them said, 'It says to do so only in an emergency.'

'This is an emergency.'

'But it isn't a *fire* emergency.'

Then the lift came, with its clashing gates.

The effects of the alarm had reached the lobby ahead of them: men and women were standing among the leather chairs, many with newspapers in their hands; half a dozen had gathered at Reception, where the panjandrum was using soothing tones to say there was no cause for panic. Carver the younger was in his office doorway, looking upwards with an expression of the deepest anxiety, as if the still-ringing alarm meant that the sky was about to fall.

Louisa, driven now by a kind of mania, tore herself away from Marie and headed for Carver. At the same time, the front doors opened and Detective-Sergeant Dunne and Cassidy burst through. She heard Dunne shout over the sound of the alarm and the panicky guests, 'Where's the fire at? How bad is it?'

But she focused on Carver. She screamed at him, 'Galt is the Butcher!'

He seemed dazed. 'It's a fire.'

'It isn't a fire, you fool! It's Galt – Galt is the Butcher! Galt is a murderer. Listen to me! *He's killed your father!*'

Her arm was grabbed; she was turned in a quarter-circle. Manion was there, his face contorted. 'What happened?'

She pulled herself away and backed a step, raising her cane to keep him away. 'It's Galt! He tried to rape me and he tortured Ethel and he's murdered three women – can't you understand? *He kills women!*'

Then Dunne was elbowing Manion out of the way. 'Tell me, Mrs Doyle.'

'The Butcher is upstairs! Is that enough sense for you? He tried to rape me, and he was going to kill me the way he's killed the others! He's got a room up there with jars of women's body parts in them, and he murdered old Carver and scalped him. You have to believe me, you fool!'

Dunne said to Cassidy, 'Who's this Galt?'

'The old man's nurse.'

Dunne said, 'Did we question him?'

'He seemed okay.'

People were pouring out of the lifts. Manion looked at them and started for the stairs to the mezzanine, his right hand inside his jacket where the bulge of his gun showed.

She screamed at Dunne. 'He doesn't know about the tunnels! Galt will be in the tunnels.'

Dunne gave Cassidy a push. 'Stop that damned

554

fool! Manion! MANION!' Halfway up the marble stairs, Manion looked back. 'You get back here! Nobody's going up there until I straighten this out. Dammit, Manion, if I have to come after you . . . !' But by that time, Cassidy had caught up with him, and he frogmarched Manion back as if he were a prisoner.

Dunne shouted at Manion, 'You stand there until I want you!' and then reached to take Louisa's arm again; she shrank away, found herself being caught from behind by Marie Corelli. Dunne said, 'Mrs Doyle, what tunnels? Tell me what I am to do!'

'Don't touch me.'

Dunne looked as if he had been slapped. 'All right, all right! How do you know this fella is the Butcher?'

'Because he has women's organs in jars and he has Minnie Fitch's face!'

Behind her, Marie, on whom she was leaning, feeling her big breasts and her belly against her back, shouted, 'He tried to break into my room to kill this poor little thing!'

Dunne looked at the two of them. His eyes went back and forth. Then he whirled on Cassidy and said, 'Get to the telegraph – it's right along there – call Mulberry, ask for— no, the Sixteenth Precinct first, get every man they got over here *now*. Don't use the Black Maria, tell them, *run*. Then telegraph Mulberry, tell them we may have the Butcher cornered in the New Britannic, I need everybody from every precinct from Fourteenth Street to Thirty-eighth. And have them tell Roosevelt. Got it? Go!' He looked towards Reception. 'And turn off that damned fire bell!'

'It isn't a matter of "may" have the Butcher,' Louisa said. 'He's here! Or he was, while you were wasting time asking me stupid questions!' She turned her head to watch several firemen come through the front doors.

Dunne's voice was weary. 'I have to have facts; I can't call out the whole police department because of your feelings.'

'I don't have any *feelings*.' She sagged against Marie. 'Have you ever been dragged through a tunnel by a madman, Detective-Sergeant? Have you ever had somebody threaten to put a knife up inside you and turn it round and round? Have you ever had a man's hand feel up inside you! I've been put through hell, and you want *facts*.'

He took his hat off and swiped his forehead with a hand. 'I can't make sense of it, Miz Doyle!'

She got her weight on her cane and pointed at a straight chair against the wall. She limped there and sat; Marie stood next to her, holding her left hand, formidable in her corseted armor. Dunne looked at them and apparently saw at last the proofs of what she had been through – the dangling manacle, the dirt on her hands and face, the tangle of her hair, the new bruises, the torn dress. He knelt but now had the sense not to put himself too close to her. 'Tell me, Mrs Doyle.'

She knew she was near hysteria. The word made her laugh at herself, the hated word, the foolish word. Her throat hurt from shouting. She couldn't focus. But she told him out of sequence what had happened and what she knew: the tunnels, the doors by the fireplaces, the peepholes. 'Old Carver built it because he was a—'

'Peeping Tom, we know.'

Her voice was hoarse. 'He photographed women. There are photographs on the walls of a room. I think it was his laboratory. Now Galt has it fitted up—' She choked and started to weep. 'He had Ethel strapped on a table with a drain for the blood and he'd stabbed her in the, the—' She laid a hand over her own breast. 'And he said how he was going to kill us while we watched each other.' She held up the manacle. 'He was going to chain me to a pipe but I . . . shot him . . .' Her sobs whirled out of control.

'You shot him? You had a gun?'

'I . . . yes . . . in my pocket. I pulled the trigger and he was hurt, but not badly because he didn't fall down and I shot him again and broke one of his jars, it had a, a, a *uterus* in it and he screamed and I shot him in the back!' She looked at Dunne with haunted eyes. 'But I didn't kill him. Perhaps you can't kill him. Perhaps he's . . .' She leaned her head on Marie's hip. 'He chased us through the tunnels and I got to Marie's room and saw them and went down the hole where the door is and he was trying to get in overhead and I—' She

557

held both hands up and mimed holding on to the hatch.

Marie smoothed her hair back and kissed her cheek. 'It's all right, my love, it's all right.' She turned to Dunne. 'She had to kick her way out – into my room, I mean – and then she was like a little typhoon, pushing the door and screaming, and he really did try to come out and get her, and she shot him again. In the arm. There was blood, I swear it. Then we put a very heavy piece of furniture against the door to keep him from getting into the room and we got out and pulled the fire box and came down here.'

He turned back to Louisa. 'I can't get this about the tunnels into my head. There are tunnels in the *walls*? So he can go into the rooms?'

Louisa leaned her head back against the chair and told him again about the tunnels and which rooms had doors. She said, 'If you go into the tunnels, Galt will kill you.' She looked at Dunne.

'We'll see about that.'

Then Cassidy came back and said he'd sent the telegrams, and he pointed at the bronze doors, where three policemen were coming through. 'From the Sixteenth, I'll bet.' Cassidy waved at them. 'Over here! Coppers over here!' But the crowd was too big and too noisy now. Cassidy said, 'We're gonna have to deal with this crowd or it'll be hell.'

'You telegraphed Mulberry?'

'I did, and then I telephoned, too. They'll get

the precincts. Roosevelt's at home; they're calling him. He's only a coupla blocks away.'

Dunne got up, his knees cracking. More policemen were coming through the door, looking belligerent and confused. Behind them, firemen in helmets and rubber coats were pushing their way in, as well. Dunne muttered, 'Ah, Cripes, it's gonna be a complete combobberation!' He pushed his way to Reception and climbed up on the mahogany desk, the panjandrum looking shocked. Carver, now with a telephone earpiece in one hand and his eyes red, looked on from his office doorway. Dunne roared, 'Quiet! Quiet down, the lot of you!' He had a parade-ground voice. Louisa flinched. 'I'm Detective-Sergeant Dunne of the Municipal Police! There is no fire! You hear me good? There is no fire! You boys from the fire department, the hallways on this floor, if you will, but please in the name of Mary and the saints, don't start dragging hose in here!' He looked over the heads of the crowd at the scattered policemen. 'I want every copper in this place to gather around me *now*! You and you and you – you hear me? Get it moving, then – now means now!' Dunne walked along the reception desk to get as close as he could to the guests. 'All of you guests, I want you to stay down here in the lobby! *Don't go back to your rooms*. We want every guest out of his room and down here, is that clear?'

After the noise and chatter of earlier, it was weirdly silent. Louisa could hear a horse-tram going by in the street, even footsteps on the pavement. Dunne said, 'We have reason to believe that there may be a dangerous criminal in the hotel.' The hubbub swelled up again; Dunne bellowed, 'Quiet! We're going to search this building from stem to stern with a fine-tooth comb! We will arrest anybody we find above this floor! I don't care who you are or how famous you are, if you're above this floor of the hotel, I'm going to throw you in the lock-up and ask questions later!'

Louisa thought, *Galt could be gone by now. They're taking too long. He's too clever for you.* She began to shake.

Dunne jumped down and headed back towards her, trailing a dozen uniformed policemen. He said to Cassidy, 'Get armed men at every exit from the building, including the ones that go to that annex next door. There's back doors the help use and the little door on Fifth. If we're really dealing with the Butcher, we know he's a clever shicer and he's twisted our nose before, so *no mistakes.*' He bent over Louisa. 'Have you seen a doctor?'

'No!'

Dunne shouted at Reception. 'Hey, you in the fancy coat – where's your doctor at?'

'He took a woman to the hospital! An injured woman – I told him to—'

'Oh, Cripes. All right, Mrs Doyle, we'll get you to a hospital ourselves.'

'No!'

560

'Look, don't give me grief, please; I know you've been through a lot, but—'

A voice as big as Dunne's bellowed from the front of the lobby, 'Follow me, men!' It was Commissioner Roosevelt.

Dunne groaned. 'Godamighty, Cassidy, tell him we're getting things organized already, will you?'

Cassidy, who had been briefing his dozen cops, tried to push towards Roosevelt. The commissioner, looking peppy and full of fight, jumped on a table and waved a six-gun as big as a meat cleaver. 'I want every policeman within the sound of my voice to rally to me at this spot where I now stand!'

Dunne squeezed his fingers into his eye sockets. His lips moved. He turned to the dozen cops and said, 'All right, six teams of two each.' He began to point at them. 'You two, Fifth Avenue door. *Move.* Nobody goes in or out. *Nobody!*' He pointed at two more. 'Mezzanine level.' He pointed at the staircase. 'Up there. Entrance into the annex. Got it? All right, you two – second floor, you reach it by the stairs; don't wait for the damned elevators, they're mobbed. Second floor, find the entrance to the annex, stay there. Nobody in or out.' He sent the remaining pairs to the kitchen entrance and what he called 'the back door.'

Roosevelt was still on his table. He bellowed, 'Where are those officers going? You there! You are under my orders! I order you to— What? What's that?'

561

Dunne stood on tiptoe. 'What a balls-up. Pardon me, ladies.' He walked away, shaking his head.

'They won't catch him,' Louisa said.

'Yes they will, *chèrie*.' Marie smoothed her hair back. 'You look dreadful, if I may say it. A hospital would be—'

'No! I don't want them to touch me.' She didn't have to say whom she meant by 'them.' She squeezed Marie's hand. 'What I want is to bathe. I feel filthy. He's covered me with his filth.'

'That's in your mind, my love. Just don't think about it. Did he . . . Did he really—?'

'He put his hand *inside me*. Is that clear enough?'

'Oh, love, don't take it out on Marie. I mean it for the best. But did he . . . I mean—'

'He couldn't do it. If I thought I was going to have his baby, I'd cut it out myself.'

Marie sucked her breath in.

Louisa had stopped weeping. She closed her eyes. Every muscle seemed to hurt. Was this shock? She wondered how she had done what she had done. If not for the gun . . . She heard voices, like the buzzing of flies: the crowd were talking again. Somebody was angry; somebody was pounding a fist on something. It was all distant, all stupid. She should get out of the hotel. She should go somewhere he couldn't find her. But she couldn't move.

She dozed. And woke suddenly. There was Marie beside here, still holding her hand. There was the crowd, the lobby. It must have been only seconds. *Where was Galt?*

She was dry-eyed now. She said, 'I didn't tell him about Newcome. Galt murdered Newcome.'

'Why would he kill a man?'

'I think they saw each other in the alley the night that Minnie Fitch was killed.'

Dunne and Cassidy came back. The starch had gone out of them. Dunne said, 'Roosevelt's in charge now.'

'I didn't tell you – Galt killed Newcome.' She told him about the Italian knife.

'We've got a kid in the lock-up for it.'

'Galt wouldn't let anybody live who'd seen him.'

Dunne sighed. He beat his hat against thigh. He jerked his head at Cassidy, then motioned with his thumb to Manion. 'You – let's have a look upstairs.'

'He'll kill you!'

'We'll be the judge of that, Miz Doyle.'

'Don't go into the tunnels. *Please.*'

'His Nibs is going to do that, as soon as his "picked squad" get here from Mulberry Street. Cassidy and me are going upstairs to gather *evidence.*' He saw her look of horror. 'It's what detectives do, Mrs Doyle. We're the Murder Squad. *Facts.*' He touched Cassidy's arm, grabbed Manion, who gave a sick look towards Louisa, and they rushed away.

More policemen went past them. Some of them came back a minute or two later as if they didn't know what they were doing. The fire alarm had stopped, she realized. Were there firemen walking

563

the corridors now? Might Galt kill one of them and take his hat and coat and vanish?

'Follow me, men!'

She looked up. Roosevelt, six-gun in hand, was standing by the staircase to the mezzanine. A dozen policemen piled up behind him as, seeing Louisa, he held up a hand to them. 'Wait here!'

He strode across to her. His eyes seemed to be open too far; his face was pink with excitement. Dropping his revolver to his side, he said, 'Are you the little lady we owe a debt of gratitude?'

'I am Louisa Doyle. And this is Miss Corelli.'

Roosevelt hardly glanced at Marie. 'You have suffered greatly, I'm told, and have persevered and come through with a magnificent display of pluck!' He held up a finger. 'We shall catch this monster for you! We shall lay him at your feet as a tribute to your courage! Now, it is best if you leave this place and seek medical care.'

'I shall decide what care I seek, thank you.'

'You need your husband in this hour of trial.'

'My husband seems not to be here.' She stared into the pincenez. She said, 'I would advise you not to go into the tunnels, Mr Roosevelt.'

'The tunnels are precisely where we *will* go! We will trap this madman in there.'

'Galt knows them and you don't.'

'The criminal mind has cunning, but it does not have intelligence. He is a criminal, and he is only one, and we are many. Fear not, dear lady.' He actually bowed and turned back to his troops. 'Follow me!'

She watched them go up the staircase. Several had dark lanterns; all had nightsticks and revolvers. She imagined them in the tunnels, Galt playing hide-and-seek, coming up behind them, going down a ladder while they went up at the opposite end, Galt going into one of the rooms while they prowled the darkness. Or was Galt so badly injured from her bullets that he was lying in his own blood somewhere? The idea swept through her like a drug; she thought, *Yes, die!*

She shuddered.

'What is it, love?'

'Only thinking.'

'Louisa, my dear little thing, a doctor could give you something to put you to sleep. When you woke, everything would look—'

'Everything would look the same! Everything will always look the same! I don't want to sleep. I want to hear that he's dead. I want to hear that he died from the bullets I put into him. I want to hear that there's some justice for those women and Ethel and me!'

Marie stroked her head. 'There, there, my love. Of course you do. And that's what will happen, you'll see. They'll find him up there and he'll be dead. And it will all be like a dream.'

CHAPTER 15

The Pennsylvania Railroad terminal was in Jersey City, which Arthur knew was in New Jersey – although barely so. It lay across the North River from New York, and it was one of the many vexations of his tour that after rattling into Jersey City and reaching the terminal, he wasn't yet at his destination but had to take a ferry to reach New York.

'It's a pity there isn't a bridge,' he had said to a man with whom he'd struck up a conversation as the outskirts of Jersey City flashed by.

'Maybe they'll build one. Or a tunnel. They can build anything nowadays.'

That seemed to be true. Wherever he had gone in the United States, they seemed to be building something new and gigantic, and they always seemed to want to build something even bigger.

'Not the happiest scenery to introduce one to New York,' Arthur had said as the train had slowed and they had passed shacks, pigsties, enormous piles of cinders, ponds of a revolting green colour and the factories that made them so. The other man had said something about Jersey City's having its pretty side, but not along the tracks. Arthur had thought that so it always was, even in England: where the railway met the city, the effect was always sour.

He got down and walked along the platform looking for something that would direct him to the ferry. Most people, he figured, would be taking the ferry into New York, so really it was a matter of following the crowd. He looked at his watch – right on time, and in thirty minutes he should be with Louisa. The thought of her wrung his heart; he knew he had been cruel to her, stupidly cruel; he yearned for her and he knew that his own stupidity had put a barrier between them. *Louisa, my little Touie . . .* Over money – stupid, wretched *money.*

What had possessed him, to be so niggardly with her? They had plenty of money; why should she not spend it on female fripperies if she wanted? But he, in his arrogance and his stupidity (as he thought of it), had hardened his heart against her to teach her a lesson! But what lesson? That he was an unfeeling dunce?

He shook his head in irritation with himself. There would be a difficult scene that he hoped would be short. He would be contrite; he would crawl, if he had to. He couldn't have her angry with him, couldn't bear it. She was his Gentle Touie, and to have angered her meant that he had been brutal, savage, a troglodyte: she might as well have a husband who carried a club and dragged her about by the hair.

So, some painful minutes of contrition, and then the pleasure of making up. And then he would show her the tickets he'd bought for her for the rest of the tour, and in a day they would be whisking along the railways together, and everything would be well.

The truth was, he couldn't bear the idea of her not loving him. If some of that love was the love of a child for her father, that was only as it should be.

He stopped at a stall outside the river end of the station and bought a bunch of bright yellow and blue iris. He supposed they had been raised in a 'hothouse,' as they called it here. He already had in his satchel a box of something called 'handmade fudge,' about which he knew nothing except that he'd sampled a piece and it was terribly sweet but delicious. He had brought only the one satchel, really an overnight bag; the rest of his luggage would be waiting for him in Philadelphia. He hoped.

He had been walking without looking for signs, actually following a party of half a dozen men who seemed to know exactly where they were going. Then he saw over their heads a sign, 'To Ferry,' with an arrow, so he knew he was all right. And he was in luck: the ferry was waiting. The men got on; he got on. One of them smiled at the flowers and then at him, as if they shared some male secret about returning to the little woman.

He stood by the rail and watched Jersey City

recede – perhaps the best way to see it, he thought. He walked to the side and watched New York City grow larger and then begin to slide by as they turned downstream. That didn't seem too odd to him; he supposed the terminal was somewhere near the tip of the city. They were supposed to dock somewhere called Cortlandt Street.

More of the city went by, mostly only the tops of buildings seen over the huge sheds of the steamship docks that lined this side of the island. Arthur tapped his foot; the scene was pleasant enough, lots of bustle and vigour, that sense of adventure that water travel always brings, but he wanted to be where he could hail a cab and hurry to Louisa.

He looked at his watch. They should be there by now; if they took much longer, he'd be late.

A large park came into view. He felt the ferry turning. Now they would be heading for the shore. But they didn't. They stayed the same distance from New York as they steamed around a green area that his guidebook told him had to be The Battery. If he had cared about history at that moment, he'd have seen it as the site of the original Dutch fortification; as it was, he was seeing it as only something that was not the terminal of the Cortlandt Street ferry. *Where* was Cortlandt Street?

He walked along the rail and said to another passenger, 'Do you know when we reach Cortlandt Street?'

'Cortlandt! This is the Brooklyn Annex Line. We're going to Brooklyn.'

'I don't understand.'

'You got on the wrong ferry, my friend. Lots of people do. It's a good way to see lower Manhattan.'

Ahead and to the left, a large bridge soared towards the sky. This, of course, would be the famous Brooklyn Bridge. The ferry began to turn away from it, heading for a shore at the bridge's far end. *Dammit to hell!*

He was going to be late. Louisa would be impatient, thus even crosser than she must be already. His plan of a speedy contrition over a nice lunch was blasted.

Hell!

He paced the deck until the ferry, seemingly hours later, bumped the dock and almost threw him off his feet. He was one of the first ones off but immediately got lost in the Pennsylvania Railroad terminal. He wanted a convenience rather desperately; he had to ask twice for directions, then got lost again finding his way to the street and a sign that said, 'Cabs Here.' There were no cabs there. When, after another five minutes, one pulled up, he threw his satchel and the flowers into it and yanked himself up on the step.

'New Britannic Hotel, and I'm in a hurry.'

'That's across the river, i'n'it?'

'Close to Fifth Avenue. Twenty-third Street.'

'In New *Yawk*.'

'In New York, yes. I'm in a devil of a hurry, really.'

'If I go inta New Yawk, I got a hell of a time

getting a fare back to Brooklyn, y'unnerstand me? I come back to Brooklyn wit'out a fare, I'm buggered.'

'You are required to take me where I wish to go!'

'Not outside a Brooklyn. Brooklyn ain't New Yawk. 'Course, you wanta pay me to come back, I can take you.'

'You'll just pick up a fare and get yourself paid twice for it!'

'I should be so lucky.'

'This is robbery.' He got into the cab. He fumed about the unfairness of it all, the wasted money, the humiliation of being duped by a clown with no more education than the horse he was driving.

The driver waved his whip at something up ahead. 'The famous Brooklyn Bridge. Toll is t'ree cents, which you can gimme now or add it to the bill.'

Arthur produced three pennies. They clopped through the toll gate and joined the traffic on the bridge. The driver, who clearly had done this many times before, began a spiel. 'This famous bridge was de wonder of de woild when completed in 1883 at a cost of fifteen million dollars. It is five t'ousand, nine hunnert and eighty-nine feet long. Four cables dat used enough wire to go mosta da way around da woild hold up da bridge, which is a hunnert and fifty-t'ree feet above da water. Hey – last week we got a moiderer, he jumped off da bridge to excape da cops, wuddya t'inka dat? And

571

he survived! Least they didn't find him. The Bowery Butcher. Some jump, huh? Where was I?'

Louisa sat on, numb. When Marie said she had to leave for a minute to visit the convenience, Louisa begged her not to go. Marie pointed to a policeman at the bottom of the staircase, but Louisa shook her head. Finally, Marie found another woman to stay with her.

The hotel's guests and staff had all been gathered in the lobby, although when the police – now led by a deputy chief until Roosevelt reappeared – saw how many there were, they allowed some to move into the restaurant and the bar. There was no food, however; the police had moved the entire staff out of the kitchens. Marie came back to say that there were long queues at both of the women's rooms on the ground floor, though the men seemed to be moving through theirs fast enough. 'Superior equipment,' Marie murmured. 'Superior clothing, anyway.'

She had drawn up a chair next to Louisa's. She thanked the other woman, a big, oddly timid woman in a kimono who drifted away; she had been complaining to Louisa about having been ousted from her room before she was dressed. She said she was outraged but sounded no more exercised than if she'd found a bonbon that had a cream rather than a chocolate centre.

Mostly, people stayed away from Louisa. She knew that word had spread through the lobby:

people stared at her from a distance, whispered to each other. She heard the word 'violated' spoken by a female voice. Only Cody came to ask her if he could do anything; Marie waved him away. Irving came towards them then but veered off when Marie shook her head. Mrs Simmons, with her little dog tucked under her arm, was allowed to come close. All the stuffing had been knocked out of her; when she got close enough to speak, she burst into tears. She couldn't kneel, but she bent over Louisa. 'I'm so sorry. So sorry. All these years I've been here, and all the time, he was . . . he was . . .' She patted Louisa's shoulder. 'You're the bravest little girl I ever saw.'

When she was gone, Louisa whispered, 'No, I'm not.' She squeezed Marie's hand. 'Do they know everything?'

'I think they've put it together, *chère*. Some of them heard you and Carver and then Dunne.'

At one point, there was a demonstration at Reception, where the deputy chief had set up his command. Several guests were demanding to be let out of the hotel. 'You're keeping us locked in here with a murderer!' But the police were taking statements and they wouldn't let anybody leave.

Then the lift descended, and everybody looked towards it before it reached the floor, because it was the first one to come down since the fire alarm had been shut off. There was a collective shrinking back and a collective holding of breath, and then the doors clashed and Manion pushed out an

573

invalid's chair with a draped something in it. Dunne and Cassidy were close behind him. Manion and Dunne both looked at her; the same expression of bewilderment came over their faces when they saw her absolute indifference to them: Louisa was looking not at them but at the chair. She saw the shape of the old man and the shapes of the bottles and jars under the white cloth. One of the jars had spilled or broken and the cloth was wet.

'I'm going to be sick.'

Roosevelt was sweating heavily in his wool jacket and thick waistcoat. His revolver felt like a fifty-pound weight in his hand. He had tried shoving it into the waistband of his trousers, but it dragged them down too much and made his braces cut into his shoulders.

It was hot and airless in the tunnels, and there was a smell. Twenty years of collected foulness whose identity he could only guess. He thought he knew men from his time in the West, and he thought he knew criminals, but he didn't know this one at all. How could a man have done such things?

He was leading half his policemen along the third floor. The other half were on the floor below, searching in the opposite direction in hopes that they would prevent the maniac from using the tunnels. Roosevelt, however, knew now how flawed his plan was: there were too many tunnels and too many ladders, and for all they knew, the murderer could be safely going up and down ladders on the other side of the hotel.

'Fire!'

'What?' His voice was hoarse, hushed. He felt exhausted.

'I smell smoke! Smell it?'

Roosevelt stopped. He sniffed. Indeed, there was a smell of heat and burning. 'It's the lanterns.'

'No, Commissioner – it's a fire. That's wood smoke!'

'Forward!' He pushed on. They followed him; he could hear their muffled footsteps, see the glow of their dark lanterns. Discipline held.

Until he got to the top of a ladder and could see the tendrils of smoke curling up in the lantern light. He could smell it, too – burning wood.

'Stay calm, men! I don't want to hear any one of you shout the word "fire"! Any man who does will be summarily dismissed from the force! I want the entire unit to right-about-face and proceed in the opposite direction until we find the hatch to one of the doors, and we'll descend and leave these tunnels. Ready? Right – *about face!*'

A sergeant who had been right behind him and was now right in front of him turned and whispered, 'What about the other boys, sir?'

'They're on the floor below – we'll disperse as soon as we're out and keep opening these infernal doors until we find them!'

He didn't question that it was his responsibility. He was picturing the tunnels as they'd been described to him and guessing where the other policemen were.

Somebody called from up ahead that they had the correct hatch and they were opening it.

'Down as fast as you can, men. Break through the door down there if you can't open it. Down you go – down, quickly, quickly . . . !' He caught the sergeant's sleeve. 'Sergeant, you take charge of getting them down to the ground floor and tell the senior man down there that there's a fire – a real fire this time.'

'You ain't coming, sir?'

'The commander must be the last man out.'

Marie hurried to lead Louisa towards the staircase. Above were the ladies' dressing and rest rooms. A glance had told Louisa that the queues for the first-floor conveniences were impossible: her stomach was heaving, her mouth salty. 'Hurry!'

'Here, now, you can't go up there!'

The cop at the stairs held out his arms to stop them. 'No admission!'

Marie looked up the stairs. 'Well, you let *her* in!'

The cop looked around. An elderly woman was coming down.

Louisa dodged around the policeman and started to climb, digging her stick into the thick carpet and pushing herself up. It was astonishing how much of her hurt, especially her abdomen and back! Below her, Marie was screaming rather operatically at the policeman, who had taken hold of her. Louisa went on without pausing, driving herself to get somewhere that she could be sick. Even after everything, she couldn't bear the idea of being sick in front of other people. Only a few feet now – there was the door to the ladies' – another step – another—

She put her hand on the doorknob and pulled. The door swung towards her and she rushed in. Her first breath told her something was wrong – *smoke* – but she was focused on her nausea, reeling from it, holding her mouth closed with her left hand. She crossed the anteroom and tore open the door to the toilets.

Heat blasted out at her. She backed. The ceiling of the large inner room seemed in flames. In a far corner, the flames were hurling themselves into a square opening as big as a chair seat.

The tunnels – it opens into the tunnels . . .

She turned away and vomited. That was quick, over; she felt dizzy but cleansed, weak. Aloud, she said, 'That old woman.'

She hobbled out, slamming the door behind her, hurrying to the top of the stairs. She looked over the crowd of heads for the dark hat the woman had worn, realized that it was Ethel's hat.

'Stop that woman! That woman – it's Galt—!'

A male voice in the crowd shouted, 'Fire! The hotel's on fire!'

A woman screamed.

Somebody was pointing at her. No, at something behind her. Louisa turned. The mezzanine was in flames. She tried to run, almost pitched down the stairs. A man dashed out of the crowd and up the stairs. It was nobody she knew; she tried to fight him off. He scooped her off the stair and carried her down, and she was screaming and pummeling him and it was only when a knot of women formed around them and she was put down that she stopped. He was young; he looked pained, puzzled.

'She was violated,' one of the women said. 'We'll take charge now.'

The deputy chief was shouting from Reception, but the mob in the lobby had stampeded towards the doors. A policeman there had had the wit to open both of the big bronze doors and hold them open with the help of a kitchen cook, and the mob poured out into Twenty-third Street.

Louisa heard the bells of more fire wagons. She was being hurried along with the crowd. Marie had reappeared, but the women who had rescued her were being jostled away from her; two of them panicked and ran, as she could not. All she could think of was Galt – that he had escaped, dressed as a woman in Ethel's clothes; that he could be any of the women around her; that she would meet him face to face, see that ferocity, the knife—

She was aware of policemen behind her, then of a knot of them with Roosevelt at the head. He was bellowing instructions about letting 'civilians' go out first. 'We must be the last! It's our duty, boys!' He had soot on his face and he had lost his glasses, but Louisa had a glimpse of a face that looked transfigured with delight.

The hotel guests tried to gather in the street but the traffic had no sympathy for them. It was New York: the tramcars and the carriages and the hurrying foot traffic had to get through. Some of the mob darted across and stood on the far side of the street to watch the hotel, but then the fire wagons were there, hose companies and ladder companies, big horses, men in rubber coats and peaked hats, men with axes and brass nozzles the size of cannons.

'Outa the way! Make room – get outa my way!'

Louisa was pulled along the pavement by somebody, then abandoned to the pressure of people behind her. She reached the corner. Barricades had been put up there, bright yellow and white with FIRE DEPARTMENT in black letters a foot high. The traffic had to stop now – two tramcars had been stalled at Madison Square; carriages and wagons were being detoured into Fifth Avenue. Policemen were everywhere out here, whistles in their mouths, arms moving, human semaphores that signalled only *Keep moving! Keep moving!*

When it was more or less sorted out, most of the guests were in a cordoned-off part of Madison Square near Fifth and Twenty-third. It was as if the police and firemen knew that the guests and the staff would be morbidly driven to watch their hotel burn. They were contained in a ring of uniformed policemen; the ostensible reason was that they had yet to be interrogated. But it was cold, and morbid curiosity or not, many of them shook fists at the policemen and shouted that they were being held prisoner.

The slowness of the ride up Fifth Avenue maddened Arthur. His flowers were wilting; his plans for luncheon were ruined. He told the driver to stop talking. He swore at the traffic. When they had to stop at Twenty-first Street and the driver told him that the police wouldn't let them go on, he was outraged. 'Why the devil can't we?'

'Fire. One a the hotels. Not my fault, so don't get on your high horse wit' me. Go shout at a copper. That'll be two dollars and forty cents.'

Arthur wanted to jump out of the carriage and tell him to go to the devil for his money, but he was a gentleman and an agreement was an agreement. He paid and got down and started trying to work his way north. The driver's words, 'fire in a hotel,' had frightened him. What if it was the New Britannic? What if Louisa was in the hotel – unable to get out – *his* Louisa . . .

An astonishingly large crowd was gathering. It was as if nobody in New York had anything to do but watch fires. His flowers were wrecked in the first hundred feet; he had trouble keeping hold of his satchel. Seeing only worse ahead, he gave it up and backtracked, hurried east on Twenty-first Street to Fourth Avenue and turned north again.

The crowd was smaller here, but everybody in

it was moving north, fortunately the direction he wanted to go – all except one old man, white hair hanging down all around his head under a peculiar old hat. He was fighting the tide. When Arthur was in his way and couldn't move fast enough, he bumped straight into Arthur, who caught himself and stepped back and said, 'Do watch where you're going!' But as he said it he saw the old man's face, deadly white, prematurely lined – with pain, the doctor in him thought; he knew that look. The old man coughed; Arthur saw a bright crimson spray. He tried to dodge, and somebody bumped into him from behind; he let himself be carried along for several steps, trying to turn to see the man.

But the old man had lurched on. Arthur looked down and saw drops on his trousers and one shoe. He knew what it was. *Blood. Arterial or lung, from the colour. I should go after him – it's my duty as a physician*— But he thought of Louisa, trapped in a fire.

He looked after the old man, but the hat had disappeared behind taller bodies and better hats. *My place is with my wife.* But he knew he had taken an oath to heal . . .

Arthur went on and reached Twenty-second Street. A remarkable number of policemen seemed to be in his way now.

He was an object of immediate interest to them. Where was he going? What was the satchel for? Who was he?

He was passed to a senior roundsman, to a sergeant, to a lieutenant.

'You can't go to the New Britannic, Mr Doyle. It's the one that's on fire.'

'But my wife's there!'

The lieutenant had read some of his stories. He was sympathetic. He apologized for the trouble and said it was because of the Butcher, which made no sense to Arthur. They were interrupted by another policeman, who said excitedly that they'd just found Foley with his throat slit and a woman's dress and hat thrown over him, so what now?

The lieutenant swore and turned Arthur over to an ancient of days with orders to take Mr Doyle to Madison Square to find his wife.

Arthur trudged along behind the old bull. All his plans for reconciliation with Louisa were spoiled, but that was unimportant now. Where was she? If she was still in the hotel, what would he do?

Louisa, perhaps because she had gained status – half heroine, half pariah? – was in the front row of the watchers. She was shivering from cold. A fireman carrying a stack of folded blankets draped one over her shoulders without a word and moved on.

Fire hoses were shooting water on both the Fifth Avenue and Twenty-third Street sides of the New Britannic. A separate cluster of hoses was drenching